THE RELUCTANT BILLIONAIRE

SARA MADDERSON

To everyone who's ever drooled over the
Diet Coke™ ad guys...

This one's for you.

SOME BRITISH LINGO DECODED!

My North American ARC readers were flummoxed by some of the British terminology in this book, so the following may come in handy before you dive in...

VEST: tank top or undershirt (Die Hard style). Key to understanding Aide's physical charms.

Lollipop man: crossing guard

OBE: Order of the British empire. A title bestowed on an individual by the monarch for remarkable public / cultural / charitable services

Keepy-uppies: keeping a football (soccer ball) airborne with your feet / lower legs / knees / head / chest / shoulders. You've probably seen them on Ted Lasso...

NFI - Not F*cking Invited

Bollocked / Bollocking - a telling-off (is that also a Britishism?!) or a stern talking to, not to be confused with **bollocks** (noun), which are testicles, or **bollocks** (adj) which means bullshit or **bollox** (noun) which means a jackass / douche / twat.

Glad we've cleared that up! Handing over to Lotta...

1

LOTTA

A community centre?'

I hope the way I've repeated my brother's words back to him conveys my intense distaste for the merest concept of a community centre. While I'm not entirely clear on what community centres actually are, or what purpose they serve beyond being, presumably, centres for their, um, communities, I know they're not for me.

He sighs. 'Don't start with your shit.'

'But why? It sounds grim.'

'Of course it's fucking grim. That's why they need our help. Fuck's sake, Lotts.'

'Why do I have to be the one to do it? Why can't we just write a cheque and send some of the guys down to help with the heavy lifting, or bulldozing, or whatever they need?'

He gives me his best *don't push me* look. It's pretty effective, actually. Gabriele Montefiore-Charlton is good at making people feel like dog shit under his Gucci loafers when they piss him off.

'Optics,' he grunts.

He makes it sound like an unwilling concession, because

he's basically admitting that my smiling face is a far more valuable commodity for our company's PR machine than his miserable one. But because my brother is a commercial shark and never one to unwillingly concede anything, I suspect he's playing me.

Appealing to my ego will net him the exact result he wants in this and every instance, and we both know it.

Still, I'm made of the same stuff as my brother. Our arguments can be as strategic—and as endless—as chess matches when we're both spoiling for a fight. Dad's suggested many times that we should have been lawyers.

'You're the CEO,' I counter lamely. I'm on the back foot here and clearly not at my best.

'And I oversaw that thing at Tower Hamlets last month. I showed my face—'

'For *one day*.'

'I shook hands and tousled kids' hair and gave a pep talk. Made myself seen. Philanthropy at our level is more than just writing a cheque. You know that, for God's sake. If Dad and I can grin and bear it, you can definitely suck it up.'

He's right. I do know that.

As the children of a painfully introverted and usually reclusive software-engineer-turned-billionaire, Gabe and I are well versed in the importance of giving back. Luckily for our quiet, British father, he's had a secret weapon all these years: Mamma, aka Chiara Montefiore-Charlton, his flamboyant and wildly sociable Italian wife who loves nothing more than throwing a party for any cause.

Gabe's as underwhelmed as Dad is by other people, though he lacks Dad's good nature. I, on the other hand, definitely take after Mamma.

It's no surprise I'm the Chief Marketing Officer of my and my brother's massive property development company,

Venus Holdings, and even less of a surprise that I frequently find myself the face of the brand, too, even if he's the commercial genius.

I mean, I have a much prettier face than my brother does, so there's that.

But I understand all too well that my high profile comes with strings attached, and that those strings don't just require me to cut ribbons and attend polo matches in head-to-toe couture. They require me to show up, to advocate for those less privileged than my family in a city with an endemic housing crisis, especially at the affordable end of the spectrum.

Not only do I get it, but I truly believe in the importance of giving back. It's been ingrained in me for my entire entitled life.

I'm still not clear on how that ties in with this community centre, though.

Or why I have to spend *two weeks* on this project. Nothing, and I mean *nothing*, pisses me off more than Gabe's inference that my time is less valuable than his. It's arrogant and sexist and flagrantly uncommercial, because my time is expensive.

'You're asking me to do a lot more than make myself be seen,' I complain now. I'm not rolling over without a fight. 'Two weeks isn't a good use of my time. You put in half a day.'

He swivels around in his chair, the South Bank behind him hazy in the London sunshine. One great perk of running a property development firm is that the office porn is seriously excellent.

'The Tower Hamlets thing is ongoing,' he points out with irritating logic. 'I'll pop back down there in a month or two to monitor the progress and pat some backs. This project will be done and dusted in a fortnight—less—and you don't need to be there the whole time. You can go back and forth. You know the council needs to see us pull our weight. You sat there and looked them in the eye and promised them this.'

He's right.

Again.

Our newest development, Elgin, was a fucking nightmare to pull off, and I have to admit Gabe worked miracles to get it over the line. A futuristic, eco double block of purpose-built flats bang in the centre of the Georgian and Victorian ice-cream-coloured streets of Notting Hill was always going to ruffle some feathers. The good councillors of the Royal Borough of Kensington and Chelsea, under whose remit Notting Hill falls, were hell-bent on turning us down.

The two main areas where we won out in the end were on the promises we made around environment and community outreach.

I have a horribly hazy memory of sitting in one of the endless meetings with pale, male and stale pen-pushers and blithely (or maybe even flirtatiously) agreeing to front the complete overhaul of some hall-slash-centre-thingy up near Avondale Park.

The park and its surrounding streets are squarely on the poorer side of an area where jaw-dropping wealth and equally shocking poverty sit cheek-by-jowl.

'I did, didn't I?' I moan, slumping in my chair in defeat. I push my foot against the white marble floor so I can simultaneously swivel the chair and take a smidgeon of comfort in the gloriousness of my new baby-pink Prada heels.

Happily, my brother's victorious smirk is interrupted by

a cursory knock at the open door before his assistant, Charlie, steps in.

'They're ready for you,' she tells him with an admiring smile.

I roll my eyes internally. Yet another secretary plotting how to put a ring on Gabriele Montefiore-Charlton's finger. She needn't bother. He's made that mistake once before and he won't make it again. I give her a month before he's got sick of her suggestive glances and given her the boot.

'How do I know what to do on this job?' I demand as my brother pushes himself up to standing, clearly dismissing me. This kind of hands-on stuff is way outside my comfort zone. I'm far happier signing off on multi-million-pound media budgets and glossy brochures and exclusive influencer events. 'How many of us do they need? I haven't got the first clue what—'

'Don't get your knickers in a twist,' he replies, flicking my hair as he walks past in a way that's puerile and irritating in equal measure. 'The foundation has it all sorted. Khalid will brief you—you just have to show up and try to be vaguely helpful. Aide'll look after you.'

'Aid?' I ask his retreating back. 'What kind of aid?' Is that some new department I'm unaware of? I mean, *Aid* isn't a bad name for our outreach efforts. It's a bit on the nose, but it's punchy, succinct.

Hmm.

'Fuck's sake,' he mutters. 'Just speak to Khal. And don't wear heels like that. They'll get trashed.'

I stare at him in horror as he disappears down the corridor, Charlie click-clacking adoringly behind him.

He's not possibly suggesting I wear flats, is he?

2

LOTTA

I have three thoughts as soon as I walk into this godforsaken place.

One. I have arrived in actual, literal hell.

Two. Henry Cavill's twin appears to have landed himself in hell with me.

Three. Hot Cavill Twin looks far less pleased to lay eyes on me than I am to see him.

And by see, I mean eye-fuck.

Because, come on. This is what I mean when I say I want a guy who's all man.

This. Right here.

An all-man man wears the hell out of a vest like this. And there's an impressive amount of dark chest hair coming out of the top of it that's somehow not wirey or pube-y but instead looks soft and manly and inviting and snuggle-worthy.

And he does proper physical work that results in said vest being grimy and dirt-marked, and in his fucking ginor-mous arms being sweat-slicked, and all the things that should be a turn-off to someone as high maintenance as me but that are, in fact, a mahoosive turn-on.

An all-man man knows how to wield his power tools, both figuratively and literally, and this guy's brandishing his huge drill in a way that screams casual competence.

Like, a literal drill.

In case you think I've already seen his penis.

You should know my competence kink is as real as my manual labourer kink.

I bet he drinks beer only in pint format and never out of bottles. I bet he goes to pubs instead of bars and washes that thick, dark hair with shower gel instead of shampoo and would have to shave twice a day if he wasn't growing a beard and doesn't believe in foreplay.

Because, you know, he doesn't need to.

I bet no woman has ever left his bed unsatisfied.

If he even bothers to use a bed, that is. He strikes me as an up-against-the-wall guy. Or a bend-you-over-the-table guy, which, you know, also works well.

You'd think someone who runs a real, live property development company would be well used to seeing builders. And I am, of course.

But not builders who look like this.

I know what I don't want in a man. Anymore, anyway. I don't want a guy whose facial schedule is more gruelling than mine or who won't fuck me because he 'needs' to spend time behind his LED mask like Hans, my most recent ex.

But I'm not sure I could have articulated exactly what I *do* want in a man until this second.

This.

This is what I want.

Not as an actual boyfriend, you understand. That would

be ridiculous, because I suspect our Venn diagrams of acceptable date venues or attire will never meet in the middle.

But as a hot-as-fuck fuck.

With eyes that have already melted my panties, because I swear to God I have never seen eyes like his.

I've been told by several adoring suitors that my eyes are mesmerising, and I've always been happy to believe it, but even I can admit I have nothing on this guy. Whereas my eyes are big and brown and usually heavily made up, his are the most unique colour I've ever, ever seen. They're icy blue, but with improbable golden flecks, which sounds like it should be weird and is in reality perfection.

He's coming towards me, and I stand there like a total muppet and gape. His hair and beard are so dark I'd say he's either Irish or Mediterranean. Probably Irish, if that silver Celtic cross around his neck is anything to go by.

Those crazy, hypnotic eyes are so heavily lashed it's just plain *rude*. All his hair is lustrous. Chest hair. Head hair. Beard. Eyelashes, for God's sake. Eyebrows. Forearms. What does one ingest for follicular health? Is it carrots? Or omega three? I can never remember.

Whatever it is, Neanderthal Drill Man must be mainlining it.

He transfers his enormous power tool easily to his left hand and wipes his right hand down the centre of his man-vest before holding it out to me.

Update: I'm gaping even harder now. Especially at the new, sweaty trail his hand has left between pecs that need zero extra definition.

'Carlotta?' he asks in a low, gruff voice that honestly has me hurtling towards orgasm.

'That's me,' I squeak. I extend mine and take his hand,

which is huge and warm, allowing it to close over mine. Every part of my nervous system goes crazy with safety cues and danger cues at the same time which I didn't even know was a thing but, it turns out, definitely is.

His face falls as though I've just confirmed his worst fears. Rude bastard.

'Aide,' he admits, gun-to-his-head style. Begrudging, much?

But also: Aide.

Ahhh.

Aide is a *person*. Who knew? I have hazy memories of Khal briefing me in the car on the way to a site visit last week, but as he talked I was manically answering emails on my phone, trying to diffuse and delay and delegate my workload ahead of this unnecessary and time-sucking fortnight.

Also, Khal, bless him, is selfless to the core and super well-meaning and also way too earnest and too fond of using his MBA-speak and therefore boring as fuck. Which means I listened to approximately two percent of his briefing, and the *Aide* thing didn't feature in that two percent.

Obviously, had Khal showed me a photo of this guy, I would have been all over him.

It, I mean. I would have been all over *it*.

The project.

As he shakes my hand, those blue eyes wander south. He's definitely checking out my rack.

Good.

'Meet the team,' he says, releasing my hand and jerking his head to the motley gaggle of individuals behind him, because, much as I wish it was to the contrary, we are not alone in this shit hole. I'm suddenly extremely glad I've come armed with a fleet of professional workmen to aid us.

Aid. Haha.

Because this gang screams *volunteers* like I don't know what.

I sigh inwardly and paste on my brightest smile.

First up is a big guy whose resemblance to James Cordon is equalled only by Aide's resemblance to my husband Henry Cavill. He gets instant points for the sincerity of his grin. At least *someone's* pleased the cavalry has arrived.

He buries my hand between two enormous paws and gives me a funny little bow. 'Gary. Call me Gaz. At your service.'

I don't miss Aide's eye-roll as I bestow my most dazzling smile upon Gaz. I like him at once. He's got a good energy, unlike Mr Hot But Hostile next to him. He's wearing a grubby blue t-shirt that says *Hays Long-Haul Logistics* on the front.

Yep. I can totally see this guy being a lorry driver. I wouldn't be surprised to find a rolled-up copy of today's *Daily Mirror* wedged in the back pocket of his jeans when he turns around.

'How do you do, Gaz?' I ask.

'All right, all right,' he drawls good-naturedly. 'Bit of a shit-tip, innit?'

My thoughts exactly, Gaz.

'Oh, don't worry about that,' I say blithely, jerking my thumb at the team behind me. 'These guys have seen worse.' I mean, I'm not sure that's actually true, but I'm not someone to piss on a person's morale in the first ten seconds of meeting them.

'Excellent, excellent,' he says. His eyes drift to my boobs and back to my face.

'This is Judy,' he tells me, stepping aside to reveal a tiny woman who's been totally concealed by his bulk. She can't be more than five foot or less than seventy, and she's wearing an actual housecoat that makes her look like an extra from *Call the Midwife,* but I can tell at a glance that I wouldn't want to fuck with her.

'Hi, Judy,' I say brightly. I take on the biggest alphaholes with glee on a daily basis, but show me a stern older woman and I'm instantly desperate for her approval and having to stop myself from rubbing myself against her leg like a needy dog and whining *like me, like me.*

God knows why. I suspect my Italian genes ensure I never underestimate a strong matriarchal figure.

She gives Gaz a shove. 'Stop staring at her tits,' she snaps. Before my jaw has time to drop open she takes my hand in a grip stronger than either of the guys'. Bloody hell.

'Nice to meet you,' she barks. 'Thank fuck you're here. These village idiots don't know what the fuck they're doing. Except Aide.' She jerks her head. 'He's all right, that one.'

'Thanks a lot, Judy,' Gaz mutters, and I'm unclear whether he's protesting being referred to as a village idiot or being called out for staring at my boobs.

'Good to know,' I say neutrally. I suspect it's a major testament to Aide that Judy's given him her ringing endorsement, but I'm not willing to acknowledge any positive attributes on his part quite yet. Except for his undeniable, shocking hotness, that is. I'm also still reeling from the language that's just come from this pint-sized retiree's mouth.

The last of the volunteers is an attractive Black woman with shoulder-length braids who I'd guess is in her fifties. She's watching the interaction of the others with a smile that straddles the line between amused and resigned.

'Sylvie,' she says. She extends a hand and shakes mine

firmly but without Judy's death-grip, which I appreciate. 'Welcome to the madhouse.'

I laugh nervously. 'So... is it just the four of you?'

'We've had a few more volunteers in over the weekend,' Sylvie says. 'There was a lot of crap to clear out.' *No shit.* 'But we'll be here for the duration.'

'Got it,' I say with a confidence I don't feel. 'Well, we've got five contractors at our end.'

I introduce Khal, who's here for today only, thank fuck, and is positively vibrating with self-righteous saviour energy, and the small team of Venus' workmen. They're all volunteering for this project on the company's dime. Aside from Reggie, who's an electrician, the others are all generalists, as capable of knocking down a wall as they are of crafting a wardrobe from scratch or inserting a window.

I hope to God that, between them, they've got enough expertise to carry the rest of us through this shit-show. They should. Khal worked on equipping the team for this project with exactly the right mix of skill-sets, and God knows they're going to need it.

The space we're in is grim and depressing and filthy and horrible. I'm used to building sites, but they're usually palatial bare-bones spaces in swanky new-builds, not decrepit community centres that look like they could fail a building regs assessment before you can say *asbestos.*

This structure is shitty. The only thing it's got going for it, as far as I can see, is its vaulted ceiling and large windows. It looks like it was erected on the cheap, probably in the Seventies, with thin exterior walls and spectacularly crappy interior fittings. The majority of it is one big room whose length I'd guesstimate at thirty-five or forty feet with a small stage at one end. There's a doorway at the other end that, at a guess, leads through to an office. Kitchen. Loo.

As far as I can tell, the volunteers have so far spent their time clearing the entire space of its fixtures and fittings so all that remains is a few of those stackable plastic moulded chairs and a crude table. It makes sense. I wouldn't want to see these guys, especially Judy, doing the heavy lifting without professional help.

What's left over is a large cluster of the new plastic-wrapped appliances and kitchen units we've preordered, bag upon bag of rubbish in a big pile, grimy-as-fuck windows, and horrific wipe-clean glossy paint in a lurid pale yellow that turns my stomach and screams *mental institution*. The floor has heavily lacquered wooden floorboards which don't look too bad.

Along one entire side of the room runs orange-y pine panelling that's retro in all the wrong ways. At least it appears, from the drill in his hand and the fact that a few panels are missing from the wall at the near end and stacked in a neat pile on the floor, that Aide has made inroads into losing the wood.

It's plain depressing.

The whole place smells of dust and industrial cleaner and hopelessness.

I make a mental note to look more closely at the scope of the refurb we've agreed to fund and see if there's any wiggle-room to expand on that. And I need to do it as soon as possible.

But first, I definitely require espresso.

3

AIDE

She doesn't remember me.

And she doesn't seem to have a clue who I am, either.

Well, well.

This should be interesting.

Judy's already bollocked me for not immediately offering our new arrivals a brew, so I let her lead the way into the kitchen. She bustles through. She can come across as an interfering old bag, but she's fucking gold. And she has a worse mouth on her than I do.

Unfortunately for me, Carlotta's back view is as decent as her front view. And by decent, I mean knockout. Her outfit's a fucking joke. She's in spray-on jeans that showcase an incredible arse and what I'm pretty sure are the Dior Air Jordan high-tops. I'm also pretty sure they cost more than six grand. When you have a nephew who's as much of a sneakerhead as mine is, you learn far more about Nike collabs than you've ever wished to know.

What I also know is that they'll get fucked as soon as she

lifts a finger in here, and it's fucking stupid of her to be wearing them on a building site.

Unless, of course, she's not planning on lifting a finger.

Nothing would surprise me less.

The biggest problem with her outfit isn't the unsuitable footwear. Or the arse-hugging jeans. Or even her tight white t-shirt with *GUCCI* emblazoned across her chest in rhinestones. I'm not sure if the OTT branding is supposed to be ironic. I have a horrible feeling it's not.

Nope. The biggest problem by far is that this woman's bra is clearly as unsuitable as the rest of her attire, because it's completely and utterly failing in its primary job.

Actually, not its primary job. I suppose its main role is to support her tits, and it's doing a fucking spectacular job of that, from what I can see. I'm just thrilled Judy called Gaz out for staring at them and not me. That woman doesn't miss a trick.

But on its secondary job? Its job of presumably forming a protective layer between her nipples and the rest of the world?

Epic fucking fail.

Because, either side of *GUCCI* it's clear that this woman is smuggling peanuts with the best of them. I know it's chilly in here, but come on. Her porn star-level nipples are beacons, and, like a car crash, I cannot look away. I can't seem to look anywhere else when they're winking at me.

Her bra must be lace, or mesh, or something sheer and sexy and totally impractical because, while its vague outline is visible, it's forming a non-existent barrier between nipples so perfect they're proof there is a God and the poor bastards who have to look at them.

The woman is undeniably hot.

That's unfair.

Hot doesn't come close to describing her. She's astonishingly beautiful with those massive brown eyes and delicate bone structure. Above the eyes are thick, shapely brows. Below, a little snub nose dotted with the faintest smattering of freckles and a full, luscious mouth. And the backdrop for these features? Skin so creamy, so luminous, it's glowing. It's literally glowing.

I can see more than a bit of her mother in her, though it's been a couple of years since I bumped into Paul and Chiara in person. But whereas Chiara is an attractive woman, her daughter is mesmerising. All that thick, dark hair cascading down her back in bouncy curls that I'm guessing are the result of a professional blow-dry.

I just wish she'd pull some of those curls forward so they cover her tits, because having the outline of her taut, puckered nipples on display like that is not fucking helpful.

It's unhelpful because Gaz or I are highly likely to do ourselves an injury while operating power tools and sneaking glances at them, and it's equally unhelpful because the merest thought of how glorious it would feel to strum my thumbs over them, or to tug up that stupid, flashy t-shirt and suck one deeply into my mouth, has my dick threatening to harden.

It's frustration at my uncharacteristic lack of self-discipline that has me snapping at her more harshly than I mean to when she asks, with a totally straight face, if we have a Nespresso machine.

'Does this place look like it has a fucking Nespresso machine?' I snarl.

Eyes on her face, mate. Eyes on her face.

She visibly recoils at my tone, and I feel like a twat.

'It's tea or Nescafé,' I say more kindly and watch as she

attempts to conceal a shudder of distaste at the idea of instant coffee. I get it—she is half-Italian, after all.

'Black tea would be lovely, thanks,' she says in a small voice to Judy, who shoots me a *behave yourself* death stare as she busies herself with filling the kettle.

To distract myself from Carlotta's epic porn star nipples, I discreetly check out the rest of her team. That guy Khalid in the blue button-down shirt has *Stanford* written all over him. I've met a million mid-level bankers who look like him, and I have a few Khalids of my own in our Finance and Strategy departments.

That said, he's been nothing but helpful and generous in all our email and phone dealings so far, and I'm grateful to him for hooking us up with Venus. I'm funding the new kitchen equipment on this project, but they're the ones with the expertise and the trade relationships for materials.

The rest of the crew look alright, too. They're quiet and polite, dressed in immaculate, identikit cargo pants and black polo shirts bearing the iconic *V* logo on the chest. I have no reason to believe they won't epitomise efficiency, and that's exactly what we need here.

We need this job executed properly and wrapped up so the people of this community can get their centre back and I can give my not insignificant day job my full attention once again.

Judy's taken over the tea service. The rest of Carlotta's team seems lower-maintenance than her, thankfully. The five guys she's brought are all enthusiastically tucking into their cuppas and helping themselves to the shortbread biscuits Judy's laid out. She may appear as though she doesn't give a flying fuck, but I can tell she wants to impress these people.

Or, if not impress them, then at least give them zero

reason to look down on us. On what we're doing here. I mean, she's put the biscuits on a plate with an actual paper doily, for fuck's sake. Who the fuck has doilies these days? She must have brought it in with her. My heart twinges at the thought.

The thing to know about Judy is that she is a fucking trooper. Heart of gold, that woman. She has a vicious tongue on her but there's no one I'd rather have in my corner. Her body may be shrinking, but that heart of hers is still massive, and there's no mistaking when Judy Jones is in the room.

I was scared to death of her twenty years ago when she was in charge of the after-school care in this very centre, and I still have what can politely be called a healthy respect for her. To Judy, I'm still the same twelve-year-old pest she knew twenty years ago. No one is less impressed by the wealth I've accumulated, though I suspect no one is more proud of how far I've come.

These four walls are forgettable, but it's people like Judy and Sylvie who've given the place a beating heart. I just hope we can get posh gits like Carlotta and Khalid to see that. To see how important this place is in our community. How established. What a gift it is to our neighbours.

Not that I care what they think.

Carlotta's valiantly dunking her PG Tips tea bag into her Good Vibes Hospice mug. I don't miss the furtive looks she's giving the kitchen.

It's a shit hole.

I know.

But anyone who measures the value of this cramped, twelve-by-twelve space based on the shoddiness of the ancient formica worktops or the peeling paint in the damp upper corners is missing the point.

Thanks to this room, kids who would otherwise go without breakfast have, for the past two or three decades, been stuffed full of toast and Weetabix and orange juice every weekday morning before going off to school with a full stomach and a functioning brain. Just ask Gaz.

Parents for whom childcare is as big a headache as paying the bills can hold down their daytime shifts in the knowledge that their kids are here after school, snacking and doing their homework under Judy's watchful eye.

Kids who qualify for free school meals during term time because there's no money at home don't go hungry in the school holidays.

Because they come here, ostensibly for activities, but in reality so they can fill themselves up on the spag bol or curry or chicken nuggets that Sylvie cooks for them with whoever she can commandeer to help her, and they live to play another day.

This old, damp, smelly kitchen is fucking *everything*. And I'll make sure it makes it through another thirty years in fine shape if it's the last thing I do.

I could fund it all myself, obviously. And that was the plan. But when one of the overzealous grads in our Executive Office applied to be a part of the Venus Holdings Corporate Charity Programme, I saw the advantage of having Venus on board.

They have resources. And construction expertise. And reach. The latter two I can't help with. I have influence, yeah, and a massive network. But my connections are concentrated in the tech world, and having a world-class construction company on board could be a game-changer for us.

If they can work out how to build without access to Italian marble and Sub-Zero appliances, that is.

The outreach programme Venus has agreed with the council will be massive for this area. It'd be stupid not to piggyback on that, not to avail ourselves of what could be a long-term strategic partnership for the Avondale Park Community Centre.

Because having links with a corporation as impressive as Venus could mean all manner of future opportunities. If we can use this project to engage them, to make them understand the level of need here, just a few streets away from their newest and most high-profile development, it could make the world of difference for the priority they give to affordable housing and investment in local parks and all the other things I know they've promised but have yet to deliver on.

Having a shiny, new community centre could be the tip of the iceberg of what we could achieve with a partner like Venus.

It's a timely reminder that I should play nicely and not piss these people off before they've done their first day's work.

4

LOTTA

I gingerly take a sip of tea that tastes oddly like pencil sharpenings brewed in hot water and focus on trying not to look at Aide, who's sitting opposite me and Frank, our head contractor, while he briefs us.

We're sitting around a plastic table in the small, depressing outdoor area while Gaz shows the others around and gets them started on ripping more shit out. It may be July, but it's fucking cold, and I wish I hadn't left my jacket inside. My nipples are so cold I feel like they're going to snap off.

From the discreet but frequent glances Aide's giving my boobs, I'm not the only one concerned about my nipples.

For some reason, that pleases me immensely. Even so, needs must. I hunch forward and cross my arms over my chest as I hold my mug to my breastbone for heat. Holding it directly to my poor nipples is a step too far, even for an exhibitionist like me. And I'm the girl who had Cher's barely-there Studio 54 costume copied for my birthday party last year.

This space seems to be a play area. Its tarmac has definitely seen better days. I don't remember seeing anything in our initial proposal about the outdoor space, but I observe idly that the kids would be better off with a ground covering of soft rubber bark chips. I make a mental note to ask Khal if we can squeeze in some love for the outdoor area.

The tarmac bears the faintest outlines of hopscotch and noughts-and-crosses grids. There are some ancient Little Tyke pieces—a rocking horse thingy and a pedal car—as well as a basketball hoop with no net and a metal climbing frame whose yellow paint has almost entirely chipped off. To my eyes, it's the bleakest possible spot for kids to hang out. The mere idea that this is a welcome space for some of them to frequent is something I can't bear to contemplate right now.

The property's perimeter is marked with a high chain-link fence through which are visible several hideous sixties' tower blocks of council flats. Honestly, this place is more like juvie than a community centre. It's frustrating, because, like my brother, I'm a perfectionist. Venus operates right at the top of its market precisely because we're both anal as fuck. Only the best will do.

Obviously, I get that there's a ceiling on how much we can improve this building and its meagre grounds, but I'm beginning to wonder why we're not razing it to the ground and starting again from scratch with a construction that'd be more durable, more eco-friendly, and more cost-effective to fund. The current brief feels as inadequate as putting a plaster on a knife wound.

Speaking of which, I wouldn't be surprised if this area gets its fair share of stabbings. It's dodgy as hell and stinks of despair.

Quite frankly, the only sight that's making my eyes happy right now, aside from the cuteness of my immaculate new Dior Air Jordans, is the man sitting across the table from me.

The man who's one of the best-looking members of the male race I've ever seen, and in a way that's far more masculine, more *raw*, than I'm used to. Let me tell you, his rugged style of handsome is compelling.

I begrudgingly remove my right arm from my chest and rummage around in my handbag for my notepad, which I place on the table in front of me. When I put my mug down, the table jolts on its uneven legs, sending the liquid slopping over the sides.

Fuck's sake. I swallow down a sigh. Today is going to be a *long* day. I risk a glance through my eyelashes at Aide. He's grinding his jaw like he's holding back, too. He probably thinks I'm some sort of rich, dizzy socialite. He has no clue what I've achieved, albeit from privileged beginnings. Gabe and I have worked our arses off.

In the Montefiore-Charlton household, there were no free handouts. Mamma may have come from wealth, but Dad is a self-made man, and he never let us forget it.

I bet Mr Sexy McJudgement across from me doesn't know that, though. I bet he sees a spoilt princess who can't hack real life. The thought of it has me sitting up straighter in my seat.

I'll show him.

And also, I'll ogle him as much as I can, because Jeeeesus Christ is this man hot. I ignore the spilt tea and pick up my pen to redirect his eye so I can look some more, trying to work out exactly what it is about him that has him getting under my skin already.

It's a combination of looks and demeanour, I decide. Mainly those eyes that are currently melting my bra and pants off and are like nothing I've ever seen before.

The brawn helps too. The massive biceps and shoulders that say *I use my body to make a living.* Not in a *Magic Mike* way. Just in a good, honest physical labour kind of way, you know?

His appearance also gives clues to his personality. He can't possibly doubt the power of his looks, but neither is there a suggestion of the slightest bit of grooming on his part. He clearly got out of bed looking like this. Though thinking about Aide in bed is a terrible idea if the shot of lust that's just hit me deep inside is anything to go by. I press my thighs together tightly under the table.

Don't think about him in bed.

Don't think about waking up with six-foot-something of that hard body pressed up against you.

Before my treacherous mind has a chance to go *there* and imagine what other hard things he might press up against me in bed, I focus on his bracelets, which are, on closer inspection, one length of thin black leather tied around his wrist a few times. It's pointless, as all jewellery is, I suppose, but weirdly effective.

I don't get the impression that the leather bracelets, or the two chunky rings in dull silver that adorn his fingers, or the silver Celtic cross hanging around his neck are in any way vanity-driven.

Which means they could be sentiment-driven.

Which gives me a pang of something. I'm not sure what. Jealousy, maybe?

Can't be. Because being jealous of the theoretical people who theoretically gave a man I've just met any of the things he holds dear is literally insane.

Like, stalker-level insane.

But, for some annoying reason, the next thing my brain leads me to wonder is what kind of women he goes for. I'm sure they're all stunners, but beyond that I have no clue. I can't see him putting up with anyone too high maintenance. He probably goes for outdoorsy, girl-next-door types who look like Jennifer Lawrence but are a lot less feisty.

Sweet. I bet he goes for sweet blondes. Something tells me he likes being in charge.

And *that* sets off a whole host of highly inappropriate but utterly delicious ponderings on just how much he likes to take charge in bed, which come to an abrupt halt when I realise he's speaking.

'The kitchen needs to be turned around in two days,' he's telling Frank. I note he's not telling me, even though I'm, theoretically, anyway, leading this project.

'That seems ridiculous,' I blurt out. The kitchen is a shocker. It needs to be completely overhauled. 'You need to give us a week, at least. Right, Frank?'

I glance at Frank, who hasn't spoken because, unlike me, he's an under-reactor. A processor. He watches Aide, waiting for him to expound.

'We can't afford a week,' Aide says, his tone clipped.

'If it's a matter of funding the extra labour,' I say carefully, 'I'm sure it won't be a problem. Is that what you're worried about?'

'No.' That one word makes it sound like he thinks I'm an imbecile, as does the filthy look he shoots me. He probably does. 'What I'm *worried* about is that every day the kitchen is closed, there will be kids going hungry. This isn't some nice-to-have place where people drop by if they feel like it and sing *Kumbaya*.'

He presses his lips together and exhales, nostrils flaring,

like he's trying to rein in his temper. Or stress. Or *something.*
When he continues, his tone is more measured. 'The
centre's really important. Especially the kitchen. Kids come
by before school and we sort them out—there are a lot of
bare cupboards around here. If we don't feed them, they go
to school hungry. The food banks can't begin to plug
the gap.

'Same after school. We feed them dinner.' He shakes his
head and looks me dead in the eye, and I see nothing but
despair in those astonishing eyes of his. 'Having the kitchen
closed even for a couple of days is a fucking disaster. I can't
emphasise that enough. If we're closed, then a hundred or
so kids get one meal a day instead of three, and that's whatever shitty school lunch they're served up, and that's not
fucking good enough.'

I stare at him in horror, tears pricking at my eyes. 'Oh,' I
say inadequately, because I didn't see *that* coming. Didn't
realise this grubby place fulfilled such a critical function. It's
hard to believe the little kitchen can fill so many stomachs.
Make so many lives that tiny bit better. I waltzed in here and
judged it, but I look at this guy, Aide, and I see how filled he
is with passion and despair and urgency on behalf of these
children.

Right now, with his ice-blue eyes radiating righteous
fury, he looks like an unlikely avenging angel. Thank God
they have someone like him in their corner. Someone to
advocate for them. Someone to *feed* them, for Christ's sake.

One meal a day? I'm out of my depth here, and I'm less
than half a mile from my and Gabe's multi-million pound
flat.

I put down the pen I've been fiddling with. 'Then we'd
better work out how quickly we can get the kitchen done

and how best to feed them while it's out of action, hadn't we?' I say.

He nods, his massive shoulders dropping a little, and I take that as a tiny win. A tiny sign that I've said something right.

'Absolute best case is three days,' Frank says. 'One to disconnect everything and rip it all out. Another to lay the flooring and paint the walls. Day three, we install all the appliances and cupboards.' He shakes his head. 'But it's a tall order, and we'll need all hands on deck.'

I'm not the expert, but it sounds unrealistic to me. Aide, however, is still shaking his head and muttering to himself.

'Can you work with three days?' I ask him.

Wrong question. He bends his head in frustration and rakes his dirty hands through his thick black hair. I should be thinking about how unhygienic it would be to have such grubby hands anywhere near my skin.

Spoiler alert: I am not thinking that.

I try again.

'What would it take,' I ask his hands, 'from all of us to make three days work? Like, is there another option? Can we feed them somewhere else?'

He drags his hands down his face and looks up at me.

He blows out a breath.

I wait.

'We can do what we did this morning,' he concedes.

'And what was that?'

'We gave them breakfast in a bag. It wasn't ideal, but at least they got fed.'

'Great!' I say brightly. Apparently, my positivity is offensive, because it earns me a scowl.

'As I said, it's not ideal. The afternoons are more problematic because they won't be able to hang out here after school and we can't give them a hot meal.'

'But we could give them a sandwich?' I suggest. 'For three days? Is that something you can get on board with so we can spend the time we need on the kitchen?'

He grimaces. 'I suppose so.'

Well, fancy that. We have a compromise.

5

AIDE

We can't waste any time if we're to get this kitchen turned around in three days. I get the crew to work. In actual fact, having ten of us in the kitchen is impossible. There's just not enough room. I content myself with the compromise of having the five people from Venus who actually know what they're doing—aka the contractors—working on dismantling the old kitchen while I put the waste-of-space one—aka Carlotta—in the main hall with Gaz, Sylv and Judy. Khalid has bid us all a suave goodbye and gone back to the office under the apparent assumption that we're in safe hands.

Good.

It's better this way. Carlotta's out of my hair, and she can focus on the less skilled task of taking down the wooden panels along the walls while Frank and I direct operations in here and Reggie, Venus' electrician, gets to work disconnecting the appliances and the ancient plug sockets at a speed so impressive he'll earn himself a slap on the back and possibly a pint this evening.

Best of all, I don't have to see her. Don't have to attempt

not to do myself an injury because I'm distracted by her perfect fucking tits and not watching what I'm doing. *And* I don't have to listen to her presumably inane chatter the whole time, either.

Instead, I can work at a fair clip alongside the Venus guys, who all seem genuinely decent. Not that I'd expect an outfit like Venus to employ anyone sub-par, but they're consummate professionals who keep their heads down and get on with the job. We stick on the radio and work in relative silence to the soundtrack of Magic's jaunty pop tunes and even jauntier DJs.

She'll be in good hands next door. Gaz is already smitten, that much is clear. She already has him calling her *Lotta*. Stupid bastard. Judy will be charmed despite herself, and while Sylv doesn't suffer fools, she's generous-hearted, too. I'm sure they'll all get on just fine, and I'm hoping that by the time Carlotta's listened to what they have to tell her about the incredible work they do here, she'll be more sympathetic to our plight.

At twelve-thirty, I'm idly considering breaking for lunch and taking people's orders for the sandwich bar down the road when a certain someone pops her glossy head around the door and smiles prettily at us.

'Wow! You've made amazing progress in here!'

I grunt in acknowledgement. We really have. Almost all the old cupboard units and appliances are now lying out in the street, ready for the skip, which should show up later. The electrics have all been disconnected, and we've made quick work of chipping off the tiled backsplash with its filthy grouting. In its place will be sheeted stainless steel— far more hygienic and easier to wipe down.

The replacement materials have been chosen not only

for their ease of use but their ease of installation, given the time constraints we're working under.

'Anyway,' she says blithely, 'lunch is here.'

That gets my attention. I look up, allowing myself to take in the willowy silhouette of her body as she leans against the door frame. 'How so?'

'Oh, we always provide lunch on these jobs,' she says. 'It should have been in the brief.'

I won't argue with that. 'Lunchtime, folks,' I say, downing tools and heading into the men's loo to wash my hands.

Lunch would have been better described as a *feast*. Fucking hell. There are huge cardboard trays on the table in the hall with far too much food from some fancy deli I've never heard of. Bagels cut in half, their colourful fillings on display. Same with the wraps. There's chopped veg in little cartons. Tubs of hummus. Slices of grilled halloumi. Even some fucking sushi. Small bottles full of rainbow-coloured juices. I check out the printed menu card propped up beside one of the trays.

Falafel wrap with slaw and chipotle dressing.

Hard greens juice.

Smoked hummus with paprika and pine nuts.

Jesus Christ. It's far too extravagant, and I can't imagine how much food we could have bought for the kids with what Venus spends on catering for a single lunch. But I catch myself, because around me everyone is absolutely fucking delighted. Sylvie is poring over the menu card and discussing whether to go for a smoked salmon or a beetroot and avocado bagel first.

Judy has already dismissed the juices as 'wanky' and has the kettle going in the hall, where the power is still on. Still, she's putting away wraps at the speed of light.

So I let it go. They deserve a treat. God knows, they work bloody hard here, day after day. Well, Judy and Sylvie do. Gaz and I are just here to help with this overhaul. But a little fancy food won't hurt anyone, I suspect. So I mumble a gruff *thanks* and get stuck in.

∽

BY THE END of the day, the kitchen is a forlorn shell, a grubby, tired blank canvas, and we're exhausted. I have an early start tomorrow. Some of the volunteers will do a Costco run this evening and deliver the kids' breakfasts here at six-forty-five in the morning. That'll give us an hour to assemble them and pack them up in paper bags before the first round of tired, scruffy little patrons hit us. Sylvie will man the production line with me.

But before that, thank God, a cold beer and a hot shower and a soft bed await me at home. I'll sleep like the dead tonight.

Carlotta seeks me out as I'm giving the kitchen floor one last brush. The revolting lino tiles have gone, to be replaced with an easy-lay laminate that comes in rolls. I've sent Frank and his guys off already, having promised them a few pints once the kitchen's in on Wednesday. Everyone's too exhausted to socialise tonight.

Or maybe it's just me. Those guys do this every day. My day job is definitely making me soft. It's a good kind of exhaustion, though, that bone-tired feeling after an honest day's work. So different from the eye-strain that gets you after a day of squinting at your monitors.

She stands in the middle of the empty space now, fiddling with her rings. She has countless thin bands of gold on all her fingers. Some are studded with tiny jewels. Others are plain. Some don't even go past her second knuckle. They seem to float halfway up her beautiful, slender fingers. I noticed them when she was cupping her mug outside earlier, in the same way I noticed how much they suited her.

Delicate.

Decorative.

Expensive.

And totally fucking impractical.

'So,' she begins, 'Sylvie was telling me the plan for tomorrow morning.'

I flick a glance at her as I sweep. Her white t-shirt has dirt smeared on it, her hair is a little dishevelled, and it's oddly gratifying that this job has dirtied her up a little. Marked that ridiculous, pristine look she's going for. Not sure how she's kept those trainers so clean, though. And her nipples are still forging ahead, trying to blaze a path through her inadequate layers.

What the fuck is up with that? Does the woman have no circulation?

While I wrestle with keeping my eyes on her face, I can't fail to miss the way her gaze flickers over my body. I'm fucking filthy, but somehow it's not repulsion I spot in those dark, feline eyes.

It's interest.

'Yep,' I say, because that wasn't a question.

'I'd like to help, if that's okay.'

I stop and give her my full attention, leaning my hands on the top of the sweeping brush. My first instinct is a harsh *no fucking way*, but I tamp it down, because it's going to be a massive stretch with just me and Sylv in the morning. I've already told Judy we don't require her help. She's seventy-five, for fuck's sake. I don't want her doing twelve-hour days here.

'With breakfast?' I say instead.

'Yeah.'

I nod cautiously. 'Okay. If you're sure.'

'I am.' She twists her rings. 'I'd like to help—I think it'd be good to see what you guys do here.'

'You're on,' I tell her.

'Great.' She gives me a smile that's objectively beautiful and seemingly genuine, and, for some reason, it pisses me off. 'Well, have a good evening.'

'Wait,' I say as she makes to leave. I hold up two fingers. 'Two things.'

She stops. 'Sure.'

'One. Lose the shoes.'

She looks down. 'What's wrong with them?'

'What's *wrong with them* is that they're six grand trainers, which is fucking unethical in itself, if you ask me. And the kids coming in tomorrow may be poor as fuck, but believe me, they all have the SNKRS app on their old, crapped-out phones and they pore over that stuff. They know every Air Jordan collab under the sun, just like my twelve-year-old nephew does.

'So if you're going to stand there and tell me you think it's okay to wear six grand trainers to hand out breakfast to kids whose parents are too broke or too high to buy them breakfast cereal, then I'm going to stand here and tell you to read. The. Fucking. Room. Got it?'

There's anger pulsing through my bloodstream at the mere fact of having to explain this shit to her. My ears are ringing, and it's heady, and I don't fucking know why. Yeah, I have an entire fucking wardrobe of Air Jordans at home, mostly purchased under pressure from my sneakerhead nephew, Woody, but there's no way I'd ever wear them here.

There's also no way I'd ever spend more than two

hundred quid on a pair, no matter how rare they are. Six grand on trainers is just *wrong*.

We stare at each other for a moment.

She blinks first.

'You are one hundred percent right, and I apologise,' she says with a grace and poise I'm not expecting. 'I wasn't thinking. Consider it done. What was the second thing?'

Well, that was easier than I expected. But I suspect she won't let my second point land without a fight.

I clear my throat.

'You need to wear a better bra tomorrow,' I say, studiously training my eyes on her face.

Her jaw drops open. *'Excuse me?'*

'You heard me. You need to put those fucking nipples away. They're distracting to the point of being a hazard.'

She glares as me. 'You're actually calling my nipples a hazard. Please tell me you're not serious.'

I'm already deeply regretting bringing this up, but if it means I don't have to spend the rest of this project expending every ounce of energy I have on avoiding the peanuts she's smuggling, then it'll be worth it.

'Us looking at them could be a hazard,' I say with less conviction.

She puts her hands on her hips, which doesn't help *at all*, because the slender curves of this woman's body are knockout. *She's* a knockout, and she knows it. 'How so? Pray, tell me why my nipples are a hazard.'

'Don't get fancy with me. They are fucking mesmerising, and I need to make sure I and all the guys here keep our focus on the job at hand and don't do ourselves an injury because we can't keep our eyes off your tits.'

Okay. That was definitely a step too far.

'This is harassment,' she says. 'I suspect you don't come

from a corporate background, but you absolutely cannot say this to people in the workplace.'

She's right. Obviously. I would never, ever dream of speaking to a colleague like this. Not only that, but Totum has a million HR policies in place to make sure a conversation like this could never happen. So what the fuck I'm doing right now, I do not know.

I throw up one hand. 'This isn't a workplace. It's a fucking community project. If you don't like it, walk. Or put on more fucking clothes. And preferably a padded bra. You'll be more comfortable. You look like you're freezing.'

'I have poor circulation,' she says through gritted teeth.

'You need to work on your vascular system,' I tell her. I know about this stuff. I've done a couple of Wim Hof weekends. 'Ice baths are great. Or cold water swimming. You can start with cold showers.'

The look she's giving me could fell a lesser man. Or a fucking oak tree, probably. 'It sounds like the only person who needs a cold shower around here is you,' she grits out. 'I suggest you take one. Maybe you can bang one out while you're in there. It might make you less fixated on the extremities of my circulatory system. Good night, *Aide.*'

I can't help but smirk as I admire the spectacular view of her retreating arse.

If I'm ice, that woman is fire.

6

AIDE

'How'd it go?' Andy enquiries twenty minutes later as he steers my brand-new Defender through the traffic-logged streets of Notting Hill. My driver and all-round house manager picked me up a couple of streets away from the community centre. Having someone drive me is one of those things that sounds wanky on the face of it but is in fact, like most of my choices, grounded purely in practicality.

I can sit on the M4 like a muppet for the best part of an hour, or I can pay Andy to sit on the M4 like a muppet while I feverishly attempt to play catch-up on my day job. Also, he's more in love with this car—his new toy—than is healthy, in my view.

I sigh and let my head fall back against the leather seat as I crack open a bottle of Pellegrino. 'I dunno. Good, I think. We're ahead of schedule. The woman running it from Venus' side's a piece of work, though.'

Understatement. I think back to our conversation just now. A conversation in which I transcended the bounds of decency so spectacularly that I'd be facing a lawsuit if we were in a formal workplace. There's no explanation other than that she—and her tits—have driven me temporarily insane.

'Is that Paul Whatshisname's daughter?' Sometimes I think Andy spends more time reading the *Financial Times* than I do.

'That's the one.' I slug some water, the bubbles hitting the back of my throat with refreshing perfection. 'Carlotta.'

Carlotta Montefiore Charlton. What a mouthful. Even her name's high-maintenance.

He laughs. 'Jumped-up little princess, is she?'

'You can say that again.' I take another swig. 'She was wearing six grand trainers. On a building site. Fucking stupid.'

'These people have no idea of the value of money,' Andy says. 'It's indecent, that's what it is. But you can't be surprised when she's grown up that minted. It's different for you. You earned it. She had it handed to her.'

'Yeah,' I agree half-heartedly, wondering why slagging Carlotta off is sitting so uncomfortably in my gut. I'm not one to sit around and bitch, but people like her are so entitled it pisses me off. They have no fucking clue. Even if what they've built at Venus is impressive.

Beyond impressive.

That said, I have no idea if she's just a pretty little figurehead or if she actually works hard. God only knows.

It's time to change the subject.

'You see Emma today?' I ask Andy. Emma's his first grandchild. I think she's around six months old. His daughter lives not far away, and he and his wife, Maggie, are hands-on grandparents. Emma's his pride and joy.

He grins at me in the rear-view mirror. 'Yeah. She's

sitting up, all by herself. Can you believe it? She's a right little sweetheart.'

He's proud as punch, and it brings a smile to my face. I can't remember when Woody sat up for the first time, but I suppose it must feel like a miracle when you witness your own kid or grandkid doing it. 'Clever girl,' I say.

'She is. She's bright, that one. You mark my words.'

We settle into a contented silence, and I begin to scroll through my emails. Andy's been working for me for over a decade now. We met when one of my seed investors sent a car to fetch me for a pitch in Mayfair. Andy was behind the wheel. I was bricking it, and he could tell. He pulled over by Hyde Park and told me to take off my shoes and socks and go take a walk in the grass.

It did the trick. I pulled myself together, and I got the funding. I also kept Andy's number and started to use him for one-off jobs. We spent more and more time together, and it felt only natural to ask him and Maggie to move into one of the cottages on my grounds when I had my house built.

When I had my house built by *Venus*, I should say.

I wonder if and when Carlotta will work that out.

Anyway, they live on-site now and they look after the place because, God knows, I'm not on the move enough during the day to warrant a full-time driver.

I already know I'll murder whatever Maggie has cooked for me tonight.

My inbox is looking borderline manageable, thanks to my amazing Executive Assistant, Laetitia. Tish. She monitors my emails with terrifying ruthlessness. She monitors my entire *life* with terrifying ruthlessness. No one gets to me on email, or by phone, or in person, without getting past her first. She has my diary organised in fifteen-minute slots, and we catch up every morning on any requests for my time that don't automatically get declined.

Tish knows I just want to be left alone to do my job. I'd die for my team, I tolerate my investors, and everyone else can go to hell. Phone calls kill me. Zooms are a necessary evil that, again, get kept to fifteen minutes. My time is too precious and my attention span too short for anything else.

Slowly, slowly, I've built up a support network of people who understand the pressures I face. Who understand how unnatural it feels for me to have this public persona. How little interest I have in cultivating that persona. And who guard my time with ferocious jealousy.

I have my family, obviously, and I love them with all my heart, but they don't always get it, and the money's a constant point of discomfort, if not overt contention. Mainly because I can never get them to take as much as I want to give them. But Tish and Andy and Maggie and the others who form the inner circle of my personal and professional lives have my back, and I'd be in a fucking loony bin without them.

~

I COLLAPSE at the massive island in the centre of my kitchen and devour Maggie's excellent Moroccan chicken as soon as I'm in the door, washing it down with a cold beer. But I'm filthy and sweaty, and I need a shower before I go anywhere near my sofa or my bed. I stick my empty bowl in the dishwasher and amble tiredly through my home and up the cantilevered staircase that floats through the centre of my entrance hall. The staggering beauty of its simplicity never fails to hit me.

This home of mine is undoubtedly my haven. Settling

outside of central London, here in Osterley, has allowed me a serious footprint inside and out. I can't see another house, thanks to the maturing groves of trees we've planted around the perimeter. My own house is built on two stories, and we went overboard on the lateral space.

My brief to Venus was to create as much space and light and fluidity as possible. The rooms flow onto each other, punctuated by huge arches or double doorways. The building faces east-west, and the reception rooms straddle it front to back, enjoying the maximum amount of daylight in both the mornings and evenings. Above them, my master bedroom complex has a fucking enormous terrace where I spend as much time as possible.

In terms of materials, we went for only the most natural. The most sustainable. This is where I'm happy spending my money. This is where it feels right to invest.

I've made peace with the vast sums I sunk into this place. I'm aware that being environmentally conscious is often the privilege of the wealthy. And while I can't stomach spending money on stuff, pointless objects to fill my home for the sake of it, I can get on board with investing in materials and pieces that are kind to our planet. That respect it.

That's where the guys at Venus really excelled themselves, to be honest. I'm sure they have clients who demand gold taps and wall-to-wall marble, and I'm sure they do a great job for them. But they were as strong on the fundamentals as they were on the design elements, and I can sleep easy knowing my home's ecological footprint is as gentle as possible.

There are plants everywhere, too. That was another priority for me. After growing up in a cramped, squalid part of London, I knew I wanted to bring the outside indoors as much as possible. The polished floors of the ground floor, made from green concrete that's far more environmentally friendly than traditional concrete, give way to numerous built-in planters of the same substance. In turn, these planters are brimming with trees and plants.

There's even a water feature in the hallway. The sound of running water and the presence of living things both contribute greatly to my mental wellbeing. When I'm at home, away from the frenetic buzz of the office and the relentless pull of everyone who demands my time, I want to be soothed. I want no distractions. No fuss.

Which is why there's so little furniture, much to the dismay of my interior designer. There are a few amazing, oversized paintings. Smooth, abstract sculptures crafted from stone. And the odd piece of mid-century furniture. But not much else.

Every single item in my home has to justify its existence.

Just like I justify my own existence every fucking day.

I wish I could tell you my mind is quiet, stilled from hours of manual labour today, but that's not true. It's the opposite, in fact. My brain is busy and fizzing, and it's not from the riot of emails I just processed in the car. It's from my day at the centre.

It's from dealing with that fucking woman.

I didn't even have much interaction with her. She was in a different room for most of the day, to be fair. But she got under my skin in every possible way, and she's still under my fucking skin even now.

And I do not fucking appreciate it.

I crank the handle in my shower, and a torrent of water hits the concrete floor of my wet room with gratifying force. Less gratifying is the reminder of my last verbal exchange with Lotta.

It sounds like the only person who needs a cold shower around here is you.

Jesus Christ. Much as I hate to admit it, she's not wrong. I hate to admit even more that a good proportion of the friction in my brain just now isn't anger or resentment or irritation.

It's desire.

Because not only is she a knockout of the finest proportions, but she's a firecracker. I mean, she's fifty percent Italian and one hundred percent entitled, so it shouldn't be a huge shock.

What's a bigger shock is that *I liked it.*

I liked riling her. Getting a reaction. And I fucking loved the fact that she was eyeing me up too, even if I suspect her physical reaction to me pissed her off just as much as my carnal reaction to her did me.

The steam coming off the water tells me I'm good to go. No cold shower tonight. My tired, aching muscles need heat. I really am getting soft—need to double up on the PT sessions when this project is over.

I peel off my vest and unzip my filthy cargo pants. Jesus, I stink. Unfortunately, there's one part of my body that's not getting soft and it's my dick.

Nope.

It is rock fucking hard and it definitely hasn't got the memo that my body is exhausted.

Fuck my life.

I shuffle into the shower and hang my head, letting the torrent of water massage my scalp and course over my sore shoulder and back muscles as I attempt to ignore my throbbing dick.

Attempt unsuccessful.

After a minute or two, I give in. I close my eyes, and I fist it roughly at the root.

Jesus fuck, that feels good.

I pump some shower gel into my hand and smooth it over my length. The glide of skin against skin has me huffing out a sigh of anguish and ecstasy, because this is what I need. A quick wank to release all that tension. I close my eyes and pull up an oldie but a goodie from the spank bank: Margot Robbie, spreading her legs in *The Wolf of Wall Street*.

She's so hot, and so golden, with that breathy voice telling Leo she's not wearing panties. She does it for me every time. She's uncrossing her legs, and—

Fuck. *Fuck*.

The second I let my mind relax, Margot's buggered off somewhere, and in her place is Carlotta, headlights on full beam.

She sashays towards me, dark eyes flashing, pulling her t-shirt over her head as she approaches. The lace bra that tormented me today is white, so pure and chaste against her tanned skin, except that I can see her taut pinky-brown nipples through the lace.

I pump harder. *Fuck,* that's good. That's exactly what the basest part of me needs. Other parts of my brain are disgusted with myself right now, but I'm past caring.

In my fantasy, I reach around and unhook her bra with one hand. It falls, and she's topless, those dark, satiny tresses cascading over her shoulders and those beautiful, beautiful tits on full display for me.

I start salivating and glance down at my dick, watching in horrified fascination at how steely it is at the mere thought of a topless Carlotta, how hard the muscles in my forearm are working.

I squeeze my eyes closed again.

She's sinking gracefully to her knees in front of me, licking those full lips and casting teasing glances my way through her thick lashes. She unbuckles my belt and unzips my trousers, shoving them down, easing my boxers down too as she presses those delicate, ring-covered hands to my quads and takes me in her mouth.

In the capable, depraved depths of my monkey brain, the wetness sluicing over me, gliding up and down my length, teasing my sensitive crown, is not my shower and my own soaped-up hand.

It's her warm, willing mouth.

I rub the pad of my thumb over the pre-cum beading at my tip, and it's her greedy, teasing tongue as she gazes up at me for approval.

She fucking has it.

I'd get to my knees for her right this second.

I'd prostrate myself at her six-grand feet.

I pump my length hard, and really it's me holding her beautiful face between my hands, my fingers clawing at her jaw through her masses of dark hair, as I fuck her mouth and she takes me all the way in like the little champ I bet she is.

The heat is building, building, engulfing me so thoroughly it'll be the death of me. I'm breathing hard as I attempt to withstand this onslaught of the purest kind of pleasure, of oblivion, there is in this life.

So fucking good, I tell her. I'm so close I can barely get the words out. *God, I'm so close. I'm so—*

I'm pumping furiously, my hand a blur of movement over my cock as I chase my high. I slap a palm against the slate wall of the shower for support as my orgasm races through me. And then it's upon me, and I open my mouth, locking my jaw in a silent scream, bucking and shaking with the intensity of the pleasure as the evidence of that pleasure erupts across the shower wall in endless hot ropes.

When I'm done, I collapse my forehead against the cool of the wall. Triumph and despair course through me equally hard, because that little fantasy I just concocted was so fucking real as to be terrifying.

7

LOTTA

Thank God for the concierge at Elgin. When I opened my front door this morning, there was a Nike shoebox on the mat containing what must be their least expensive, least exciting trainers in my size.

They're surprisingly comfy, though. Almost bouncy. That's the reason I give myself, anyway, for the spring in my step when I turn up at the centre at six-fifty-five prompt.

I mean business today. My hair's tied back in a perky ponytail, I'm in head-to-toe Lululemon under my lightweight trench, and my Nikes will inspire envy in precisely no one. I look ready for action, if I say so myself. I was up till midnight signing off on which event sponsorships Venus should bid on for next year's summer season, but for some reason I'm feeling galvanised as hell this morning.

Especially because I got a Nespresso machine couriered to my flat last night, and I have it with me, boxed up with about three million pods.

Someone must already be here, because a long folding table is set out in the play area, near the front gate. There are rows upon rows of paper bags, all unfolded and standing stiffly to attention.

I really hope we don't get a gust of wind.

Aide emerges from the building, an insane number of carrier bags hanging from his forearms and a couple of massive industrial chopping boards in his hands on which are balanced a few tubs of butter. He dumps the boards on the table and the bags on the ground next to it before giving me a once-over.

He could not look less pleased to see me, but he manages a gruff *morning*. I did wonder if he'd regret the way he spoke to me yesterday, but it would seem not.

'What can I do?' I ask.

'Bagels. You can cut them or butter them.'

'Um, butter?' I ask. I venture over to the table and peer into the paper bags. No wonder they haven't blown away—they're each weighed down with a bottle of smoothie.

'What do they get?' I ask, grabbing a board and taking the lid off one of the butter tubs as Aide reaches into one of the carriers and pulls out several packs of bagels. He disregards the sticky tie around the top of the first one and cuts the plastic open with a bread knife.

I treat myself to a little peek as he holds the first bagel between two fingers and slices it cleanly through. He's in an unbranded navy hoodie this morning and a clean but otherwise identical version of the heavy-duty cargo pants he had on yesterday. His hood is down, his hair is slightly damp and deliciously tousled, and the neckline of his hoodie is low enough both to show off his cross, lying happily against that perfect smattering of dark hair, and to suggest another tank top underneath, because there's no sign of a t-shirt.

Yep. That'll do nicely, thank you.

The guy is so fucking hot it's frankly ridiculous. He is

hands-down the most *male* man I've met in real life, while still being unfairly beautiful. In this stance, the insane thickness of his eyelashes is more obvious as he focuses on the lucky bagel. He's tugging at his lower lip with his teeth while he finishes slicing.

The fingers holding the knife are long. Manly but shapely, covered in grazes. Obviously, he cuts the bagel with perfect precision and lays it on my board. If he touches his women with the same care and finesse that he touches his bagels, then they must be very happy.

Very happy indeed.

'Butter it, then foil,' he says, pointing at the enormous roll of Costco-branded foil next to me. 'They get a smoothie, bagel and a mini box of Cornflakes.'

I must have made a face, because he says, 'No, it's not the most nutritious breakfast on the planet. In the centre we can usually give them some hot protein, but today we make do. And they're fussy little shits. You'd be amazed how many of them refuse to eat the wholemeal bagels, so we're stuck with white.'

'Fair enough,' I say. He's been doing this longer than me, and I'm not about to second-guess him.

'What's in that box?' he asks, nodding at the ground.

'Nespresso machine. And a tonne of pods.'

He rolls his eyes. 'Course it is. Jesus Christ.'

'Hey. Don't knock it. I'm much more efficient when I'm caffeinated. And I saw you putting two tea bags in your mug yesterday, so you're not exactly one to judge people's beverage choices.'

I finish buttering the bagel and wrap it up. One down, ninety-nine to go.

Sylvie turns up a minute or two later and takes over the buttering from me, leaving me with the decidedly low-skilled task of wrapping the finished goods. Her silent and low-level grumpy demeanour suggests she's not a morning person, so the three of us work in silence.

～

THE FIRST COUPLE of kids trickle in around seven-forty—a boy with who I assume is his younger sister. They both have pale, freckled faces and fiery red hair, and they wear a navy and grey uniform with *Avondale Primary* printed across the fronts of their sweatshirts.

'Alright, mate?' Aide asks the boy as I hand him and his sister a bag each.

'Yeah,' he whispers.

'Good man. You gonna get some footie in at school today?'

'I hope so, at lunch.' His voice is so quiet I can barely hear him.

'Keep practicing those keepy uppies, yeah? I wanna see what you've got next week, when we're back up and running.'

The boy nods. 'I'm up to fifty-two now.' His voice is a little louder and filled with a pride that has the corners of my mouth turning up.

His sister already has her hand in her paper bag and is tugging off the foil so she can get stuck into her bagel. There's an enormous gap where her two front teeth used to be, but she rips an impressive chunk off. She stares at me, wide-eyed, taking in my appearance, and I'm suddenly very glad I'm wearing the least desirable trainers known to man.

'Fifty-two? That's awesome, mate!' Aide holds up his hand, and the boy high-fives him. They grin at each other. It's definitely the most animated I've seen him so far. 'Well, you'll be wiping the floor with me next week for sure.' He shakes his head in mock despair. 'Fifty-two keepy uppies. Jesus. Will we see you for dinner?'

'Mum wants us back home after school,' the little girl pipes up, her mouth full.

Aide and Sylvie exchange a glance.

'No probs. Sylv or I'll drop something round, yeah?' Aide says. 'Here, take another bag in case that doesn't touch the sides, okay? You need to keep that strength up if you're going to be the next Marcus Rashford.'

The boy's face lights up again, and I'm unclear if it's the mention of a football hero or the prospect of more food that's done it. 'Thanks a lot, bro. See ya,' he says.

As they leave, Aide and Sylvie exchange another glance before Aide trails them slowly to the gate. He leans against the post and watches as they walk down the street.

'Are they okay?' I ask Sylvie tentatively. Something about their pale little faces doesn't sit well with me.

She sniffs. 'Not really. They're always first up. Always starving.'

'Did they miss dinner, do you think?'

'Almost certainly. They're their mum's carers, basically. It's been enough of a struggle getting them to do a full day of school without them being able to sneak out for dinner, too.'

'Fucking hell,' I mutter. 'So, will Aide bring them food?'

'Yeah.' She smiles fondly in his direction. 'He takes it so personally—he's on a mission to keep the tummies of every child in this neighbourhood full. And to make sure they get to school okay.' She nods at the gate.

'They look far too young to go on their own,' I say worriedly. 'Are they allowed?'

She laughs, but there's no humour in it. 'Forget about

allowed. Their mum's housebound. Their dad's long gone. If they don't take themselves, they won't ever go.'

I look at Aide. His body is slumped against the gatepost, all the joviality he showed the boy gone from his demeanour. He rubs his forehead with his thumb, his gaze still fixed in the same spot.

'Is he watching them?'

'He's keeping an eye out for as long as he can. Don't worry—it's not far, and there's a lollipop man down the street.'

Oh, Aide. Aide. Don't do this. Don't be a rude, inappropriate, grumpy prick and then tear that heart of yours out and let it bleed on your sleeve for some kids you can't save.

I don't think I can handle it if you do.

8

AIDE

Whatever grudging tolerance that's grown in me for Carlotta as she's mucked in the past couple of mornings disappears as soon we get inside each day and she takes off that coat, because under its blessed shapelessness is lycra for days and *no fucking bra.*

I didn't think the situation could get worse than it was on Monday.

I was wrong.

Today, for example, she's serving us up spray-on leggings in dark grey. They're so tight they could pass for body paint, and Jesus Christ, do they hug every perfect curve.

Her arse.

That *arse.*

It's so smooth, so pert, I could get to my knees behind her right now and press my nose to the seam running between her cheeks and die a happy man.

The leggings hint at toned, athletic thighs and finish halfway down her calves, showing off trim, tanned ankles.

And the front view is even worse.

She has one of those ultra-lightweight, zip-up yogi

jackets on. It's practically a second skin. The zip is only closed to just below her tits, offering a peek of bronzed skin and, so help me God, a shot of cleavage above the hot-pink sliver of whatever top she's got on underneath.

But that's not the worst part.

Oh, no.

The *worst* part is that the thin layer of jacket and the thin layer of top and the fucking useless layer of what's presumably a zero-coverage sports bra is totally bloody inadequate in the fight against her pneumatic nipples, and their outline is poking through her clothes clear as day, perky as you like, once a-fucking-gain.

I stand corrected.

Turns out, that's not the worst part. When I take a break from the kitchen an hour later, I find Carlotta, Gaz, Judy and Sylv having a grand old time together, laughing away behind their face masks as they sand the glue remnants off the parts of the wall where the panelling was previously.

It seems Carlotta's worked up a heat, because her flimsy jacket is nowhere to be seen. Instead, she looks like she's on the brink of leading an aerobics class.

Her irritatingly jaunty ponytail hides nothing.

Her front and back view are now even more affronting.

Killer figure in a skimpy, strappy vest and yoga pants? Check.

Nipples that look likely to tear through the fabric of said vest any moment now? Fucking *check*.

Nightmare sports-yogi-whatever-bra peeking out with zero protection in the front and a zillion of the most alluring, impractical teeny straps criss-crossed over the tanned skin of her upper back in a way that would make anyone want to go full caveman?

Check.

Check.

Check.

I can't do this. I don't know what the hell is wrong with me, but I can't be in the same building as her when she looks like that. I can barely even think straight.

See straight.

Mum would say I'm going blind from too much wanking.

She may not be wrong.

My dick is chafed from wanking in the shower. In bed. Even my outdoor ice bath hasn't helped alleviate my frustration.

I turn on my heel and stomp back to the kitchen for my phone.

'I need to run out for an hour,' I growl at the guys. We're on the clock here, but needs must. Besides, we're nearly done in here. The Venus team works *hard*.

Twenty minutes and one hired Boris bike later, I'm dumping the bike in front of Harrods and running inside.

'Women's underwear?' I ask the doorman, trying to catch my breath. He looks me up and down in a way that's more confused than snotty.

'First floor, sir,' he says.

'Ta.' I take off at a peg and climb the escalator two steps at a time.

Once I've navigated the warren of seemingly endless rooms of women's clothing, I find myself in the bowels of the store, surrounded by lingerie. A cursory glance tells me Carlotta would look fucking amazing in all of it, and none of it is what I need in my life, and I will be requiring some serious help.

I look around again and spot a sturdy-looking older woman wearing a tape measure around her neck and a name badge that reads *Audrey*. She'll do nicely. I already have a feeling Audrey will take me in hand. Help me through my misery.

'How can I help you, sir?' she asks, graciously ignoring my dusty trousers. I'm sweating in my hoodie after that frantic bike ride, but I suspect grimy vests aren't welcome in Harrods so I'll keep it on till I get out of here.

'I'm looking for a bra,' I blurt out.

'Ah.'

We stare at each other.

She presses her lips together then, when I'm not forthcoming with further detail, says, 'And will that be for yourself, sir?'

'Jesus, no!' I practically shout.

She raises her eyebrows at me in a schoolmarmish manner.

'No,' I repeat, more quietly this time. 'For a… friend.'

For a gorgeous prick-tease non-*friend with fantastic tits and porn-star nipples who's quickly becoming the bane of my—and my cock's—existence.*

'Right you are. Any particular style you're after?'

I swallow. This is excruciating. I've bought lingerie for women before, but that usually involves me giving their vitals to Tish and having her order from Matches or Net à Porter.

I should totally have called Tish for this.

I'm way out of my depth here.

'I'm after something…'

Ugly.

Asexual.

Man-repelling.

Dick-shrivelling.

'...full coverage. Something really plain, so you can't see anything through clothes. Like no patterns, or outlines, or...'

I shoot her a long, pleading, and hopefully telepathic look.

'Nipples?' she suggests.

I give her a curt nod of relief. 'Exactly.'

'Ah. So a t-shirt bra, then? Something that won't show any lines?'

'That sounds great. Yes.'

'Well,' she says, 'we have plenty of those. What colour?'

I think. 'White?'

'That's fine. Just be aware that white can show up under thinner light-coloured fabric.'

The panic rises up in me again. 'Oh, no. Don't want that. What else is there?'

'How about nude?'

Nude? No, that sounds terrible. A sudden vision of Carlotta in some fucking see-through, mesh, *nude* bra, everything on full display, has me light-headed.

I shake my head frantically. 'No, you don't understand. She—my friend—has nipples that need serious reining in. Like, remember that Sofia Vergara movie where she shoots bullets from her t—breasts? They're like that. *Nude* won't cut it. She needs serious buffering.'

She's staring at me, and I realise belatedly that *Machete Kills* may not have been the under-rated gem for her that it was for me. Thankfully, she takes pity on me and pats me on the arm. 'Nude's a colour, dear, not an opacity descriptor. It sounds like you might be after a skin-coloured bra, is that right? That way you'll get minimal outline.'

'Yeah,' I breathe. 'That sounds perfect, thanks.'

'Well, let's take a look then, shall we?' She bustles off and calls, 'What size?'

What size?

What size?

Oh, Jesus. I attempt to mentally measure Carlotta's tits with my fail-safe 'handful' methodology while not actually lifting my hands in the middle of Harrods and forming them into actual cup shapes.

'Thirty-two D,' I say. 'No, wait. C. No, D.' She's definitely a D cup, especially with that slight frame of hers.

The salesperson wisely waits.

I nod with a confidence I do not feel. 'Thirty-two D.'

Five minutes later, I'm emerging into the July sunshine, a staggering one-hundred-and-twenty pounds poorer and in possession of the ugliest bra I've ever seen. It's the colour of granny tights and about a hundred times thicker.

If Carlotta's nipples are bullets, this is a bulletproof vest.

Perfect.

9

LOTTA

'And I said'—Gaz stretches out his arms theatrically—'gimme the fucking fiver, mate.'

He collapses with the utter hilarity of his punchline, and the rest of us follow. I have no clue what he's talking about half the time, but we've been falling about laughing for the past hour. This guy cracks me up. It's his delivery. The stories he's telling about his and Aide's juvenile delinquency are pretty funny in their own right, but the way he tells them is priceless.

'Tell her about the time you and Aide pulled the plastic fork stunt at school,' Judy urges him.

I gape. 'You were at school together?'

'Course we were,' Gaz says. 'All the way from Year Seven. He was a lot cleverer than me, but he always managed to get us into trouble.'

Judy shakes her head mournfully. 'He was a troublesome little twat at school, he was. Mark my words. I'm glad he managed to pull his head out of his arse and do so well for himself.'

I don't miss the warning shake of the head Sylvie gives

her, though I have no idea what she's talking about. And, while it's not obvious that Aide has done particularly well for himself, I've seen enough this morning not to judge. I know the gap between rich and poor in London is a travesty, but this morning really brought it home to me just how poor *poor* can mean.

So if these guys see Aide as a success story, then maybe he is. He's here, showing up every day to support his community, isn't he? That's got to count for a lot.

Anyway, I'm more interested in what Judy said before that.

'Troublesome little twat, you say? Tell me more.'

Gaz points at me. 'You, my friend, are going to need a cuppa for this. Boy, has Uncle Gaz got some stories for you.'

'Let's make it espresso,' I suggest. No way am I drinking more of that pencil sharpenings shit.

When Gaz, Judy and Sylvia have sorted themselves out with cups of tea and I've produced the perfect coffee—thank you, Nespresso—we take a seat outside in the play area. We've earned a break, and I could do with some fresh air. It's gorgeous out now. I sit back in my shitty plastic chair and stretch luxuriously. My arms are stiff from the sanding.

Gaz dips a hobnob so far into his tea, and for so many seconds, that I'm positive it'll disintegrate and drop to the bottom of the mug, never to be seen again.

But nope. He fishes it out, soggy but intact, and pops the entire thing in his mouth. Judy snorts.

'Right,' he says when he's swallowed it. He rubs his hands together. 'How naughty do you want to go? Cos we were very naughty.'

'You mentioned plastic forks?' I say with trepidation.

'That was a good one,' Gaz says, a nostalgic grin on his face. 'The thing you've gotta know about our Aide is that he is a sneaky. Little. Fucker. Came up with the most amazing concepts. He was the big picture guy. I was the executor.' He points his thumbs at his chest.

'Otherwise known as Aide's gimp,' Judy says, nodding sagely as she brandishes her hobnob.

'Now, now, Judy. That's not very nice,' Gaz chides. 'I was his henchman.'

'And you usually got the rap,' she retorts.

He inclines his head. 'Harsh but fair. Anyway, our devious little Aide liked to play mind games with the teachers.'

'Why?' I ask.

'Boredom,' Gaz and Judy say together.

Gaz shrugs. 'Right. He was too smart for his own good, he was. The teachers didn't know how to keep him busy. So he used that magic brain of his for all sorts of nefarious purposes. Anyway, the forks. Aide rounded up a whole gang of us for that one—must have been five or six of us. We got up stupidly early in the summer term and stuck plastic forks into the grass all over the games pitch.

'They used it for everything, but it would have been a cricket and athletics pitch that term. We got two thousand forks from Poundland, and we stuck all of them into the grass, prongs down, all over the pitch. Mr Hell, that's the PE teacher, went fucking ballistic. His name was Mr Hail, but we called him Mr Hell because he was such a sadistic twat.'

'Oh my God,' I gasp. This is brilliant. 'And *Aide* did this? He seems so serious.'

'He's seriously twisted,' Gaz clarifies. 'He's an evil genius. He'd stew over this stuff for hours and hours. You have no idea. Honestly, you don't want to get on the wrong side of him. This one time'—he stops to guffaw and slap his knee— 'Oh my *God*, this one time, the girls' school across the road put a stop to any socials between us and them because apparently some of the girls complained to the teachers that the boys were a bad influence on them.

'So Aide made this banner. It was, like, eight feet long. And he hung it across their entrance.' He's doubled over, laughing so hard that I can't help laughing too, even though I have no idea where this story is going. 'It said.' He laughs silently, his fist to his mouth. All I can hear is his wheezing. Judy's watching him with the most affection I've seen her show anyone. Sylvie and I exchange an amused glance.

'Sorry.' Gaz straightens up and uses his hand to fan his face dramatically. 'I will prevail. It said *VIRGIN MEGAS-TORE* in massive capital letters. It was fucking. Brilliant. Honestly, I'm glad that guy finally put his brain to good use.'

I can feel my mouth hanging open. 'Virgin Megastore? Oh my God. They must have been livid.'

'Fucking ironic, if you ask me,' Judy says, crossing her arms. 'Those St Bernadette's girls were little sluts, every last one of them. Still are.'

I dip my head to my espresso cup so she can't see how hard I'm trying not to laugh. These two are the ultimate comedic double act. They should be on stage. I'd definitely buy tickets.

Gaz tuts. 'Judith, Judith. We've talked about this. The year is 2023. You cannot slut-shame women in this day and age. It's called *embracing your sexuality*.'

'Sexuality, my arse,' Judy says, nonplussed. 'I'm sure some of them are on the game.'

'As long as they're their own boss, that's called entrepreneurship,' Gaz tells her. 'You have a lot to learn, my sweetling. Stick with me and Lotta here, and we'll set you straight.'

'Call me your *sweetling* again and I'll break your arm,'

Judy says. She pushes her glasses up her nose and smiles sweetly at him.

Bloody hell.

I'm totally out of my depth with this lot.

But back to Aide, who's becoming more of an enigma every second. I can't believe this shit.

'So when did someone put the stick up Aide's arse?' I wonder out loud.

Sylvie sniggers.

Judy shoots me daggers.

'He settled down in Upper Sixth,' Gaz muses. 'I think A Levels finally kept that brain of his busy. And he got a girl-friend—Mary. Fucking hell, she was hot.' He shakes out his hand. 'She kept him distracted, if you know what I mean.'

I have no explanation or justification for the tremor of jealousy that courses through me and makes me shudder.

Mary. Ugh. She sounds wholesome as fuck.

'Was she from that girl's school?' I ask neutrally.

'Yeah. But she definitely didn't belong in the Virgin Megastore by the time he finished with her, dirty bastard.' Gaz rubs his hands together in glee. 'Fuck, he's always got the hottest girls. Total stunners. Still does. Lucky bastard. If he wasn't my best mate, I'd hate his guts.'

'He's a looker,' Judy observes. 'And he has a huge ding-dong, if I'm not mistaken. I think it's the girls who are the lucky ones.'

I'm so shocked that I go to inhale and instead manage to choke on some air, resulting in a massive coughing fit. Sylvie gets up to rub my back.

'You okay, love?' she asks.

'Yes,' I wheeze. I sound like I'm dying.

I *feel* like I'm dying.

I cannot believe what just came out of Judy's mouth.

'She's not used to you, Judy,' Gaz chides. 'You've got to watch that potty mouth of yours. You can't just go around dropping Aide's ding-dong into the conversation or being a dirty little cougar. It's unseemly. Got it?'

'Then someone should tell him not to strut around the place in tracksuit bottoms with no briefs on,' Judy argues. 'It's not right, letting it all hang out like a boa constrictor.'

'I cannot with you today, Judith,' Gaz says, getting to his feet and pretending to pick her up. 'I just cannot. It's time for your nap, dear.'

'Fuck you,' Judy says.

I get myself upright and pat Sylvie's hand to thank her. She's the only normal one around here.

Gaz sits back down. 'Remember, though, the vaseline thing? And the KY jelly, if we're on a lube theme?'

I grimace. 'I really don't think I want to know.'

'Oh, don't worry. They were separate incidents,' Gaz says. 'One time, Aide sellotaped a massive tube of KY to our RE teacher's board eraser, and another time we vaseline-d pretty much every door in the school.'

'Let me guess,' I say drily. 'Before dawn?'

'Yep. He did his best work in the early hours of the morning. It was definitely his MO—sneak in before dawn and wreak utter havoc.'

'Remember when he took a single screw out of all the desks in, what was it, Year Nine?' Judy asks. 'And then he went to the Head and presented him with a bucket of screws. Zero context. Said "Sir, I've found these". What an impudent little bollox he was. You both were.'

'Best days of my life,' Gaz says, stretching.

'Hang on.' I lean forward. 'How come you know so much about these two, Judy?'

'Well, dear, Gaz is my secret love child,' she says.

My eyes widen.

'Only kidding.' She laughs heartily at her own joke.

'You fucking wish,' Gaz says.

'I really do not. I've run this place for years, Lotta. Years and years. Twenty-five, to be precise. And I had the bad luck to have these little turds here every bloody weekday afternoon for a few of those.'

I look between the two of them. 'Gaz and Aide came here?'

Judy lets out a sigh of fatigue. 'Did they ever? They were the bane of my life.'

I rub the toe of my trainer against the ancient tarmac and stare at it to hide the fact that I can't quite look Gaz in the eye right now. I wasn't sure how he and Aide were connected to this place, because I didn't like to ask. But I certainly didn't suspect for a minute that they used to avail of it.

That they may possibly even have *depended* on it.

The children I've seen this morning and yesterday morning have haunted me. It's something about that mix of resignation and resilience in their demeanour that hits me right in my stomach whenever I think about it. They've accepted their utterly shitty lot, and they get on with it.

They're kids.

They deal with it.

But *fuck*, they shouldn't have to.

That little ginger-haired duo, the brother and sister, hit me especially hard. They were first through the gates this morning, too, grabbing their breakfast bags and thanking Aide for the pizza he'd had delivered the previous night.

I can't remember what I ate for breakfast when I was their age, but I do remember Mamma accompanying Gabe and me to school every morning in the back of a chauffeur-driven Mercedes.

I make a mental note to grab Sylvie as soon as this is over and discreetly request that pair's address. I'll call my local deli and see if they can't send over something home-made and microwavable—lasagne, maybe. Or shepherd's pie.

It's the very least I can do, and it's so far from enough it's not funny.

10

LOTTA

Aide slips back in through the front gate as I'm ruminating. He's taken off his hoody and is holding it in front of him like a weird bundle. It's a bit odd, but I don't think much about it because I'm far too busy ogling the fine, fine view that is him in his vest top and work pants. He looks even hotter when he has his tool belt on, but I can handle him without it, too.

There's a fine sheen of sweat on his skin. It glistens on his arms, enhancing the sculptural beauty of his delts and biceps and making it hard for me to think about anything except licking a trail through it. He turns to look at me, and the cross so perfectly nestled against that dusting of chest hair glints in the sunlight.

Maybe God's reminding me not to have carnal thoughts about this poor man. My *nonna* would definitely say so.

Now might be a good time to confess I've been taking as many photos as I can for Venus' social media, mainly fly-on-the-wall shots, and would you know, a lot of them have turned out to be of Aide?

Aide wielding a power drill.

Aide handing out breakfast bags. (I didn't snap the kids. I'm not that awful.)

Aide's muscles flexing as he helps carry the enormous old industrial oven out of the kitchen.

I may or may not have spent over an hour studying the Aide-porn at home last night, a glass of chilled and well-earned Gavi in hand.

'We were just telling Lotta about our escapades at school, mate,' Gaz informs him now.

Aide raises an eyebrow. 'None of it's true,' he tells me with a straight face.

'Shame,' I say, 'because you've definitely gone up in my estimation in the last ten minutes.'

He rakes his sweat-dampened hair off his face, and I swoon a little. 'How so?'

'It sounds like you were a lot more fun in those days,' I say archly.

'I was a lot more fucked up, that's what I was.' There's an ominous undercurrent to his tone.

'That's what I said,' Judy says. 'And look at you now. We're all so proud of you.'

'Thanks, Jude,' he says, shooting her a small smile. He makes as if to leave us to it, but Gaz stops him.

'Mate. Remember when we stuck the plastic forks all over Mr Hell's pitch?'

Aide's smile turns real in an instant, and his entire face lights up. 'Fuck, yeah. That was the highlight of my academic career. Jesus, he was such a wanker.'

'He didn't have an issue with you,' Judy reminds him.

'He treated Gaz like shit, though, so that's all that counts,' Aide says.

'Because I was fat as fuck and crap at sports,' Gaz says.

'Doesn't matter. He made your life a living hell, and he

needed some of his own medicine. Oh my God—remember the Rice Krispies?'

He claps his free hand to his mouth, still clutching his bundled hoodie like it's a newborn baby with the other. Gaz gasps and shakes out his wrist.

'Fucking hell, mate. That was *magic.*'

'I lied about the forks,' Aide says. 'The Rice Krispies were the best moment of my life.' He turns to me, his expression animated. 'So Mr Hell used to make us play sports in all weather, yeah? Even when it was pissing it down. He was such a twat. But he'd always bring this massive golf umbrella along to keep himself nice and dry.'

He shakes his head at the memory, and I smile despite myself. I love seeing him like this. Lit up from within. 'God, that used to piss us off no end. What a tool. So, one day we had rugby training, and the weather was shite, and we knew, right, we just *knew* Hell would make us get out there and play. Jesus, the pitch was totally churned up—it was like something out of The Battle of the Somme. I think it was double PE after lunch. Did we sneak into his office at lunch, Gaz?'

Gaz nods, looking pleased. 'Yes we did, my friend, yes we did.'

Judy presses her lips together and shakes her head primly, like she wants to be disgusted but, in fact, knows she will be tickled pink by this retelling.

'So we find his umbrella,' Aide says, hitting his stride, 'and we open it up and empty in a whole box of Rice Krispies.'

He's beaming now, while Gaz has already lost it. He's bent over double in his chair, shaking with laughter. I giggle.

'We close it back up and fasten it nice and tight, right,' Aide says, miming the action, 'and we leave it. So then, after lunch, we're all filing outside for rugby and it's fucking horrible—like, seriously pissing it down—and Gaz and I are just watching. And waiting. And sure enough, Mr Hell puts his umbrella out, all self-important and smug, and opens it.'

He pauses for effect, and the rest of us wait for the punchline. Everyone except Gaz, that is, because he's still laughing uncontrollably against his thighs.

Aide gestures with his hand. 'And they go fucking. *Everywhere.* All over him. All over the ground. He starts screaming, and he kind of shakes out the brolly, and kids start shrieking as they get hit with Rice Krispies. But it's chucking it down, right? So the ones all over his head and shoulders go instantly soggy.' He chuckles like he's recounting his favourite childhood Christmas. 'And they all stick to him. He's covered in all these soggy things that look like warts. Hundreds of them. It was, hands down, the best thing I have *ever* seen.'

'Oh my God,' I say, shuddering and laughing because that is just grim beyond belief. 'They must have gone down his top, too.'

'They did,' Aide agrees cheerily. 'They went *everywhere.* He had to go and have a shower, and he called his wife to bring in some fresh clothes for him.'

'Did you guys get caught?'

'Nope.' He winks at me conspiratorially, and the earth stills on its axis for a moment. 'I mean, he knew exactly who it was, but he could never prove anything.'

'Best prank I've ever heard,' I tell him, earning myself another devastating smile. Let me tell you, when this guy lets go and enjoys himself, it's truly beautiful.

I wish he'd do it more often.

As if he can read my mind, his smile vanishes, and it's as instantly chilly as if the sun's just gone in.

'I need a quick word.' He jerks his head towards the building.

'Okay,' I say, unfolding myself from my chair. Uh oh. Aide avoids me like the plague, so if he wants to talk to me then he probably has a gripe.

'Good times, mate, good times,' a barely recovered Gaz says to him as he passes. Gaz holds out his hand, and they high-five before gripping each other hard.

I follow Aide inside and into the small office next to the kitchen. We've made good progress these past couple of days. The main interior already looks airier without that dreadful yellowed pine panelling. The floor in the big hall is wooden and in good shape, so it's staying. Painting and decorating will make up the bulk of the next week's labour. We may even finish up early. Weirdly, the thought depresses me, mainly because I won't be able to ogle *this* arse when I'm back in my office.

Not that I'll miss his personality.

'What's up?' I ask as he closes the door behind us.

He burrows under his bundled-up hoodie and thrusts something into my hands that I realise after a second is a small Harrods carrier bag.

'I got you something and I need you to wear it tomorrow,' he says. 'It doesn't have to be a big deal, so don't make it one.'

I stare at him, gobsmacked, then down at the bag. 'Okay,' I say slowly.

Aide has bought me something to wear.

From Harrods.

My mind is racing. So's my heart rate. I have no idea what it could be or what I'm supposed to do with this new information.

He nods curtly at the bag. 'Go on.'

I peek in and see only tissue paper. Carefully, I pull the package out and put the bag on the counter so I can use both hands to unwrap the tissue. It's really light. I open it.

It's a bra.

A bra that may be the ugliest, most industrial-level undergarment I've ever seen.

I gape at in confusion and then up at him. He's quiet, those pale blue eyes watchful.

I fling it at him. 'What the fuck is this?'

'It's a bra,' he says, attempting to put it back in my hands, but I hold them up in a *back off* gesture. 'It's for you.'

He's lost the plot. He's actually insane.

'It's hideous, and you have no place buying me a bra. This is totally inappropriate. And also, you know, really creepy.'

'I need you to wear it,' he says, and I'm amazed to hear the pleading tone in his voice. 'Seriously, Carlotta, I need you to put your fucking tits away, properly, in a proper fucking bra, once and for all. Or I'll—'

'You'll what?' I say. My voice is shaking, which is no surprise, because my entire body is also shaking. I'm trembling with rage, and shock, and the intimate, affronting and totally bizarre nature of this interlude with a man I do not know and yet feel uncomfortably attracted to.

He lets those eyes of his drift closed for a second. When he opens them, he looks straight at me. They're as pale as ever. As beautiful. But instead of their usual ice I see heat. 'I'll be in very grave danger of doing something so fucking inappropriate that this, right here, will seem about as tame as a royal garden party.'

I swallow and press my thighs together. We're so close. We're a foot apart, max, and in these damn trainers I'm several inches shorter than him. I can smell him—sunshine, and sweat, and a kind of earthiness, and good, honest laundry liquid. I bet he shuns cologne, but he doesn't need it, anyway.

He smells incredible just like this.

'What would you call *fucking inappropriate?*' I ask in a small voice.

He shrugs, but there's nothing offhand about his voice when he speaks. If anything, he sounds hungry. Starving.

His gaze flicks from my eyes to my mouth to my boobs and back up again. 'I'd stick a chair under the door handle and sit you up on that desk,' he says, 'and I'd pull off that stupid top. And then I'd slide that fucking useless sports bra off you, and I'd feast on your beautiful, beautiful tits. I'd go to fucking town on them. I'd lick those mind-blowing nipples of yours, and I'd suck them, and pull at them till you came just from that. Because I know you could. I have no doubt I could make you come.'

Our eyes are locked. My boobs and my clit are growing heavy, achy, at the mere thought of Aide ministering to them like that, with so much hunger and desperation. At the thought of sitting there, bare-breasted, while he devours me. Ravages me. Of taking everything he has to give me.

His voice is lower and rougher than I've ever heard it, and yet it feels like a caress. Hearing this stoic, gruff man put graphic, sensual language to the dark attentions he's dreamt about lavishing on me is too much.

I can feel his mouth on me.

I can sense the wet warmth of his tongue, his lips, on my nipples. The pulls of his fingertips on my sensitive skin.

I can imagine the noises both of us would make.

I know just how it would be between us.

But even better than the picture he's painted is the knowledge that I've driven him to this.

Me.

This guy gives nothing away. He's as closed off as they come, from what I've seen. But, somehow, my boobs and I have worked him up so much in the past three days that we've driven him to go to a department store, buy me an actual—if revolting—bra, and express his darkest fantasies to me.

That's almost headier than what he's threatening to do to me if I don't wear the bra. And yeah, it's definitely a threat, not a promise.

Unfortunately.

I stare at him. He's breathing hard through flared nostrils, and we're so close I can feel the faint warmth of his breath on my face.

I wish I could reach up and drag my fingers through that dark, neatly clipped beard. Rake them through his hair. Pull his head down to mine and tug that full bottom lip between my teeth.

But he's made it clear that, for whatever reason, he is intent on *not* pursuing anything akin to that scenario with me.

Probably because, aside from my tits and my looks, he finds me utterly dreadful.

Although none of the above means I feel remotely compelled to play fair. So I open my mouth to say what I want to say, because we've pole-vaulted way over the line of *appropriate* now.

'I have no doubt you could, either,' I tell him. 'And if you made me come like that, I'd definitely let you jizz all over them afterwards.'

His face contorts as if I've actually kneed him in the balls.

'Fuuuuuck,' he grits out, and it's so anguished that my pussy echoes its pain.

I arch what I'm aware is a perfectly groomed brow at him. 'I bet you'd like that,' I whisper seductively. 'Wouldn't you? Imagine shooting your load all over my amazing tits. Imagine your cum dripping off my nipples.'

Yeah.

I'm mean.

More than mean. Evil.

But he can't just pull me into a room, and order me to wear a grotesque bra while describing in graphic detail how he wants to make me come by sucking on my boobs if I *don't* wear it, and not expect me to fight back.

Hard.

He has no idea who he's messing with here.

I give as good as I get.

Also, it's just plain annoying. Because in the time it's taken for us to have this pointless argument and unsuccessful, unwelcome gift-giving attempt, we could probably both have made each other come.

Those gorgeous black-lashed eyes drop to my boobs again, and he groans. He stuffs the bra and its nest of tissue back into my hands and waves a finger in my face.

'And *that* is precisely why you need to wear the fucking bra,' he barks, before wrenching open the door and storming out of the room.

I'm not sure if he realises he's just given me the best pitch of all time on why I *shouldn't* wear the fucking bra.

11

AIDE

She is not wearing the fucking bra.

She turns up at lunchtime—apparently she had some work calls this morning that she couldn't get out of—and shimmies out of that trench coat to reveal denim cutoffs, a tight white t-shirt, and absolutely none of the 'clean lines' or 'full coverage' Audrey at Harrods assured me the overpriced bra would deliver.

Instead, I'm treated to the faint, tantalising outline of lace and the not remotely faint but even more tantalising outline of her nipples, which are standing to attention like they're on duty at fucking Buckingham Palace. I shoot her what I intend as a withering look of disapproval, and she shoots me a sunny smile that's nowhere near as innocent as it pretends.

She knows exactly what she's doing to me.

And it's all my fault.

I shouldn't have said or done any of that yesterday. Shouldn't have bought her a bra. And definitely shouldn't have given her a pornographic blow-by-blow of what I was in danger of doing to her if my years of carefully constructed willpower failed me.

She had a hell of a comeback for me.

One I thoroughly deserved.

And one that had me shooting my load in the shower *again* as soon as I got home.

I'm the only one who has an issue with her. Gaz is smitten. Being the jovial bastard that he is, he seems to enjoy gawping at her physical perfection while bantering away with her as if their lives depend on it. Sylvie referred to her this morning as *a very kind-hearted young woman*, and Judy actually pulled me aside before Carlotta came in and told me to make more of an effort with her.

Unbelievable.

They're all dropping like flies.

It was quiet without her around this morning; I'll admit that much.

Still, things are progressing around here. We got the kitchen finished off last night. By the skin of our teeth, but still. The Venus guys ended up staying late. So late, I didn't get to buy them a pint to say thank you.

I have to say, it looks great. There are vast stretches of shiny, easy-clean stainless steel between the splash backs, the work surfaces and the appliances themselves. The industrial ovens run floor to ceiling, and Sylvie is ecstatic. She and some of the usual volunteers got in at six-thirty this morning, I believe, so we could offer the kids a full breakfast. They couldn't wait to get their hands on their shiny new toys.

Because the main hall's still out of action, we've stuck to the takeaway breakfast service we've run this week, but at least we were able to offer the kids some hot food—sausage

baps and banana porridge in cardboard pots which went
down a treat.

With the main structural work out of the way, Reggie,
Venus' electrician, has taken his leave, along with another
guy, Ian. The bulk of the labour now is cosmetic. Sanding
down the remainder of the walls where the panelling was.
Washing all the ancient paintwork down. Replastering or
caulking the millions of little spots where the cheap plaster
has come off. And, finally, painting the whole fucking
building before setting up the new furniture.

I'm stood at one end, watching the progress and the
chaos from a slight distance as I mitre the edges of the new
skirting boards we're putting in. I don't get to do this kind of
thing very often, but I enjoy the precision of it. The total
focus it requires. The reward of the end product. Gaz, who
trained as a joiner before he gave it up to sit behind the
wheel of heavy goods lorries, brought his old mitre box in
this morning and is humouring me by letting me do the
mitring while he nails the skirting boards to the walls.

He's got Magic FM blasting from our digital radio. One
of the Venus guys, Jack, is patching up the plasterwork while
Frank and their other colleague, Marv, install brand-new,
cheap but far superior, toilets, urinals and washbasins in the
poky loos.

Sylv is back in the kitchen with Charmaine, another of
our regular volunteers on the catering side, chopping and
prepping for the big pasta bake we'll be handing out to the
kids outside later for their dinner. That leaves Judy and
Carlotta, who look thick as thieves.

We've replaced a couple of the old internal doors. One of
them in particular had the shit kicked out of it by a kid with
anger issues years ago and never got replaced. Carlotta and
Judy are applying a base coat of primer to the bare wood. As

far as I can see, they're doing a half-decent job of it, though they'd be a lot quicker if they shut the fuck up and focused on the task at hand.

Carlotta looks beautiful. Someone's given her a black Venus-branded t-shirt, which is already splattered with primer, but thank fuck it's covering her up. Pity we couldn't find some full-length painting overalls for her, because those legs of hers are every bit as long and tanned and glossy as I imagined they'd be, and they are not helping my libido one bit. It feels like every time she covers up one body part, she puts another on show for me.

I'm saved by a sharp rapping on the open internal door. I look up to see Noah Thierry standing there, wearing a bright orange Good Vibes Hospice t-shirt and a wide grin. He holds up a foil-covered oblong that I have good reason to hope is a homemade cake. 'Thought you might need sustenance,' he says. 'Brought you a loaf of lemon drizzle.'

I down tools and walk towards the doorway so I can shake the man by the hand. He's one of the most genuinely decent people I've met. He runs a progressive and incredibly inspiring hospice on the other side of the square, and he happens to have a chef to hand who's a dangerously good baker. All visitors to the Good Vibes hospice know you want to visit at three o'clock. Afternoon tea-time.

'My hero,' I say, and we bro-hug around the cake. 'Your timing is fucking perfect.'

'It's looking good in here,' he says charitably, because in reality it's still a total mess. The sunlight pouring through the huge window is lighting up every single speck of dust, and there's shit everywhere.

'Not yet,' I tell him, 'but we're getting there. Kitchen's done.'

'Sylv must be thrilled,' he says. 'It's been a long time coming.'

I nod. 'She's a patient woman.'

Noah is one of the good ones—a doctor who's found his vocation in helping the dying pass in peace and with grace. Though I think he's even more valuable to the loved ones they leave behind. The man's a saint and a plugged-in member of the local community.

He's also married to one of the most beautiful women on the planet—Honor Chapman, a massive celebrity who left her even more famous action hero husband for Noah here.

Sometimes, the good guy really does win.

We've built up a quiet, easy friendship over the past couple of years. We met at a few local community events and hit it off. As a former NHS doctor, he can appreciate the value Totum adds, and we've sponsored a few fundraisers for the hospice here and the one they're opening in North London. We also may or may not have discovered a fondness for drinking excellent whisky in companionable silence in the square together from time to time.

I'm just about to piss him off by asking him how his beautiful wife is when I hear a jaunty *Noah!*

What the actual fuck?

I spin around. Carlotta's coming towards us, all bronze-limbed and sparkly-eyed and perky.

'I thought that was you!' she cries. 'What on earth are you doing here?'

What on earth are you *doing?* I think.

'My hospice is across the square,' he tells her, leaning in for a double kiss. Charming French bastard. Seriously. Not content with bagging Honor bloody Chapman, he has to be pally with Carlotta, too? My warmth towards him is cooling by the second.

'This is a new look for you,' he tells her warmly.

'Right?' She looks down and laughs. 'So attractive.'

She means it sarcastically. Self-deprecatingly. But the oversized, paint-splattered t-shirt and the cutoffs are, in my view, fucking perfection. They make her look girl-next-door in a way her usual get-ups don't, even if the result is more accurately girl-next-door-I'd-like-to-bang.

'How come you're here?' he asks.

'Venus is doing an outreach programme with Aide here. We're sprucing this place up.'

I can't last another second. 'How come you two know each other?' I grunt.

Carlotta beams at him adoringly. 'I know Noah's wife, Honor. We have mutual friends.'

Of course they do. Of course Carlotta hangs out with the rich and famous. I employ every fibre of my willpower not to roll my eyes.

'Lotta's friends, Elle and Nora, know Honor.' He wrinkles his nose as if summoning a memory. He's on *Lotta* terms with her too, then. 'You were at uni with those two, right?'

'Well remembered. You going to Elle's wedding?'

'I hope so, given she's having it my family's chateau,' he says.

Her eyes widen and she pats him on the arm. 'Of course! Duh. Oh my God, I can't wait.'

'Cosy,' I say. I aim for light snark, but it comes out heavier than that. Noah's family owns Chateau des Anges, a vineyard near St Tropez that produces a great rosé. Even so, all this socialite stuff is way out of my comfort zone.

He grins at me. 'Seriously, mate. I'm still getting used to the high life. Elle Hart and Josh Lander's wedding—should be fucking amazing. I'm not complaining.'

'Oh Jesus. *That* wedding? Good luck to you,' I say, to hide the inexplicable fact that I'm jealous. Not that these two are off to the wedding of two of the biggest movie stars on the planet. More that Noah's getting to do something like *that* with Carlotta. Something exotic and decadent and glamorous, where she'll look like an angel. And dance like a she-devil on steroids, no doubt.

I stand there like a muppet, holding the loaf of lemon drizzle that Noah's passed to me, and listening to the two of them prattle on about people I've never met, when the screams of pain and terror start.

12

LOTTA

I jerk around at the noise.

Oh my God. It's Gaz, and he's screaming his head off. There's a scuffle as we all run towards him from wherever we're standing. Sylv appears from the kitchen. It's a horrible noise Gaz is making, almost inhuman.

We crowd around him and I see him on his knees, bent over in front of the skirting board he was fitting and wailing. I have no idea what the hell's just happened, but it looks like it's not life-threatening, thank God.

'Let me see, please,' Noah orders firmly. The reassuring sound of his doctor voice has everyone stepping back and giving him space. 'What's happened, Gaz—oh, I see.'

'What's he done?' Aide barks. His tone has me looking up. His face is all red and twisted.

'Nail gun injury to the finger. I need a clean towel or cloth, please, as soon as possible.'

'On it.' Sylv takes off at a run towards the kitchen.

'Oh my God,' Judy exclaims. 'The poor lamb.'

I suck in a breath at the horrifying array of possibilities the phrase *nail gun injury to the finger* presents. Poor Gaz is whimpering *fuck fuck fuck*. I can only imagine how agonising it is.

'Shit!' Aide shouts. 'You stupid fucking idiot. Why weren't you wearing gloves?'

Noah interrupts him. 'Not now, Aide. Right, mate, I'm going to hold your arm up to stem the blood flow, okay? We'll bandage you up, but we'll need to get this out in a hospital. Any idea when your last tetanus shot was?'

'No fucking clue,' Gaz manages through gritted teeth. He's gone as white as a sheet.

'Not a problem.' Noah slowly lifts his arm up and oh my *Lord*. Holy mother of God. There's an actual nail sticking through his fucking fingernail, and there's blood everywhere. It's like something out of a horror show. I think I might barf. Or faint. It's the most revolting thing I've ever seen.

'Any sign of the cloth?' Noah shouts.

'Got it!' Sylv returns, breathless. 'Found the first aid kit, too.'

'Well done.' Noah continues to hold Gaz's arm aloft. 'Open it for me, will you? Grab any antiseptic wipe you can find and open it up for me, please. Aide, take this.'

He transfers the arm attached to Gaz's injured hand over to Aide, who kneels beside him. Then Noah's a blur of efficiency, wiping at the wound, which is gushing blood, before wrapping gauze around it and then the cloth Sylvie's procured.

All the way through it, Gaz is sobbing and swearing, and I feel so helpless. It's so awful. The poor, poor guy. I'm only semi-aware of getting to my knees beside Aide and behind Gaz and putting my arms against Gaz from behind as I lay my head against his shoulder.

'It's okay,' I tell his back. 'It's going to be okay. You're so brave. It must hurt so much.'

He shifts gingerly and reaches up to squeeze my hand with his good one. 'Thanks, babe,' he says through gritted teeth, and I hug him harder. I feel so bloody helpless.

'Can you take it out at your place?' Aide asks Noah, who shakes his head.

'Afraid not. It's A&E for him. Hammersmith's your best bet. He'll need a tetanus shot, too.'

'I'll take him,' Aide says.

'No you won't.' Judy crouches down. 'I'll do it. You'll be a blubbering idiot, and you're more use here than I am.'

'It should be me,' Aide insists. 'I'm his best mate.'

'I. Will. Take. Him,' Judy insists. 'If you want to make yourself useful, get us a cab.'

Within minutes, Aide has a black cab outside, its meter running. He bundles Judy and Gaz in and returns to the hall, where we're surveying the damage. It looks like someone's staged an amateur production of *Texas Chainsaw Massacre*. There's blood spattered across the wall where Gaz was working, all over the floor, and soaked into the bare wood of the skirting board he was in the process of fitting to the wall.

Frank lifts the piece of skirting and stands it on end against the wall. 'I'm really sorry about this, mate,' he tells Aide. 'I should have been supervising him more closely.'

'He used to be a fucking joiner, for fuck's sake,' Aide says, raking a hand through that mass of dark hair in frustration. 'He knows how to use a nail gun. Why the fuck he wasn't wearing gloves, I don't know.' He looks down at the blood, and his shoulders visibly slump. 'Why don't you guys get out of here. I'll clear up.'

'No you won't,' I say. 'I will.'

He shoots me a look that telegraphs his utter lack of belief in my ability to clean up a bit of blood. Even when he's devastated, he manages to be rude.

'I'm not saying I'll get it all out,' I say, holding my hands up, 'but I'll have a go.' At least the wooden floorboards are so highly varnished that the blood is pooling on their surface rather than soaking in like a murder scene. Thank God. A lone skirting board is easier to replace than an entire floor.

He hesitates.

'Go on. You look a bit shaken up. Go and have some of Noah's cake, or a whisky or something.'

'I've lost my appetite,' he says, but he does what he's told and ambles back to the other end of the hall.

While I mop the blood off the floor, Frank has the others clear up their tools and stack all their equipment and massive toolboxes in a neat pile under the window, which he covers with a paint sheet for the night. My end of the hall looks less tidy when I'm done. Most of the blood comes off the floorboards, as I hoped it would, but the skirting board is going to need a fair few coats of paint to cover the stain, and the walls end up with ominous pinky blotches.

At least they're all due a new paint job, too.

I drain the bloody water out of the mop bucket in the little scullery off the kitchen and leave the mop standing upside down to dry. The kitchen itself smells deliciously of garlic and onion and tomatoes.

'Have you seen Aide?' I ask Sylvie, who's peering into the oven at her vast trays of pasta bake.

She jerks her head towards the office next door. 'I think he's still in there. You okay, sweetie?'

I grimace. 'I'm fine. I just feel so bad for Gaz. It's so horrible.'

She gives me a comforting nod. 'I know. Not nice at all.

But he'll be fine. He's had a nail through his foot once, you know. Stood on it. Went right through the sole of his work boot and all.'

I gasp in horror. 'Oh my God. That's revolting.'

'Yup,' she says. 'This ain't his first nail gun rodeo. But you think he'd be a faster learner, wouldn't you?'

That makes me giggle. 'Seriously.' Poor Gaz.

'Stupid twat,' one of the women helping her says. It's mean, but it makes me giggle even harder.

'You head home,' Sylvie says. 'We've got this.'

'If you're sure.' I back towards the door. I feel really drained, all of a sudden. An unexpectedly long evening in my luxurious, blood-free flat sounds amazing. 'I'll just go say bye to Aide.'

I pause for a second outside the closed door of the office, pulling out my hair tie and shaking out my hair before knocking. I hear an irritated-sounding *Come in.*

Yep, that's definitely Aide in there.

He's sitting on the desk, facing the door, his legs spread wide and his shoulders slumped. His fingers are curled around a glass, and there's an open bottle of whisky beside it. He doesn't smile, but neither does he tell me to get out.

'I'm going to head off,' I tell him.

He looks down at the glass. Tilts it in his hand.

'Want some?' he asks, raising his head to me. Despair is etched onto his gorgeous face. His blue eyes are reddened. Tired.

I nod and back up against the door, pushing it shut with my bum. 'Why not?' I'm not much of a whisky drinker, but I've developed a taste for it over years spent with my dad and my brother. Gabe has a stupendous collection at our flat. He favours scotch, obviously, but I'm more of a Bourbon girl. It's kinder. Sweeter.

He picks up the bottle and sloshes, conservatively, three shots into the glass before holding it out to me. 'Drink.'

I step forward and put it to my lips.

Wow.

Definitely scotch. It's good stuff, smooth, but bloody hell does it burn.

'Yikes,' I say, wiping my mouth with the back of my hand.

He laughs gruffly. 'Not your poison?'

'I don't mind it, but I'm more of a champagne girl.'

'Course you are,' he says, but it's not unkind. He gestures towards my leg. 'You've got blood on your thigh.'

I look down at my bare thigh. There is indeed a smear of Gaz's blood across my skin. 'Nice. At least I didn't wear yoga pants today. Skin's easier to wash.'

His gaze lingers on my thigh before he drags it upwards.

'You okay?' I ask hesitantly. He's a grumpy bastard at the best of times, and I don't want to poke the bear, but I also don't want to go without making sure he's not too shaken up. I know he and Gaz are close, and I've already learnt that Aide thinks everything and everyone are his responsibility.

'I'm fucked off,' he says. He accepts the glass I hold out and takes a swig before handing it back to me. There's something about sharing a glass with him that feels intimate. Sensual. 'Fucked off with him for not sticking to super fucking basic safety rules and fucked off with myself for not noticing.'

'He's not your responsibility,' I say. 'He's a big boy. At the end of the day, it's down to him to keep himself safe. But it was also an unfortunate accident. These things happen.'

I raise the now-almost-empty glass to my lips again and take a slow sip, allowing myself to enjoy the burn. To revel in the incredible, almost medicinal warmth of the liquid as it coats my throat. My oesophagus. Heating me, soothing me from the inside.

When I look back down, his eyes are on me. On my mouth, more precisely.

'I know that in my head,' he says to my mouth. 'I mean, I know you're right. But I still feel sick to my stomach. We're here trying to do a bit of good, and now my mate is sitting in fucking A&E, waiting to have a bloody nail pulled out of his finger, and there's nothing I can do about it. I'm just sitting here, drinking like a useless twat and spiralling. It's stupid. But I can't get out of my own head. I can't stop obsessing about it.'

He raises those despairing blue eyes to meet mine, and we're locked in place for a moment. I don't know why, but Aide deigning to talk to me, to let me in, has me feeling more lightheaded than the whisky has.

'I know,' I say, and I step closer, between his legs, setting the glass down on the desk. I'm thinking this guy needs a good hug, so I act on instinct and put my arms around him, pulling him in towards me. Given he's sitting and I'm standing, the hug ends up being more like suffocation by boobs. I hold his head against my chest and move one hand up so it's cupping the back of his head through all that glorious, silky hair.

He stays frozen for a few seconds before his entire body slumps against me and he lets out the most enormous shuddery sigh. *'Fuck,'* he groans, and I feel the heat of his breath through both my t-shirts.

We stay like that for what feels like an eternity until he lifts a big hand and places it right on the small of my back, pressing me in closer to him. I stagger forward half a step and allow myself to rake a hand through his hair as I lower my face to the top of his head.

To say it feels *good* like this is a gross understatement. It's elemental. It's two people who don't particularly enjoy each other's company coming together and offering each other comfort with parts of themselves that transcend personality.

Being here with him like this, my body cradling his and his cradling mine, feels right in a way that's quiet and tentative and yet revelatory.

It's also hot as hell. Aide is coursing through my bloodstream like a drug, this proximity to him messing with my brain. He looks up at me, his face pained but open.

Questioning.

And I know what my answer is.

13

LOTTA

I release him and take a step back, crossing my arms in front of me so I can tug my oversized Venus t-shirt over my head and chuck it in the far corner of the room.

'What are you doing?' he mutters, his gaze roving over my chest, with which he's now perfectly at eye-level. He presses his hands to his thighs, palms down, fingers splayed in a way that feels intentional. Like a predator trying to talk himself out of attacking.

'Giving that brain of yours something else to obsess about,' I tell him. 'Watch.'

I cross my arms again and pull my white t-shirt up, shaking out my hair as I pull my top all the way off. Aide's sharp intake of breath when he finds himself at eye-level with and inches away from my boobs encased in their pale pink, lacy bra is *the* best sound I have ever heard.

'Jesus fuck,' he groans. 'Oh my God.' I doubt he's aware of it, but his hands go straight to grip my hips, holding me in place through my cut-offs.

His breath is warm on my breasts. His face is anguished.

His fingers dig into my hips. And I want this man's mouth on my nipples like I've never wanted anything in my entire, charmed life.

'Take off my bra,' I tell him.

His laugh is choked. 'No, Carlotta, I—'

Fine. If he's going to go all shy on me, I'll take matters into my own hands. I reach behind and unhook my bra, letting its straps slide down my arms before it lands on his thigh. He doesn't bat an eyelid, because his stare is fixated on my now-bare breasts.

'Oh my God,' he says again. He pants out a breath. 'Fucking hell, you're so beautiful. Jesus Christ.' His words are slurred already, and all he's done is look.

I know objectively I have great boobs. They're decent-sized and pert and shapely and fabulous. But I have never in my life wanted a man to appreciate them like I do now. I want him to adore them. Worship them. I want them to give him everything he needs in this moment. And I'm not sure my nipples have ever been pinched so tight. So aching.

I want him to *go to fucking town on them*, like he threatened to the other day.

I put my hands on his shoulders. He's wearing one of his sexy builder-vests, and under my palms his shoulders are huge and taut, the skin smooth. 'I want you to touch me, Aide,' I tell him. 'I really, really need you to touch them.'

'Oh fuck,' he rasps, and it has my lady parts clenching madly under my shorts. He looks up at me, his eyes dark and hooded, his lips parted. If this is the way he looks *before* he touches a woman, I can't begin to imagine how he looks when he's inside her.

Just imagining that feels unwise.

Dangerous.

Because a mere look like this, from a man like this, isn't something you recover from easily.

'You sure?' he mouths, his fingers flexing around my hips, and I give them a little thrust in his direction.

'Please,' I beg. I'm standing here with my boobs out for him, my skin bare, and his breath warm on them, and his mouth so close it's torture.

He slides his hands up my sides. They're warm, and his fingers are calloused, and they send a scatter of goosebumps over my skin and a flurry of butterflies through my stomach.

His eyes flick back up to my face one more time. I suspect what he sees there is the equivalent of a big fat *yes please* tattooed across my forehead, because he allows his hands to skate higher until they're framing my boobs and his thumbs are stroking along the creases of their undersides.

I groan, because his touch, and the anticipation of more of it, is already igniting me. My noise seems to catalyse him. He dips that dark head and runs his nose and lips over my skin, back and forth over my décolletage and the tops of my boobs before he kisses right between them.

I grip his shoulders harder in encouragement, and he acts.

His mouth moves to my right nipple. He teases it with the tip of his tongue before taking the entire thing in his mouth and sucking hard.

Oh my God.

Oh my God.

The pleasure is so instant, so intense, that I gasp aloud and arch into him, stroking my hands over his shoulders before letting one get tangled up in his hair again.

My encouragement seems to stoke him. He continues to suck, to tease my nipple with his mouth, his teeth catching it lightly so he can strum at it with his tongue, while he palms my other breast. Kneads it. Rolls my nipple around under his calloused skin. His other hand finds my back again, and he splays his huge fingers across me as it roams up and down my spine.

I'm lost in a stupor of sensation. My legs are shaking, and I'm conscious only of Aide's touch. Of where he's devouring my skin with his mouth and his hands. He makes ravenous humming noises at the back of his throat, and I press against him harder, clutching his head to my body and gasping whenever his mouth switches nipples.

He was right the other day. I could come just from this. I totally could, and I possibly will. It seems I'm not the only one being wound higher and higher, because next thing he's pushing off the desk and standing, dragging his mouth from my chest and up my neck, teeth and lips and tongue exploring me, his breath coming in harsh bursts.

He wraps me in his arms, one arm banding tightly around my shoulders as the other one finds my shorts and cups my bum. Hard. As he holds me flush against him, I have the singular, exquisite pleasure of being surrounded by Aide. Completely consumed by him. Most pressingly, his dick is rock hard and wedged against me, the fabric of his work trousers rough against my bare stomach.

His heart is hammering against me, as I suspect mine is against him. The hand around my shoulders finds my hair and fists it, tugging my face upwards. I'm treated for a second to the glorious, otherworldly sight of this godlike man staring down at me with starvation and awe wrought in every gorgeous feature, and I gaze back with what must be utter adoration, because I am gone.

And then his mouth is upon me, hot and hungry, and I'm really, really gone, because it seems Aide's found his stride. It seems he's finally unleashing himself, unleashing himself *upon me*, and I know I will take every last morsel this man is prepared to give me. Even if it slays me. Even if he pushes me to my limits, and stretches me, and challenges me, and demands every last ounce of my strength, I will take it all.

And I will give him everything.

His mouth is soft and hard all at once. His beard is ticklish and abrasive against my lips, my chin, and all I can think is *I need that between my legs.*

There's no hesitation now.

No restraint.

No barely there self-control.

No poor attempt at manners.

It's all gone, blown to smithereens, and all that's left in its place is Aide's unsated appetite. His tongue thrusts straight into my mouth, and I groan and arch my hips as hard against his erection as I can while my tongue fights with his. We entangle, and dance, and spar. The sensation of being overpowered by him is like nothing I've ever known.

I wriggle with need against him, my bare boobs squished against his hard chest, the fine ribbing of his vest rubbing at my nipples exactly the way I need. He responds by grabbing my bum harder, his fingers stretching low and burrowing under the frayed hem of my cutoffs so he can dig them right into the crease where my cheek meets my thigh.

I need them further up. Further *in.* I want him to consume me with his tongue and his fingers and his dick. I want to be conscious of nothing else on this earth but this man.

I tug at his hair and kiss him harder, moaning into his mouth, and he makes a pleased, approving noise in response that nearly undoes me. I'm desperate for as much of him as I can get, desperate to make it count. He tastes of whisky and he smells incredible: sweat, and hard work, and so many sex hormones that I feel like a mare in heat. I manage to get my other hand under the hem of his vest, and my fingertips encounter sweat-slicked skin.

He releases my mouth and tugs at my hair again, this time to pull my head to one side. Then he's kissing back down my neck and pulling away enough to wedge his hands between us. 'Look at me,' he says, his voice low. Rough.

I open my eyes and gaze up at him in a fog of lust. His lips are wet and swollen, his eyes glazed and hooded. 'How's this?' he asks. He cups both my boobs and strums his thumbs over my nipples again. I knit my brows together at the unutterable pleasure that is Aide touching me with those big, calloused thumbs while staring right into my eyes. The intensity is overwhelming. I'm laid bare for only him to see.

'Amazing,' I tell him huskily. 'Harder.'

His answering smile is smug, and I fucking love it. 'That's my girl,' he says softly, and he ups the ante, pinching my nipples hard as he watches my face. 'Think you can come like this?'

'I know I can,' I tell him on a gasp, 'but I'd much rather you played with my clit, too.'

He chokes out a pained laugh. 'I bet you would. I can't wait to see what you look like when you come.'

'I can't wait to see what you look like when you come all over my tits,' I retort, and he shakes his head like he just can't handle that idea.

Like it's a bad idea for us to even go there.

He releases one nipple and goes to unbutton the flies of my cutoffs but, before he can, there's a loud rap at the door that has us both jumping out of our skin.

'Aide?' Sylvie cries. 'You ready to dish up?'

'Fuck,' I whisper. She has got to be kidding me. This is the worst timing ever. I look around on the floor for my bra.

'Jesus,' Aidan curses under his breath. He looks as gutted as I feel, which is something, at least. 'Give me five minutes,' he shouts at the door. 'I'm on a call.'

'Okay,' she sing-songs.

I look up at him.

He looks down at my bare boobs.

'I need to go,' he tells me.

'I know,' I say. 'It's cool.'

It's stupid, but I feel bereft. Like this fragile intimacy between me and a man who otherwise refuses to give me the time of day has been snapped. Broken. Like we only got this tiny fragment of time, and it's already dissipated, and he'll be back to giving me the cold shoulder in the morning, and—

My thought process stops right there, because he's gathering me up in his arms and kissing me again, smoothing my hair down my back in firm strokes. I lean into him. Into the hungry glides of his mouth. The decisive tautness of his tongue inside *my* mouth. Into this feeling of being tiny, and desirable, and bare, and completely engulfed in Aide's huge arms.

Most of all, I lean into the heady relief of knowing that, right at this second, he has no regrets. That Sylvia's abrupt interruption was as unwelcome to him as it was to me.

That he's not leaping away from me in horror, or coming to his senses just yet.

I loop my hands lazily around his neck, fondling the clasp of his silver chain with my fingertips. 'Do you want some help with the food?' I ask, because I really, really don't want to walk away from him.

He smiles lazily against my lips. To have made him smile, to have taken him out of his head for a few minutes, makes my heart happy. 'Not a good idea,' he murmurs. He nudges me gently with his erection. 'Can't serve the kids with a raging boner, and I can't get rid of it if you and your tits are hanging around, can I?'

'I see your point,' I whisper, pleased that he's admitting I affect him like that.

Pleased that I might continue to affect him after we leave this room. After I walk away.

I kiss him once more before extricating myself and hunting around for my bra. He gets to it first and holds it up for me like a gentleman helping a lady on with her coat. I put my arms out, and he slides it on me before moving behind me and scooping my hair over my shoulder.

'Very pretty bra,' he says against my ear, his fingers lingering against my back after he's fastened it. 'I'll see you tomorrow. Don't think I've remotely finished with you.'

14

LOTTA

The distance between the centre and my flat is half a mile. Far too short to justify a cab, especially on a gorgeous evening like this. Even if my legs are threatening to give out on me after the manliest, gruffest, most rugged, most enigmatic man I've ever met has just now almost brought me to orgasm with the decadence of his tongue and the fire in those dangerous eyes and the filthily ominous threats in his parting words.

I can't quite believe we just did that.

That is to say, I can totally believe that I just ripped my top off in front of Aide and got my boobs out for him. I've never done anything quite that shameless or brave before, but it's not a massive step out of character for me.

No.

What I really mean is that I can't believe Aide let me. Went along with it. *And then some*. He may have been full of warnings—or promises—yesterday of the things he wanted to do to me, but I wouldn't have expected him to follow up on them. Not because he wasn't as desperate as I was, but because he's seemed so stoic and sensible and repressed all this week.

He's one of those guys who takes the weight of every last thing, and every last person, on his shoulders.

What I didn't see coming was that when that weight got too great, he'd snap. Break.

And he'd let me comfort him. Or distract him, more accurately.

I was as good as my word. I told him I'd give him something else to obsess over aside from poor Gaz's accident.

Judging from the smile I put on his face and the bulge I put in his pants, I succeeded.

If he hadn't said what he said as he left the room, I'd probably be feeling, not insecure, exactly, but pissed off. Wistful that something so good had been nipped in the bud so quickly.

But his gorgeous, growly *don't think I've remotely finished with you* will go down in history as the sexiest thing any man has ever said to me, and it makes me think tomorrow will definitely be worth showing up for.

I don't even know the guy, I think as I meander dreamily down the chaos of Ladbroke Grove, side-stepping hoards of kids in uniform who I assume just got out of school. And yet, being the sole focus of his attention after just a few days of being fascinated by him, horribly attracted to him, was like nothing I can describe.

I suspect anyone who knows me would say I like the limelight, that I'm an attention whore, but this wasn't like that. I didn't crave Aide's attention to make a point or give myself a cheap thrill. I didn't think I had the remotest shot at getting any of his attention, to be honest, except in the form of the begrudging desire and overt disapproval he's been dishing out all week.

But just now was more... special than that. It felt like a distinct privilege to be there, alone with him in his arms. His hands and mouth on me, his dick hard for me, and that look of rapture and hunger on me that was so intoxicating it could have brought me to my knees.

Literally.

He's got this weird gravitas about him I can't explain. A quiet authority. A way of making people sit up and pay attention. He draws people to him—I've noticed we all want to be in his orbit. He's just a normal guy, doing a normal job, yet it's not only me who feels it. Gaz hero-worships him. Sylvie and Judy clearly adore him.

And I've known from the second I laid eyes on him that he's someone you don't forget. Someone special. I suppose the term I'm looking for is Big Dick Energy.

It's not just his outrageous, ridiculous looks, or his size (generally speaking, not his dick size, though I have my suspicions on that front).

It's *him*.

And for a few blissful minutes just now, I got to be the one he focused those icy, mesmerising eyes and that elusive approval on.

I got to be the one who nearly unravelled him. And I would have, if Sylvie hadn't unwittingly cockblocked us.

I would have climbed that man like a tree.

I allow myself a cat-who-got-the-cream smile, even though I'm the opposite of satisfied. I'm turned on and frustrated, my erogenous zones throbbing and my head spinning with salacious fantasies about how it would have been with him if we hadn't been interrupted.

My plans for this evening are now to spend serious quality time with my vibrators.

～

AIDE

'What the hell are you doing here?' I demand as Gaz breezes into the main hallway.

'Try and keep me away, my friend,' he says.

'You're injured. Go on, get out.'

He holds up a cartoon-style bandaged finger. 'It's amazing, but they say I'll live.'

'Ha fucking ha.' I put down the skirting board I'm mitring so I can give him my full attention. 'You're a liability. Can't have you on a building site when you're injured, mate. You know that.'

He scoffs. 'Come on. It's not a building site—it's a basic refurb. I'm fine.'

'A basic refurb where you shot yourself with a nail gun, you incompetent twat.'

He has the grace to look embarrassed about his utter ineptitude.

'I know. I'm a nob. But I've taken two weeks off work, haven't I? Just give me a paintbrush or something. I can't sit around at home.'

I sigh. Gaz has indeed taken two weeks' holiday from driving lorries so he can help out. I know how dear he holds this place—just like we all do. And he can't do that much damage with a paintbrush.

Can he?

'Fine.' I bark. 'Painting and nothing else. If I see you going anywhere near a single power tool, there'll be hell to pay.' .

'Got it,' he says cheerfully. 'I'll hang out with the girls. They love my chat.'

By *girls*, I assume he means Carlotta and Judy. I glower at him, but before I can say anything, Carlotta's upon us.

Speak of the devil.

'Heyyy!' she cries, throwing her arms around Gaz, who hugs her tightly and winks at me over her shoulder. 'You're back! How's the finger?'

'Pretty grim,' he tells her as he releases her. 'I actually fainted when they were stitching it up.'

'You poor thing!' she coos as I roll my eyes behind her back, because boy will Gaz milk this for all it's worth. 'I'm not surprised. How long were you in there for?'

'Eight hours, all in. Fucking brutal. Judy was a doll. She bought me a couple of Toffee Crisps from the vending machine.'

'Shouldn't you be at home?' Carlotta insists. So far she's completely failed to acknowledge me, which would be bad enough if she hadn't had her tits in my mouth last time I saw her.

'I'd be bored shitless,' he says. He jerks a thumb at me. 'And Stalin here says I can stay if I stick to painting.'

'Oh, goodie! You can paint with us,' she says before turning and deigning to acknowledge me. 'Morning, Aide.' She flashes me a coquettish smile that I don't return.

'Carlotta.' I nod curtly. She's in a bright pink baggy sweatshirt made all the worse by a massive Versace logo printed all over the front of it. At least she's still got the cutoffs on. I'm a big fan of those. The very brief encounter my fingers made with the soft underside of her arse cheek yesterday is emblazoned on my mind.

Among other things.

Suffice to say I did *not* get much sleep last night.

'Who'll put the skirtings on?' Gaz insists with the confidence of one who's too fucking stupid to understand when he's pushing his luck.

'I will,' I say through gritted teeth. 'Or one of the guys. They've pretty much finished the bathrooms.'

'I can help,' he says. 'I mean, I can tell you where to put them.'

I give him my most exasperated glare. 'I think I can manage. They're *skirting boards*. It's not rocket science.'

He shrugs. 'You're the genius. Go for it.'

'Your blessing means the world to me,' I tell him, and I sweep past them both towards the kitchen. I'll never admit it, but that Nespresso machine is a godsend.

I find Judy bending Sylvie's ear in the kitchen.

'What're you doing here?' I ask her. 'You should have slept in. What time did you get home—midnight?'

'Something like that,' she says. 'But you know me, the older I get, the earlier I wake.'

I gather her up into my arms. She's so tiny she barely comes up to my chest. 'Thanks for staying with him,' I say gruffly into her hair.

'Now, now.' She clasps me around my middle and pats me hard on the back. Judy gives excellent hugs. Always has. 'He's a good boy. You're both good boys. All's well that ends well.'

'Was it bad?' I ask, releasing her. 'At the hospital?'

'It was a total shitshow.'

'Apparently it was an hour before they even triaged him,' Sylvie says.

I shake my head. 'Jesus.' Our NHS gets stretched thinner and thinner every year. I don't know how we're still limping along. If ever I developed a serious masochistic streak, I'd go in and sort the whole circus out for them. It needs such a huge overhaul it's not funny.

'How are you finding the new kitchen, Sylv?' Judy asks her as I amble towards the Nespresso machine and stick in a pod.

Sylv runs a loving hand over the stainless steel work surface. 'It's a dream come true. It makes everything so easy I could weep.'

I exhale as I watch the machine with bated breath. These fucking women. Asking for so little. Giving so much.

'You two are the real deal, you know that?' I say to my coffee cup. Carlotta even brought in a stack of those little glass Nespresso-branded espresso cups for us to use.

Course she did.

Sylv comes up behind me and slides her arms around my waist. Her head rests against my back. 'And you're our favourite secret softie, isn't he, Jude?'

'I've said it before, and I'll say it again,' Judy pronounces. 'He's a keeper.'

Sylv sighs into my back. 'Marry me.'

'Let's do it,' I tell her. 'I've got expensive lawyers. I'm sure we can get around the bigamy thing.'

'I'll take Ray if he's going spare,' Judy says.

Ray is Sylvie's husband of, I dunno, twenty-five, thirty years. He has a few inches on me and he's built like a brick shithouse.

Sylv laughs. 'I couldn't do that to him. You'd eat him for breakfast.'

'Don't joke,' Judy warns. 'You know I'd eat that man for breakfast *every* morning. He's delicious.'

I groan, but Judy's words trigger something I've been meaning to ask Sylv.

'Connor and Kate thanked me for their shepherd's pie this morning,' I say over my shoulder. 'They said it was yum. I hadn't a clue what they were talking about. Ring any bells?'

Connor and Kate Jones are basically carers for their mum, and I know they're not eating anywhere near as regularly as they should. I sent them over some pizzas the other day, after they told me they couldn't get here for dinner, but I haven't sent them anything since.

She releases me, and I turn to face her. She's eyeing me up thoughtfully, as if weighing her words.

'What?'

'I have a feeling I know where that shepherd's pie came from,' she says.

'You?'

'Nope.' She shakes her head and purses her lips together. 'I'd ask Carlotta.'

Carlotta?

What the hell does she have to do with it?

15

AIDE

I corner her after our now usual lunch feast of ginger and turmeric juices and chicken-pesto-avocado wraps. And by corner, I mean I drag her into the office with me and shut the door behind us.

Just like yesterday.

She swapped out her lurid sweatshirt earlier for her black Venus painting t-shirt, and now she's standing in front of me in that and those fucking cutoffs, arms crossed. I lick my lips as I look down and take her in.

It would be a lie to say I've stopped thinking about her since we were in here yesterday. Don't get me wrong; I am far from celibate. I do alright for myself. But it's not every day I allow myself to get into any of the situations I've already found myself in with her.

And by *found myself*, I mean thrown myself into headfirst.

Except for yesterday, actually. That one I didn't see coming. Didn't expect her to strip for me from the waist up and challenge me to feast on her and forget my troubles among her spectacular curves.

I certainly didn't expect to have the fucking nipples I've tormented myself over all week *in my mouth.*

It's pretty clear we have little in common. Our bank balances may be more similar than she realises, but our outlooks on life, our lived experiences, are worlds apart.

Even in a paint-splattered t-shirt, she still screams *high maintenance.* The fine gold bands still adorn her slender fingers. Her ponytail is long and sleek and perfect. Her makeup is light but perfectly applied, to my eyes, anyway. It enhances her huge, dark eyes and kisses her high cheek-bones with a rosy blush.

She was beautiful aged sixteen, when her dad invited me to join his family for dinner at their Holland Park mansion. Such an honour—such a *milestone*—for a piss-poor twenty-year-old from a London council house, but, it would seem, not remotely memorable for her. Obviously, I wasn't going to repay Paul Montefiore-Charlton's mentorship, his faith in me, by hitting on his barely legal daughter and the apple of his eye.

Not that she would have given me a second glance.

But if she was beautiful then, she's exquisite now. Her features are finely wrought, her colouring perfect. And, much as it pains me to admit it, I quite like her cockiness. It's growing on me. She's a stunner, and she knows it. She's not coy or falsely demure—that would piss me off.

She owns it all. Her looks. Her sexuality. Her attraction to me, and her certain knowledge of my attraction to her.

Let me tell you, that is very, very hot.

And on top of all that, she may be less of a blinkered princess than I've given her credit for.

I take a step towards her. 'Know anything about a certain shepherd's pie that found its way into a couple of hungry bellies last night?' I ask in a low voice.

Her face flickers with surprise. She wasn't expecting that.

'Maybe.' She leans against the door and narrows her eyes, assessing me.

'How did you know?' I ask.

'I was there the other day when you were talking to them outside. Sylvie filled me in afterwards.'

'So you sent them some food?'

She shifts. 'Yeah. Well, I had Judy sort it out cos she said she couldn't share their address. But yep.'

Her gaze drags over me, from my eyes to my mouth and down to my chest. I'm already covered in sawdust and grime. My vest is damp with sweat and my trousers have all sorts of crap on them. But she's looking at me like it's all good, like every stain is a mark of my masculinity. Like the dirtier I get, the more I do it for her.

Like she wouldn't mind me dirtying her up, either.

Which is ironic, because with most women I fuck I'm wondering whether they're just after my money. It's refreshing to be objectified by this princess purely for my body and whatever bad-boy, bit-of-rough kink she's decided I can feed for her.

Even if I'm not quite the rough diamond she sees me as.

I plant a palm against the door, next to her ear. 'Well, thank you,' I tell her. I look her in the eyes so she knows I mean it. I'm not messing around. That those kids touched her heart enough to galvanise her into action really fucking touches *me*. 'It means a lot.'

'I didn't do it to suck up to you,' she says, a note of defiance in her voice. 'I did it for them.'

'I know.' I nod. 'Even better.'

We stare at each other.

'You and I have unfinished business,' I tell her gruffly, dropping my eyes to that pink, plump mouth.

She lets her head drop back against the door. 'If by *unfinished business* you mean you owe me the orgasm you promised me, then that is correct.'

I allow myself a smirk at her lack of filter. 'That's exactly what I mean.'

'But if you're looking for a peep show today, you'll be disappointed,' she says blithely, 'because I'm wearing your bra and it's hideous.'

A flush rolls over my skin at the prospect of her wearing something intimate that I bought her, even if its entire, though impossible, purpose is to render Carlotta as unappealing as possible.

'Show me,' I say.

She raises her eyebrows at me.

'I don't mean strip. Just take off this layer—you've got something on underneath, yeah?'

She shakes her head. 'Nope. Too hot. Just the bra of doom. If you want to see it, you do the honours.'

I lick my lips before moving in closer, picking up the hem of her oversized t-shirt.

She nods again. 'Go on,' she says, her voice amused.

That does it. I tug the t-shirt straight up and yank it off over her head as she raises her arms for me.

She's in just the bra and her cutoffs now, and I survey the picture. Fuck, the bra is ugly—a shiny, depressing beige with sensible, supportive straps and not a nipple in sight. Still, it has her tits practically on a platter and it gives her one hell of a cleavage. When I drag my eyes downwards, the soft, tanned skin of her stomach draws me in.

'Grim, isn't it?' she says.

'There is nothing grim about you, Carlotta,' I say. 'Nice cleavage.'

She smirks. 'You've sucked my boobs. I think you can call me Lotta.'

I ignore the invitation. It sounds too *matey* for my liking, and there's something about saying her full name that gives me a kick.

Instead, I run my knuckles over the skin of her stomach. God, it's soft. So soft. Up and down I go, and she shivers.

'Unfinished business,' I repeat, watching her face.

Her bravado's gone, and in its place is watchfulness. Need.

'Mm hmm,' she agrees, looking dazed. 'Here?'

I laugh. 'Nope. Up against a door with Judy on the other side isn't really my style.'

'Really?' She pouts. 'That's disappointing. I really thought it would be.'

'Because that's what happens in your *bang a builder* fantasy?'

'Basically, yeah,' she admits with refreshing honesty and a total lack of shame.

Turns out being objectified is absolutely fine with me.

I dip my head so my mouth is inches from hers. 'I need you in a bed, Carlotta,' I tell her. 'Naked. I need hours with you to do all the things I want to do to you.'

Her eyelashes flutter as she skims her gaze back over my pecs again. 'I can—we can find a bed.' She sounds breathless. 'I thought this would be—you'd be, you know—quick and dirty.' She shakes her head. 'But, yeah, a bed is good. Great.'

I grin. 'It won't be quick, sweetheart. Not at all. But it'll be very, very dirty.'

～

LOTTA

Because Aide is one of those self-controlled sado-masochists, and also, possibly, because he's a nice guy who knows how to look after his team, he insists on buying everyone an end-of-week drink at the local pub before he and I can abscond for our slow and dirty evening of sin.

'These are long overdue,' he says as he hands pints of lager around to Gaz, Frank, Jack and Marc. Sylvie and I have opted for white wine, which seems high-risk in a place like this, and Judy's on the Bailey's. Aide requests bags of crisps and dry roasted peanuts, which is great, because I'm starving, and extracts a wad of notes from his wallet before peeling off a few tenners for the server.

I smile to myself. Such a cliché—the builder who gets paid in cash.

We're all covered in dust and paint and grime, but no one in here seems to care. In fact, no one's spared us a second glance except for the server, who's been eye-fucking Aide so hard while she pulled his pints I'm amazed they didn't all overflow. He seems totally oblivious, though. And I can't blame the poor woman.

He's absolute perfection. Standing in this dreary old man's pub, surrounded by us lot and a load of randoms, he looks like a film star.

Seriously.

He looks like he's just wandered off the set of those Diet Coke ads Mamma used to love, or like he's getting ready to do a remake of Die Hard. He just needs a machine gun strapped to his back. Move over, Bruce. This guy has *brooding action hero* written all over him. Even filthy and sweaty and exhausted, he exudes this leading-man magnetism that makes my jaw drop and my panties *threaten* to drop and my legs weak.

It's everything. The beard. The incredible eyes. The mop of dark, sweat-slicked hair. That vest showing off those insane guns.

It's the way he holds himself. His natural unselfconsciousness, like he has no clue how much he draws the eye.

As I watch him pass the drinks around our little gang, I marvel at the fact that, in an hour or two, I will be attending to some serious unfinished business with this guy.

Sex.

Hot, languid, sweaty, athletic sex, where the intensity of having Aide's body wrapped around mine, and his eyes on me, and his dick inside me, may actually finish me off.

The anticipation, the tension, has been building since he took my top off earlier this afternoon. His attentions to me have been subtle, but they've given me goosebumps every time. He brought me an espresso earlier—unheard of. He defended me when I suggested to Frank that we could (unfortunately) get this job wrapped up a couple of days ahead of schedule next week.

And he keeps touching me whenever he can.

A hand on my lower back as he guided me through the doorway just now.

Knuckles grazing my arm earlier when no one was looking.

The lightest pinch on my waist through my t-shirt.

His fingers brushing mine as he hands me my wine glass, those eyes sweeping over my body.

It's like he wants to remind me what's coming. Not that I could forget for a second what I have in store tonight.

'Cheers,' he says when everyone has their drink. 'To all of you. Thank you for making this project possible.'

'To Gaz, for sacrificing a finger for the cause,' Judy says, holding her Bailey's aloft. 'Stupid fucker.'

We all laugh, and Gaz holds up a hand. 'Now, now, Judith. Where's your Christian charity?'

'I've used it all up on those poor kids,' she retorts. 'There's none left for idiots who don't know how to use a nail gun.'

'Happens to the best of us, mate,' Marv offers. 'I've seen more nail gun accidents than anything else in my twenty years on the job.'

Gaz clanks his pint glass against Marv's. '*Thank you*, my friend. See that, Judith? Nobody likes a beeotch.'

Sylvie's eyes go wide as she brings her glass to her lips. 'Children,' she says when she's taken a sip. 'Why don't we try to be grownups for an hour? Especially in front of these nice people who've helped us out all week?'

'Nah,' Gaz says. He rests an elbow on Judy's shoulder, which is not difficult for him to do given he has at least a foot on her. 'I'm going to get Judy drunk and then her filter will really come off. That's when the magic happens. Let's you and I get on the whisky after this, Judith, my love.'

'You'll be absolutely twatted if you do that,' Judy tells him, wriggling out from underneath him. 'I can drink you under the table. I could drink anyone here under the table except for the mighty Aidan Duffy.'

Aidan raises his pint to her and smirks. Amusement and arrogance are written all over that gorgeous face, and it's hot AF. 'Happy to meet that challenge anytime, Jude. Just say the word.'

Everyone's laughing, including me, but there's the

funniest feeling in my brain. I feel dizzy. Ungrounded. Like the earth just shifted beneath me.

Aidan Duffy.

Aidan *Duffy.*

That name is familiar.

My lightheadedness is growing. I put my wineglass down on the bar. 'Mind that for me, will you?' I ask Sylvie. 'I just need to make a call.'

I make my way outside as fast as I can, tugging my phone out of my handbag and typing in *Aidan Duffy.*

Oh my God oh my God oh my God.

It's fucking him.

16

LOTTA

I clamp a hand over my mouth as I lean against the wall and stare at my phone in disbelief.

Aidan Duffy.

A name I know well, and yet have never put a face to. Google has a subtitle below his name.

British entrepreneur.

Below that is a carousel of images. The first one shows Aide—*my* Aide—smiling and holding an award. He's in black tie.

Black fucking *tie*.

And oh my sweet mother of God does he look beautiful. Divine. He looks like a film star accepting an Oscar. He also looks genuinely happy. Proud. Two expressions I haven't seen much evidence of on that ridiculous face of his since I've known him.

The next image has him standing, arms folded and face unsmiling in a deep blue shirt, in front of a bank of what look like massive servers.

There are more.

Aide in a recording booth, headphones on, a BBC mic in

front of him.

Aide standing on a podium.

Aide surrounded by smiling youths, all wearing Prince's Trust t-shirts.

Aide with a beautiful blonde.

Aide with *another* beautiful blonde.

I scroll down to the Wikipedia entry Google is showing right beneath the photos.

Aidan Cuthbert Duffy, OBE, (Cuthbert? What the hell? And OB fucking E?) *is a British entrepreneur, software engineer and philanthropist. He is founder of data security firm Totum and youth charity Fresh Start and is an Ambassador of The Prince's Trust. He was awarded his OBE by Queen Elizabeth II in 2022. His net worth is estimated as four-point-two billion pounds. He was born in Notting Hill, London on February 6th, 1990.*

I slump against the wall. There's a myriad of emotions hitting me right now, and I understand precisely none of them. I'd expect myself to feel smugness, triumph, even, at my proximity to bedding, if not bagging, a real live billionaire who, for once, isn't a total wanker.

Instead, I feel...weird.

Disappointment rolls through my belly, curdling that revolting white 'house wine' that didn't even sport a grape type. I've had a very clear vision in my mind of who Aide is, and that is a handsome, hunky, Henry Cavill-esque builder whose filthy mouth will be equalled, I'm sure, only by his filthy bedside manner.

And it appears the guy who's been sucking my boobs and buying me bras and whispering dirty things to me is not that. Not at all.

He's someone altogether different. Someone who's been having a laugh at my expense.

Forget disappointed. I feel betrayed, and really fucking cross.

My dating history over the past two years has been a long string of rich pricks. Sure, there've been highs. Portofino, Paris, New York, Cannes. Candlelit dinners and galas and yachts and diamonds.

And yep, there's been some great sex amid the average sex—mainly because I know what I like, and I'm not afraid to ask for it, and I'm even less afraid to provide a running commentary if someone needs a manual.

But I've been colouring strictly within the lines. I've dated and fucked exclusively in my social circle of elite Londoners and Europeans and Americans. I've been snooty and predictable and clichéd.

Aide is *supposed* to be the antidote to all that. He's supposed to be the guy I succumb to just because he's hot and insanely masculine and capable of that fuck-me, swoon-worthy throw-down I crave so badly.

He's supposed to be the all-man man. The female fantasy. He's supposed to be everything the female gaze wants... and he is.

But he also isn't.

He's an insanely wealthy, jaw-droppingly successful guy who's also a public figure and probably has a blue tick on Instagram.

I had a fun, steamy, sweaty little dalliance planned, where I'd live out some kind of porno fantasy that's a mix of *Lady Chatterley* and Pulp's *Common People*. And with a couple of words out of Judy's mouth, that's just—poof—evaporated.

Into thin air.

Gone.

Obviously, he's still hot. Like, otherworldly hot. But he's

been playing me, and I swear to God nobody plays Carlotta Montefiore-Charlton.

I'm so angry now that adrenalin's flooded my system and I'm shaking. I'm furious with him, and I'm furious with myself for being so dim. So obtuse.

How the fuck did I miss this?

I have a degree from Cambridge, for God's sake. I run a ten-figure business which I co-founded. I am a highly intelligent and wealthy woman in my own right, and yet this idiot has seen fit to pull the wool over my eyes. I try to rack my brain for all the clues I missed, for the times people like Khal probably spelt out for me who Aide was and I didn't pay attention.

My God, he must think I'm ridiculous.

I'm ready to lay into him. Fuck knows, I'm so angry I could march back in there and throw his stupid working-man's pint all over his stupid face in this stupid, smelly working-man's pub. And I'm so close to doing that, I swear.

But *Aide*, my hot, manly builder, promised me a seriously filthy night.

And I'll be damned if *Aidan Fucking Duffy*, international hotshot businessman and tech billionaire who still believes he's outwitted me, is going to ruin my little fantasy.

∼

I PLASTER on a smile for the next two rounds and attempt to ride out the conversation which, to be fair, is hilarious. Gaz switches to pints of bitter with whisky chasers, which seems ill-advised, and Judy matches him on the latter. Sylvie, who's definitely more of a listener than a spotlight-hogger, seems content to stand with me and watch the banter between them.

And Aide, or should I say *Aidan*, dips in and out, an abnormally good-natured grin on his face most of the time. He seems blissfully unaware that his full name has belatedly triggered my mental cogs. His eyes seek me out so often that I'd be a puddle on the floor if I was unaware that he was lying to me through his teeth.

To be fair, it's no hardship to eye-fuck him right back. I have a vivid imagination. No matter what this guy's failed to disclose to me, he is utterly, flawlessly gorgeous, and the reality of having him stand across from me in stained work trousers and boots and a sweaty vest is more than enough material for me to work with.

My manual labourer kink remains happily intact.

I watch in disbelief as he peels a few more tenners off the wad in his wallet to pay for the next round of drinks. What tech billionaire walks around with wads of cash? Doesn't he have his platinum Amex on Apple Pay like most self-respecting rich pricks? Surely things with the tax man can't be so bad that he's wheeling and dealing in hard cash?

As I stand at the bar to help him with the round of drinks, he brushes his knuckles discreetly down my bare arm.

'You want to get out of here soon?' he murmurs.

Fuck, yes I do. 'Yep,' I tell him. I lick my lips. 'Long and dirty, remember?'

He grins, his eyes sweeping over my face and lingering on my mouth. 'You're about to see me neck the quickest pint ever,' he says, and he turns to distribute the drinks.

I attack a bag of crinkle cut crisps so the wine doesn't totally go to my head. I give the cheese and onion flavour a wide berth, because there's nothing erotic about onion breath, plumping instead for salt and vinegar. They complement the pure vinegar of my wine nicely, I decide. And they definitely hit the spot.

Aide's as good as his word. He downs his pint in the space of two minutes and wipes his mouth. 'Got to go see my mum,' he tells us all. 'She'll have my guts if I'm late.'

'I'll walk with you,' I announce. 'I have a drinks reception to go to.'

'Course you do, darling,' Judy says, patting me on the arm. 'Be a good girl for me.'

'I have no intention whatsoever of being a good girl,' I tell her with a wink.

'Even better,' she crows delightedly. 'See you Monday, Aide.'

'I'm not in on Monday,' Aide says. 'I have something at work. I'll see you all on Tuesday.'

Probably a mega-deal to broke, I think bitchily as we saunter out. *A knighthood to receive, perhaps. An orphanage to open.*

Fuck Aide, and fuck his lying ways, and fuck me for finding out about this right as I'm about to do the deed. Because ignorance would most definitely be bliss tonight. If I was strolling home with Aide, my gorgeous builder, right now on this glorious summer evening, with the prospect of hot, no-strings-attached sex lined up, I'd be delirious.

As it is, the anger still simmering in my blood is both ruining my anticipation and somehow adding a frisson.

I can have fun with him *and* have fun with him, if you catch my drift.

'We can go back to mine,' I suggest airily as we saunter down a sun-soaked Ladbroke Grove, the bulky muscles of his upper arm grazing mine, 'unless you live nearby?'

'I live out west,' he says. 'Osterley. Yours sounds great.'

'Ah.' Half an hour ago, I would have imagined some

depressing terrace house on the way out to Heathrow. Now
I'm recalibrating. He probably has a fucking estate. 'My flat
is five minutes away,' I tell him. 'I live in our most recent
development. It's called Elgin.'

'As long as it has a shower and a bed,' he says with a
sideways look so scorching it makes me full-body shiver, 'it
works for me.'

A shower.

A shower *with Aide.*

Jesus.

It's a prospect so tantalising that, for a second, I almost
don't care that he's a lying twat. Because, at the end of the
day, no matter what his actual identity is, his physical reality
is real. It's real, and it's outstanding, and nothing will stop
me from enjoying this man tonight. From letting him show
me what he's capable of. Whatever else I may think of him,
it's clear 'Aide' is capable on far more fronts than I initially
gave him credit for.

So let's see what he can do.

17

LOTTA

As I press my fingerprint against the lift button in my building, Aide's hands snag on the sides of my waist. He follows me into the lift, shuffling behind me so he can bury his nose and lips in my neck. The mirror shows me in a state of dishevelment and early arousal as a gorgeous specimen of a man kisses my skin, one hand sliding around to caress my stomach.

He's already doing everything right.

And I'm already in danger of losing my head and succumbing to him completely.

'Nice place,' he observes neutrally from behind me as I open the door to my flat. Technically, Gabe lives here too. He's staying with me while he recovers from his divorce, but he's in Paris this week.

'Thanks.' I bend to untie my basic-bitch Nikes before toeing them off by the door. As I said, I feel a damn sight less awkward about Aidan Duffy seeing my palatial pad than I would have done about Aide seeing it a couple of hours ago.

He's crouched down and is taking off his steel-capped work boots. As I stands, those shocking pale eyes trained only on me, I have a weird flash of self-consciousness. But then he's pulling me into him, one big hand splayed across my back as the other fists my ponytail, tugging my head back, and I sag, squishing my boobs and their armoured bra against his hard chest as he lowers his face and his mouth finds mine.

This is real. The attraction between us. The need. The wet heat of his mouth as he coaxes mine open with his tongue. The scrape of his beard over my chin as he angles my face just how he wants it and deepens his access. I wrap my arms around him and hold on tight as I drown in the smell of his sweat and the faint taste of beer on his tongue and the slick bulk of his muscles under my fingertips.

I despise myself for thinking it, but no matter who this enigmatic guy is beyond these walls, right now I've got him all to myself, and it's magic. He's got me wrapped up in his enormous arms, and he's doing things with his tongue that make me need it between my legs, like, yesterday, and he's growing so divinely hard against me that my head is spinning.

For the next hour or two, this will be all that exists. Him and me. And if I give him everything, I'm bloody well going to take everything I can from him, too.

'Any chance of a shower?' he asks against my mouth. His voice already sounds husky, and it makes everything clench between my legs.

'Solo or together?' I ask. *Together. Together.*

'What do you think?' He plants a lingering kiss on my lips. 'Lead the way.'

I wriggle free of him and sashay off to the master bedroom, which is spectacular, if I say so myself. I'm sure Aide's been in many a woman's bedroom, a fact I have no desire to dwell on, but he may never have seen anything quite this girly. He's going to look like some oversized cartoon beast ravishing the princess in her enchanted palace.

Come to think of it, that's not a bad analogy for this situation. Nor an unappealing one.

My carpet is white. My bed is four poster and epic. And my walls are papered in hand-painted De Gournay panels whose palest green backdrop showcases perfect pink cherry blossoms and green-gold hummingbirds. It's a work of art. In the main part of the flat, I went for pale colours and bold artwork, but here, in my sanctuary I've gone ultra-feminine.

I've gone similarly indulgent in my bathroom. I'm not a huge fan of the current penchant for minimalist wet rooms. I wanted my *bagno* to echo the most spectacular penthouse bathrooms I've ever stayed in. Shitloads of marble. Shiny chrome. Gorgeous sconces on the walls and flattering mood lighting, given there's no natural light.

'Come on through,' I say, uttering a silent prayer of thanks to Venus' lighting engineers as I select the button for low-level, sultry lighting. The wall sconces come on low as do the spotlights around the base of the bath. I know from previous encounters that this setting will showcase every shadow of every one of Aide's beautiful muscles to perfection.

I crank the lever—old school chrome—to turn the shower on. A torrent of water immediately hits the tiles of the enormous, four-person enclosure. From my position by the vanity I watch Aide approach me in the mirror. He puts his hands on the marble surround, caging me in, and presses his erection against my bum. I wiggle shamelessly against his hardness, because boy does it feel amazing. Like the best kind of promise.

He meets my gaze in the mirror as tugs the band off my

ponytail. When my hair is loose, he reaches up and runs his fingers through it. I have a lot of hair, but it falls lightly, thanks to its excellent cut and the bouncy professional blow-dry I had last night.

Aide keeps me pinned against the vanity with his dick as he arches his top half back slightly and pulls off his vest before planting his hands either side of me again. He's tall enough and bulky enough that I have a good view of his bare shoulders above mine.

The mass of his body around mine.

The tantalising Celtic cross around his neck.

I bet it'll hit me in the chin when he ranges over me and fucks me, again and again.

God.

I watch as he slides his hands towards my waist and gets a grip of the hem of my top. Up he pulls it, up and over my head. I shake my hair out.

He grimaces as he eyes up the bra he gave me. 'You can burn this,' he says as he unhooks it. Those eyes darken as he slides it down my arms and sees my boobs come into view in the mirror.

'Don't worry,' I tell him. 'I plan to. I only wore it to make a point.'

'Point made.' He reaches around and cups me. The warmth and the friction of those big, rough hands palming my boobs is so divine I shiver.

Slowly, deliberately, he runs the calloused pads of his thumbs over my nipples. We both watch in fascination through the mirror as they stiffen even more under his touch. I suck in a breath through my teeth at the perfect abrasion, as well as what a compelling picture we make.

We're both dark-haired.

Both olive-skinned.

Both topless.

Aide looks so fucking huge and commanding, and I look petite framed in his arms. Pliable. He may only be holding my boobs, but my entire body and soul are in his hands right now. Beside us, the water thunders against the floor of the shower.

'Look at you,' he groans in my ear. 'So *fucking* beautiful.'

'Mmm,' I manage, leaning back further against him and relishing the brush of his soft hair against the back of my arms.

'What do you like?' he asks gruffly, kissing along my jawline.

Clearly, I've already lost several IQ points, and the man hasn't even brought me to orgasm yet. I tilt my head, offering him better access to my neck. 'Huh?'

'What kind of sex do you like?' he clarifies. 'Want to give you what you want.'

Oh.

I'm suddenly alert. Not only is he physical perfection, but he's asking me for input up front? Perhaps he offers a menu of services? This man could definitely ace the gigolo thing if his billions turn to ashes.

'Um,' I say. I'm not backward about articulating my desires, but he's caught me off guard.

He rolls my nipples between his fingers, and I grind my bum against his dick. 'Come on. Don't be shy.' I detect a teasing note in his voice. Could Bedroom Aide be *playful?* Curiouser and curiouser.

I meet his eyes in the mirror. 'Put it this way. I'm sick of dating rich twats who can never undo their years of all-male public schools. I want a real man who'll throw me down and give me a good seeing-to.'

He may be a rich twat, but I bet he can handle some throw-down.

He raises his eyebrows and smirks. I can tell I've surprised him. 'I thought you'd want to take charge. You're such a pain in the arse during the day.'

'Hilarious,' I say with as much archness as I can muster given the man is massaging my boobs. 'Don't get me wrong, I can give you a running commentary, but I'd much rather I didn't have to. Think you can handle it?'

18

LOTTA

My little pep talk seems to galvanise him.

Maybe the phrase *rich twat* hit a nerve, because he backs away enough to spin me around in his arms.

'Look at me,' he growls. 'Does anything about me tell you I can't handle giving you exactly what you need?'

Oh my God.

No, it certainly does not.

'No,' I squeak, putting my palms on his chest as I look him over in all his shirtless glory.

This man is beautiful. Just beautiful. It's fair to say I have an eye for the dandies, the European playboys who live in London and summer in the Med. But never have I seen such a perfect example of the male form in all the virile splendour it's meant to embody. Aide is *built*. Rugged. Muscles for days. I've been ogling his huge fucking biceps, but seeing his abdomen laid bare for me is a pleasure beyond compare.

I called it the second I laid eyes on him, but the distribution of this guy's body hair is actually weird. There's the perfect, most even dusting of fine dark hairs over his impressive pecs, before it tapers down to dust a line between his finely delineated abs. Just like everything else about him, it's flawless. And drool-inducing.

I allow my hands to roam over the curves of his pecs. His shoulders. Flat-out awe is probably written all over my face, but I'm past caring.

My admission earns me a little smile. 'Let's get you in the shower, sweetheart,' he says softly, unbuttoning my cutoffs and backing away so he can slide them down my legs. I wiggle an ankle to kick them off and watch with gratification at his face as he takes in my teeny hot pink Agent Provocateur thong.

'Fuck,' he grits out. 'You been wearing that all day?'

'I *always* wear sexy underwear,' I purr. 'Except when overbearing dickheads buy me ugly bras.'

He shoots me a look that's supposed to be ominous and is instead profoundly sexy. 'Take it off, sweetheart.'

There's something in his voice—barely controlled frustration and desire—that has me shivering. I hook my thumbs into the thong and lower it till I can step out of it. His once-over of my naked body is searing.

He finds my gaze again and holds the most intense eye contact as he unbuckles his belt, biting down on his full lower lip as he does. He takes out the battered wallet from earlier, rummaging behind his wad of notes for a strip of condoms, which he throws on the vanity.

'Good thinking,' I croak. I'm glad someone has it together enough to think about practicalities. Also, this presumably means he's planning on fucking me in the shower, which is truly excellent news.

Then his trousers are off, and he's standing in front of me in nothing but that blessed cross and some tight black Boss boxer briefs. Best of all, the crown of his dick is making a break for freedom and peeking out of the waistband. It's shiny and purple and *angry*. There's even a bead of moisture pearled at the top.

Good.

I want it to be angry. I want to tease him and rile him and piss him off until he can't take any more and he wedges that angry dick so far inside me I'll never be the same again.

It's too prettily angry to resist. I reach out and daintily swipe at the moisture with my index finger before sucking it into my mouth. Mmm. Aide inhales sharply at the touch before staring at me with what looks like awed disbelief.

I wiggle my eyebrows and suck on my finger.

He bends and pushes his boxers down and I eye his cock shamelessly as it springs proudly free.

Fucking hell.

It shouldn't come as any surprise given the general physical perfection level of this guy, but that thing's a beast.

I was right about that Big Dick Energy of his. *I knew it.*

God, it's going to fill me up so well. My mouth is watering already.

'Wow,' I tell him. 'You are *huge.*'

'Get in the fucking shower, Lotta,' he says wearily.

I've already broken him.

I make for the shower, and he follows right behind me. As soon as we hit the torrent, he tugs me around the waist and spins me around, crushing me to him so that gorgeous dick of his jerks between us. The water cascades over us, soaking our bodies so our moves are slick.

It feels like a cocoon in here, with the spray thundering around us. I'm conscious only of Aide's hard body against me, engulfing me as his lips drag over my face and neck and his hands explore my curves. I open my eyes in the dim light for a second and absorb a vague impression of wet, starry lashes, and dripping hair, and his hungry mouth bearing down on me.

There's no game-playing now.

Just need.

He grabs handfuls of my flesh, kneading my bum and squeezing my waist and sweeping down my arms. I give as good as I get, determined not to waste a second in exploring his body. The body that had me at hello. That's been the subject of my most porno fantasies since I met him.

Jesus. His bum is rock fucking hard. I have a decent glute game, thanks to my sadistic PT, but this man's arse is carved from stone. I give it a good grope. It's delicious. I'm just about to slip a hand between us and explore that dick of his up close when he spins me around so I'm facing the wall.

'Hands on the tiles like a good girl,' he whispers, winding my hair into a manageable mass before slinging it over my shoulder. He steps up right behind me and grips my hips tightly as I slam my palms against the tiles. He sucks in a pleased breath as he digs his fingers harder into my hips.

Oh my God, he's pressing himself up against me and I can feel every inch. I wasn't paying him lip service when I complimented his dick. He's fucking huge.

Hmm. I really want to pay lip service to that dick.

'What are you doing?' I ask.

'Washing you.' He doesn't move.

'Novel technique,' I observe.

He releases my hips and slaps my bum lightly. 'Don't move.' A moment later comes the squelch of shower gel being pumped and lathered, and then he's smoothing it up my back. Over my armpits. Down my arms. Back up my arms and over my breasts, where he lingers so he can soap them up lasciviously.

Mmm. I moan a little and wiggle my bum at the decadence of having Aide's large hands massaging my boobs as his cock presses against me. I need him inside me sooner rather than later. He slides his hands back down my sides.

A moment later, one hand is reaching between my legs while he drags his cock between my cheeks. He finds my clit with his fingers as his crown probes me from behind, and it's so perfect I whimper.

'Jesus,' he grits out. His finger moves in a lazy circle against my flesh.

'God, that's good,' I gasp, widening my legs.

'You are fucking spectacular,' he chokes out. 'I need to fuck you.'

'Do it,' I urge him, my enthusiasm hopefully making up for my basic prose.

'In a sec,' he replies. 'Wider. Bend over more.'

For some annoying reason, he can carry off basic Neanderthal speech in a far sexier way than I can. But no matter. If my hairy caveman wishes me to bend over and spread 'em for him in the shower while he grunts single-syllable instructions at me, he will find no pushback here.

I shuffle to one side so I can grab onto the edge of the inbuilt shelf and he bends, sliding my feet apart. I'm expecting Aide to go grab his condoms, but instead his hands slide down my legs before coming back up, fingers spreading my cheeks apart. And then his magical tongue is *right there*.

Testing my entrance.

Breaching it.

Fucking it.

Oh my Lord.

He makes a ravenous, appreciative humming sound deep in his throat before he extricates himself and moves to my clit. Licking it. Lapping at it. Sucking it as the water pours over us, lubricating everything. His fingers find my entrance and thrust deep inside, and the combination is so otherworldly good that I arch back into him and clench my fists in an attempt to hold it together.

'More,' I gasp. 'Harder.' Scratch that. 'Aide, I need you inside me. *Now*.'

'Which is it?' His mouth vibrates against my pussy in a way that's very hot.

'In me,' I pant out.

He pulls away and streaks out of the shower. I turn my head and admire the spectacular view that is Aide gingerly rolling what is presumably an XL condom over his engorged length as he grits his teeth in frustration. He fists the sheathed monster in front of me. 'You sure?' he asks.

I glare at him. 'Get in here.'

He smirks, which is hot and obnoxious and arrogant and yet totally justified, because I'm a writhing mess.

But I forgive him as he gets back in and stands right behind me, the hair of his thighs tickling the backs of mine as he lines his dick up right where I need it.

He pushes in.

Fuck.

'Wait,' I tell him as I attempt to breathe through this breach. I suspect this is the vaginal equivalent of my eyes being bigger than my belly. I've been eyeing up that dick like it's my next meal, but I don't have much bravado now.

He stiffens. 'Shit. Sorry—you need lube?' I can hear, in every word, the effort it's taking him to hold off from thrusting all the way in.

'Nope. Just go slow. I can do it.'

'I know you can.' He caresses my bum, and I push back against him slightly. Whew. Feels like another inch is in.

He lets out a pained laugh. 'You have no fucking clue how unbelievable you look taking my cock from this angle.'

Well, that'll do it. Praise and filth for the win. I groan and tell him, 'Do it.'

'Tell me if it hurts,' he says and drives the rest of the way in.

'Fuck,' I groan, twisting my head so I can bite down on my upper arm if I need to, because this. Is. Intense. I'm so full of him I can barely move for fear of hearing actual flesh tear, and yet it's staggeringly, spectacularly wonderful, too.

His ragged breaths tell me this is having quite the effect on him, too. 'You are very, very tight,' he says. 'Jesus Christ.' He flexes his fingers around my hips.

'You can move,' I tell him.

He drags himself out of me, and it's no exaggeration to say I can feel the imprint of his dick on every single nerve ending lining my inner walls. It's heavenly and achy and torturous all at once, but it is absolutely *nothing* compared to when he slams back in with a single smooth drive.

Holy hell.

I let out some kind of low, weird cry which I assume is my body's way of saying *your enormous dick is actually touching my womb and it's frankly excellent.*

'Fuck, Lotta.' He rolls his hips in a way that's so good it should be illegal. 'I'm going for it.'

'Give it to me,' I pant. Every thrust from him seems to be taking me one rung further down the evolutionary ladder, but if I end up as a chimp, that's okay. As long as I'm Aide's chimp. The contractions, the ache, are worsening deep inside my core, and every wonderful, miraculous barrage from his best-in-class artillery has them building.

Snake Hips here has not only size but rhythm. I should have made him do me over the vanity, then I could have watched in awe and fear as he fucked me deep and slow in stunning, rolling thrusts.

Maybe it's better this way.

I don't think that's a sight I'd ever get over. I'd never be able to brush my teeth over the washbasin in ignorant bliss again.

'I'm close,' I manage before I bite into the wet skin of my arm so I can better survive this pounding.

'Me too.' Thrust. 'God, you are so *fucking* perfect.' Thrust. 'Best sight I've ever, ever...'

He loses the power of speech around the same time that my entire pussy harnesses the sensation Aide's perfect pumps have been feeding to my body and just plain deto-nates. I squeeze my eyes shut as colours and sunspots collide behind my eyelids and the insane heat that's been building inside me floods my entire body in wave after wave of sheer pleasure.

He rams into me again and again as I ride out an orgasm of biblical proportions, and I'm vaguely aware of his thrusts and grunts growing more desperate before he stills and jerks out his release in some part of my body I didn't know existed until ten minutes ago.

I'm floppy and sated and shaky-legged when Aide pulls carefully out of me. 'Give me a sec,' he says. I straighten up with difficulty and ogle the incomparable view of his firm backside while he loses the condom. I'm smiling like the cat that got the cream when he turns. He tugs me to him with an arm around my neck and kisses me slowly. Languidly. But also deeply. Powerfully.

He kisses like he fucks.

That works.

'You sore, or can you do another round?' he asks, that intense gaze scrutinising my face.

Every part of me that makes me my avaricious self clenches in delight. 'Another round,' I say, practically before he's finished the sentence. He chuckles, and my ovaries twerk.

'That's my greedy girl,' he says, and hoists me up into his arms. I wrap my legs around him, koala style, and cling on, kissing and slurping at his delicious, wet shoulder, teasing the fine chain bearing his cross with my tongue.

He carries me back into my bedroom, swiping the strip of condoms as he goes, and halts by the bed. 'Do you care if we get your bed wet?' he asks.

I snort into his shoulder. 'I do not give a flying fuck about anything except having your dick inside me again.'

'I knew I should give you a chance,' he says, and I slap his back hard.

'Un-fucking-believable,' he mutters. He disentangles my arms from his neck. Next thing I know, I'm flying backwards and landing on my bed with a thump.

Ladies and gentleman, we have throw-down.

I lie there, sprawled on the bed in a tangle of wet limbs and soaking hair, letting my arms fall above my head and my legs drop open, watching as Aide looms over me. His hair's falling over his eyes, his dick is already fully hard again, he's rolling on another condom, and he is eye-fucking my naked body so hard I reckon it could get me pregnant with triplets.

Let me tell you, the second time is dreamy. It's slow. Decadent. He braces over me on one elbow, his other arm pinning my wrists in place above my head and that dick buried up to the hilt inside my body. There's so much intoxicating eye contact that I suspect I could come just from the astonishing pleasure of having Aide's eyes bore into mine.

I feel laid bare for him. I'm stretched open, pinned

under him, impaled on him. Giving him everything I have. And let me also tell you, right now I wouldn't care if Aide was the devil incarnate, because this thing right here between our bodies feels so shockingly good, so extraordinarily right, that any other labels we attach to ourselves in this contrived world feel artificial and pointless.

That feeling of transcendence, of awe, lasts until he's brought me to a second orgasm, one so beautiful it almost —*almost*—brings tears to my eyes. Until he's climaxed in my body and I've swallowed up his heart-wrenchingly deep groans inside my mouth as he kisses me like a man possessed.

It lasts until he collapses on top of me and rolls our wet bodies onto their sides, throwing a heavy, hairy leg over me and winding a huge arm around my shoulders and bending his forehead to mine in a way that says *that was fucking otherworldly* and *I am in awe of you* and, more scarily, *I am in awe of how good it is between us.*

Because it is.

That was no run-of-the-mill fuck.

That was *insane.*

And I would love nothing more right now than to drift off for a little naked nap in the cradle of Aide's glorious body before waking for possibly naked takeaway pizza and a probably naked heart-to-heart and a definitely naked third round and an undoubtedly excellent, also naked, night's sleep together.

But I can't do that, especially the third bit, because Aide doesn't trust or respect me enough to tell me the truth, despite the fact that I've let him inside my body.

Twice.

It's best for everyone, but definitely for me, if I get rid of him and take tonight for what it was: a strictly physical encounter so spectacular that it's easy to mistake it for something more.

So when he nudges my nose with his nose and whispers against my lips, *Should I stay? We could go get some food?* I lie and tell him I have to catch up on work.

And I pretend not to notice the flash of disappointment and possibly hurt on that beautiful face of his, because he has no one to blame but himself.

I'm sure he can helicopter himself back to his estate from here.

Meanwhile, I have a hot date with Uncle Google.

19

AIDE

'How's Gaz doing?' Mum asks.

'Good, I think,' I reply absently as I fetch the ancient rattan placemats from their drawer in the dresser.

Yesterday evening was weird.

Amazing, but weird.

Either Carlotta is far more of a *fuck 'em and leave 'em* type than I would have guessed, or I did something wrong. She seemed happy, or as happy as three orgasms can make a person, but she shot me down when I suggested staying.

Maybe she just likes her own space.

Maybe blowing hot and cold is normal for her.

Maybe she came, saw conquered—or rather saw, conquered, came—and promptly lost interest.

It made a change from clingy post-coital women, but still. I'm a little pissed off, to be honest.

Should have got her number. At least we could have flirted over the weekend.

Fuck, she was hot. I knew she would be. Knew she'd be even more stunning when I got her naked. I suspected, from the way she got her tits out for me the other day with the unselfconsciousness of someone shaking my hand, that she'd show me a good time in the bedroom.

But she was so much more than that. She was passionate and responsive and willowy and lithe and hot for me. A mental image of her bent over in the shower, my dick disappearing between her smooth, pert cheeks, assaults me. Another one for the spank bank, as was the moment she swiped my pre-cum off the tip of my cock and sucked her fingertip between those beautiful lips. Second time around was different. Slower. More intense.

Caging her in.

Pinning her down.

Unable to look away from each other as I moved inside her.

Jesus Christ.

I wish she'd let me hang around for round three. I could have managed it after a brief recovery period in Lotta's beautiful but totally fucking OTT bedroom.

I subtly adjust myself as I pull out the napkins. Mum would have an aneurism if we sat down for dinner without napkins.

Oh, shit. She's saying something.

'Huh?'

'She means the nail, you wanker,' my brother Pete says, earning himself a clip around the ear from mum. 'Ow!'

'I will not tolerate language like that in my home,' Mum tells him. She turns to me. 'I can tell when your head is in the clouds. I'm asking how Gaz's hand is.'

'Oh.' I return to the present moment with a bang. 'Yeah. Dunno. He seems okay. Turned up for work yesterday, and all. I read him the riot act, but he said he'd taken the time off work and wanted to get stuck in, so I let him do a bit of painting.'

'I expect he'd be bored stiff at home,' Mum muses. 'He can't come to any harm with a paintbrush.'

I raise my eyebrows. 'You'd be amazed. He was out last night, though. When I left, he was getting Judy fu —trolleyed.'

'That woman is a marvel,' Mum says.

'She really is,' I agree. 'She hasn't stopped all week. But she and Carlotta have got through far more work than I thought they would.'

The second Carlotta's name is out of my mouth, I regret it. Well, I regret it with everything but the tiny part of me that gets a kick out of hearing her name on my lips.

Her name is just like her. Beautiful. Elegant. Exotic. Classy.

'Who's Carlotta?' my twelve-year-old nephew, Woody, pipes up. He and his mother, Laura, are by far my waste-of-space brother's biggest achievements.

I turn back to the dresser and count out five knives, forks and spoons. Not that any of us will use knives except Pete, because even Woody is civilised enough to know you use a spoon to twirl your spaghetti around your fork when you're eating spag bol.

Not Pete.

He still likes to cut his up into little bits.

I'm surprised he doesn't still ask Mum or Laura to do it for him.

'She owns a company called Venus,' I tell Woody, keeping my voice natural. 'They build houses and flats, and they're helping us on the project. They've donated all the equipment, and a team of them have been helping out all week. They're good guys.'

'Is she fit?' Pete asks, a sneaky tone to his voice that makes me want to punch him in the face.

I mean, it's not his tone that makes me want to punch him. It's his spectacular lack of maturity, of accountability, that makes me despise my brother.

All the other shit is just icing on the fucking chocolate fudge cake that is his life.

'She's pretty,' I concede in what I hope is my most off-putting tone. 'But, you know, high maintenance. She's from a very wealthy family.'

'What's her full name?' Laura asks. Clearly, my off-putting tone needs work.

I sigh. If my brother was asking, I'd shoot him down, but I can't be rude to Laura. She's far too lovely, and she has enough on her plate dealing with Pete day in, day out.

'Carlotta Montefiore-Charlton,' I say. 'She's Paul's daughter, Mum. You know, my mentor.'

Mum purses her lips. While I'm sure she's grateful to Paul and Chiara for everything they've done for me over the years, I know the wealth level of people like that make her incredibly uncomfortable. Her eldest son may be worth ten figures, but in her eyes, I'm still me. It helps that I do everything humanly possible to act the same when I see her. My net worth is an abstract concept to her, and she'd prefer to keep it that way than deal with the inevitable change that comes with life-changing money.

It's difficult for me. It's not like I won the fucking lottery and became rich overnight. I worked and worked and made decisions and took steps and worked some more and got lucky. My rise may have been what *The Economist* likes to call *meteoric*, but it's been gradual enough for us to accommodate.

Unless you're Veronica Duffy and you've been brought

up in a culture that teaches you never to abandon your religion or your political stance or your social class, even when they no longer serve you. So she's stayed staunchly Catholic and Labour-voting and working class all her life. And, if I didn't know better, I'd be tempted to think I let her down by finding professional success and 'abandoning' my honest, working roots.

Even this house is a joke. Yeah, it's better than the shit-hole I grew up in, the one I persuaded her to sell after Dad died. But it's still a small terraced house in an uninspiring road in North Kensington.

I've done the best I can. I never expected her to up sticks and move somewhere swanky, so I bought her the best house I could. It's secure, and clean, and not damp. It has double glazing and a nice little garden and a kitchen that had been newly installed when we bought it. When I look around, I feel I've failed her, but here's the thing.

She would never allow herself to upgrade more than this. To 'move up in the world'. Because, God forbid, her small-minded, backwards-looking friends and neighbours would think she'd got too big for her boots.

Just like I have, apparently.

Pete's another matter entirely. To say my brother has embraced my wealth is an understatement, and that's caused more friction than anything else.

'I've seen their house in *Hello!* magazine,' Mum says now. 'It's very tacky. Money can't buy taste, you know.'

'I don't remember it,' I say, even though I do. I was definitely too young and too skint to understand taste levels in the way I do now. All I knew back then was that the Monte-fiore-Charlton home was a palace. Everything glittered. But I have no interest in perpetuating this conversation, because Mum seems determined to be mean-spirited about the people who gave me my first shot at success and worked hard to deserve their own.

'Oh my God,' Laura says. 'She's *gorgeous*, Aide.'

I steel myself and lean in to look at the phone she's waving in my and Pete's direction. It looks like Carlotta's Instagram account, which is a roundabout way of saying I *know* it's her Instagram account because I feasted my eyes on it over the weekend before finally following her.

To say her feed is a reflection of the hedonistic bubble the woman I bedded lives in is an understatement. Everything in her life, from her clothes to her friends and her holidays, is beautiful. She's radiant in every fucking photo, but natural, too. It's not like she's sporting some Kardashian-esque pout. She's beaming and moving and shining in all of them.

Just like in real life.

'This is what pisses me off,' Pete says, grabbing the phone off his long-suffering partner. 'You become a billionaire and suddenly you have all these smoking hot women hanging off you. It's so fucking wrong. It's not like you're a rapper—you're a fucking tech nerd. Do they even realise that?'

'*Language,*' Mum spits.

Pete shrugs.

Woody grins.

'Pete,' I say, exasperated, 'I met her on a *community project*, for God's sake, not a super yacht. She's 'hanging off' Gaz and Judy more than me. If you could be bothered to get off your backside and volunteer, then you'd get to meet her, too. But you can't be arsed.'

It's true. I asked my brother to help out, and he laughed in my face. He doesn't even have a job at the moment, as far as I know. His concept of *needing* to work has become far too skewed since I started gifting my family money, and while it's a struggle to get Mum to take a penny, Pete's bank account is a black fucking hole.

I grab Laura's phone off him and hand it back to her. She scrolls wistfully through Lotta's feed, and I feel a pang towards this woman who's living with my fuckwit brother and managing to raise an amazing kid.

I make a note to do something nice for Laura—something I'll pay for directly so Pete can't intercept the money with his dirty mitts. Maybe a spa day one weekend, or lunch for her and her girlfriends. An overnight, even.

No Pete. No Woody. None of the scabby teenagers she teaches science to.

I'll ask Tish to look into some options later.

'You're gorgeous, too,' I tell her, partly because it's true and partly to piss my brother off. Laura has that natural, girl-next-door prettiness that Pete and I have always gravitated to.

Or at least, I did until I was bewitched by a Mediterranean stunner with a penchant for six-grand trainers and athletic shower sex.

Pete rolls his eyes. 'So you gonna bang her or what?'

'Peter!' Mum exclaims. 'Stop that right now. Aide. Parmesan.'

'I'm not going to gratify that with an answer,' I say with the moral outrage of a man who absolutely did not spend his Friday evening banging the woman in question.

'Aide doesn't go for girls like that,' Mum says, bustling over with the saucepan of drained spaghetti and putting it on the cork mat in the middle of the table. 'She's far too fancy for him. He should stick with what he knows.'

And there you have it.

Predictable as clockwork.

My mother's total refusal to accept that I may be deserving of choosing my own future.

My own place in this world.

And my own companion in it.

Now, all that remains is to sit down for dinner and place a private wager on how long it'll take my brother to pitch me the latest harebrained investment scheme he wants me to fund on his behalf.

I stand at my place at the same kitchen table we've had since I was a kid, the table whose varnish has long been scrubbed off, and proceed to dole out the spaghetti.

20

LOTTA

I jump straight into it with my brother as he pours me a glass of Krug. We have *Elgin Residents and Friends* tonight, a soirée that one of our celebrity neighbours is generously hosting on his roof terrace, and we both require some social lubrication first. He because he's a miserable bastard who, to be fair, is having a shitty divorce, and I because I have barely emerged from my *who exactly is Aide?* rabbit hole of the past twenty-four hours.

'Thanks. So. You know Aidan Duffy, right?' I say with false bravado as I accept the flute from him. Even saying Aide's full name feels weird. Forbidden, somehow.

He stares at me blankly. 'You know I do. How do you think your community project got kicked off?'

Um. The answer to that is *I have not once wondered that.*

I shrug. 'I dunno. Randomly?'

'He and I came up with the idea over drinks one night.'

Excellent. They're not only acquaintances but *drinking buddies*. This is information I really could have done with having a week ago.

'Did he not mention he knew me?' Gabe asks.

'Nope.' *Among other small details he didn't mention. Like, that he was thirty-second on the* Sunday Times *Rich List last year.*

'Why do you ask, anyway?' He takes a slug of Krug.

I hesitate. 'I'll tell you, but I need you not to be a judgemental arsehole for like, five minutes. Okay? Can you promise me that and just be nice?'

He raises his eyebrows. It's a common reaction to my outbursts. But, to his credit, he follows it with a nod. 'If that's what you need.'

'It is.' I take a deep breath and a long sip. God, that's delicious. Right. 'So I didn't realise it was him. As far as I was concerned, he was just this guy Aide on our project.'

Gabe stares. 'But you've been working with him all week, haven't you? How the hell did it not come up?'

Exactly, mate. Because someone's a devious little fucker. I shrug. 'I have literally no idea.'

'So?' he asks. 'He giving you grief?'

'Not exactly.' *Just a whole wedge of dick, actually.* 'But we've been... flirting all week.'

He narrows his eyes. The man is right to be suspicious. 'Right.'

'And I fucked him. Last night.' I flick my sleek curtain of hair over my shoulder. It's blowdried dead straight tonight.

Gabe grins. 'You dirty little wench.'

'Helpful. Thanks.'

'Good for you. He's a catch, or so I'm told. So what's the issue? He bang you and leave you?'

'No, dickhead, he did not. I kicked him out, I'll have you know, and he looked pretty gutted. The issue is I didn't put two and two together until we were in the pub last night with the whole crew, and I went ahead and brought him back here anyway, but he doesn't know I know who he is.'

Gabe edges away from me and refills the flute he's already drained. 'Fucking hell. Sounds like an Oscar Wilde play.'

'It's definitely farcical,' I concede.

'So what's the bottom line?'

Such a Gabe question. He's bored already.

'The *bottom line* is that I'm really, really pissed off with him. I feel like he played me. But I also had a great time with him. And now I don't know what's real. Like, is the fact that he's actually this billionaire and didn't tell me the real part, or is it that I had the most amazing shower sex of my life with him—'

Gabe holds a hand out in front of his face as if I'm about to throw acid in it. 'Fuck's sake, Lotts. I don't want to know.'

'Sorry.' I wait. 'But I'm not sure what to do.'

'It depends solely on what you want from him,' he says with the characteristic clarity that explains why they pay him the big bucks. 'Do you want a replay? If it was just one night, then it doesn't really matter who's played who. I mean, you won't see him again after next week.'

That's a chilling thought.

No more Aide.

It hits me right in the gut, and I'm not happy about it.

'But if you're interested in pursuing this, then you and he should try behaving like grownups and having an actual conversation,' he continues.

I deflate, because I know he's right.

'You are aware we built his house, correct?' he asks.

'What?' I stare at him in horror as my brain immediately flips through every standalone project we've done in living memory. Our focus is mainly on building blocks of super-exclusive flats with all manner of amenities. That's where we excel. But we do the occasional house build for our highest net-worth clients.

'Osterley,' he says. 'Two, three years ago? Mid century vibe. We had all that planning shit with his pool house.'

'Holy crap. That's his house?' I remember it well. It's a stunning showcase for what can be achieved without compromising on the ethics of materials or building techniques. A bright green poster child, if you like.

We built his fucking house.

Shit shit shit.

I'm feeling stupider by the second.

～

THE DRINKS PARTY IS DELIGHTFUL, actually, and exactly what I need to get out of my own head. The twelve flats across the two purpose-built Elgin blocks are all occupied now, and the list of residents is pretty epic. It's heavy on billionaires and celebrities, with a decent overlap between the two. The journey to get here was utter mayhem, and at times it nearly broke me.

But the flats are sold, the investors are thrilled, and the media buzz I helped create around the entire project has been so successful that we've already sold half the residences in our next project in Knightsbridge off plan.

Our host for this evening falls smack bang in the middle of my mental celebrity-slash-billionaire Venn diagram. Santiago Vale is the eldest son of the Vale musical dynasty, headed up by his father, the great tenor Dominic Vale. Not only did Santi inherit his father's singing talent, but he showed remarkable business acumen by forming a record company and buying back all of his father's rights from Sony before signing a whole host of other classical artists.

The Vale family, however, is a walking soap opera. Daddy Dom is on wife number two, who can't be that much older than Santi, and Santi himself has recently and very publicly extricated himself from his own marriage to the famous soprano, Vanessa Vale. I can only imagine the mess that's caused, given how intrinsically their careers and fortunes are linked.

I'd put a lot of money on Vale Entertainment having held onto all Vanessa's music rights, though.

Maybe Santi and Gabe can cry on each other's shoulders this evening and exchange single parenting tips.

Even if something tells me neither of them will stay single for long.

Tonight's setting is picture-perfect. Santi's roof terrace has a beautiful view of Notting Hill's ice-cream-coloured streets, of verdant trees, shady gardens, and private parks aplenty. His guests are all equally beautiful. In one corner a DJ is providing chill-out vibes, and there's a chic all-white bar in another. All that's missing is his adorable Staff, Luke, who's usually his faithful shadow but whom I assume is NFI this evening given his penchant for canapés.

I give Santi my most dazzling smile as he leans down to greet me with a kiss on both cheeks. A year ago, I would have been all over this gorgeous, eligible divorcé. He's sheer perfection in a black shirt that skims his trim torso perfectly. His looks are as intoxicatingly dark and his bone structure as dangerously sharp as Tom Ellis, he has a voice that brings women to their knees, and he's a majorly successful businessman who wields serious clout in the music industry.

What's not to love?

For some unfathomable reason and by some cruel twist of fate, however, I'm pining over some lying Romeo who wears the hell out of a filthy vest and knows how to get his hands dirty by day and fuck me like a caveman by night.

Worse, rather than celebrating the fact that he's secretly rich as sin, I'm actually bemoaning it.

What the utter fucking hell is wrong with me?

'Hello, darling,' Santi drawls in that entitled posh-boy accent that usually gets my juices flowing. Jesus, he smells amazing. He casts an approving eye over my short, frothy canary-yellow dress. 'Looking ravishing, as always. Is that new season Giambattista?'

'You're good,' I tell him with a saucy wink. Honestly, this man is perfection. A straight, hot male who can identify what label *and* season you're wearing at first glance *and* is on first-name terms with the designer?

The guy's officially a unicorn, and I am officially swooning.

Just, unfortunately, not in a sexy way. More's the pity.

He grimaces. 'I've spent more time than I'd care to in his Paris showroom recently. Four hours of my life I'll never get back.'

'Is he kitting you out with some nice gowns for your next gig?' I ask.

'I stick to Chanel for the gowns,' he deadpans. 'Nope, but he's kitting Ness out with many, many gowns for our next gig.'

I accept a flute of champagne from a passing waiter. 'Cosy.'

He sighs. 'Tell me about it, darling. Unfortunately, I still get eargasms every time that woman opens her mouth to sing. There's no one better in the world to duet with. If only she stuck to singing and not whining.'

'You'll find someone,' I tell him unsympathetically. 'I

can't believe for a second women aren't crawling all over you.'

'They are.' He lowers his voice. 'They're just... predictable as fuck. *You* know. Sometimes these social circles of ours feel endlessly samey.'

I lay a hand on his arm, feeling slightly more sympathetic to his plight. 'I know exactly what you mean, believe me.'

'Too many rich playboys?' he asks, faking fatigue.

I narrow my eyes at him. 'I'm not sure. Maybe, or maybe the opposite—it's kind of complicated. I haven't worked him out yet.'

'Sounds intriguing,' he tells me. 'Go forth and report back with your salacious gossip from your little enigma.'

$\sim$

I'M NOT ashamed to admit I spend the rest of the weekend spiralling.

I go into our records and examine every photo Aide's interior designer sent us of his house. You know, the one *we* built, that I had no memory of. While it's a little minimalist for my taste—I was raised by an Italian woman who favours Versace rugs, after all—it's undeniably stunning. Even better, it has such structural and environmental integrity that I want to swoon.

It's come back to me now, how much he dug his heels in over making the environmental footprint of his home as light as possible. How hard he pushed us to find innovative solutions to ensure it worked in harmony with, rather than against, nature. How impressed we were, and what a learning curve it was for the Venus team even while it became a pain in all our arses.

Next, I scroll through every single image Aidan Duffy Official (ugh) has ever posted on Instagram, which tells me that I am a pathetic stalker with a love-sick (and still marginally sore) vagina and that he is, unfortunately, a decent guy.

You can get such a good idea of a person by what they post. Aide's Instagram is horrifyingly uncurated. On the one hand, there's lots of random candid shit, like a fish he caught or a sunset he dug or his trashed, abandoned trainers after the London marathon.

No selfies.

No pics of him on his own, accepting awards or giving speeches or anything like that.

Nada.

The other main purposes for his IG account appear to be lending his weight to worthy causes and showcasing them to his three million followers. He shares a lot of stuff from The Prince's Trust and from his own youth charity, Fresh Start, as well as from other causes he deems worthy.

He also doesn't mince his words. On one post, about the teachers' strikes in the UK, he's simply written *When the government stops stealing from the education budget, our teachers will stop striking. Understand?*

Probably the biggest rabbit hole I fall down, though, is his company, Totum. From what I can see, its core business is data management software for the healthcare industry and its mission is to allow regional and specialist healthcare providers in the public sector—namely our very own NHS —to fully and confidentially share patient data, allowing doctors and other healthcare professionals to make more educated calls with a far fuller picture of all background and history pertaining to their patients.

Not only does it sound impressive, but its list of investors reads like the great and good of the British and US private equity industry. Its latest funding round, the one on which Aide's current net worth is based, valued the company at north of fifty billion pounds.

I watch several videos of Aide talking articulately and intelligently about stuff I don't have the faintest idea about. With every word that comes out of his mouth, my stomach sinks further at the extent to which I've underestimated this man, and my core clenches, because he's impressive and genius-level clever, and it's outrageously arousing to have this side of him suddenly made available to me. I'm Alice, going down the hottest, most jarring, rabbit hole *ever*.

How is it fair that listening to him spout tech jargon is just as much of a turn-on as having him grunt one-syllable caveman words as he fucks me?

It's not fair at all.

There's also a recording of him being interviewed on Bloomberg, where he asserts for what is apparently the millionth time that he won't be seeking to take Totum public at any stage, because he's not prepared to prioritise shareholders at the expense of their clients and the members of the public whose data they safeguard.

All of this stuff sounds like the Aide I know. All of it sounds like he's using his wealth and his platform as forces for good.

Still, all of it makes me really fucking angry.

Angry with him for shying away from embracing who he is.

And angry with myself for taking him at face value.

I am going to tear strips off this guy on Monday.

21

AIDE

I'm pacing at my treadmill desk in the corner of my office, trying to ignore the building feeling of disquiet I've had since Carlotta kicked me out on Friday night. Another few peeks at her Instagram feed tell me she spent Saturday night hanging off that classical singer Mum loves, Santiago Vale, on some roof terrace somewhere.

She looked breathtaking.

He looked smug as fuck.

I ramp up my pace just as Tish pops her head around the door.

'There's someone at reception to see you. She's not in your calendar.'

'And?' I ask distractedly. My laptop is perched on the high desk rigged up in front of me, and I'm attempting to pour over why our subscriber acquisition costs have drifted up year to date. I have a meeting with Permira, one of our largest investors, later today, and I want all my ducks in a row before I get on the Zoom with them. Unusually, though, the numbers swim before my eyes.

'She's called Carlotta Montefiore-Charlton,' Tish says.

That has my attention.

My head snaps up, and I stare at my assistant in horror.

'She says she runs Venus, the company you're doing the community project with? She also says she's not leaving till she's seen you, and that if you don't want all the funding pulled you should let her come up. She seems really, really angry.'

Tish's facial expression tells me exactly what she thinks of being railroaded like this.

'Send her up,' I say, punching the stop button on my Peloton Tread.

'I can get rid of her like that if you want.' She clicks her fingers.

Despite the growing sense of doom in the pit of my stomach, I swallow a smirk. Tish against Carlotta would be a lot of fun to watch.

'Send her up,' I repeat. 'Thank you.'

After Tish has pursed her lips and left, I pace my office.

Fuck fuck fuck.

She's outed me, and she's going to see me like this, in my wanky corner office, which is the absolute worst.

I'm a dick. I thought I'd ease her into my truth. She's made it very, very clear this past week what kind of kink I'm fulfilling for her, and the billionaire kink it is *not*. I was the backstreet guy to her glossy uptown girl, to paraphrase Billy Joel, and that dynamic certainly did it for her, and I was delighted to oblige.

But my little lie of omission has backfired massively, and I may have done myself out of a chance of ever being inside her beautiful body again.

I straighten up my shirt collar and stick my hands in my pockets for something to do, and I wait.

Jesus Christ.

She's a vision.

Don't get me wrong. She's a knockout in a t-shirt and cutoffs, but like this, in full battle mode, she takes my breath away.

I am so fucked.

She sashays through the doorway in a slim-fitting, fire-engine-red dress. It's sleeveless and it skims over her curves in a way that's feminine and sensual and powerful. Her heels are sky high and red. Her full lips are painted scarlet, and her dark hair is all sleek curls, billowing out behind her. She's wielding an enormous handbag like it's a kettle bell. I'm sure she'd like to take a swing at me with it.

Best of all, she's spitting fire. Those gorgeous eyes are huge and dark, and I can practically see flames coming out of her nostrils.

She is fucking spectacular.

I would very much like to relieve her of that dress and gather up that all that hair in my fists and get her on her knees, but I'm not delusional.

In this mood, she'd probably take a chunk out of my dick.

'You look beautiful,' I say softly, both because it's true and because I'm a fucking coward and I'd like to disarm her.

Doesn't work.

Obviously.

She drops the dangerous-looking handbag at her feet, which I have to say is a relief, and eyes me up and down as she plants her hands on her hips. There's no vest and steel-capped boots today. Instead, I'm in my standard investor-friendly uniform of black trousers and a white shirt, courtesy of Mr Ford. I tolerate spending money on good clothes, primarily because they last and also because people seem to expect it of 'someone in my position,' or so my team tells me constantly.

'Aidan fucking Duffy,' she says. 'Well, well, well.' She looks around, taking in my oversized office, as I try in vain to keep my eyes off her nipples, which, in a shocking twist, have come to join this little party.

'How fascinating to see you in your natural habitat,' she goes on. 'Quite the office you have here.'

'I like my own space,' I say, which is both lame and true. I despise the implied status commandeering this much square footage gives me while absolutely loving the privacy it affords me. The space to think amid the circus.

She ignores my comment, meeting my gaze, which I've managed to drag back to her beautiful face, defiantly.

'You must think I'm really stupid,' she says. The determined tilt of her jaw hints at vulnerability, which has me feeling even worse.

'I don't think you're stupid in the slightest.'

'Were you ever going to stop lying to me?' she asks. 'Or did you just feed me whatever you needed to feed me to get me into bed?'

That has my hackles rising. 'Hang on a minute,' I tell her. 'I've never lied to you. Not once.'

She rolls her eyes. 'You tell yourself that. Failing to mention something this big is a lie in my book. You let me believe you were someone very different.'

'Carlotta,' I say, attempting to keep my temper, 'you took me at face value, and you saw exactly who you wanted to see. I'm not stupid. You actually told me in your bathroom the other night that you were sick of rich guys and wanted a quote-unquote *real man*.

'You've objectified me since the second you laid eyes on me, and I think I represented exactly what you wanted and needed in the moment. That's fine by me, but don't try to tell me any of that is my fault.'

'I'm pretty sure you objectified me, too,' is all she has to say to that truth bomb. 'I'm not sure you looked away from my boobs long enough to see much more.'

I flinch, because it's not strictly inaccurate. 'I was dazzled by them at first,' I say, 'and I fully admit I may have underestimated you at first. But I don't now. I think you're fucking spectacular in every way. Every single thing about you impresses me.'

She crosses her arms, but she shrugs like she's dubious. Like she wants to believe me but can't quite risk it.

'Do you think,' I say tentatively, 'maybe we both underestimated each other at first? You saw a rough-and-ready builder, and I saw a spoilt princess, and we were both a little hasty?'

She nibbles on her scarlet lip as she takes in what I'm saying. I brave a step forward and put my hands on her bare upper arms. 'Do you think if we took the time to get to know each other better, it would be worth it?'

Silence. Her deadly glare tells me I'll have to work a lot harder to convince her.

I hesitate, choosing my words. 'I know you think I deceived you, but quite honestly, the version of me you've got to know this week is the real me. It's the part of me I keep hidden from most people, and it's felt really fucking good to be on site with my old mates who know me as Aide and don't fawn or do me any favours.

'All this stuff is fine, and it's fun, but I don't do it for the money, and the money is a major issue for me. So forgive me if I don't like bringing it up when I have a chance to forget it for a while.'

'Most people wouldn't want to forget they had four billion pounds,' she says.

I laugh at that. 'That's a paper valuation. It could all be gone tomorrow if this thing blows up.'

'It won't,' she says quietly. She uncrosses her arms and places her palms flat over my pecs, her eyes watchful. It feels like she's a stray I'm coaxing out into the open. Any adverse moves from me and she could flee.

Or bite.

Of that I have no doubt.

'I have something to tell you,' I say. I close my hands over hers.

She rolls her eyes again. 'Now what.'

'We've met before, you know.'

'Oh, come—' she starts to say, but stops when she sees my face.

'We have.'

She frowns. 'Where? I definitely would have remembered you.' She accompanies that line with a squeeze of my pecs.

'Thank you, but clearly not. I'll let you off, though. You were only sixteen.'

I have her well and truly confounded now. '*What?*' she asks in disbelief.

'Your dad invited me for dinner.' I laugh at the shock on her face.

'You know my dad?'

'And your mum—well, I've met her. And your brother.'

'I know that after this weekend,' she says in a way that makes me think there's more to the story. 'Go on. So you know my entire family, basically. Excellent.'

I release her hands and wrap my arms around her waist, drawing her into me. 'I was twenty when I came over, and

I'd just dropped out of uni because Totum was growing like crazy, and uni was costing my parents so much. I just wanted to get to the bit where I made some money and paid my way, you know?

'Your dad was amazing about it all. I met him through a mentorship programme at uni. He was the first person beyond my professors who saw the potential in Totum and in me. He held my hand when I took the jump and dropped out. Even got on a call with Mum, who was hysterical—I was the first person in my family to do any kind of further education, so it was tough for her to see me walk.

'Anyway, he talked her off the ledge, and he gave me my first chunk of seed capital. Introduced me to two of his friends who invested, too. I met them that night at your house.'

'I have no recollection of this,' she says, shaking her head in wonder. 'Literally none. Were you a late bloomer? If you were this hot at twenty, there's no way I would have forgotten.'

I smirk. 'I did alright for myself.'

'Ugh, of course you did,' she groans. 'Judy and Gaz told me that. But what was I doing at the dinner?'

I pause, choosing my words again. 'Lotta, you wouldn't have been interested in me. First, I was babbling about software as a service all night, which I doubt did anything for you. Second, I wasn't your type.'

'You're everyone's type,' she counters, but I shake my head.

'Nope. Not yours. I was this young guy who was scared shitless of being in your palatial home, and even more fucking terrified of blowing this massive chance your dad was giving me. I was totally intimidated. I wouldn't have been on your radar at all. You were in the middle of your GCSEs, so I think you were preoccupied with those, too.'

I slide a hand around her neck, under that mass of hair, and stroke her skin with my thumb. 'I was dazzled by you, you know.'

She smiles, embarrassed. 'I'm sure I was an entitled little shit.'

'You definitely were,' I say teasingly, 'but I think that was part of the impression you made on me. You were four years younger than me and so fucking confident. I'd never seen that kind of confidence. You sat there and talked about your studies and your friends and your social life, which sounded glittering, even then. Oh, and you were going to St Tropez after your GCSEs were done—I remember that very clearly, because I'd never even heard of the place.'

The memory is clear. The gulf I felt between myself and that beautiful, wealthy princess that evening was as wide as the Atlantic. She may as well have been a creature from another planet.

'Clearly, I haven't known how to read the room for a very long time,' she says.

'Don't say that. I told you, you were dazzling. And so fucking beautiful. But you didn't give me the time of day, and even if you had, I wouldn't have gone within a mile of Paul's innocent, barely legal daughter.'

She smirks. 'I was far from innocent. I popped my cherry that summer in France, actually, with some rich Parisian dude who was on holiday with his parents. And that kind of opened the floodgates.'

I groan. 'I really didn't need to know that. But basically, you can't blame me for not introducing myself when I know your entire family and I've sat across a fucking dinner table from you. I couldn't believe you didn't know who I was when you rocked up last week—I kept waiting for you to put two and two together.'

'As my brother tells me, I can be incredibly obtuse,' she sighs.

I drag my thumb over her soft skin. 'When did you work it out? Did Gabe spill the beans?'

She stiffens in my arms.

'Lotta.'

'In the pub on Friday night,' she admits, meeting my eyes. 'When Judy said your full name, bells started ringing, and I ran outside and googled you.'

I frown. That doesn't make sense. 'But we—'

'Fucked? Yep.'

'You didn't say anything,' I tell her.

'Nor did you,' she points out. 'I let you inside my body and you still didn't come clean, so I wasn't about to. I was really, really fucked off, Aide. I was so fucking furious with you for lying to me, and I think I was even more furious that you'd just ruined the hot builder sex I had planned for the night.' She shrugs. 'So I ignored it and went ahead and dragged you home anyway.'

I stare at her in disbelief. This fucking woman. She was so unbelievably hot for me the other night, but she knew the truth and kept it to herself?

'Are you saying you used me?' I ask her, raising my eyebrows in a way I hope is intimidating.

'Absolutely,' she says decisively. 'And you railed the living daylights out of me, and I considered it the least you could do.'

I let the hand on her waist slide lower to grab her arse. 'Is that why you kicked me out afterwards?' I ask in a low, ominous voice.

She doesn't flinch. 'Yep. I may have enjoyed your body,

but I wasn't about to let you get intimate with me up here'—
she taps her temple—'when you had no intention of telling
me who you were.'

'You should have come clean,' I tell her.

I swear her dark eyes have ignited with anger. '*You should
have come clean* is not a line you get to say to me, dickhead.'

I can't help the grin that breaks out. 'Touché.' I cup her
arse harder and press her against my thickening cock as I
tighten my hold on her neck, my mouth lowering to her ear.
'So, are you telling me you're only attracted to me if you
convince yourself I'm some sort of rough 'n' ready builder?
You're not attracted to me now you see the full picture?'

'Nope,' she says breathily against me, her hands flexing
against my pecs. 'No interest whatsoever. I told you, I'm sick
of rich pricks. I only want the animal version of you.'

'Hmm,' I say, massaging her arse through this very sexy
little dress and trying not to laugh, because she is ridiculous.
'What a shame.' I flick her earlobe with my bottom lip and
feel her shudder gratifyingly in my arms. 'So I should take
you back to that shitty pub again if I want my way with you
—you're not remotely interested in me fucking you in my
office.'

She turns her head towards me, pressing her jaw against
my mouth. 'Does absolutely nothing for me,' she lies
smoothly as she grinds her pelvis against my dick.

It's time to call her bluff. 'Got it,' I say and release her,
stepping backwards.

She stares at me in shock from hooded eyes before her
gaze drops to my crotch. She actually gapes, in fact. Her
nipples look set to rip through the fabric of that expensive
dress at any second.

'Not fair,' she stammers.

I smile, the corners of my mouth curving up in evil glee. I'm really enjoying this.

'You should know before you go,' I say, 'that if you think for a second there isn't an animal lurking in plain sight here, you're even less observant than I thought you were, and that's saying something. Anyway, I'll see you tomorrow. Tish'll escort you out.'

She pouts. 'Aide.'

'Yeah?'

'I want you to show me.' She takes a step towards me.

'Show you what?' I ask, although I already know.

'Show me what's underneath. I want to see what you're capable of. All this'—she throws her arms wide—'has me rattled. I need to know you're the same guy I—'

'The same guy you what?' I prompt gently, because this vulnerable, soft, unsure version of my little hellcat has my heart beating faster even than the cocky, knowingly seductive side.

'The same guy I couldn't stop fixating on last week,' she says haltingly, 'and all weekend, after you left. Otherwise it's like I fucked someone who doesn't actually exist, and that's just depressing.'

'Jesus, Lotts.' I close the space between us and grip her jaw in my hand, angling her face up towards me. 'I fucking exist. *Everything* from the other night was real, okay? And I'm so sorry if I made you doubt that.'

'Then show me,' she says, her eyes huge.

'I will,' I tell her. 'Get on the sofa, sweetheart. On your stomach.'

22

AIDE

I t hasn't escaped my notice while running my hands over her body that this dress of hers has a chunky zip running its entire length. A zip I suspect will be my ally now.

She turns towards the huge, modular sofa, glancing at me over her shoulder, and I nod my encouragement.

Yep.

I was right.

I could have that dress on the floor in two seconds flat.

But I might just take my time.

I press a button on my desk. Instantly, the door locks with a loud click and the windows along the wall separating my office from the rest of our workforce turn opaque.

'Is that your *sexy times* setting?' Lotta asks. She drapes herself across the sofa on her stomach, her heels waving in the air, ankles elegantly crossed and face turned back towards me so she can bat her eyelids at me. 'Use it a lot?'

'It's usually my *I have to bollock someone* setting,' I tell her, taking a couple of steps towards her. The curve of her arse, the dip of her lower back, looks so enticing right now.

'You can bollock me any time,' she tells me with a coquettish smile, and I'm instantly assaulted by the visual of being balls-deep in this one as she grinds her face into the sofa cushions in her efforts to accommodate me.

I stand next to her and bend, fondling the zipper at the hem of her dress, because of course I'm going to start at the business end.

'Dangerous words, sweetheart,' I whisper, and she gives a little wiggle of her delicious bottom which has me pushing her ankles down and lifting a knee so I can straddle her.

It's a knee-length dress, and the bottom few inches of the exposed zip are already undone, leaving a little slit. I grab the chunky silver zip pull and drag it upwards. It chugs against the metal teeth, and they part for me, offering me access. Inch after inch of bronzed thigh comes into view, so alluring that I sink my teeth into my lower lip.

I'd rather be sinking them into her skin.

Then, as I run the zip pull over the curve of her arse, I'm rewarded with a sight that has me going even harder. Carlotta's twin, shapely cheeks, divided by a scrap of red lace.

Jesus Christ.

I tug hard on the pull, unzipping her the rest of the way so I can part her dress like curtains and marvel at her rear view. Flawless skin and the delicate scarlet lace of her thong and bra.

'Would you look at that,' I say on an exhale, running my hands over her body. 'So, so beautiful.' I glide them over her arse and up her back, brushing her long hair out of the way so I can toy with the closure on her bra before I slide my thumbs back down and under the waistband of her thong.

I have no idea where to start. I want *everything*. Want to flip her over and admire those tits in their red lace before pulling her cups down and feasting on her nipples. But my instinct is to slide a firm hand under her stomach and raise myself up high enough on my knees so I can get her on *her* hands and knees for me.

That's what I'll do.

First, I lower my full weight on top of her so my still-clothed dick is pressing between those beautiful, plump cheeks and my mouth is next to her ear. She smells incredible. Heady. Expensive. Her floral fragrance pervades my nostrils and wraps itself around my brain.

'Did you wear this underwear for me?' I ask her, running my lips along the soft spot just below her ear. Her head is to one side, cradled in her arms. I loop my thumb and fingers loosely around the wrist next to her face, marvelling at how daintily she's constructed.

'No.' She sounds genuinely affronted. 'I told you, I always wear stuff like this.'

I grind my pelvis against her, and she moans a little.

'Hope you're not too fond of it, because it might not come out of this unscathed.' What I really mean is that neither she nor I may come out of this unscathed. 'You asked for real, sweetheart. Things are about to get real.'

She tries unsuccessfully to wriggle beneath my weight. 'I'll believe you when you show me.'

I laugh softly and press a kiss to her jaw. 'My little hellcat. I'll show you, alright.'

Raising myself up, I pull back to my knees and give her a little slap on that gorgeous bare arse. 'Up you get. Hands and knees.'

She does so with a sexy little noise of approval, her sleeveless dress sliding down her arms and fully off her. I nudge her legs apart one by one and position myself between them. Her arse is exactly where I need it, and I allow my hands to roam over those cheeks, to savour the dip at her waist, my thumbs to explore the curves of her hips.

I could spend hours worshipping her body, and I will, just not right now. For one thing, I won't last that long, and for another, she needs me to prove a point. She needs me to show her that the gruff, pretty fucking basic guy she's inexplicably responded to over the past week is still there. That the fancy Tom Ford get-up means bugger all.

That I am every inch the dirty, primal animal she seems to want me to be.

Shouldn't be difficult, because that's what this pampered, gorgeous, sparky little princess turns me into, whether I like it or not.

But I'm very, very glad she likes it.

I bend, sliding my hands up her sides until they cup her tits. Fuck me. They sit full and heavy in my hands, encased in their beautiful lace. My morals over the money this woman likely spends on outfitting her gorgeous body fly out the window, because there's something about knowing that the delicate, gossamer-thin lace through which I'm palming her bullet-like nipples cost a bloody fortune that goads my inner beast even more.

I'll shred this bra, this thong, to pieces if I have to.

As I knead harder, pulling and pinching her nipples and revelling in the breathy, needy little moans already coming from her mouth, the realisation hits me that I want her to desire this version of me as much as my community centre persona. I may have been at my most comfortable there, this past week, but, like it or not, I spend most of my time in this corner office, working on my laptop rather than hammering and sawing.

I owe it to this version of myself to win her over.

I push the lace down roughly so I can roll her gorgeous,

berry-ripe nipples between my fingers just as hard as I like, and I grind my erection against her.

'Aide,' she moans.

'You know what?' I tell her, my voice hoarse with desire. 'Tomorrow, I'll find a way to get you up against the wall in that shitty little office and bang you as hard as you want.'

I release one perfect breast and slip a hand between us, running a couple of leisurely fingers over the soaking strip of lace covering her pussy. 'But today, I'm a CEO, and you are here in *my* fucking office, on your hands and knees for me with nothing protecting you except this sexy little excuse for underwear.'

I press a finger directly to her clit through the lace, and she shudders and sobs out a strangled *God.*

'So you'll take every inch I have to give you, and you'll take it like a good girl. Got it?'

'Y-yes,' she manages, bowing her head.

'Right answer,' I say, and I unsnap her bra. Next, I peel her thong over that glorious arse and down her legs. She raises one knee and I slide it off, removing her stiletto as I go before doing the same on the other side.

She's naked, and stunning, and quivering for me. I scoot backwards, giving thanks for this enormous sofa, and admire the un-fucking-believable view that is Lotta's pussy, bare and already glistening with arousal, just for me. It's the most tantalising thing I've ever seen, and I kneel, using my hands to spread her folds wide open before I put my tongue right where it belongs.

I can't help the ravenous groan that escapes my lips as I begin to feast on her. I give her one long, decadent swipe of my tongue from front to back before proceeding to tongue-fuck her, slowly and luxuriously. I had a taste in the shower the other night, but that was pretty quick. Now, it's just me and her, and my prep for the Permira meeting can go to hell.

Worshipping this high-maintenance princess' body with mine? Showing her I know far better than she does that I'm capable of giving her what she needs?

That's far more important.

As is, I'm ashamed to say, showing her who's boss. Or, at least, showing her she doesn't call all the shots here. I meant what I said. I have her in my office, and I won't be happy until she's surrendered to what we have. Till she's come so hard and screamed my name so loudly that there's no doubt in her mind that this version of me can own her body just as wholly as the version who fucked her, hard and slow, in her shower and in her bed.

Just the way she wanted it.

Usually, I steer clear of the CEO thing. I feel uncomfortable thinking too much about the power it gives me. Feel even more uncomfortable wielding that power.

But here in this moment, with Carlotta, it's heady. I feel the need to win her respect and have her crave being on the receiving end of every last bit of the power I wield.

I slide my tongue out of her and move it to her clit. Fuck, it's so swollen. I flick at it, and she pushes back against my face.

'God, that's amazing,' she pants. 'Aide, *God.*'

Every time she succumbs, every time I get closer to that elemental part of her, something loosens in my chest.

'You are fucking delicious,' I grunt out, rubbing my nose in her pussy as I pause my licking. 'You're going to come so hard on my tongue.'

'I know,' she manages.

'Down on your elbows, sweetheart,' I say, and I ramp up my onslaught, sliding a couple of fingers inside her as my lips and tongue lave her exactly where she needs it. Fuck, she's so wet and tight, her muscles gripping my fingers. I add a third.

She lets out some kind of strangled noise of approval, and I finger fuck her harder.

'Fuck,' she says. 'Your *beard*.'

'Too rough?' I ask between licks.

'*No*. It's, *God,* it's so perfect. I can take it harder.'

The upside of having your community project turned upside down by a knockout hellcat is that, once you get her naked and get your hands and mouth on her, that fire of hers fucking ignites. She's moaning and writhing and twisting her body, her face grinding against the sofa cushions exactly how I imagined.

She's so close now. Every exhale is a moan. My fingers and mouth are soaked in her arousal. I'm lost in this sensory paradise. Can't get enough of the taste and smell and feel of her slickness.

I work her as hard as I can. I know she wants it. Needs it. I know she can take it all.

And then she's coming, her pussy shuddering beneath my tongue and contracting around my fingers, the fucking amazing sounds she makes telling me she's lost somewhere deep inside herself, that I've transported her to another realm.

And I want her to take me there with her.

23

LOTTA

oly hell.

That was the most intense orgasm ever, thanks to Aide's magic mouth and hands. I attempt to catch my breath, gather my wits, as I rub my forehead into the sofa cushion.

'Jesus, you're delicious,' he says behind me. He presses a kiss to my clit as he slides his fingers out of my body. I'm instantly bereft. I'm going to need to fill myself up with a lot more Aide, and quickly.

I rear up to my knees and stretch like a cat as he collapses on the sofa behind me. When I turn, he's sitting, his head lolling on the back cushions and his face watchful. Intense. A glance at the insane tent in his trousers tells me the poor guy must be in some discomfort.

He is a sight for sore eyes. I may have bawled him out for his deception and given him some grief about not being interested in this monied version of him, but I'd be lying if I said the man in front of me isn't spectacular.

Powerful.

Arousing.

It's a lot to process. I came in here pissed off and devastated that Aide wasn't the guy I thought he was, and I'm reeling.

Reeling because we've had so many connections in our past, and I failed to spot any of them.

Reeling because I honestly thought the billionaire thing would be a massive turnoff where Aide is concerned and yet I'm blown away by and desperate for more of the man I see before me.

And, you know, reeling because he's just delivered me one of the best orgasms of my life.

Basically, it's all broken my brain.

I gaze into those incredible blue eyes of his as I edge towards him on my knees and throw a leg over him. The stuff he was saying to me when he was going down on me, about him being a CEO and me being in his office, got me so hot before he even put his mouth on me.

I'm not going to lie; it felt kind of porno, and in a really *great* way. You know, *Fucking the CEO*. I'm also up for its sister title, *Sucking the CEO*. I'm the co-founder of a massive business and a major power player in my own right. I usually scoff at the idea of some guy using me as his plaything, using me to make him feel more powerful. But in this moment, the dynamic is seriously doing it for me.

It's partly to do with how fucking hot Aide looks like this. Obviously, the guy could dress himself in Lidl carrier bags and he'd look gorgeous. But the immaculate white shirt and perfectly cut black trousers really enhance his looks, his demeanour, his *everything*. I was here for the BBB —Basic Builder Brawn, where all his primal charms were laid out for me on a platter.

But here, in his office, clad in the beautiful custom

uniform that's supposed to denote restraint, civility, his animalistic side is even more alluring.

The uniform is a foil. A pathetic, inadequate shield against the man Aide really is. He's just shown me the tip of the iceberg.

I think back to his words just now.

If you think for a second there isn't an animal lurking in plain sight here, you're even less observant than I thought you were.

I mean, fuck. How is a girl supposed to respond to a line like that when it's growled at her while said animal fixates her with his predatory blue eyes?

When he said that, I knew I didn't stand a chance against him. I didn't *want* to. I knew in that moment that the throw-down with this new version of Aide might be even more savage than what I've experienced at his hands so far.

I was right.

I take him in as I lower myself down into his lap, grinding my still-sensitive pussy against his erection. I bite my lip. Jesus, that feels good.

He is a seriously beautiful man. That dark beard of his looks more neatly trimmed than it did last week. It showcases the sharp jut of his jaw and the generous curves of his lips, which still bear evidence of my arousal on them. His eyes are hooded as he observes me from under that thick black canopy of lashes. The top button of his shirt is open, but I need more. I need to see my gorgeous, hairy Aide in all his glory.

He shudders as I lower my mouth to his, running my tongue slowly over his lower lip and tasting myself on it. With one hand, he grabs the back of my neck, pressing me to him as his tongue finds mine. He kisses me like a man who's been pushed past the point of reason, his lips hard against my mouth and his tongue taut. Invading me. I open myself up for him and grind myself harder against him as his other hand goes to my bum, kneading and pulling me against him.

'Fuck,' he grunts against my lips. 'I could come like this.'

'Condom,' I say breathlessly. I sit back as he arches his back, digging in his pocket for his wallet. I take advantage of the moment to slip his shirt buttons through their button-holes, tugging the shirt out of his waistband so I can finish opening it.

There he is.

I smirk as I survey my handiwork. 'Hot as hell,' I murmur. The crisp white shirt lies open, giving me the perfect view of Aide's hard, tanned, hairy body underneath, that intricate Celtic cross resting right between his collar-bones. God, he's a work of art, and exposing his raw masculinity beneath his custom tailoring is like unwrapping the perfect present.

I take that back as he holds up a condom for me. 'Put it on me, sweetheart.'

This is unwrapping the perfect present.

Unbuckling his understated but very nice belt.

Unzipping those lustrous Italian wool trousers.

Tugging down the waistband of his black boxer briefs so I can extricate his dick.

Oh God, *yes*.

Would you look at that.

He's ready to explode.

I rip open the foil and position the condom over his angry, swollen crown before rolling it carefully over his length. He rumbles low in his throat and palms my boobs, weighing them, kneading them in his hands as his fingers strum my nipples, sending new flashes of heat straight to my core.

'Fuck, I missed these,' he tells me with a pained grin as I raise myself far enough off his lap to position myself directly above his cock.

We stare at each other as I lower myself down onto his thick length, inch by inch. As the glorious sensation of fullness sweeps over me I explore his body, sliding my hands under his shirt, along the bunched muscles of his shoulders, over his pecs. '*Yes,*' I tell him through clenched teeth. Sweat prickles on my skin as I attempt to accommodate him because gosh is it a tight fit.

He groans, his big hands sweeping over my bare skin, eyes searching my face. 'Fuck, sweetheart,' he says. 'You okay?'

'Yeah,' I manage. 'It feels amazing.'

'You're nearly there.'

Nearly. Bloody hell. I force myself to exhale, to relax, to allow my body to take him in more fully. Then I give, and he jerks, and he's fully sheathed inside me.

'Give me a second to enjoy this,' he whispers, 'because I'm not sure I'll last long.'

I nod, bending my head to kiss him deeply as I marvel at the sensation of being completely full of him. His hands are everywhere, stroking me, caressing me. They worship my boobs, and rake through my hair, and slide down my back, and grip my hips.

There's something about being completely naked while Aide remains fully dressed that's infinitely arousing. It's as if he's reminding me of his power. He's the one in charge. He's the one sitting back in his crazy office, his business on hold while he prepares to fuck a stark-naked woman, to have her writhe and purr for him in his lap.

The idea of it, and the physical reality of being impaled on his dick, is overwhelming.

My body needs more.

I grab onto his shoulders and drag myself up his dick. The friction is indescribable. I pause when only his crown remains inside me and hold there.

'Fuck, Lotts,' he murmurs, taking advantage of my height to dip his mouth to my breast and take a leisurely taste of my nipple. He snags it lightly between his teeth and flicks it with his tongue, making a ravenous humming noise as he does it. God, it feels amazing. I whimper and rake my fingernails through his thick hair to show my appreciation. He switches boobs, his fingers working my still-wet nipple, and I feel his crown pulse against my entrance.

He releases my nipple with a pop and sits back, jerking his hips towards the front of the sofa so he can recline more fully. I almost lose my grip on him.

'Ride my cock hard, sweetheart,' he says through gritted teeth. 'Hard as you can.'

This time, I almost lose a lot more than my grip. Because, in this moment, he looks every inch the mega-successful businessman, his clothes just undone enough to reveal the animal beneath. That chest is flawless. Hairy. Masculine. His cock's everything I need. He may think he's putting me to work, which is hot in itself, but really, he's letting me unleash myself on him.

Feast on him.

Go to town on him.

I arch my back and toss my hair back over my shoulders as I sit back down. Hard. Taking every inch, feeling him hit the place deep inside me that he found the other night. It's so otherworldly good my mouth opens in a silent scream.

Aide, on the other hand, lets out a loud grunt. 'Fuck. Me.' He finds my bum and gives it a *go faster* smack before smoothing his palm over my skin.

It seems my caveman is back.

Sweaty, grimy vest and work pants.

Impeccable Tom Ford tailoring.

It's all the same, apparently.

Because the man beneath both disguises is my absolute favourite beast.

If he wants me to ride him like the best, sparkliest show-girl, I will. I feel wanton astride him like this. Carnal. I'm totally bare for him, my boobs rubbing against his eager mouth and my bum brushing against the fabric of his trousers every time he bottoms out in me.

It seems I've well and truly brought out the animal in him, too. He's not holding back on any front. As I grind against him, he meets me as best he can, thrusting up into me with hard drives, those gorgeous abs of his rippling with effort as he does. For someone who told me he's close, he's holding out admirably, though I can see from the slick of sweat on his forehead and the pained awe etched on his gorgeous features that the effort is taking its toll.

He's restless, hands roaming, fingers and mouth on my breasts. My face. He tugs at my lower lip with his teeth before dragging his mouth down my neck and sucking hard between muttered compliments. Curses. Hoarse words of adoration. Encouragement. It'll mark where he's sucking me, but I'm past caring.

I *want* him to mark me.

I grind against him as the inevitable ache builds and builds deep inside me. The more fiercely I bear down on him, let him fill me up, the more exquisite the feeling becomes. Pleasure blooms deep within me, blissful tendrils of it unfurling in my core and creeping through my body, oxidising my blood and lighting up my nerve endings as I lose myself in this ageless rhythm with Aide.

It's not just having him reach those parts inside of me.

It's *everything*.

The scent of him and the slickness of his sweat and the bulk of soft hair and warm skin and taut muscle under my fingertips and the primal need shining from those eyes of his and rasps of our ragged breathing and the wet sounds of my body sucking him in.

It's too much.

He uses a hand to grip my hip, the impressions his fingers make on my skin telling me how desperate he is to guide me to ride him just how he needs. His hands, his eyes, his noises beseech me, but I'm conscious enough to know that I'm doing this for myself as much as for him, that, above all, I'm listening to the call from within my own body for *more, more, more.*

'I'm gonna—*God*, I'm—' And with that, the wave that's been cresting breaks, and I splinter into a million fragments around Aide, bucking and grinding and crying out and biting down onto the cotton covering one huge shoulder in an attempt to absorb this shockwave.

He follows me over the edge, one hand still on my hip and the other gripping the back of my neck as he holds me down, impaling me on him as he jerks out his own violent climax inside me.

'Fuck, Lotts,' he grunts incoherently. '*Fuuuuck.*'

His thrusts stop.

His hands still.

I wearily raise my heavy head from his shoulder and lean my forehead against his for a moment before I find his mouth. He kisses me hungrily, stroking my mane of hair back from my face. Off my shoulders. He gathers it up and winds it around his fist as he continues to worship my lips.

When his kisses slow, I ease away, putting enough distance between us to look at him.

His face is sated, relaxed, his features wiped clean of the frustration, the need they reflected a few moments ago. Those astonishing eyes are soft, and he's smiling gently at me.

'Hope that convinced you I'm still me,' he mumbles in the manner of one who hasn't quite recovered his power of speech yet.

'It most certainly did,' I tell him, and I lean forward to capture his mouth again.

24

LOTTA

Aidan Duffy is grinning at me.

Full-wattage, underwear-melting grinning.

Let me tell you, it's spectacular.

We're in the kitchen at the community centre. We're alone, but the door is open and the volume of Sylvie and Judy's conversation tells me they're just on the other side of it.

That isn't deterring Aide, who's making a beeline for me as I await my perfectly executed Nespresso. He comes to stand on the other side of the counter, which is probably a good thing, because if it wasn't for this three-foot-wide barrier of stainless steel, I'd probably be wrapped around him already.

Having fucked me good and proper yesterday in his huge corner office like the power player he is, this morning he's catering to my blue-collar fantasies in boots, cargo pants and one of *those* vests. It's pristine, but I don't give it long before that changes.

'Morning,' he says in a low voice.

'Why, good morning,' I singsong cheerily.

'You still staying at mine tonight?' he asks my chest.

'My boobs are still planning to spend the night with you, yes, and I was going to come along too if that's okay?' In truth, I've thought of little else except being with Aide in his home, in his *bed*, since he suggested it yesterday.

He has the good grace to look embarrassed. 'Sorry.'

'No you're not.'

'Nope. I'm not. You got your overnight stuff?'

'Yeah. It's in the hallway,' I say, jerking my head.

He raises his dark, shapely eyebrows. 'I didn't notice a full-size Louis Vuitton trunk out there.'

'Hilarious, aren't you? You want to get laid or not?'

He glances at the doorway, then skulks around the island towards me.

Uh-oh.

'Yes, smart-arse,' he says, pushing my hair behind my shoulder so he can press the most delicious kiss to my neck. He drags his mouth up to my ear. He smells freshly showered and fucking amazing. 'I want to get laid,' he whispers. 'By *you*.'

'Mmm,' I say, leaning into him. 'Goody.' He is so, so gorgeous. I raise a hand and trail it over his shoulder and down his arm, marvelling at how such soft skin can coexist with such hard muscle.

He straightens back up, his hand going to squeeze, to caress, the dip of my waist. He seems to love that part of my body. I take advantage of the small distance between us to touch one of *my* favourite parts of *his* body—that chest hair. I hook a couple of fingers into the scooped neckline of his vest and brush my knuckles over the downy coating.

'Such a neanderthal,' I coo. 'Got any power tools for me today?'

'I'll have one tonight,' he jokes. He pauses, then adds, 'Can't wait to have you in my bed.'

I shoot him a smile that telegraphs how similarly I feel. 'How will we get back to yours?'

'My driver, Andy, will pick us up.'

I snigger. 'You've got so many personas I'm getting whiplash. I was indulging in some verbal foreplay with my bad boy builder, and then you throw bad boy billionaire into the mix. It could confuse a girl with a lesser intellect than mine.'

He smiles, then leans back in to kiss me on the cheek. His beard tickles my skin gently. 'It's all the same guy, sweetheart. Remember? It's all real.'

It's all real.

Jesus, Aide. What are you doing to me?

'I remember,' I tell him softly.

'I've got to stick around for a bit after we finish,' he says. 'That little lad you fed—Connor. Told him if he managed to get him and his sister to come for a bite this evening, I'd kick a ball round with him for a bit. He's footie mad. Hoping it'll do the trick. You happy to hang around?'

I keep my hand on his chest and place it over his heart. The thud-thud of it is grounding. I could put my ear to his chest and listen to that sound all day long.

'Sure—not a problem,' I tell him with my words.

You are a good man, Aidan Duffy, I tell him with my heart.

~

HE IS A GOOD MAN.

I assist Sylvie and Judy and another volunteer called Carl in a token way with dinner duty. The main part of the hall is looking great, and we'll be finished tomorrow—two days early. Meanwhile, the kids are still being fed outside. These guys claim to have the dinner service handled, but I can't exactly sit around and do nothing while they work, so I pretend to pack the bags and hand them out to the kids while really ogling my brand-new man.

The football has got slightly out of hand, in that so many other kids wanted to get involved when they saw Aide coaching Connor that it's turned into a big kick about in the too-small space. Aide ended up digging out a net of balls from one of the cupboards in the hall, and now at least a dozen kids, boys and girls whose ages I'd put somewhere in the seven-to-twelve range, are engaged in keepy-uppies and a bit of dribbling.

But my eyes aren't on them.

Nope.

They're on the man who's coaching them. Who's exhibiting best practice, and breaking down the stunt, and, if I'm being honest, who's worked up such a heat in this west-facing inferno of dark tarmac that he's lost the vest and trousers and is wearing only his socks, trainers, and a pair of Spurs shorts, all of which he must have brought along for the occasion.

And holy *hell* does he look fine.

I swooned alongside the rest of the world when *Maverick* came out and treated us all to that delicious dogfight football scene. But honestly, Rooster and Hangman and their waxed-chested cronies and their aviators and Californian sunlight can take a running jump, because I will take Aide Duffy with his chest hair and fucking incredible body and endless goodheartedness, on a shitty-ripped up piece of tarmac in West London.

Any. Day. Of. The. Week.

'Bad luck, mate!' he shouts to one little boy who's inadvertently kicked his ball too hard, sending it away from himself. 'Try catching the ball between every keepy-uppy for the moment, yeah? Means you won't be running around as much.'

It's lucky I'm wearing sunglasses, because I am eye-fucking that man so hard it's indecent. Especially when there are so many kids around.

'Here you go, honey,' I say to a gangly girl with braces. I practically stuff the paper bag into her arms as I crane my neck to watch Aide doing keepy-uppies. The kids are standing around him, keeping a noisy count, but luckily I'm well positioned to watch him through the gap.

'Sixty-eight!' they chant. 'Sixty-nine! *Seventy!*'

His movements are measured and seemingly effortless. He keeps the ball in the air with the lightest of flicks from his feet, but I notice, to my intense gratification, that with each kick, the corresponding pec flexes, and my pussy clenches in sync.

He's sweating hard, and I'm not surprised. The heat's been building all day, and it's now sweltering. He rakes his damp hair off his forehead, and I swoon. Sweat glistens on his abs. His pecs. His biceps.

And I swoon. Again.

Every single thing this man does seems fated to make me swoon, basically.

Which is why I cannot wait till we get back to his place to show him how much he turns me on.

~

As soon as the last child has reluctantly left his impromptu football practice, I tell him I need him inside. Urgently. I lead the way into the office, which is stuffy but cooler than it is outside.

'Fuck,' he says, wiping his forearm across his forehead, 'I'm sweating like a pig.' He tilts his head back to take a swig from his water bottle, and I pause from my task of ramming the back of a chair under the unlockable handle of the office door to watch his Adam's apple work as he drinks.

The pure masculinity of it has me pressing my thighs together.

'Mmm-hmm,' I say, closing the distance between us. I touch my fingertips to the damp valley between his pecs and let them trail down his slick abs.

God.

He's good enough to eat.

He pulls his water bottle away and looks down at me with interest. 'What's going on here?'

'I'm showing my appreciation for how insanely sexy you look like this,' I say. I turn my hand so my knuckles follow the damp path of his happy trail down past his waistband to graze lightly over his cock.

He inhales through his teeth. 'I'm sweaty and disgusting,' he says, but his eyes are already flicking to my boobs. He arches into my touch, probably unconsciously, and I stand there and palm him shamelessly, loving how he grows harder and heavier right there in my hand.

'You're sweaty and *delicious*,' I correct him. I stand back so I don't take him out with a rogue elbow as I tug off my painting t-shirt and my hot-pink *Barbie* logo-ed vest top. I'm in a matching pink bra today. It's ridiculously cute and shows off a lot of nipple.

He groans out an anguished *fuck me, Lotts.*

I sink to my knees in front of him.

'You don't have to do this, sweetheart,' he pleads. 'Seriously, I can wait till I've showered.'

'Well that makes one of us,' I say tartly, and I pull down his shorts. It seems he lost his briefs, too, when he changed, because his cock springs out, thick and far readier than he's letting on.

I look up at him and flick my tongue lightly over his crown as I grip him hard, and he rewards me with a low rumble of approval. He's damp everywhere, slick and hot beneath my fingers.

I wave my free hand at him. 'Water.'

He hands me the metal water bottle and I take a slug. As I hoped, the water's ice-cold. I keep it in my mouth and wrap my lips around his cock again, basking in his shocked, delighted jolt, his pained sigh, as I bathe his heat in cool liquid, my tongue moving more easily now as it sluices him down. Some drops escape my mouth, trickling over my chin and hand. I blindly stand the bottle on the floor and resume my onslaught, my free hand going to cup, to knead, his already-heavy sac.

I find my rhythm.

Pump him with my fist and mouth.

Swirl my tongue around his silky crown.

Caress his balls.

Swallow the water when it loses its coolness.

Take a swig from the bottle, rising up on my knees slightly as I drink so I can glide Aide's tip between my lace-cupped breasts.

Repeat.

And, above all, revel in the glory that is this man coming undone around me as he shifts, and moans, and claws at my hair, my shoulders. As he begins to move his hips to meet my wet, willing mouth.

After one swallow, I look up. 'Fuck my mouth,' I tell him, and I swig more water. When my liquid-filled mouth takes his length in again, he takes heed. He puts one hand on my jaw, another around the back of my neck, holding me steady as he works those hips. He starts off hesitantly, picking up strength as I moan and suck harder so he's pistoning his hips against me, forcing me to take everything.

I let my eyes flutter closed and focus on my rhythm, on giving him the maximum amount of sensation I can, and on not gagging, because this guy is *big*, and he's going for it.

'So *fucking* good,' he grits out, his hands gripping my hair even more tightly.

There's nothing like this. Nothing like being on my knees for him, worshipping his cock with my mouth while he desecrates said mouth with said cock. Nothing like feeling and hearing his entire body struggle to handle how I'm making him feel. Feeling and hearing him get closer and closer.

It's fucking amazing.

I'm already well-versed in how well-endowed Aide is, but feeling every hot inch of him down my throat is a whole other experience. He's overwhelming me, and I'm overwhelming him, and I let him know with my moans and my sucks how eager I am to bring this home.

'I'm close,' he tells me, and I nod.

'Lotts—' He releases my head and tries to pull out of me, but I grip him harder, the hand on his balls moving further back to hold him against me by the arse.

He's so close. The balls I just cradled are so tight. And then he's coming with a low roar, his head hitting the wall with a noisy thud as he jerks his orgasm into my mouth.

When his shudders have subsided, I swallow it all and suck him clean before I stand. He's staring at me like he's shell-shocked. Then he grabs my jaw with both hands and hauls me towards him, kissing me hungrily, his tongue rampaging through the exact space his cock just occupied. And as he slides a hand down my back, pressing me towards his sweat-slicked body, I marvel at having had the unique privilege of undoing Aidan Duffy with my mouth.

25
———

LOTTA

I t's clear from the moment Aide's driver, Andy, steers us up his driveway that this is more than a home for him.

It's a sanctuary.

Okay, so it may be the polar opposite of my opulent, over-decorated flat (I am my mother's daughter, after all) and not to my usual taste, but I can see exactly why he's gone for the aesthetic, the vibe, he has.

I'm beginning to understand that this success, and the lifestyle and demands that come with it, don't sit well with Aide. He seems naturally introverted, so it makes sense that he'd build himself a refuge.

In fact, it makes me feel better just knowing he has this place to escape to.

The weird thing is how familiar everything about Aide's home is before I even step foot in it. I recognise the signature of Venus' architectural team everywhere. In the seamless bank of Crittall and glass doors to one side. In the shallow gables. The impeccable finish whose very simplicity screams quality.

I feel a stab of pride at the beauty around us. It never gets old, seeing our work. Dad may have built his company from ones and zeroes, but I like *things*. I like having something concrete to show for my efforts. And what's better than buildings that house all manner of human experiences and stand the test of time far long after we've passed?

Aide's house may scream *Venus*, but the look and feel he's gone for is all him. The way the structure interacts with the softly landscaped grounds in which it stands feels far more organic than most of the intimidating steel-and-glass blocks of flats we tend to build back in the city.

We usually like our creations to stand out, but this masterpiece's success rests on it fitting into its surroundings.

Our hallmarks are even more apparent when we head inside. I take a few steps into the airy, double-height entrance hall he ushers me into, an instant and overwhelming sense of peace hitting me. It's in the light. The tinkle of running water. The abundance of plants. The way he's left the space alone and unfurnished to just *be*.

The polished concrete floor is spectacular. The curved wooden banister of the stairs has a lustre so beautiful I want to run my palm over it.

This man may still be mostly a mystery to me. But it's obvious that he's exactly where he belongs. That he's built a home whose authenticity, and serenity, and understated profundity reflect the same qualities in him.

Most notably, it's rock solid.

Just like him.

'Shower?' he asks me now as we stand side by side. 'Or swim?' There's a hint of shyness masquerading as offhandedness in his voice, and it strikes me that he probably doesn't bring too many people here—especially women he doesn't know all that well (in the non-Shakespearean sense, anyway).

I lean into him, twisting my face up to his so I can smile coquettishly. 'I didn't bring a bikini.'

'You won't need one.' He grazes my lips with his before looping his hand around my waist and leading me through the majestic living space into the huge kitchen. He's been like this since we left the community centre. Attentive. Affectionate. He held my hand the whole way here in the car.

'I want a full tour, too,' I tell him, looking around curiously. I'm itching to check out every inch of our handiwork.

'Sure,' he says, 'but maybe after we've eaten, because I know once I get you in my room I won't let you escape easily.'

The kitchen's gorgeous. Again, I recognise Venus' signature touches, but this room has a more organic feel to it than most of our kitchens, which tend to be shiny and attention-grabbing and heavy on the appliance porn. I suspect a few of our clients never actually cook in their own kitchens—the spaces are often showpieces.

Aide's version, meanwhile, has vaulted ceilings and off-black handle-less cupboards. The work surfaces are gorgeous slabs of poured concrete, and above the main island hangs a wooden shelf, suspended on chains from the vaulted ceiling and bearing a riot of greenery whose tendrils cascade over its sides. The overall effect, once again, is of bringing the outside in.

He opens a cupboard door concealing a giant fridge and grabs two bottles—a beer and a white wine.

'Greco di Tufo okay?' he asks, and I hide a smile. I wonder if it's a coincidence that he has his fridge stocked with Italian wine.

'Wonderful,' I say airily, leaning my elbows on the island as he deftly uncorks the wine and pours me a generous glass. He cracks open his beer and clinks it against my glass before leading the way through one of the open French doors.

The trees and plants in the garden still have a way to go before reaching maturity. This must only be their second or third summer. That said, the garden is gorgeous. There's a massive weeping willow that must've preceded the house by decades. The lawns aren't overly manicured, and the flowerbeds are a jumble of heavenly purples, blues and whites. I spy hydrangeas, delphiniums, anemones. There are fruit trees galore.

It feels like a proper English country garden that's miles and miles from London. My blood pressure is dropping just by being here.

The pool is tucked away behind a fence concealed by a laurel hedge.

'Were you not tempted to have it nearer the house?' I ask, thinking he's missed a trick. It would be amazing to have it over by the kitchen terrace.

He unfastens the gate bolt and holds it open for me. 'Not really. If I have kids, I want to know they're a hundred percent safe when they're running around outside. I couldn't relax if there was a pool bang in the middle of the garden.'

'Makes sense,' I say, but my heart goes pitter-patter.

This man kills me. Of course Aide designed this place with a family, and the safety of his unborn children, in mind. That's the kind of guy he is. I should have seen that coming.

He wants to look after everyone.

To keep them safe.

It's his entire MO.

Hidden or not, the pool is spectacular. It's lined in grey slate and surrounded by a flagstoned area featuring my favourite type of sun loungers - heavy and wooden, with deep white mattresses. There's a matching daybed at the far end, its huge mattress covered with scatter cushions and sheltered by billowing sheets of white muslin. On every lounger is a perfectly placed rolled-up towel with thick slate-grey stripes. A huge wicker basket neatly stacked with more matching, rolled-up towels sits next to the first lounger.

Beyond the flagstones lies a thick lawn, on the other side of which is a sizeable, bad-ass pool house. Built in the same brick as the main house, its front boasts a line of Crittall French doors similar in style to those leading from Aide's kitchen.

So this was the structure that caused all those paper-work headaches for my colleagues.

Looks like it was worth it.

Next to it is an epic summer kitchen with a bar, an abso-lutely enormous barbecue, and a glass-fronted drinks fridge. I suppress a smile. It's reassuring to know my ascetic fuck-buddy spends his money somewhere. Even Aide Duffy isn't immune to the charms of boys' toys.

'I bet you have some good parties here,' I observe, putting my wineglass down on one of the sturdy wooden tables dotted between the loungers.

He lowers his beer from his lips and rakes his eyes over my body before he answers. I've ditched my painting t-shirt and am instead in another pair of cutoffs, given the heat, and the same *Barbie* vest as earlier.

'Mmm-hmm,' he says, 'but none as fun as the party you and I are about to have.'

Challenge accepted, darling.

I raise an eyebrow? 'Is that so?'

'Most of my parties don't feature beautiful, naked women or happy endings,' he says, strolling towards me. He put his vest back on for the car journey home but is still in his football shorts. It's a testament to this guy's Big Dick Energy that he can seem so powerful, so menacing, in such casual clothes.

'That's very presumptuous,' I say, standing my ground.

He reaches me and wraps a strong arm around my waist, hauling me to him. I look up and smirk. He's so fucking hot, with that strong, beard-covered jaw and those melting blue eyes. I don't stand a chance.

'I forgot to mention the happy ending's for *you*,' he says in a low growl, dipping his head so his lips are millimetres from mine.

My breath hitches, and I allow myself to swoon a little, because come on. 'Now you're talking.'

'I already had my happy ending. It's your turn.' He slides a finger under the strap of my vest and strokes my skin. 'Now *strip*.'

Before I can tell him the night is young and he most certainly has more happy endings coming his way, he's releasing me and stepping backwards, a grin on his face that's hungry and expectant and hot.

I salute him. 'Yes, sir.' And with that, I peel off my top to reveal my matching bra, and his grin turns even more wolfish.

'It's amazing how tolerant you are of my bras these past few days,' I muse as I unbutton my shorts and slide them down my legs to reveal the bottom half of my very cute matching set.

'Risk-reward,' he mutters.

I pause with my fingers on my bra clasp. 'Oh, yeah?'

'Yeah. Lose the bra, Lotts.'

'How so?'

'The stakes have changed. Before, it was all downside for me, having to deal with those nipples in my fucking face all day.'

I unhook my bra and let it fall from my body. 'These nipples?'

His eyes darken, and he shakes his head in defeat, his gaze riveted to my boobs. Basic as fuck. God bless him.

'Yeah.' He takes a step towards me. 'But now I get to see your bras, and take them off your beautiful body, and suck on those tits whenever I like, and—'

'Well, I wouldn't say *whenever* you like, but I take your point.' I bat my eyelashes and hook my thumbs through the sides of my pink thong. 'You were saying?'

I pause, and he blinks. 'Huh?'

'Something about risk-reward.' I put the poor man out of his misery and slide my thong down my legs, stepping daintily out of it. I grab it with a finger and toss it to him.

'Yeah. Um.' He stares at my nearly bare pussy with its immaculate strip of hair as he balls my thong in his hands. 'The risk-reward's in my favour, now,' he mutters. 'So I can handle it.'

I beam at him and put a hand on my hip. 'Spoken like a true entrepreneur. Your turn, Mister. Get them off.'

Instead, he looks down at my balled-up thong and brings it slowly, deliberately to his nose. He inhales deeply, unhurriedly, and my mouth falls open, because this dirty bastard is hot as fuck.

'Mmm,' he groans before lifting his head and tossing my thong on the nearest lounger. Then he's stripping off his vest and tugging down his shorts. Merely watching him take his clothes off is a joy. Skin coming into view, muscles flexing, abs contracting, dick hanging heavily between his legs. He's already nursing a semi.

The man is a living work of art, and I am here to pay homage.

He's on me with no warning, lifting me up against him. I wrap my arms and legs around him and nuzzle into the crook of his neck, revelling in the skin-on-skin contact. The air out here is far less sticky than it was after a day of trapped heat building in central London. Here it's heavenly: warm with a light breeze. The perfect conditions for a skinny dip with my sex-on-a-stick hottie.

26

LOTTA

The near end of the pool has an elegant, shallow flight of steps which I assume we'll descend in a dignified manner. It's too late when I realise that what's actually happening is Aide is marching us to the deep end and, without notice, takes a huge leap into the water.

He's launched a fucking double cannonball.

We crash into the pool and go deep under. It's colder than I was expecting. Shit. My instinct is to disentangle myself from him and get myself to the surface, where I gasp for breath and flap around in shock. A second later, he's surfacing, dark hair slicked back, eyelashes wet and starry, and possibly the most gleeful, carefree expression I've yet had the privilege of seeing on his handsome face. He's absolutely thrilled with himself, and it's beyond adorable.

I close the distance between us and pretend to put him in a headlock so I can dunk him. 'You dick!'

He licks his lips and smirks at me. 'I wouldn't do that, sweetheart. You know I'm a lot stronger than you.' He leans right in so our mouths are almost touching. 'In fact, you shouldn't try to resist me at all in this pool. It won't end well for you.'

I abandon all pretence of a headlock and wrap my other arm around him, slithering against him and wrapping my legs around him, too. My boobs are smushed against his hard chest. It seems that's not the only part of him that hard, because something very, very appealing is pressing against my pussy in this position.

'Is that a fact?' I ask breathlessly.

In response, he hoists me up so I'm even more flush against him and puts his mouth to mine as he walks us further up the pool. I cling to him and allow his firm, wet lips to part mine, his warm tongue to seek mine out. He smooths my hair off my face and slides a hand beneath its soaking curtain to find my neck, which he grips. We stand, cool water submerging us up to our shoulders as the warm sun shines down upon us, and we kiss. We explore. We communicate with our mouths.

My arms are draped lazily around his neck now. I allow the water to take my weight and Aide's arms to hold me in place as I float, suspended in some kind of sensory heaven. His mouth is supple. Responsive. His damp beard abrades my chin gently as we kiss and suck and lick.

With my eyes closed, I'm more conscious of the sounds around us: lapping water, and birdsong, and Aide's breaths. The tiny noises he makes in the back of his throat as his tongue strokes mine.

Not sure I've ever known peace like it.

After a few moments of the type of languid kissing that has me lulled into a blissful stupor, Aide's hand moves down from my neck.

'You are so captivating,' he whispers against my mouth.

I hum my thanks.

'And you give amazing head. That was fucking incredible, earlier.'

I laugh. 'Anytime.'

His hand cups my bum before sliding between my legs. 'Told you it was your turn.'

Mmm. Just his words, and the feel of his fingertips against the very top of my inner thigh, are enough to have my nerve endings standing to attention. I let him resume his dreamy kisses as his fingertip finds my entrance and circles it. He pushes in one knuckle deep, and I wriggle.

I want more.

He finds my clit with what I think is his thumb and teases it. His skin feels calloused through the water, and I jolt as the sharp pang of pleasure hits in exactly the right spot.

'Just there,' I murmur between kisses. 'Mmm.'

We float there, entwined, as Aide continues to stroke my needy flesh, circling and flicking and pressing and fingerfucking me in ways that have my body spiralling. I love having his mouth and hands on me like this. My breathing turns to whimpers, to soft little moans, as he coaxes a world of sensation out of me.

Then his hand leaves where I need it most and clamps around my bum as he pulls away from my mouth.

We're on the move.

'What are we doing?' I manage.

'Need to spread you out and taste you,' he says.

I can roll with that.

I stretch luxuriously in his arms as he exits the pool—using the steps, this time—and makes for the covered daybed at the far end. He tosses me down in the middle of the enormous terry-towelling-lined mattress, and I take a moment to appreciate the beautiful irony of having wanted a 'real' man capable of throw-down and having found one who can do so in the context of his insane swimming pool.

I could get used to this.

Aide crawls between my legs and looms over me, pausing to lift my head gently and place one of the scatter cushions under it. He's such a sweetheart. I smile up at him, enjoying the stark look of desire on his gorgeous face as he takes in the sight of me laid out like a feast for him. His cock is thick and hard and pointing straight at me. I engage my abs to make a grab for it, but he halts me.

'Not yet. My turn.'

Aaand we're back to the two-word sentences. I adore this version of him.

He plants his hands on either side of my face and braces, dipping his head to kiss me again before his mouth grazes a trail down to one of my nipples. He takes it between his lips and flicks at it with his tongue, groaning as he does so. His touch is light, but it stokes the flames he's been fanning in the pool and I arch into the sensation as I abandon myself to Aide.

With kisses and licks, he works his way down my wet body, pushing my legs further apart so he can crouch between them. He has me so worked up that I practically shoot off the bed when his tongue hits my clit.

He laughs, a low, delicious rumble. 'That good?'

'*Yes,*' I hiss, pushing my bum down the bed so I can shove myself closer against his magic mouth.

'Good girl,' he says, and resumes his ministrations, parting my folds and holding me wide open for him. My pulse beats insistently between my legs as he licks and sucks, his tongue skilled. Hungry. Determined. He slides a couple of fingers inside me without warning, and I push into the heavenly intrusion.

Because this is heaven, surely.

A man like Aide.

Devastatingly beautiful, but without an ounce of the artifice so many guys I've dated—or fucked—have.

Kind.

Humble.

Generous and skilled and ravenous in bed, with a way of making me feel like no one else exists for him but me in this moment.

I gaze up at the white sheets billowing around me and try to absorb every single unique bolt of pleasure he delivers. I'm so turned on from the pool, and the blowjob earlier, and the shirtless football, and just from being around Aide all day, that it won't take much to send me over the edge.

And it doesn't. The hard, hungry swipes of his tongue, and the twists of his fingers, and the low noises of appreciation and arousal he's making in his throat all conspire to wind me tighter and tighter. I find my nipples and pinch them hard, my touch intensifying the pleasure even further.

'Please,' I tell him, 'I'm so close. I need it really hard.'

He groans loudly at my words, but the thrusts of his fingers become harder, crueller, as he licks me more ruthlessly. The heat where his mouth is on my flesh sears through my core, through my entire body, as sensation crescendos in my clit. His tongue hits me again, and again, and again, and my damp skin breaks out in a sweat as I yield to this onslaught. Nothing else matters except Aide's mouth on my flesh. Except chasing this wondrous build.

He rams his fingers inside me hard and twists them, and I cry out as the heat explodes into nothingness and my soul soars through the warm evening air. This one is intense. I buck, and I shudder, and I arch as Aide's mouth and tongue and hands wring every last drop of my orgasm from me.

When I've drifted down from my high, he crawls up my body, his eyes hooded. Heavy. He finds my mouth with his and kisses me like a starving man. I pull him down towards me, needing more of him. Needing him to fill me up.

'Get inside me,' I gasp.

He growls and lowers his delicious weight onto me, his rock-hard cock pressing against my entrance, his hips rolling restlessly.

'Fuck,' he gasps suddenly. 'I need a condom.'

'I mean, we can go without,' I offer. 'I'm on the pill, and I got tested recently.' And I really, really need your huge cock inside me right now, pal.

He shoots me a look that could politely be called dubious as he rolls off me, bracing on one elbow next to me. 'Me too, but I've never—I have a very strict condom policy.'

Realisation dawns, and I start to laugh. Aide stares at me in bewilderment.

'Oh my *God*,' I say, my eyes wide and head twisted in his direction. 'You're worried I'll try to get myself knocked up with a little billionaire baby and take you for all you're worth! That is *hysterical*.'

'No,' he protests, a little too forcefully. 'Of course not—not with you. I just have to be careful.'

'Aide,' I tell him, leaning in to stroke his cheek and still sniggering. 'Darling, darling man. I don't want to trap you. I have zero interest in any Baby Aides. I have plenty of money of my own. I just want to *fuck* you. But if you want to use a condom, you knock yourself out. I'll wait here.'

I collapse back on the mattress and make a show of interlocking my hands behind my head. I gaze at the billowing ceiling and wiggle my toes, shimmying my hips and knowing full well that Aide's gaze is raking over my naked, sated body.

Next thing I know, he's rolling his massive bulk back on top of me and tugging my hands out from beneath my head, pinning my wrists above me.

'Quite the comedian, aren't you?' he grunts.

I shrug as best I can given my pinned wrists and the enormous bear of a man weighing me down. 'I amuse myself, yes.'

'Open your legs.'

Biting down on my lower lip, I stare up at him. At the naked hunger and pissed-off-ness in his eyes.

I should poke the bear more often.

I let my legs fall open.

'I'm going to fuck you bare. What do you think of that?'

'Yes,' I moan. 'Please.'

'Fucking hell,' he grumbles. 'Keep your hands there.' He releases my wrists and raises off me a little so he can line the smooth, angry crown of his dick right up against my entrance.

I'm so ready for him. Already savouring how it'll feel. Then he's pushing inside me in sharp thrusts, like he can't be sheathed in me quickly enough.

'Ok?' he asks, and I nod.

I can't take my eyes off him as he slides home inside me. Maybe it's the incredible orgasm I just had, but each time he enters me, it feels a little easier to accommodate him.

This position is so intimate. So intense. So confronting as to be almost overwhelming. I'm surrounded by Aide. Weighed down by him. *Consumed* by him.

He begins to move with the fevered drives of a man not far from the brink. I slide my arms over those domed shoulders I adore and squeeze his biceps, showing him I can take it. Showing him how much I need him to fill me up. He ranges that incredible body above me, ploughing into me over and over, those blue eyes boring into mine.

The electricity between us is undeniable. It crackles and fizzes where we're conjoined. It takes my breath away, actually. The power this man has over me, when we're together like this. All our differences stripped away.

This is what I needed when I said I wanted it real.

'You're so, *so* beautiful,' he tells me, his face etched with his efforts at self control. I smile a cat-like smile at him. 'But I need to fuck you from behind so badly,' he huffs out, and I laugh.

'*God.* Do it.'

He pulls out and flips me over easily with an arm around my waist, tugging me up to my hands and knees. 'On your elbows or I'll fuck you right off the bed,' he warns.

I'm not sure if that's a promise or a threat, but I sink to my elbows, and he's pushing back inside me almost immediately, his hands stroking over my hips, my arse, squeezing my waist as he sinks so deep inside me that I almost lose my mind.

Fuck that's intense. I blow out the kind of exhale I've seen labouring mothers use on *One Born Every Minute.*

'You okay?' he manages on a groan.

'Mmm-hmm,' I squeak, because my lung capacity has just halved. 'Just fuck me hard.'

And he does.

With the punishing pace of his thrusts, and at this angle, the sensation of Aide filling me up has me losing my mind. I claw at the towelling fitted sheet and dig my elbows in in an attempt to stop myself from shooting off the bed like he warned me, but really, all I can do is hold on for dear life and ride out the pressure that's contracting and building deep inside me.

Aide runs his hand up my sides and back down as his hips roll and his dick does magical things to my internal tissue. One hand stays wrapped around the back of my neck, holding me in place, while the fingers of his other hand dig into my waist.

I'd sell my soul never to stop hearing the low, rough grunts he makes each time he bottoms out in me.

It's coarse and primal and perfect, and the swell of need inside me grows so great as to become a white light, a beautiful thing, engulfing me and stealing my consciousness as my vision leaves me and I succumb to this somehow other-worldly but very earthly pleasure.

Aide, who seems to have the world's greatest willpower —figures—lasts a few more thrusts before his own climax comes crashing over him. Every part of his powerful body shakes with the violence of his release. His fingers grasp me harder. His dick jerks inside me. He collapses on top of me, his chest against my back, his heart hammering against my skin.

27

AIDE

Dark curls on my white pillowcase.

Smooth, tanned limbs against my sheets.

Slender, ring-adorned fingers interlocked with my thick, work-roughened ones.

I scarcely dare admit, even to myself, how good Carlotta Montefiore-Charlton looks in my enormous bed.

Or how good it feels to be lying next to her.

The evening is warm enough that the French doors to my terrace are open, the bedsheet draped low on our hips as we lie on our sides, two commas facing each other.

Athletic fucking after an equally hard day's work has worn us out. I'm impressed I had the energy and the stamina to put in a decent performance after all those keepy uppies I did, but Lotta's willing mouth and beautiful, dangerous body seem to galvanise a guy.

We cooled down from that unbelievable fuck with another dip in the pool, followed by dinner on the terrace. Maggie had left out an array of salads and tuna tartare that we ate while wrapped around each other on the huge, modular outdoor sofa.

The food recharged our batteries sufficiently that we managed another round just now, the glow of whose aftermath I am currently wallowing in like a spaniel in a puddle.

Contented is not the word. It's as if a master masseur has spent the evening walking up and down my body. Every ache is gone. My muscles, usually aching after a day at the community centre, feel loose.

And best of all, my mind is clear.

If I behaved like a fucking animal on that daybed—literally, a *fucking* animal, unleashed on the most beautiful, captive prey I'd ever encountered, this last round was an exercise in restraint.

In taking it slow.

Letting Lotta open herself up to me while I enjoyed every inch of her body and fucked her so hard and slow that I had her screaming for me to put me out of her misery.

I liked that a lot.

If Lotta is the kind of woman it's impossible to look away from at the best of times, then being the one she allows to see her come undone feels like an unfathomable privilege.

This time, I wedged a pillow under her arse and stayed above her, powering into her till I thought I'd go mad from the desire. But holding off was worth it, because seeing *her* come undone as I kissed her felt like a front-row seat to the greatest show on earth.

Now I drink her in as she brushes her knuckles down the cleft between my pecs.

She's loose too. Relaxed. Her face is soft, those huge eyes limpid with fatigue and, I hope, satisfaction. Her hair is less immaculate than usual, thanks to our swim and, I hope, my manhandling of her. It makes her look younger. Less the worldly businesswoman she usually is.

Much as that version of her captivates me, this one

entrances me just as much in ways that, frankly, scare me. Because when it's like this, just the two of us in a bed, every last difference between us seems stripped away and all that remains is her and me, laid bare for each other.

And the problem with *that*, the reason it's dangerous, is that then I forget exactly why she's not the type of woman I can or should or will go for, my heart focusing instead on all the ways in which she's perfect for me.

This, therefore, seems like the appropriate moment to remind myself that it's not my heart doing any of the focusing.

Nope.

When my heart gets involved, it's because those kids from the centre aren't going to get fed tonight, or because Sylvie's slaved away long enough in sub-par conditions and deserves a new kitchen, or my oldest and most extroverted friend is lonely as fuck driving those heavy goods vehicles day in, day out and could benefit from being included in a project.

Those are all excellent examples of me thinking with my heart.

Right now, I'm thinking with my dick. With my monkey brain that's so orgasm-addled it can't think straight. Lotta has dazzled me and the others from the get-go.

That's what she does.

She waltzes in and blinds us all with the force of her beauty, and glamour, and fucking relentless good-natured-ness, and her seeming and, honestly, irritating ability to see only the positives in life. It's an ability that's only possible for someone who's never been disappointed. She is a wonderful, impressive, successful product of the privileged bubble she's been raised in, and none of us stands a chance against it.

Against her.

If Gaz and the guys knew about me and her they'd have a field day. Sure, Gaz is smitten in a boyish-crush kind of way. He'd be tickled as fuck if he knew I was messing around with Lotts.

But come on.

I've already done enough. Moved on while trying to keep everything that makes me me intact. Tried to always remember my roots. And for the most part, I've been semi-successful, except that I'll never again know financial worries. Even that feels like a betrayal of my family and friends. Of the community and culture and values and moral codes I was brought up with. That form the backbone of who I am.

Lotta's hand twists between my pecs, her fingertips running higher until she's holding my crucifix.

'Tell me about the cross,' she whispers. Her eyelashes cast shadows across her cheekbones, and for a moment I'm transfixed.

'It's a Celtic cross. Mum bought it for me when I was christened. They'd been on a pilgrimage up to Holy Island —Lindisfarne, up in Northumberland—just before they conceived me, and Mum's always been convinced that's why I came along. They were having problems getting pregnant before that. Anyway, they named me after St Aidan and St Cuthbert, who were the two early Christian saints who made the island famous.'

Her face opens up like she's just had a revelation. 'Ahh. I wondered why your middle name was Cuthbert?'

'How'd you know that?' I ask, and she looks shifty.

'Wikipedia, I think.'

I laugh and slide my hand up the smooth arc of her spine. 'Stalker.'

'When people lie to you about who they are, *Aidan*,' she retorts, 'you have to take matters into your own hands.'

We lie there, grinning at each other like idiots.

'So, all this roots stuff is important to you.' It's not a question.

'Suppose so.' I pause. I've over-thought this topic so much in the past decade, as I've been on my crazy journey, but it's hard, and sometimes painful, to articulate it. 'I think roots are important for all of us as human beings—we latch onto them. But I also think when you have very little, maybe you make them a bit too important.'

'How do you mean?' she asks, shifting closer and releasing my cross. Her hand drifts over my shoulder and down my arm, and I like how good her easy touch makes me feel. How safe.

'Well, take our family. We had no fucking money. Nor did any of our neighbours. So you cling onto other stuff. Tradition. Cultural identity—Mum was second generation Irish and Dad was first generation. He moved over as soon as they let him leave school. I dunno. Religion. That played far too big a part in our lives for our liking.

'Also things like... reputation. Shame. Pride. Dignity. Values. Codes of conduct. When you don't have much, you live and die by how you act. Poverty can make people strong and resilient, but often it brings out the worst in humanity, too. That neighbourhood I grew up in was just petty. No one wanted to see anyone else doing better than them. Getting out. It wasn't fair. It was resented.'

She purses her lips. 'So you're saying you had nothing but your roots, and who you were and who your family was informed your whole identity, and tough shit if you didn't like that identity because you didn't feel you had the right—

or maybe even the currency—to change any of it? Nor did you feel you could leave?'

I laugh, but there's no mirth in it. 'Something like that, yeah.'

'Fuck, that's depressing. It's like the song *Common People.*'

That makes me grin properly. 'If I'm Jarvis Cocker, you know who you are in that song, right?'

'Fuck off. But also, *obviously*.' Her fingers run up and down my arm. 'Where's your dad now? I haven't heard you mention him.'

'He died a few years ago.'

She really does have the most expressive eyes. Face. The way she's looking at me almost undoes me.

'It's okay. He was sick for a long time. Got sick after my brother, Pete, was born. MS. He couldn't work. Not really.' I let out a heavy sigh. 'Mum was a nurse, but she also took care of Dad until I was old enough to help.'

Her beautiful dark eyes narrow. 'Wait. You were your dad's carer?'

I exhale. I really do not want to make a big deal out of it. 'Yeah, but not full-time. They never let me miss any school. But Mum's shifts were all over the place, so yeah, when I was older I had to step up so she could earn her salary. Even then, she ended up going down to part time because it all just got too much once Dad lost the use of his legs.'

'Jesus,' she groans. 'Is that why you used to go to the community centre?'

'It got us out of Mum's hair when she was at home,' I say, 'and when she was at work, it meant she knew we could pop down there for dinner and not go hungry. Judy is a living saint. That woman was like a second mother to me.'

'I'm glad you had her,' Lotta says softly. 'Thanks for telling me. I'm sorry you had a shitty time of it.'

'It wasn't unhappy,' I say, anxious to make her understand. 'It was just... stressful. I worried about stuff that I wouldn't want my kids worrying about, and I saw my mum upset a lot. I'd never want that, either. But honestly, I'm amazed she didn't fall to pieces. It was a lot for her to deal with. She's so fucking strong.'

'It must be amazing to know you can look after her now,' she says, and I roll my eyes.

'You'd think so, right? But she's also fucking stubborn. And she refused to move away from this area. So she's in a better house, but it's nowhere near as nice as I'd like her to have.'

'I mean, I get that,' Lotta muses. 'If she's raised her family here, she's probably got strong ties. Roots, even.'

'Yeah, but I don't think she's staying purely for the right reasons. Sure, she knows this place—she didn't want to start from scratch, which I get. But it's also that shame thing again. She's super proud of me, but when the neighbours start whispering about how Veronica Duffy's getting too big for her boots because her son was on the news, or on breakfast TV, or any of that crap?

'Her way of dealing with that is to show them she's exactly who she's always been, and she's not going to put on airs and graces just because I'm doing well for myself. I swear to God, every working class person I grew up with seems to be terrified of putting on *airs and graces*, which is what I would call self-improvement or dreaming big, and it really fucks me off.'

Lotta's quiet for a moment. Then she says, 'Well, that's shitty for her, because she's kind of cutting off her nose to spite her face, but it must be really hard for you, too. I bet it makes you a lot more conflicted about what you've achieved than you'd probably like to be.'

I lie there and drink her in. The dark tendrils of hair curling over her neck. Her shoulder. That jaw-dropping face, its full lips parted and huge eyes fixed on me. Her extraordinary beauty makes it tempting to dismiss her as anything more than a stunning facade, but I've begun to think differently for a while now.

'You nailed it,' I say more lightly than I feel.

'I mean, you do seem to have a *lot* of airs and graces.'

I laugh. 'I should probably work on being less of a poncy twat.'

She smiles at me, and it's breathtaking. 'You're definitely too big for your boots. Maybe it's time to remember your roots.'

'She rhymes, too,' I mutter.

'Seriously. Do they give you shit for it? Or maybe it's just *you* giving yourself shit for it. There's no way it's easy to make the kind of money you've made and not have it raise a bit of existential angst.'

'All of the above,' I say, tugging her against me. She throws a long leg over my thigh and nestles closer.

'Poor little rich boy. Do you have a therapist?'

'Yep. I bore the shit out of her every week.'

'Good.'

'What about you, poor little rich girl? Do you lie in that fancy bedroom of yours every night full of existential angst?'

'Nope,' she says, popping the *p*, and I laugh. 'But I grew up with it. It's all I know. And you might think I'm over-privileged, but I've worked my arse off to be where I am. So, no. I'm very comfortable with my millions of pounds, thank you.'

'You never worry about that sense of entitlement?' I ask. When it comes out, it sounds more dickish than I intended it to, but she speaks before I can qualify my question.

'Aide.' Her plush lips are so close to mine.

'Mmm-hmm?' I ask dreamily.

'Entitlement is not a dirty word. I know society's turned it into one. If you're asking me if I take my wealth for granted, no, I do not. But if you're asking me if I've ever known anything different, also, no. I've never expected handouts, and my dad was never going to be that guy.

'Yeah, his incubator gave me and Gabe our seed capital, but you should have seen them put us through the mill. It was terrifying. Our business plan was like a Harvard Business School case study. So, in my mind, we've earned every pound Venus has made for us and we are *entitled* to that money because we've earned it with a tonne of work and all-nighters and sacrifices.' She pokes my pec lightly. 'Just. Like. You.'

The world Carlotta inhabits is easy. Fair. Where hard work reaps just rewards. To use her own words, she is entitled to that perspective because it's been born out of her own experience.

But I've seen another world.

A world that isn't fair or just.

Where the relationship between hard work and success is not linear.

Where people slave away all day long in factories and hospitals and on building sites just to keep the fucking lights on.

Where the stakes are sky high and the margin of error paper-thin.

Where hardworking men get sick, and there's no insurance or critical illness cover to allow for that.

Where hardworking women have almost no time for sleep between caring for their patients at work and at home.

I have a foot in both camps. I've been straddling that

uneasy divide for a decade, and I still have no fucking clue where I belong in the world.

Any hope people might have that the UK is becoming a classless society is utter bullshit. There's social mobility, yes. I'm proof that if you take a chance on someone, they can come good. But, while the money has made my life easier in many ways, it's also made it more complicated.

It strikes me that, in the small microcosm of the world that forged me, there's more shame in having too much than in having too little. Poverty can be born with quiet dignity, if you choose.

It's wealth that destroys you. Money, rather than the lack of it, that people fear the most.

Now *that's* fucked up.

Lotta is the kind of girl who'll end up with a minted twat. Some guy with a hedge fund and a yacht. Obviously, I'm minted now, but it's not who I am in my essence. Whatever she wants to think, and however hard she's worked to be where she is now, she was born with a silver spoon in her mouth.

She was always going to be okay.

I've soared in my professional life, but the tethers that bind me to my roots are far fucking stronger and more insidious than I'd like.

Twenty-year-old me took one look at Carlotta Montefiore-Charlton and knew she wasn't an option for me. Knew that to touch her would be to play with fire.

I've come so far. Yet it seems my twenty-year-old self was wiser than the guy I am today in a lot of ways.

Unfortunately, knowing all this and acting on it are two very different things, because I cannot. Stay. Away.

28

LOTTA

I could get used to waking in Aide's arms.

To his kisses on my neck. His hard—and I do mean *hard*—body pressed up behind me.

To him bringing me a perfect espresso as I blow-dry my hair and apply some light makeup in a dressing room so vast it's totally wasted on him.

To being tugged into his huge shower for a highly satisfying quickie before being served up more perfect espresso and scrambled eggs on the terrace by his very sweet, very smiley housekeeper, Maggie. She seems even happier than me that I spent the night, and that's saying something.

I adore my ultra-feminine flat, and I love Notting Hill, but there's something about waking up out here that's pretty special. I know in an hour we'll be surrounded by chain-link fences and overlooked by rundown blocks of council flats, but right in this moment I could easily imagine I'm on holiday.

The only sounds are birdsong and the chinking of cutlery against crockery. Given we're just a couple of weeks past midsummer, the sun's already high in the sky, casting short shadows over the gardens. All those gorgeous flowerbeds are throwing off their scent, aided by some early-morning sprinklers.

Peace.

Peace is what I feel here. Splendid isolation, like Aide and I are the only two people in the world. Like the trials and tribulations of the rest of humanity are faint. Muted.

I wonder if that's why Aide based himself out here. It's clear he's a guy who, despite his grumpy facade, feels things deeply. Maybe he needs somewhere like this to create some proper distance between him and all the shit he has to deal with. The pressures and the conflicts, the critics and the freeloaders.

I'm really, really glad he has this place. All the stuff he was saying last night suggested he hasn't really left the chains of his poverty-stricken upbringing behind. That his 'emancipation' is, in reality, far more complex and less complete than it may seem.

I'm glad he's harnessed enough self-love and self-belief to create a little slice of heaven here, just for himself.

My heart sinks as we walk to his car. Andy's already stowed my overnight bag in the boot. As a delightfully dirty mini-break, it's been way too short. I refuse to consider whether I'll ever be back here.

'Last day,' Aide says, reaching for my hand on the cream leather of his back seat and clasping it with an easy familiarity.

'Are you sad?' I ask.

He leans his head back against the seat and stares at the ceiling of the car. 'Yeah. I'll miss everyone. It's been good working side-by-side with my old mates, you know?'

'Hmm,' I say, and he drops his head to the side to look at me.

'What?'

I hesitate. 'Nothing. I mean—I'm sure you'll miss them. It makes sense. I just—I wonder if it's also a bit bittersweet because you won't be around to help them any more.' I turn my hand palm up and intertwine my fingers with his. 'I've seen what an amazing job you've done here, and I'm sure it's hard for you to walk away.'

When there's so much work still to be done in this community.

I don't say the words, but I can feel them hanging in the air between us. Aide's so loyal, so committed, and I know he feels he owes Judy and the community centre the world. I've seen how stuck in he gets. I think he even prefers playing footie with the kids and doling out meals to getting his hands dirty with the building work.

For someone like that, being perceived to be 'walking away' must be a real wrench.

'Yeah,' he says quietly, letting his head fall back on the headrest once again. 'Tomorrow I'll be sitting in my cushty office, eating fucking sushi, or something, and these guys will be slogging it out again. And again. Every fucking day. It's never-ending, the work they have to do.'

'I know,' I tell him. I try to seize on the silver lining. 'At least they'll have a nice new centre to do it in. Sylvie seems really thrilled with the new kitchen. Everything doesn't have to be perfect all the time. It being *better* is a start.'

He squeezes my hand hard. 'Thanks.'

'What's your charity about?' I ask. 'Is it linked to the centre?' I've heard him mention his charity, Fresh Start, a few times, and it came up during my online stalking, but I don't know much about it. Given how heavy the traffic looks as we head into London, now seems like a good time to get to know more about it.

He screws up his nose. 'Kind of. So Totum has a foundation, and one thing it does is support community centres across the UK. Some of the money for the refurb has come from that, and some of it from me. But Fresh Start's different. It runs before-and-after-school enrichment clubs in London, and hopefully, at some point, we'll expand it across the country.'

'What kind of enrichment clubs?' I ask. 'Like, coding and stuff?'

'Among other things.' He shifts in his seat, but he doesn't let go of my hand. 'Most state primary schools run a pretty limited syllabus. I mean, they cover the basics, but there are very few specialist teachers outside of PE. The kids don't get a chance to explore many subjects until they hit secondary school, so we're trying to change that. It's also a good form of childcare for the parents.'

'Go on,' I say.

'So we'll go into a school. Take over the school hall, or any decent-sized space, and we'll run two or three clubs a day, so ten to fifteen a week. Everything from dance to coding to sculpture to parkour. It's just about trying to enrich these kids' experience, open their eyes to talents and interests they wouldn't get to explore otherwise. A lot of schools don't have the capacity to set this stuff up themselves, and even if they could, the parents can't afford to pay for clubs. So we make the classes free, and the kids who qualify for free school lunches get priority.'

'Free school lunches...' I frown, trying to get it straight in my head.

Aide grins at me. I'm sure he's thinking I'm a rich, clueless princess, but he doesn't say it. 'Some families get free school lunches because they've been means-tested and shown not to be able to afford them. So we know they're the families in each school who are struggling the most financially. Chances are, their kids aren't going to be doing piano and tap-dancing after school.'

I nod. 'Thank you,' I say quietly. 'It's a really cool idea.' I mean it. It is. I can't imagine how much work it is going into God knows how many schools. Managing the logistics and red tape. Dealing with the admin side of schools who are totally overwhelmed already. It makes me tired just thinking about it.

Does Aide ever get tired?

Not of this stuff, I decide. This guy has a fire so powerful lit under his arse it's like jet fuel. He's on a mission to save every kid in Britain from his own fate, it seems.

The thought makes my heart hurt.

No wonder he has an OBE.

I reach over and cup his face with my free hand. 'You are a very, very good guy, Aidan Duffy,' I tell him, looking deeply into those blue eyes that once seemed icy cold and are now anything but.

He wriggles his shoulders like the compliment makes him uncomfortable. 'I'm really not. I got a lucky break—I want to give back and make sure more children get the chances I got.'

I raise my eyebrows sceptically. 'You did not *get* a lucky break. You made your own luck, from everything I've heard. You've worked your arse off to be here, but I'm glad you've found something you find rewarding.'

He gives me a tight smile. 'It's by far the best thing about having money. Getting to put it to work. The plan is to give it all away before I pop my clogs. Don't think I'll rest till I do.'

This man. Be still my beating heart.

'What about you?' He strokes his thumb over my skin

and looks down at our conjoined hands. 'You must be dying to get back to normality.'

Ugh. The mere reminder that I won't be spending my days with Aide makes my scrambled eggs curdle in my stomach. We were born out of a totally unexpected, and initially unwanted, proximity, but the heat between us is undeniable.

Not just the heat. Last night felt like a step forward for us in terms of getting to know each other better. Getting to understand each other. But I have no fucking clue what happens from here.

And I'm no longer so convinced that my *normality* is quite so normal.

I hold his gaze as the car progresses down the narrow lanes. 'I'll miss the view,' I say lightly. I let my eyes drop to his insane pecs below their—currently pristine—white vest and back up.

'I'll miss the view, too,' he says, his eyes dropping to my boobs in their tight, cropped t-shirt before he leans in to kiss me lightly on the lips.

Good, I think.

'Do none of your co-workers get their boobs out for you in your day job?'

He drops me a panty-melting grin. 'Thankfully, no. There's only one pair I want to see, anyway.'

I give my shoulders a happy little shimmy.

'I cannot *believe* I told you to put them away that first day,' he says, dragging his free hand over his face. 'You were right. That would have been a lawsuit waiting to happen.'

I grimace. 'I really hope you don't say things like that to your employees. Nobody likes a sex-pest boss.'

'No fucking way,' he says. 'Seriously. Not in a million

years would I ever. I think I must have gone temporarily insane—it's the only explanation.'

'I'm glad they're capable of driving good men to the brink of sanity,' I say. 'Always useful to be aware of one's powers.'

His grin drops away, and he chews on his lower lip before replying. 'I want to keep on seeing you.' His voice drops to a whisper, and he leans in to my ear. 'In case my complete inability to keep my cock out of your body hasn't made it clear, it's insane between us. I want to get to know you a lot better.'

I swivel my head so my lips are level with his. His beard brushes my chin. There's no way I can be this close to him and not kiss him. Not feel his mouth on mine.

'Glad to hear it,' I tell him, and I take his full lower lip between my teeth.

29

AIDE

Today should be the easy day. The fun day.

We've done the hard, back-breaking work, and now we get to reap the benefits. To enjoy the part where we put all the new furniture and toys and games into the refreshed community centre and marvel at the transformation we've made. There's even a new air hockey table which Venus has generously donated. It turned up yesterday out of the blue. The kids will lose their fucking lives over it.

The whole thing has Lotta's fingerprints all over it.

The kids will see it tomorrow morning, when the sit-down breakfast service will recommence. God knows how Judy and Sylv will get the kids out the door in time for school. They won't want to leave.

They'll definitely have to keep the air hockey table turned off till the afternoon session.

So yeah. It should be a happy occasion. The team's done a great job. We can be proud of ourselves. Between us, we've managed to keep a twice-a-day food service going from the play area while Lotta's excellent team of professionals has turned out work of the highest calibre.

The room I'm standing in today is unrecognisable, frankly. The new paint job and doors and fixtures have worked wonders in elevating the atmosphere to one of playfulness. Optimism. Hope. Ian's team installed massive cupboards which will now hide the majority of the necessary clutter, giving the kids more room to play.

Today, the clever new tables go in. They're stowaway ones like primary schools use, with little round stools attached to them. Outside of mealtimes, they'll flatten up against the wall of the hall like gym apparatus. They're genius.

We've even got Gaz's blood off the skirting board.

So I should be feeling less melancholy, less deflated, than I am.

Everything Lotta said in the car was right. I feel guilty, and I shouldn't. I dislike the idea of Judy and Sylv and all our volunteers being left to manage things here while I swan off to run my multi-billion-pound empire.

I've been through this circular argument with myself a million times in my head.

Judy and Sylvie are both salaried. It's not much, but they're paid a respectable amount for the amazing work they do.

As Lotta said, they're not measuring things by the same exhaustingly high standards that I am. They're fucking thrilled, dizzy with excitement at the improvements in the centre. This, for them, is a huge win, and I need to remember that.

And I'm not bailing on them. I'll still come and help out one afternoon a week, like I've always done. I'll be here to kick a ball around with the kids and catch up on how things are going at home. At school. I'm still ploughing a lot of cash into this place, both personally and through Totum's foundation.

It's still a part of me. And I'm still a part of it.

Jesus. I should be glad to get out of here. Improved or not, it's still fucking depressing. It's still a reminder of what I endured as a kid. Of how far I've come. I should be putting as much distance as possible between me and this part of town.

But, as I told Lotta last night, roots are strong, stubborn fuckers, and it's far harder to uproot yourself, reinvent yourself, than anyone ever gives you credit for.

It's not—

I lose all track of what it's not, because at that moment, Lotta sashays past me into the kitchen with a smile on her face that's aimed squarely at me, turning my brain to instant mush. I follow her through to the kitchen, grabbing the pockets of her denim shorts as I catch her up and tugging that delectable little arse of hers firmly against my dick.

I couldn't give a shit who sees us. I'm done playing games and hiding my infatuation with her.

Life is short. Today's our last day working together. If I want to spend as much of it as possible with my hands on her, everyone's going to have to deal with it.

She looks like a fucking supermodel. I was slightly concerned her morning routine would make us late, but she just ran a hairdryer through her hair for five minutes and dumped it all on top of her head in a big, messy pile. Huge gold hoop earrings dangle against her slim neck, and worst of all, she's wearing a t-shirt that may well bring me to my knees. It almost led to round two when she put it on in my bedroom earlier.

It's tight and white, with *Chanel* written across her tits in the sparkliest, most look-at-me manner possible. It's written in gold sequins, for fuck's sake. Worse, it stops far too high, exposing inches of flat, soft stomach.

I thought Lotta's tits were my favourite thing about her. Now there are too many to count, but her skin is right up there. If I was a poet, I'd write sonnets to her skin. It manages to be creamy and tanned and glossy and so fucking soft.

I. Cannot. Stop. Touching. It.

Earlier, I sat on my bed and pulled her to stand between my legs so I could kiss that smooth belly of hers. Her skin feels like heaven to me. Like home.

Now I've secured her against me, I press a palm to said stomach, my fingers splaying out so my thumb brushes the hem of her top and my little finger toys with the button on her shorts.

Skin on skin.

There's nothing like it in the world.

I bury my face in her neck and inhale the intoxicating combination of my shower gel on her skin as we shuffle to her beloved Nespresso machine. 'Tell me you'll put on your painting t-shirt shortly,' I beg, my lips dragging over her neck.

She laughs and puts her hand on her stomach, on top of mine. 'But we're not painting today, darling.'

'We're doing *stuff*. This'll get filthy. *You'll* get filthy.'

'Maybe you'll have to come back to mine later and wash me off,' she coos.

I tense in anticipation. 'Yeah?'

'Yeah.'

'I didn't bring a change of clothes.'

'We have an overnight laundry service at Elgin.' Her hand tightens over mine, and she pushes her arse back against me. 'I can handle having you naked in my flat for a few hours.'

'It's a date,' I tell her, tugging lightly at her neck with my teeth. That reminds me, I want to take her on a proper date. Something Lotta-worthy. So far, she's had a drink in a shitty old men's pub with me and the team.

I think I can do better than that.

'Don't forget to take that thing home with you tonight,' I say about the Nespresso machine.

'Oh God no. I got this for here. I have them coming out of my ears. Besides, Sylvie's become addicted to the *Vaniglia*. I couldn't do that to her—I've got a few sleeves of them on their way for her.'

She's sweet. So sweet. And hearing her tongue caress a single Italian word like that, in the beautiful, melodic way it's supposed to be spoken, almost makes me hard.

'Will you speak Italian to me in bed?' I ask. 'It's really fucking hot.'

She laughs and says something that's unintelligible and husky and suggestive and absolutely perfect.

'What did you say?'

She grabs a Nespresso pod and puts the little glass cup into the machine. 'I said I'm going to bend over for you later and ask you in Italian to fuck me really, really hard and really, really slowly,' she says seductively.

'Jesus Christ,' I moan, dropping my forehead to her shoulder. This woman is sex on legs. I can't think straight around her. I'm barely surviving being outside of her body. God knows what I'll be like tomorrow at work when I don't get to touch her all day.

I might have to pay a visit to her office. Return the favour, as it were. I grin to myself as I rub my forehead on the cotton of her t-shirt.

'Well, well, well,' comes Gaz's highly amused voice from behind me. 'What do we have here, then?'

'None of your fucking business,' I say gruffly, but I make no attempt to extricate myself from whatever pheromones Lotta's skin is emitting.

'Morning, Gaz,' Lotta says, sounding amused and a tiny bit self-conscious, which I really love. I wrap my other arm around her middle and squeeze.

'I bloody knew it!' Gaz says. 'Oh shit.'

'What?' I mutter against Lotta's neck.

'I owe Judy twenty quid,' he says. 'She called it. Judith? *Judith!* Get in here!'

Lotta giggles.

I snort. 'Jesus,' I say. I turn us around and lift my head in time to see Gaz's smirk. Whatever he's lost on his little bet, I suspect he's gained in satisfaction at catching us like this.

Judy appears behind him. 'About fucking time,' she says, looking us up and down. I can tell she's trying not to grin. 'Knew you two were fucking.'

Gaz tuts. 'Language, Judith, language. Look at these two. Adorable. I might just have to...'

'Nope,' I say as he comes towards us. But it's too late. He envelopes us both in a massive hug, throwing his arms around me and squishing poor Lotta completely in the process. He reeks of deodorant, which I should probably be grateful for. I laugh, and she groans. Then Gaz moves his head so he can plant a big wet kiss on my forehead.

'Fuck off, mate,' I say.

'I'm just so happy for you both,' he says in a faux-emotional voice. 'You'll make such beautiful babies together.'

'Jesus Christ,' Judy says. 'Man the fuck up, Gaz.'

'I can't breathe,' Lotta gasps between us.

I push out of his arms. 'That's enough, okay? And keep your hands off her,' I add as an afterthought.

'What'd I miss?' Sylvie asks, barrelling in, vape in hand. I roll my eyes.

'These two are an item,' Gaz volunteers, right as Judy says, 'They're fucking.'

'Oh!' Sylvie gasps out the words. Her kind brown eyes are wide. Her lips press together like she's trying to stop herself from beaming, and she puts her hand to her heart as she takes a tentative step forward.

Fuck's sake. This woman kills me.

'Get in here,' I tell her with another eye roll, and I tuck her under my arm while pulling Lotta out of Gaz's clutches. Lotta rests her head against Sylvie's, and the older woman lets out a contented sigh.

'I'm not missing this,' Judy says, bustling over so she can get in on the action. She presses herself against Lotta. She only comes up to her shoulder.

'Quite right,' Gaz says. 'We need to hug this out. The two most gorgeous human beings I've laid eyes on are humping. This is cause for a lager shandy later, Judith, my friend.'

'Have some self respect,' Judy tells him. 'Lager shandy, my arse. We'll have some of that expensive whisky Aide's got stashed next door.'

I stand there and I fucking suck it up as my friends insist on hugging me and Lotta half to death.

I'd rather die than admit it, but I'm really going to miss this lot.

30

LOTTA

A casual supper in the Montefiore-Charlton household is never casual. Not with my mother at the helm.

When I let myself into their massive townhouse in Knightsbridge, I'm immediately hit by a gorgeous wall of music courtesy of the sound system. Someone is belting out *Una Furtiva Lagrima* at full force. I'd put money on it being Santi's dad, Dominic Vale.

In the centre of the high-shine, monochrome tiled floor sits an elegant antique table bearing a complex, multi-vase arrangement of flowers that would put the Mandarin Oriental's lobbies to shame. One of Mamma's many extravagances is having fresh flowers around the house at all times. It looks and smells like paradise, so I can't complain.

Often, Mamma and Dad's chef cooks Mediterranean, but tonight she's cooking Asian. The table in the huge kitchen where they prefer to eat unless they're entertaining formally is set with one of Mamma's favourite Hermes dinnerware sets, their geometric Balcon du Guadalquivir design in iconic tomato and white.

Delicate bud vases bearing perfect sprigs of white flowers and greenery line the entire length of the table. Blue-striped Murano wine glasses and tumblers adorn our place-settings. Murano glassware is another of Mamma's weaknesses. The effect is stunning, if a little OTT for a quiet family supper.

'Hey,' the chef, Sabrina, calls out from the far end of the kitchen where she's plating up food on the island. She's technically not their chef—more a wellness consultant who Mamma hired a few months ago to overhaul her and Dad's health.

Mamma's a lot more into the idea than Dad is.

'Hi!' I reply, making for her end of the kitchen. 'Why does it smell like Nobu in here?' I round the island and give her a hug.

She laughs. 'Must be the miso black cod. It's in the oven.'

'I think it's everything,' I say, eyeing up the spread appreciatively. This looks incredible. Sabrina's cooking is an excellent reason to visit my parents more often. 'What's that?' I point to the sauce she's spooning over what looks like yellowtail sashimi with infinite care.

'Just yuzu and soy sauce.'

'I hope my Dad appreciates this.'

'You know he won't.'

'He still giving you grief?'

She cocks her head, and her long, sleek ponytail swings. She's a gorgeous Californian blonde who exudes good health and outdoor living every time I see her. She's definitely a great advertisement for her own services. 'More like puppy eyes?' she says. 'He looks super sad whenever I put his food down in front of him. Like he's asking *really? That's the best you can do?*'

I snort. 'Oh God. The guilt trip. That's tough—I'm so sorry.'

'Yeah,' she says. 'It's brutal. He's started counting down the days till they go to Mustique. *In front of me.*'

'Well that's just rude,' I say. 'Will you not go with them?'

'Nah. Your mom said they have someone out there who looks after their place and does all the cooking, so they don't really need me.'

'That's true. When do they go?'

'Mid October.' She takes a tiny pair of tongs and painstakingly places a ring of jalapeño on each piece of sashimi. My mouth waters.

'What will you do?'

'I dunno. I wanna go to Israel for a while—maybe Lebanon, too. Israel for sure, though, so I can do an Ottolenghi pilgrimage.'

'That sounds amazing,' I say. I'd much rather be a food pilgrim than a religious one.

'I'd love to go home for the holidays, but it makes more sense to stay here. London's such a great base for travelling. So if you hear of anyone looking for someone in my field, please let me know.'

'I definitely will,' I say, 'though I'm not sure how many takers you'll get for a wellness consultant over Christmas. New Year's more likely.'

She laughs. 'Right? Can you imagine how pissed your dad would be if I was hanging around at Christmas?'

I pretend to shudder. 'I dread to think how *rude* he'd be.'

～

MAMMA AND DAD materialise a few minutes later. While Dad plods, Mamma wafts. She's in a full-length Pucci kaftan with a low-cut V neck that looks amazing on her and gives serious *Elizabeth Taylor receiving guests at home* vibes.

Mamma instilled in me from a young age a preference for Italian designers. Cavalli. Pucci. Gucci. Dolce and Gabbana. Versace. *They understand women's bodies*, she explained. *They celebrate them.* That's always stuck with me. I love how unapologetic Italian labels are. How colourful. How they do indeed celebrate our curves. Showcase them.

Not that Chiara Montefiore-Charlton needs much help showcasing anything. People tend to notice when she enters a room, Pucci or no Pucci. It's not just the noise factor, which is not inconsiderable. Mamma is effusive with a capital E. She's also an old-school Italian siren with bucket loads of flirtatious charm. My quiet father, on the other hand, has always been happy to have her absorb the limelight so he can better avoid it.

It's probably not a million miles from my and Aide's dynamic, to be honest.

Once we've installed ourselves at the table and Dad has poured some champagne, I raise the subject I've come here to discuss. Our family's not known for its subtlety, so I dive right in with the same gusto that I'm diving into this insane yellowtail.

'Talk to me about Aidan Duffy,' I demand, my sashimi poised between chopsticks next to my mouth. As usual, a frisson runs over my skin when I allow myself to say that delicious man's name out loud.

'Aide?' Dad asks, perking up notably. A moment ago, he was picking at an edamame bean with an *I wish you were a sausage roll* look. 'They don't come better than him.'

I've swiftly reached that conclusion by myself, but it feels great to hear Dad's knee-jerk reaction.

'Aide is a very sweet boy,' Mamma coos. 'Very sweet

indeed! And so clever.' She tuts, pursing her glossy, cherry-red lips, and lays her bejewelled hand fondly over Dad's. 'Even more clever than your Papa, I think.'

'That is a fact,' Dad says. 'How do you know him?'

'I've been doing a charitable project through Venus that we finished up last week,' I say. 'A community centre in Avondale Park. Anyway, Aide's been leading it from his side —he and Gabe cooked the whole thing up together. And... we're kind of dating.'

Dad raises his eyebrows, which is as much of a reaction as anyone usually gets from him, but Mum clasps her hands together, hugging them against her chest, and gasps theatrically.

'This is marvellous!' she cries. 'He is a good boy, *tesoro*.' She smiles indulgently. 'Remember that very first time he came for dinner? He was so shy, so *handsome*. Even then. You were quite taken.'

'I don't remember,' I say, throwing my chopsticks down. Why does everyone remember that evening apart from me? 'He told me about it, but I have no recollection.' I keep thinking maybe I remember, but I know I'm just making the scene up in my head based on what Aide's told me.

'I'm sure the conversation got pretty technical that night,' Dad says. 'You probably zoned out. But you two are getting on well?'

There is no reality in which my dad needs to know quite how well I'm 'getting on' with his former protégé. Since the first night I spent at his place, however, it feels like something has shifted.

Before, we were hooking up based purely on chemistry. It was physical.

Now, it feels a lot more than that, and not solely because

we haven't spent a night apart since. This is our first evening apart, in fact.

'How did you meet him?' I ask my dad, because it seems my thirst for information about Aide grows every day. I've heard Aide's side of the story, including his very sweet memories of the allure of my sixteen-year-old self, but I want to hear it from as many sources as possible.

Dad pauses, leaning back in his chair to allow Sabrina to place a large bowl of salad on the table as well as the platter of miso black cod, which looks and smells spectacular. Mum and I both make hungry noises of appreciation, while Dad turns his face to Sabrina.

'Thanks, Sabrina. Don't suppose there's any rice?'

'I apologise, Paul,' she says. 'Not today.' She looks at my mum for assistance, but Mamma shakes her head sharply.

'No carbs, *caro*.'

'There's salad, though,' Sabrina says. 'It's a Thai salad. With cashews.'

'I'm sure it will be delicious, thank you, Sabrina,' Mum says with a gentle incline of her head and the air of one breaking up a playground fight. 'Paul, do not make her feel bad for doing her job.'

'I would never,' Dad says. He visibly slumps in his chair. 'Thank you,' he says to Sabrina in the tone of a defeated child.

'Where was I?' he asks when she's left us. 'Ah, yes. Aide. It was through UCL, I suppose. They were one of the feeder universities for our incubator—still are—and he must've applied through his professor. However it happened, I recall that his application was standout. Quite extraordinary.'

He lays his hands flat on the table and stares off into space, and I know in this moment that Dad's terrifying brain has transported him to a world of zeroes and ones, as it so often does.

Shaking his head, he continues. 'But when I met him—that's when I knew he was special. He was, you know, a bit rough around the edges. He didn't have that obnoxious polish some of the others we saw did. He was shy. Yes, shy. But articulate. Quietly confident, you know? Very much unshakeable in his vision, but it wasn't born out of arrogance. More intelligence and the moral certitude of what he wanted to do.'

I blink. That might possibly be the longest speech I've ever heard my dad utter when he's not standing on a podium with a proverbial gun to his head.

'Wow. What was his vision?'

I mean, I know Totum is a medical data company. But, to be honest, I pretty much had brain freeze as soon as I read the words *medical* and *data*. I haven't read much about Totum, because I kind of assumed I wouldn't understand much of it. I may be smart, but I do *not* have my father's type of brain.

My parents exchange a glance.

'You remember?' Dad asks Mamma softly.

'I do.' She pretends to wipe a tear from her eye. 'It was a very good pitch.'

'It was,' Dad says. 'That's the thing about Aide—he's always been equally compelling on the quantitative and qualitative fronts.' He spoons a mound of Thai salad onto his plate with a deeply sceptical look.

'He had a friend,' Mamma prompts.

'That's right. A friend, or a boy from school, maybe? Or from his community. I can't recall. Anyway. This young person died at the hands of his father. Beaten to death.'

Oh my *God*. I clap my hand over my mouth.

'It turned out, in the aftermath, that there had been a pattern of abuse,' Dad continues quietly. 'Broken legs. Arms. I don't recall the details. But here's the thing.' He leans in and grimaces. 'The injuries were each treated at different hospitals, *in different London trusts.*'

I frown, trying to put the pieces together. 'So...'

'So the trusts didn't share data. It transpires that the father had taken the child to a different hospital each time to avoid any healthcare professional spotting the pattern of abuse. Therefore, each time, they treated it as an isolated incident. The abuse was never spotted. Social services were never brought in, and the child went unprotected.'

Dad sits back, spreading his arms wide. He doesn't need to say any more.

Until it was too late.

I stare at him, shocked. 'What do you mean, they didn't share data?' I cry. 'That's the most ridiculous thing I've ever heard.'

Dad shrugs. 'Patient confidentiality. The NHS had to prioritise that, and it didn't have a way to make data available between individual trusts without risking a data breach. Until a young, precociously intelligent, and very, very angry young man decided to do something about it.'

'Aide,' I whisper.

I am shellshocked.

I had no idea there was such an emotive story behind Aide's success. That the software, the massive company, he's created was born out of anything other than the wish to scratch an intellectual itch.

'Yep,' Dad says. 'He found a way to build data systems that were shareable while adhering to the strictest security standards. He found a way to have NHS trusts all over the country speak to each other, instantly, which is far trickier than it sounds, given the jumble of out-of-date, non-compatible systems our healthcare service uses. The name, Totum, means *all* in Latin, of course.'

Of course it does. I'm a Classics graduate, and yet I haven't thought about the meaning behind the name until now. *All. Totality.* Aide brought visibility, transparency, to our healthcare data, fuelled by his deep sense of injustice. Of frustration that anyone he knows should be left unprotected.

Or anyone at all, for that matter.

'Most of its objectives are more prosaic, of course,' Dad continues. 'But that's not to say they aren't incredibly important. If you take a cancer patient being treated across various modalities and trusts, even, Totum's functionality means every professional, oncologist or otherwise, can see all the clinical data and treatment history at a glance, no matter what hospital treated the patient. That may seem basic stuff, but I can assure you, in our dear, decrepit healthcare system, it's not. And he's sold the data globally. Most countries around the world have adopted Totum by now. It's indisputably the market leader.'

'He was so—what is the word—unassuming, that evening,' Mamma muses. 'But still very impressive. So impressive. And so handsome.' She smiles fondly.

I'm still reeling at how deep Aide's altruism runs, and how powerful a force for good this guy is, when Mamma asks with a devious grin and a shoulder shimmy, 'So, *tesoro*, will you invite this very good-looking young man to Elle's wedding?'

31

AIDE

I've put myself in Lotta's work calendar.

The lunchtime slot.

It seemed appropriate given I plan to eat her.

Venus' offices are, unsurprisingly, glossy and stylish and beautiful and expensive-looking.

Just like one of their founders.

It's only been a few hours since we took our leave from each other, but I'm looking forward to seeing her in her working environment. The building's lobby is white, sleek and flower-filled, with huge, muted canvases. White sofas flank low glass coffee tables on which rest big leather books. When I leaf through one, I realise they're portfolios of Venus' work, everything shot in black and white.

Fuck, these guys are good at what they do.

The pretty redhead behind the lacquered front desk blushes and smiles as she hands me a security pass and ushers me to the bank of lifts. I shoot her a grin that's more apologetic than encouraging, because, more often than not, my looks tend to be a curse.

Sometimes they work in my favour, though.

Like on shitty building sites when glittering, captivating heiresses so far out of my league it's not funny decide, for some unknown reason, that they like how I look wielding an electric drill.

Then I thank whoever's up there for them. I might give a nod to my old man, too. He was the original black-haired, blue-eyed charmer with the gift of the gab and the roguish Dublin charm. I may have inherited his colouring, but the charm's definitely gone astray somewhere.

No matter.

If Carlotta likes the way I look, and speak, and touch her, the way I can make her feel, then my cup is full.

I exit the lift and make my way across an open-plan floor of sleek desks, accompanied by a sleek young MBA-type. He doesn't need to open his mouth to tell me he's American— the white t-shirt peeking out from under his immaculate blue shirt gives the game away immediately.

The space is smaller than ours. At Totum, we went for a lateral layout in a huge repurposed warehouse in Kings Cross, whereas here at Venus they have several floors. But whereas our office is bright and friendly and screams creativity, the vibe here is more grownup. More sophisticated.

Carlotta's standing in the doorway to what must be her office. I grin, because she's a sight for sore fucking eyes. She's in the same longish, floaty floral dress she put on this morning and some fuck-me heels that I'm a big fan of. The best thing about the outfit, though, is undoubtedly the tantalising row of buttons that run the whole way down the front of the dress. She's got her arms crossed and bright red lips that instantly makes me want to wipe her lipstick off.

With my cock.

But that's not why I'm here.

I'm here for *her*.

'Thanks, Ash,' she says to the guy as she stands aside to usher me inside. 'Hello, stranger,' she says to me.

I stroll through, hands in my pockets. I'm absolutely thrilled to see that her office has walls and a door, both of which are completely opaque.

All the better to ravish her behind.

I close the door and turn the lock before pressing her up against it. Her hands go straight to my head, pulling at my hair as she guides my mouth to those beautiful, pouty lips. She's fucking beautiful, and she seems as hungry for me as I am for her, which is a miracle. I cup her jaw with one hand and the underside of her breast with the other while busying myself with kissing off that lipstick.

God, she's perfection. I use the hand on her jaw to tilt her head so I can lick and nip down that swanlike neck and inhale her gorgeous floral scent. Her hands are moving over my shoulders. Down my back.

'How the hell are you in a three-piece suit?' she gasps. 'I left you looking like Mark Zuckerberg this morning in your t-shirt.'

'I've got a few hanging in the office.' I pause to kiss her collarbone. 'I've got a meeting later and a *very* hot date tonight.'

'Mmm,' she says, arching into me. 'Very hot. Yeah. You should wear this all the time.'

'Not my favourite outfit in July.'

'I get that. Just stay indoors. You look so gorgeous.'

I pull away and grin at her. That red lipstick is looking nicely smudged against her ripe, swollen lips. The buttons on her dress are a bit of a pain in the arse, but I can take them.

'Why don't you give me a tour of your office?' I ask,

stroking my fingertip gently down the slope of her adorably pert little nose. It makes her look younger, somehow. Her freckles are clearer, her skin more sun kissed, after spending most of the weekend by my pool.

'With pleasure.' She spreads her arms wide. 'This is my office. Now I really want to get under that suit.'

I tut. 'Not going to happen, sweetheart. I'm just here to service the boss. Are you her?'

'I am.'

I lean in and lower my voice, taking her hand in mine. 'Come with me, then. This your desk?'

'Yes.'

'This your chair?'

'Yes.'

I hold out my hand. 'Please, have a seat.'

'Thank you.' She sinks gracefully into the leather swivel chair and I look down at her, admiring the view.

'This place suits you. It's very *you*.' I mean it. It's an equally stylish but more colourful version of the lobby, with oversized arrangements of fresh flowers everywhere, stunning, hyper-feminine canvases in muted pinks and blushes, and a couple of blown-up building shots that look similar to the ones in the leather portfolios downstairs. Against one wall is a long sofa whose grey-green velvet looks a lot more luxurious than mine and reminds me of the colour and texture of the sage leaves in my garden.

'I love it.' She looks around the room, and I see pride and possession on her finely wrought features.

She's earned this.

She's worked her arse off for this office.

This is a microcosm of her kingdom, and she is its queen.

And what a fucking queen.

I step between her desk and her chair, pushing the chair backwards, and get to my knees in front of her.

'It's a lovely room,' I tell her. 'You've got great taste. But you're the most beautiful thing in it by a million miles.'

She raises a shapely eyebrow. '*Thing?*'

'Thing,' I confirm, cuffing her ankles with my hands and nudging her feet apart. I slide my hands up her legs, hitching the hem of her dress higher as I go. 'Very tidy desk, by the way.'

'What? Oh, yeah. I don't like clutter. I like fabulous things, but not random shit everywhere.'

'Makes sense,' I say, but I'm thinking *I know exactly how to make use of that very tidy desk surface.*

'How has your morning been?' I ask evenly, staring down at her knees, her smooth thighs, as they appear from under the light, frothy fabric.

'Tiring,' she says, but there's an edge to her voice that suggests anticipation rather than weariness. 'I feel like I'm still playing catch-up.'

'Poor baby,' I say. I've got the dress almost all the way up now. My thumbs drag up her inner thighs. 'How about you let me be the boss for a few minutes?'

'Sounds good,' she says in a breathy voice I decide I really, really like.

'Good girl. Wouldn't it be nice to have a guy who turns up to make you feel better every time it all gets too much?' I bend and kiss her knees. Softly. Chastely. 'Who does all the work?'

'Mmm-hmm,' she agrees. I doubt she's aware, but she's just opened her legs a little more for me and I spy a glimpse of the pale pink thong she was skipping around her bedroom in this morning, driving me crazy while we got ready for work.

It's payback time.

~

LOTTA

I stare at the beautiful man kneeling between my legs.

His suit is so perfectly cut, its wool so fine and lustrous, I could weep. But it's not where my focus is, because I can't stop looking at his gorgeous face. At the seriousness in those intense blue eyes, as if he means business. They rove over my body, tracing a path from my face to the apex of my parted thighs and back again, like they want to drink in every part of me.

Being the sole object of Aidan Duffy's attention is a wonderful, mesmerising, heady thing. He's *Aide*. He's amazing and open-hearted and an exceptional human being. He's also the most magnificent *thing*, to use his language, I've ever set eyes on.

His hair is slicked back today with a bit of gel—not enough to make him look like a wanker banker, but enough to neaten up his unruly mane of unfairly thick hair. It shows off the lean, gorgeous planes of his face. The hard jut of his jaw, covered by his neatly clipped beard.

Aide Duffy is like no one I've ever seen.

And he's kneeling between my legs like a penitent.

I just hope he's planning on worshipping me.

He must be able to see my thong by now, and he goes to push the fabric of my totally sick new Dolce dress up even further, then reconsiders. With dextrous, careful fingers he locates the placket and starts undoing my buttons, one by one. The silk chiffon tumbles south on either side of my legs as he goes. He doesn't stop once he has my thong exposed, but keeps on going until the entire dress is hanging open.

His satisfied smirk turns to something darker once he's got me completely exposed for him. My nipples, encased in their pale pink lace, are already hard. He takes them in and then looks up at me. His pose may be one of supplication, but in this moment there's no denying who'll be calling the shots here.

He will.

He runs his hands over my body. Up my thighs, brushing over my thong far too fleetingly before he strokes my stomach. The sensation of his large, calloused hands on my bare skin sends butterflies flitting below the surface. I watch, rapt, to see what part of me he'll touch next.

My boobs.

Obviously.

He cups them, and weighs them with pleased, approving noises that make me restless, running his thumbs roughly over my nipples so the lace scratches them in the best way.

'God, your tits will be the death of me,' he groans, resting his forehead on my stomach. I allow myself the pleasure of raking my fingers through his hair as I revel in the heat of his breath on my lower stomach and the pressure of his hands on my boobs.

'I can smell you,' he grits out. 'Fuck. Need a taste.' He lowers his face, dragging his lips and nose down over my skin until he reaches my already damp thong. I claw at his hair, but then he's pulling away from my hands and looking up at me again, hunger in those dangerous eyes.

'Pull your thong aside for me, sweetheart,' he mutters. He tugs on his full lower lip with his teeth, a gesture that has my pussy contracting, before continuing. 'Show me what's waiting for me.'

I slide my bum forward in my seat so I'm reclining further. It has the bonus of thrusting my pussy further towards Aide's beautiful mouth. Without taking my eyes off him, I hook my thumb through one side of my thong's central strip and pull it aside.

'That's my fucking girl,' he says. His breath is already laboured. His words reek of thinly held control.

And it is so fucking hot.

'Hold it right there, okay?'

'Okay,' I say, and let my head sink back.

'You. Are. So. Wet,' he says, dipping an experimental finger into my entrance. I moan. What parallel universe am I in, to find myself sequestered in my office with a delicious, dirty man who wants to take control of me? Undo me right here, with my team on the other side of that locked door?

He pushes his finger in hard, and I gasp. God, that's good. Aide's touch, and the almost feral look in his eyes, and the filth of this entire scenario, will be the death of me. He bends his head and touches his tongue almost reverently to my clit.

Sweet Jesus.

'Mmm,' he says, his voice rumbling against my needy flesh. 'Fucking delicious.'

'So good,' I manage breathlessly.

He stops and looks up. His eyes are already glazed with desire. I bet he's rock fucking hard already. 'Lotts.'

'Yeah?'

'Tell me what you fantasised about me doing to you when you first met me.' He watches my face for a moment before dropping back down and pressing a soft kiss to my pussy. Then his tongue finds my clit again, and Holy Mary, Mother of God, that feels right.

He should stay there forever.

'Um.' I struggle to recalibrate enough to answer his unexpected question. 'Well, I thought you were a grumpy, hostile dickhead.'

He stops.

'Okay, okay,' I say hurriedly. I close my eyes and take myself back to that first day. 'And I wanted you to rail me really, really hard virtually as soon as I laid eyes on you.'

'Mmm hmm.' He hums out his approval and rewards me with a magical swirl of his tongue around my clit that has angels breaking out in song around my head.

'Um. It was your eyes. I'd never seen anything like them. Never. I wanted—I just wanted them on me. On my skin. I remember I saw you looking at my boobs, and I had this feeling, like *how would it feel if I had those incredible eyes on my naked tits?* Like I could have come just from the way I knew you'd look at them. Like the way you did look at them when I got them out for you that day in the office.'

'Fuck, yeah,' he groans. *Lick.* 'Touch them for me.'

I hold on to my thong for dear life with one hand as I take the other to one taut, aching nipple. It's pinched into a little ball of need, and my frantic fingers feel so, so good as they rub it. Roll it.

'God, I remember that first time you sucked them,' I moan. 'It was like nothing else I've ever known. I needed your mouth on them so, so badly.'

'Mmph,' he says, and it sounds pretty agonised. He rewards me by adding another finger inside me. Holy *fuck*, his fingers are big. I arch my back as much as I can in the chair to accommodate him and look down. The sight of his dark head moving between my legs, working the very core of me, is one that will be emblazoned on my mind on my deathbed.

Aidan Duffy will be emblazoned on my mind on my deathbed.

He is not the kind of man you recover from.

A wave of emotion crests over me, even more potent than the imminent orgasm threatening to build inside me, that has my heart squeezing. It's all I've wanted, really, since that first moment I saw him. His question has me remembering oh-so-clearly.

I wanted his attention.

His eyes on me.

His body tending to mine. Making me feel everything I knew he was capable of.

I was so right.

His tongue picks up. His licks become rougher. The twists of his fingers inside me grow harder. The heat coursing through my body grows ever stronger.

'Fuck me hard when you're done, honey,' I say softly, and I hear a low, pained grunt which I'll take as a resounding *yes*.

When I peak, it's a thing of such beauty it takes my breath away. My soul soars as my entire body tenses with the effort of not screaming out. Instead I allow myself ragged, breathy whimpers as I shake out my orgasm on Aide's magic, generous tongue and mouth and fingers. I'm barely through it before he's clambering to his feet, and hauling me to mine, and unhooking my bra, and shrugging it and my dress off my shoulders, and kissing me desperately, before he spins me around and bends me over my plexiglass desk.

My thong is peeled down my legs and then he's stepping right up behind me and pressing his wool-clad legs against mine as he lines himself up and pushes inside me, hard.

I gasp as my cheek hits the cool plexiglass, as Aide's

hand brushes my hair impatiently out of the way so he can hold me in place with a firm hand against the base of my neck. With his other hand, he grips my hip tightly as he begins to move inside me.

Jesus Christ. It feels *so fucking good*.

'Fuck, Lotts,' he's panting out. '*Shit*. You feel like nothing else. Fucking *hell*. I want to fuck this beautiful cunt into next weekend.'

Somehow, I've found myself spending my Thursday lunchtime naked and bent over my desk at work, being railed from behind by a gorgeous billionaire in a three-piece suit, whose oversized dick is matched only by his oversized heart.

He is revelling in this. My beautiful Aide, who usually bears the weight of the world on his shoulders, is allowing me to be the channel for his unravelling. These aren't the thrusts, the grunts, the filthy muttered endearments, of a man holding back.

They're those of my favourite caveman. The only person on earth who's capable of making me feel like this.

I *knew* it.

I knew, as soon as I saw him, that he'd be very, very good at getting his hands dirty.

32

AIDE

I may be in the type of swanky, wanky Mayfair restaurant I usually avoid like the plague, but I'm feeling pretty pleased with myself, and that has nothing to do with the swanky, wanky crowd around me and everything to do with the woman sitting opposite me.

The woman whose in-fucking-credible body I devoured in the quiet splendour of her office at lunchtime.

The woman who let me *inside* her body, let me bend her over and fuck her hard and fast on her desk because I was so far past being able to hold back.

I gaze at her.

I still cannot believe I get to be *inside her body*.

She, of course, looks like she was made for this place. I suppose I do too, to the untuned eye, in my Savile Row suit and Armani tie. But, unlike me, Lotta's totally at home here. She's also the most beautiful woman in the room by a mile, and, let me tell you, there are a lot of *very* expensive hookers loitering by the bar area. And it's not just her beauty. It's the whole fucking package. Her elegance. Poise. Intelligence. Charm.

Carlotta Montefiore-Charlton is a class act.

She shifts in her seat a little as she peruses the drinks menu.

I lean forward. 'Feeling sore?' I enquire in a low voice.

I love the self-conscious smile that washes over her face at my question.

'A little tender,' she admits, inclining her swanlike neck. It's on full display given she's put her hair up. She's also applied heavier eye makeup for this evening, and whatever she's done makes her look even more goddess-like, makes the huge brown doe eyes staring at me even more mesmerising.

'Poor baby.' I reach across the table and brush the pad of my thumb over a couple of her rings. I give her a wolfish grin. 'I'll make it all better later.'

The part of me that's a civilised human being is gutted that I've made her sore, but a horrifyingly large part of me loves that she's sitting here in this flashy restaurant, surrounded by posh twats, and that it's *my* cock she can still feel in the place that none of them will ever get near.

Not on my watch, at least.

Her mouth twists. 'I bet you will.'

I order us a Meursault from the bottom of the wine list, because I know she loves her big, buttery whites, and one thing I struggle to feel guilty about spending money on is seriously decent wine. Besides, the most extravagant thing we've done in the past week is order Wagamama's on Deliveroo. There's no harm in splashing out every now and again.

I'm not tight. I enjoy high quality. I've developed a *taste* for high quality, in case you couldn't work that out with a single glance at my new, beautiful girlfriend. I'm not that clichéd rich-as-sin miser who'd rather count his money than spend it. I couldn't be less like that. I'd rather give the entire load away. But I still struggle with guilt over ostentation. Throwing my money around.

That is not, however, an issue to worry about tonight. Because tonight, I'm the luckiest guy in the world, and I intend to have fun.

I'm casting my eye over the menu when Lotta gets gracefully to her feet. A tall posh bloke in a seriously nice suit is loitering. He looks far too confident for my liking yet strangely familiar.

Lotta leans in for a double air kiss. 'Santi!'

'Darling,' he drawls in a deep, cultured rumble I suppose the women go crazy for. 'You look stunning, as always.' I roll my eyes internally at his suaveness before fixing a smile on my face, because I left that chippy, insecure boy behind a long time ago, and Lotta deserves a far more socially competent dinner partner than that.

'Santi,' she says, 'allow me to introduce Aidan Duffy. Aide, this is Santiago Vale.'

Santiago Vale. Vale Music. Fucking hell—he's a massive player in the music industry. Mum's had a crush on his dad, Dominic Vale, for as long as I can remember.

And the bloke cuddling up to Lotta on her Instagram feed.

Bingo.

I rise to my feet, cogs turning as I put out my hand. 'The music guy?'

'The very same,' he says, shaking it with a surprisingly firm grip. 'And, far more glamorously, this one's neighbour.' He has that faux self-deprecating air that so many former public schoolboys have, but I don't hate him. I suspect everything's a bit of a piss-take with him. Besides, he's properly talented. No wonder his speaking voice sounds like warm treacle.

Before I can reply, he jerks his head in my direction and says to Lotta, 'So, is this your little "enigma"?'

To my surprise, she blushes and shoves him on the arm. 'Thanks a lot,' she hisses.

'Enigma?' I ask. I have no clue what he meant, but seeing Lotta flustered is amusing.

She rolls her eyes. 'Santi threw a party last week weekend after you and I...' She huffs. 'I may have mentioned, briefly and *in confidence*'—this last part aimed at him through gritted teeth—'that there was someone in the picture who I couldn't quite figure out. You know, because you were a dirty little liar.'

I close the gap between us and kiss her on the cheek, because the fact that she was ranting about me to her mates after kicking me out makes me inexplicably happy.

'Did you, now?' I murmur.

'Oh, yes, darling.' Santini clasps his hands together. 'You two are perfect. Look at you! Am I correct in thinking you're *the* Aidan Duffy?'

I'll never get used to being recognised, nor do I enjoy it. But I laugh, because Lotta's groaning beside me.

'Think so,' I say. 'If you mean the tech bloke.'

'Exactly!' Santi points at me. 'I knew it.'

'So I'm the only person on the planet who didn't know who you are,' Lotta whines. 'Fucking excellent.'

'Darling, get with the programme. Nerds are the new hotties,' Santi says, looking me over approvingly. 'Anyway, you two are divine. So adorable. You should have his babies.' He nods at Lotta.

This guy is fucking weird, but also hilarious. I also don't disagree with him on the last part, which is even weirder.

An image of her pregnant, so fleeting it's almost subliminal, flashes through my mind. Her tits would be so fucking luscious. I blink.

'*Anyway*, Santi, how are you doing?' Lotta asks through still-gritted teeth, a not-so-subtle way of indicating her desire to change the subject away from my filling her with my babies.

'I've been singing *O Holy Night* all fucking day, if you must know,' he says, putting his hands in his pockets. 'You may think it's July, but the festive season is officially upon us. We're recording our family Christmas album. Dad's even roped poor Vi into it.'

'Violet's Santi's daughter,' Lotta tells me. I nod and slip my hand further down the small of her back till I can feel the waistband of her thong through the thin silk of her dress. I like standing here with her like this, in the middle of this restaurant. Like she's mine. Like it's not the biggest miracle on earth that she's in my arms.

'She's ten,' Santi says. 'The exploitation of every last generation of Vales for commercial purposes is relentless. If Dad could record the fucking dog, he would.'

'Maybe you should put him on the album cover anyway,' Lotta suggests.

'Nope. Tried that. Dad vetoed it. Said he wasn't "pretty" enough.'

Lotta gasps. 'Luke's the prettiest boy in the world!'

'Exactly. His beauty is rivalled only by his quiet stoicism. But you know Dad. He said a Staffy wasn't "elevated" enough for the family brand. Wanted to hire a golden spaniel for the cover shoot. A fucking *golden spaniel*! Can you imagine?'

'I am really, really pissed off on Luke's behalf,' my little hellcat says, crossing her arms.

'As am I, darling. As am I. Anyway, the stress of the

whole thing's getting to us all. Dad's blood pressure's through the roof, his cholesterol's a fucking disaster, and Mum's going ballistic about his health. She said I'm working him too hard, when in reality it's completely the other way around. God knows, I'm going to need a fucking guru just to keep him alive for the next six months. It'll be a marathon—the planned publicity around it is a total circus.'

'Ooh—I have someone,' Lotta says. 'My parents will be away from October and they have an amazing person they won't be requiring for winter—she's a wellness consultant. She's from California, and she's extremely well-versed on the whole holistic thing, and, you know, complementary medicine. And nutrition too, obviously.'

Santi grimaces and rakes a hand through his dark hair. 'Dear God. An American, and an alternative one at that. She sounds utterly *ghastly*.' He really is a fucking drama queen, this guy.

'She is not *ghastly*,' Lotts says firmly. 'She's *delightful*. And she's an amazing chef. She is also a total smoke show, for your information, *Santi*, so I would thank you to keep your ill-informed opinions to yourself.'

He shoots her a filthy look, then rolls his eyes. 'Fine. Send me her number.'

∼

'Let's play a game,' I say when we've got rid of Santi and are each nursing a glass of Meursault. 'Quick fire get-to-know-you.'

'I'm in,' she says with a sexy smile.

'Let's see—favourite subject at school.'

'Classics,' she shoots back. 'You?'

'IT, obviously. And Maths. Why Classics?'

'Dunno.' She sticks out her delicious lower lip as she thinks. 'I suppose a lot of it was Italian history, which I loved. But I think it was just learning about ancient civilisations. We're so smug about how sophisticated we are—you know? But there was so much wisdom and insight back then. They had it a lot more figured out than we do. I ended up doing it at uni, too.'

This I did not know. 'Where did you go to uni?'

'Cambridge. Emmanuel College.'

'Course you did,' I say, smiling at her.

She laughs, and it's fucking beautiful. *She* is fucking beautiful. 'What's that supposed to mean? That I'm awful and entitled?'

'*No*. That you're very fucking intelligent.'

She narrows her eyes at me. 'Nice recovery. You were at UCL, right?'

'Yeah, but I never finished. I dropped out, thanks to your Dad's help.'

'He told me why you started Totum,' she says softly, stretching across the table to take my hand. 'I'm sorry.'

'Thanks,' I say. I can feel myself stiffen at the thought of that poor, poor little fucker, Jerry Smith. He was a skinny little thing. Stunted. I look down at our conjoined hands.

'I didn't mean to upset you,' she says. 'I'm so sorry.'

'Nothing to apologise for,' I tell her. 'It was a long time ago. I wasn't in a position to be able to fight child abuse, not then, but I could sure as fuck do something about making sure the NHS never let that stuff fall through the cracks.'

'It's absolutely amazing, what you've done.'

I blow out a breath and plaster a smile on my face. 'I want to be happy tonight. I'm sitting across a table from the most stunning woman I've ever seen, so I refuse to be a miserable bastard. Okay?'

She presses her lips together and smiles. 'Okay.'

'Why did you start Venus?' I ask. 'Where did the idea come from?'

'I can't take much credit,' she says, twirling the stem of her wine glass between her fingers. 'Gabe started it when I was in my final year at uni and he asked me to come on board. He felt there was a gap at the very top of the market for a design-led property developer that also refused to compromise on ethics and integrity. Some people that loaded don't give a shit about the planet, obviously, but others, like you'—she gestures at me—'care a lot and can afford to make the right environmental decisions, even if they cost a lot more than doing things the wrong way.'

'How did you divvy things up? Was it just the two of you at the start?'

She laughs. 'God, no. We had a *go big or go home* strategy from the get-go. We each invested a chunk of our trust funds as start-up capital—I turned twenty-one that year so mine freed up at exactly the right time—and Dad invested through his incubator, as I think I told you, and personally. He also made introductions.'

She looks down at her glass. 'So it was intense, but it wasn't like it was for you, where you had to do it all yourself and start from scratch. We hired analysts and architects and planners—it was a big operation. We had a *lot* of help.'

'Hey,' I say. 'Don't be ridiculous. It's totally different. You can't run your kind of start-up out of a basement. All I needed was me and a laptop, and some more computer scientists as I ramped up. You were building fucking *buildings*. It's far more capital intensive. And at that end of the market you need to show a professional front from the outset.'

'You're right, I suppose,' she says with a shrug.

'Was all the branding your responsibility?' I ask.

She grins. 'It was, and it was so much fun. While Gabe was dealing with buying land and haggling with councils and fucking town planners'—she shudders—'I was drawing up glossy brochures and commissioning beautiful artists' impressions and schmoozing everyone in my network, so that before we had our first block ready to start building we could sell the whole thing off-plan. And we did. That ramp-up phase was fun.'

I return her grin. 'Yeah. It really is. It's such a rush. And I bet you were the best marketer ever. I mean, who's going to say no to you?'

She rewards my compliment with a bat of her eyelids that makes me laugh. 'No one.'

'Exactly. I'm just wondering why I never got to meet you —that fucker Gabe kept me safely away from his little sister.'

'Probably because you were an incoming. No need to get the marketing team on a client if they come to us. It's a pity, though.' She licks her lips. 'I definitely would have enjoyed helping you seal the deal.'

'And I would have greatly enjoyed any freebies you were willing to throw in,' I counter. 'Though if I'd turned up in a suit, without my power tools, you might not have looked at me twice.'

'I'd have eye-fucked you even if you'd turned up in a *Minions* onesie,' she retorts. She leans forward. 'And I know exactly where you keep your power tool, gorgeous. And how good you are at using it.'

'Because you can still feel it,' I say.

Her eyes are soft in the dim light. I watch her lips annunciate *because I can still feel it.*

33

LOTTA

When your jaw-droppingly beautiful boyfriend asks you to be his date at a 'boring black-tie thing'—his words—and you find out it's a super-important event for the tech industry in London, and that said boyfriend will be the *keynote speaker*, and it's your first official engagement together, you make an effort.

And when you set the bar pretty high with your daily sartorial choices, you know it's time to pull out the big guns.

So you do.

It's weird, because I've dated a lot of guys who are successful at what they do—even if that success has been handed to them on a plate. And, obviously, I attend a tonne of these sorts of things already in my capacity as a C-suite-level representative of a large company.

But Aide and I got together in an environment completely outside of all that corporate schmoozing and incestuous London networking, and neither of us were trying to impress each other with our professional credentials. Which is code for *he was entranced by my tits and I was entranced by his biceps and—at the time confusing—Big Dick Energy.*

Which makes tonight's little outing on his arm feel like a step-change for us. We're doing something formal, work-related, as a professional couple.

That feels very grownup.

Happily, I *look* very grownup, thanks to my sweet and insanely talented fashion designer friend, Astrid Carmichael. I only gave her a couple of weeks' notice, but she's worked her usual magic. The dress is emerald green super weight crèpe de Chine, which is her signature fabric. It hits the floor, but there's plenty of skin on display thanks to an epic thigh slit, plunging keyhole neckline and cutaway waistline. It's sensational, if I do say so myself, even if it's not the most practical choice for a sit-down dinner.

The makeup artist I use for such occasions has excelled herself, giving me a fabulous smoky eye and applying high-lighter to every inch of visible skin on my body. My hair's in a sleek, low ponytail to one side, and the extensions my stylist added in have it falling in a silky snake almost to my hip. Green satin Louboutins, chunky gold hoop earrings and a pair of gold Chanel cuffs complete the look.

I hope the good people of London's tech industry appreciate my efforts. I bet they won't. I'm sure most of them have had to be dragged kicking and screaming out of their hoodies for the occasion.

Actually, forget the tech industry.

Because when I walk—okay, maybe I sashay—through the double doors of my bedroom to where Aide's waiting in my living room, the expression on his face is everything. *Everything.* It goes from gobsmacked to feral in a second flat.

'Fucking hell,' he growls, standing and coming for me

like he plans to throw me over his shoulder and take me back to his cave. 'You are magnificent.'

Yes *please.*

'Don't touch her!' Amanda, my makeup artist squeaks from behind me. Aide stops like a kid who's been caught red-handed.

'You can touch me.' I slink towards him, loving the hunger in those blue, blue eyes. 'You can *always* touch me. Just don't mess up my makeup.'

He closes the gap between us, sliding his hands around my bare waist with an appreciative hum before tilting his head to the side of my neck not sprouting a ponytail and pressing his lips to my skin. There's a hint of tongue, and I sag into him, clutching at those biceps through his impeccable Tom Ford tailoring. Jesus Christ, this man gets me horny. How can he be just as hot in a custom tux as he is in a grimy, Die-Hard-style vest?

How can that be fair?

He looks like Henry fucking Cavill on the red carpet at Cannes. Actually, forget Henry, because it's Aide who has true star quality.

It's Aide no one will be able to take their eyes off tonight.

I'm just the candy on his arm, and I couldn't be prouder.

～

THE SHALLOW STEPS leading up to the Natural History Museum's gothic entrance are covered in a wide strip of red carpet and lined with paparazzi. It turns out the guest list tonight goes way beyond the tech industry to politicians, lobbyists and celebrities, all of whom are invested in enhancing London's reputation as a hospitable base for high-growth global tech companies—not easy when Dublin has cornered the market thanks to the low Irish corporation tax rate.

As our driver drops us off and we walk along the scarlet runway to the steps, I spot the Chancellor of the Exchequer, Stella McCartney, the sexy tycoon Anton Wolff, and even Sheryl Sandberg.

Holy crap.

'Sheryl Sandberg's here and *you're* the keynote speaker?' I mutter in the direction of my hot date. 'No offence,' I add.

He laughs. 'None taken. It's ridiculous, I agree. She's speaking later, but they've asked me to open up the speeches on behalf of London-based tech companies. I'm the warm-up act.'

'No you're not,' I say. 'It makes sense, putting you on first. Also, you're hotter.'

For someone who likes to make out that he's some poor little imposter in this field, my date is every inch the suave billionaire entrepreneur this evening. He seems relaxed, jovial, and he looks a million fucking dollars. When I asked him in the car if he'd like to run through his speech with me, he shrugged the offer off.

'Nah. I don't usually overthink these things. I'll just see how it goes,' he said.

Okay then. That's impressive.

'I'd much rather spend the journey imagining finger-fucking that pussy of yours under the table later,' he added huskily in my ear. 'I cannot fucking wait to get inside you tonight.'

I quickly crossed my legs at that comment, to minimise the chances of turning up here with a wet spot on the back of my crêpe de Chine.

It's totally out of character for me, but for once I'm happy to be in someone else's shadow. I just want to sit back and bask in the reflected glory of my hot, clever boyfriend's speech.

And maybe enjoy his attentions when it's done and dusted.

∼

WE'RE SITTING beneath the vaulted ceilings of The Natural History Museum's stupendous Hintze Hall. As darkness falls, the white and pink uplighting around the space grows more dramatic. Hundreds of tea lights in glass votives flicker on the iconic Beauty-and-the-Beast-style staircase at the far end of the space.

We've drunk excellent champagne, nibbled on the prettiest canapés, and, of course, mingled. When Aide isn't being a grumpy bastard, he's effortlessly charming. No one talking to him would ever, ever be able to tell he wasn't a social animal. That he'd rather be in his quiet garden in a pair of football shorts, nursing a cold beer.

What's unsurprising is how popular he is. How many people make a beeline for him—both men and women. How many bro-hugs and back-slaps and hearty handshakes (from the men) and lecherous kisses (from the women) he gets.

What's a little more surprising, but maybe shouldn't be, because he's a sweetheart, is how intent he is on showing me off. Introducing me. Tonight's his night, but he ensures I'm involved in every situation. That my glass is always filled. That he never leaves my side.

I adore the property sector, but tonight I'm envious, because the energy in this vast room is palpable. Obviously, the numbers at stake in the tech industry are dizzying, but it's an industry I have surprisingly little exposure to, despite my dad's background. I can instantly feel the power, the money, the excitement, the ambition here.

Everyone is smart.

Hungry.

Scarily young, considering what they've achieved (Exhibit A: Aidan Duffy).

Everyone makes 'thinking big' sound like a four-year-old's imaginary play.

Sure, there are lots of nerds here, but there are also lots of folks from the commercial side, and I can smell their ambition a mile off. These people have Big Hairy Audacious Goals—BHAGs—and they are not afraid to put them out there into the universe.

I fucking *love* it. It's intoxicating. And I'm lightheaded with pride that my man plays such a central part in driving such a critical part of the economy.

Not just driving. Nurturing. Because surely, having role models like Aide, who are driven by their heart and soul, is everything when it comes to attracting the next generation of engineers? Data scientists?

My parents are here, obviously. Dad looks quietly, politely pained—he's a lot like Aide, but a lot worse at hiding it—while Mamma's wearing a couture dress from Dolce and Gabbana's last Alta Moda collection and loving every minute of this shindig. They are loving Aide and me being together, and I can't deny it's a kick to have them see us here like we're a proper couple.

Which we are.

Obviously.

My man's speech is electric. Fuck, he's amazing. He's amazing because he doesn't give a shit about any of the optics but he gives far too many shits about the real stuff, and that authenticity, that fervour, just radiates out of him.

Also because he's scarily smart and fluent and articulate and passionate. He makes it sound like he's just coming up with his beautiful, thought-provoking speech in the moment. All that, and his movie star looks, mean every person in this room is in his thrall.

He talks about the friend he lost and why he started Totum. He doesn't over-egg it; he tells the story and connects it to the wonder of technology.

Technology is hope and possibility and limitlessness. It is working with the very best of humanity and leveraging that. It is here not to replace us, but to offer us transparency. Liberty. Dignity. He talks about the awe he felt as a young teen when he discovered that the most elevated concepts in the world—love and wellbeing and community—could be transcribed in ones and zeroes. Could be captured. Quantified. Made real.

His words are poetic, and inspiring, and achingly beautiful, but they're not pompous or exclusive. Maybe that's his greatest gift—that he can speak to everyone's hearts. He's Aidan Duffy, but he's also Aide, and whatever he says about his inner conflict, about his discomfort at straddling both sides of him, I know they're one and the same.

Ladies and gentlemen. I give you *Aide Fucking Duffy*.

There isn't a person off their feet when he finishes. The soaring ceilings of the museum echo the resounding applause and cheers of what must be close to five hundred bastions of industry, politics and education. Because my Aide has touched everyone in this room tonight.

When he gets back to the table, which is a tougher journey than it sounds given the number of people who stop him for back slaps and handshakes en route, he's smiling and bashful and emotional, but I can tell he's proud of himself.

And so he fucking should be.

As for me? I'm a shaking, teary mess as I sit there with his Totum colleagues (Aide turned down the top table, apparently. Course he did). I feel shallow and inadequate and star-struck. I make a great living in a very frothy part of the market, catering to people richer than God.

My boyfriend changes lives and pools knowledge and transforms industries.

I give back and pay forward in a perfunctory, efficient and duty-fuelled way, because I know it's the right thing to do, and I know how lucky I am, and I low-key believe in karma.

My boyfriend gives back and pays forward because he has a fire in his belly, and that fire is altruism. It's a desperate desire to do better by the people who have less than him.

It's almost laughable to me now that I saw his attraction as skin-deep at first. Sure, I came for his pecs.

But I stayed for his heart.

And I'm falling for *him.*

When he gets back to the table, I jump up before any of his colleagues can get to him and throw myself smack against his chest. 'You were amazing,' I breathe against his neck. I'm sobbing. I'm totally bowled over. I hug him tighter. 'So, so bloody amazing. I'm so proud of you.'

'Hey,' he whispers, his hands moving over my bare back. 'Thank you. And I'm proud of you, too. Every day. But there's a problem.'

'What's that?' I ask with an unsexy gulp. I am in real danger of ruining my eye makeup like this. Aidan Duffy and his panda-eyed girlfriend.

He moves his mouth closer to my ear and slides a hand down over my bum. 'It's a glass-topped table,' he says, and I burst out laughing.

34

AIDE

I need *her*. Now. I've needed her all night, in fact, and I cannot wait another fucking minute.

Gabe's away, thank fuck, so the moment she closes the door of her flat behind us, I'm on her. Claiming her sweet little mouth. Clawing at her clothes. Trying to work out how the fuck to get this dress off.

Tonight was a good night—a rare work occasion where I really enjoyed myself and got swept up in the atmosphere in the room. I'd usually come home and succumb to an exhausted, introverted crash, but I hold Lotta accountable for the desire coursing through my body right now as much as I held her accountable for the grand time I had earlier.

Having her by my side all evening, watching her dazzle everyone in her path and allowing myself to drink up all that energy she shed, transformed my night from samey to special.

She's been getting me worked up in the car the whole way home, too. I'm not enough of a dick to have tried anything with the driver sitting right in front of us, but simply having my hand on the warm, smooth thigh that slit in her sexy-as-fuck dress exposed for me as she told me over and over how proud she was, how amazing I was, had happiness and hunger burning through my veins.

She also had her hand too high up my thigh in that car. Far too high.

Good job it was a fifteen-minute journey.

It seems I'm not the only one worked up. She shoves my jacket down my arms and tugs my bowtie loose and begins unbuckling my belt, her movements unusually clumsy.

'Just take my dick out,' I grunt, trying to get her hand away so I can undo my zip, but she slaps it away.

'No. Want us naked,' she practically sobs, wrenching my trousers down my legs.

That makes two of us.

'Take your dress off then, sweetheart,' I plead. 'I can't fucking get it off.'

I undo my screw-in dress shirt buttons at the speed of light and lose my shoes, socks and trousers as Lotta locates some hidden zip over her arse. Then she's undone the neck of her dress and the entire thing falls to the floor, a heavy emerald curtain that leaves her stunning body on display in just a green lace thong.

Jesus fucking Christ. Sorry, St Aidan, for the blasphemy.

She's in my arms in a second and on the rug a second after that. I crouch over her and peel the thong down her shapely legs, leaving her stark naked aside from those green fuck-me heels and her jewellery, and oh my God. I have never, ever seen anything more beautiful, or carnal, or inviting in my life.

'Aide.' Unbelievably, she's looking at me with what seems like an equally spellbound, ravenous expression. She reaches out for me with both arms and I crawl over her like a fucking predator.

And I am.

Because I am going to fucking devour her.

I sink down, bracing on my elbows so I can dip my head and take as much of one glorious tit as possible in my mouth. There's no finesse. I don't have time for it. I'm shaking with need. I lave at her skin, I suck on her nipple, I grind against her with my lips and tongue and beard and she's fucking crying out and writhing under me, pushing her tit into my mouth as she winds her legs around me and attempts to pull me against that needy, glorious pussy. A stiletto heel digs into my arse, and the sharp pain has the flames of my desire licking higher.

Jesus *fuck*.

I release her nipple and find her lips as I crash my mouth down upon hers, invading it with my tongue, ravaging it and swallowing up her incredible, throaty whimpers. Sliding one hand under that fine arse of hers, I hold her in place as I position myself at her entrance. I'm hard as fuck and I'm being too hurried, but she's already slick and ready, thank God, and I push in. Hard.

Oh my God. Oh my sweet mother of Christ.

She is so fucking tight. As her intimate muscles clench around me, and she gasps into my mouth, I experience a jolt of pleasure so intense it almost has me blacking out.

'Fuck,' I mumble. 'You okay?'

'Fuck me, honey.'

'I won't last,' I say hoarsely, because the climax of heat, of pressure at the base of my spine and in my balls is almost upon me, I can tell.

'I need it hard,' she pants. 'I'm close. Just—oh my *God.*'

God is what she says as I take her invitation at face value, pulling almost all the way out of her and ramming back home as hard, as roughly as I possibly can.

I'm a fucking animal. I have this impossibly beautiful, delicate creature writhing below me, impaled on my cock, and I won't rest until I've railed her so hard she won't walk for days. Fucking hell. I'm barely conscious, barely functioning. My primal brain takes over and I do all I'm capable of, which is kissing this beautiful woman while I rut into her, hard as I can.

Her hands are around my arse too, working in tandem with her heels to keep me driving into her. Her moans are wilder, deeper than most of her orgasms. Her touch spurs me on. Her cries spur me on. The unfuckingbelievable sensation of her interior walls sucking me in spurs me on.

I'm close.

Jesus, I'm so close.

Our skin slicks damply together as we move in tandem. My rhythm is punishing, but I couldn't slow down if I wanted to. I'm in freefall. I've ceded all control to the most ancient parts of my makeup.

'I'm—I'm—oh my God!' she cries, and then she's convulsing around me, her walls squeezing my dick all the way to heaven as her long nails dig into my arse cheeks. It's too much, too much sensation, and emotion, and intensity.

Too much *everything*.

I freeze for a second as the white-hot blaze of my orgasm races through my balls and down my dick and then I'm bucking and rutting like a fucking madman, spilling myself into Lotta's willing, miraculous body until I'm emptied. Wrung out.

I collapse on top of her, speechless and dazed, kissing her neck. Smoothing her ponytail. We're both slick with sweat. She runs her hands up my back and hugs me as hard as she can.

I never want to leave this place.

◠

LOTTA

The glow in my heart is real this morning.

The spring in my step belies the tenderness between my legs.

Because, clearly not content with having movie-star looks, a heart of gold and a brain that's frankly terrifying, my boyfriend has to be the best kind of animal between the sheets.

And on the rug.

We made it to the bed at after that first attempt and fucked twice more. I swear something shifted last night for both of us. Maybe it was being on our first official public engagement together. For me, seeing him up there on that stage, making everyone in that vast museum fall in love with him and his heart and his vision, was the best kind of turn-on.

Knowing a guy with Aide's undeniable magnetic pull wants to come home to me, wants as much of me as he can get, wants me so badly he fucks me right there on the floor, is on a different level entirely. It makes my heart swell so much in my ribcage that I might burst.

Every day, it seems I uncover more of this man's essence. He's layered like no one else I've met. Nuanced. And a little damaged. But the parts of his soul that I know still hurt are the same parts that make him good and real, that give him depth and spur him on.

He still carries the weight of the world on his shoulders. Everyone can see how much good he does, but it's never enough for him.

It'll never be enough.

And if I'm someone who can help him forget those burdens, if he can find peace and relief and oblivion and ecstasy in my arms, then I am the luckiest, most privileged girl in the world.

Because whether he's shooting his load inside me, or smiling down at me, or simply letting that dangerous mouth of his roam over my body, he's choosing to see me as a safe place to lay down his worries and allow himself to indulge.

To be.

And there's nothing on earth like knowing I can give him that.

I would give this man everything if I could.

Everything.

That gets clearer every day. I'm falling so hard for him. My feelings are a never-ending vortex, every layer he uncovers for me sending me deeper into this abyss of white-hot lust and adoration. I mean, the physical side is actually insane. Yeah, I'm a physical creature. I enjoy touch. I have a healthy sex drive.

But I've never been like this—so utterly addicted to another human being that I would crawl under his skin if I could, that I can barely function when he's not inside me. I've never felt so clearly like heaven and earth are colliding as I do when I'm with Aide. In his orbit.

I'd say I'm in trouble, but it's the best I've ever, ever felt. The happiest I've ever been. And, while we haven't talked about our feelings outright, I'm growing quietly confident that he's not immune, either. He doesn't strike me as an emotionally slutty guy or someone who'd lead me on. On the contrary, he's straight as a die. And he's been doing an admirable job of not letting my shallow, extravagant lifestyle freak him out too much.

In fact, I bit the bullet and asked what I've been wanting

to ask him for days now. The thing I was afraid would have him running for the hills, because it really, really could.

I asked him to be my date to Elle Hart and Josh Lander's fabulous, star-studded wedding at Noah's parents' chateau in a couple of weeks.

Basically, I was asking him to do everything he hated. Put on a tux (again), hang out with wealthy, entitled people in their wealthy, entitled bubble, make small talk, deal with unwanted attention, and not freak out over the—in his eyes —excess he'll bear witness to for the entire weekend, even if I know Elle and Josh will put on a classy and gorgeous and dreamy few days for us all.

I was also, it turns out, asking him to miss the kids' party the community centre is throwing to celebrate the start of the summer holidays, which I feel awful about. The irony of asking my gorgeous and deserving, if reluctant, billionaire, to forgo an event that close to his heart to party with the rich and famous isn't lost on me.

But you know what?

He said yes.

35

AIDE

'There was an article about us in the *Post* today,' Lotta says. 'Did you see it?'

'Nope.' I put my finger in my cold war thriller and close the book over, twisting onto my side so I can give her my full attention. We're sprawled next to each other on the huge sofa on my terrace, our stomachs full of Maggie's excellent barbecued chicken and salad. I've been lying on my back, a few scatter cushions stuffed behind my head.

Lotts is on her front in a t-shirt and those obligatory cutoffs, bare feet up and waving in the air as she devours some mafia romance with a terrifying-looking guy on the cover. She told me the plot. It sounds fucking awful, except for the bit where she mentioned I'd make a brilliant mafia boss and that maybe we could do some role-play where I kidnap her and fuck her brains out.

I'm not sure what fucked-up part of me really likes the sound of that, but it does, and I'm game if she is. Shouldn't be much of a hardship.

It's a low-key Wednesday evening. We've had a quiet week socially so far, but we fly to Toulon on Friday for this bloody wedding, so I'll take my quiet, intimate evenings while I can. Lotta is more excited than I've ever seen her about the wedding, and that's saying something for a woman as naturally effusive as her.

Between the couture dress she's had made for the ceremony, and the uni friends she's looking forward to seeing, and the A-list celebrities who may or may not show up, she hasn't stopped talking about it. While I love seeing her like this, I certainly can't muster up much excitement about a celebrity wedding. It's bound to be a total fucking circus. I just hope babysitting my sorry arse won't be too much of a shag for Lotts.

I am, however, very much looking forward to escaping the circus on Sunday and absconding to an idyllic boutique hotel near St Maxime with my stunning girlfriend for twenty-four hours of, hopefully, nudity.

'What was the article about?' I ask now. I slide my hand onto the small of her back, tugging up the hem of her t-shirt, and splay my fingers over her bare skin.

Everything is better when I'm touching Lotta.

'Well, it was about you, really. I'm just in it as the glamorous love interest.' She smiles like she knows she's a lot more than that but like it's kind of tickled, her too. 'They called it *Aidan Duffy's Charmed Life*.'

'What the actual fuck? That's a fucking joke. Did they erase the first twenty years, or something?'

'That's just it. They said your story is like some Jeffrey Archer rags-to-riches novel, like you're the plucky hero who's full of ambition but has never lost sight of his roots, you know?' She tosses her hair jokingly. 'And meeting the beautiful heiress is the icing on the cake. You'll be glad to know you've officially arrived, according to the *Post*, at least.'

'What a bunch of horseshit,' I say. I hold her more

tightly and flip her onto her side, pulling her in flush against me. 'Except for the bit about the beautiful heiress,' I murmur as I lower my mouth to capture hers.

~

THE ARTICLE IS, as I suspected, total fucking horseshit. It also has a tone I don't appreciate, like I'm supposed to be in this smug, self-congratulatory bubble of knowing I've got the money, the trappings, and the girl.

None of it sits quite right with me.

None of it feels accurate. I suppose it's easy for them to judge, easy for them to see some clear story arc, a hero's journey of such linear upward momentum that it looks like a fucking hockey stick, when really, the wealth is uncomfortable, and the trappings are as limited as I've been able to keep them.

The *girl* part's true, though. The odious journos at the *Post* are right—she's the ultimate prize. But not because she's some gorgeous, lithe, impeccably stylish trophy like they've insinuated.

No fucking way.

Because women don't come much more impressive than Carlotta Montefiore-Charlton. It's occurred to me gradually over the past few weeks that historically I've had a type: the shy, wholesome girl next door who tends to lean on me. I don't need Freud to tell me I feel validated when I'm needed.

Lotta definitely doesn't need me, and it's refreshing. It's good for me. She's a professional powerhouse with a seemingly endless appetite for work. For fun. For *life*. Her energy is infectious. *She's* good for me. And while she seems to appreciate me and my company, she's not needy. We're not co-dependent. For all our differences, this closeness, this intimacy that we're building, is born out of each of us finding our equal in the other.

And I really, really love it.

I still feel an element of unease, though, at this seemingly relentless upwards journey. At how well everything's going, both with Totum and with my personal life. So when I get a text from Judy, I actually laugh in horror, because it's as if my inner self-saboteur has conjured this shit-show up.

With one simple text, my obligations to my past and my fragile hopes for my future are strung up against each other like contestants in an amphitheatre.

> Shayla's in labour. Five weeks early. Can u
> help this weekend?

Fuck fuck fuck. Shayla is Sylvie's daughter. Five weeks early does not sound good—this is a shit show. And of course Sylv will want to be by her side the whole time.

This is a fucking disaster.

Fuck.

I text back tentatively.

> Oh no. I'm sorry. What kind of timings?

She comes straight back.

> Setup tomorrow. Party 11-4 sat

I grimace and suck air in through my teeth as noisily as if someone's just punched me in the gut, because that's what it feels like. Could this timing be any worse?

> I'm supposed to be somewhere. Is there anyone else who can help? Gaz?

I stare anxiously at the three little dots.

> G couldn't organise a piss-up in a brewery. Anyway he's on a long-haul to Europe.

> Will get more volunteers but need someone who can lead this or it'll be a total shitshow

There is no easy solution here; I know that much. But fuck, most of the state schools break up for the summer holidays tomorrow and our kids and their parents are staring down the barrel of seven weeks off school with none of the structures or entertainment or childcare or fucking *meals* they have in place during term-time, and this party is a big deal for them. It's our way of reminding them that the summer can be fun, that they've nailed another whole school year, and, most importantly, that we're here for them.

The bottom line is that they need me and Lotta doesn't. Sure, she wants me there; she's excited to introduce me to her mates. She's excited for our first trip abroad together. But she doesn't *need* me. She'll know tonnes of people there and she won't have to worry about babysitting me.

She'll get over it.

The kids won't get over it if their party goes south.

Fuck.

> Got it. I'll be there.

I drag my hand over my face before hovering my finger over Lotta's number.

~

LOTTA

'Hi, honey,' I coo. 'Guess what? The dresses just arrived. They're *amazing*.' Not amazing enough to remotely risk upstaging the bride, who's going to look so beautiful I can't even imagine it, but amazing enough to feel very good about being on my boyfriend's arm this weekend. The rehearsal dinner one is a slinky, silk jersey coral number by Astrid Carmichael, while the gown for Saturday's ceremony is Chanel. It's pale aquamarine tulle, and sparkly, and to die for.

The smile on his gorgeous face is weak and tired. 'I bet you'll look gorgeous in them.'

I swivel away from my desk in my chair. 'What's up?'

'Lotts.' He closes his eyes and frowns. 'I'm so sorry. I can't make it this weekend.'

'You can't—*what?*' I stare at him in horror, waiting for him to grant me eye contact and explain himself, because it sounds like he's standing me up.

He opens his eyes slowly and squints at his screen like he's afraid of what he'll see on my face.

Damn right.

'There's been an emergency,' he begins. 'Sylvie's daughter, Shayla, is in labour. She's five weeks early.'

'Oh no!' I clap my hand over my mouth. Sylvie's been so excited about this baby. It'll be her first grandchild. But even I know five weeks premature is far from ideal. 'Is she okay? Is the baby okay?'

'I don't have many details—I just got a call from Judy. But it's the summer party at the centre this weekend and

Judy can't make it. They need someone in there running the kitchen so it doesn't all go to shit, so I've agreed to do it.'

'But you're not a chef,' I say, 'and they've got other volunteers who can help in the kitchen, don't they? Can't they get someone else to do it?'

He sighs and rubs his thumb and forefinger over his eyes. 'They've got some volunteers, yeah, but Sylv and Judy run that place. Judy can't do it by herself, baby. She's too old. She needs someone there who knows the place like the back of their hand. I can take care of it all for her.'

And there we have it.

I can take care of it all for her.

Fucking Aide and his fucking saviour complex.

'I'm so sorry about Sylvie's daughter,' I say, making a concerted effort to keep my temper. 'It's absolutely awful. But the community centre isn't your problem this weekend, because you already made a commitment. *To me.* Remember? You can't pull out of a wedding just like that.'

'I hate doing this to you,' he tells me, finally raising those big, blue eyes to me. I know he believes he's telling the truth. 'But I have no choice. I can't let those kids down, sweetheart. They need me a lot more than you do.'

Oh, for fuck's sake.

'They'll always need *help* a lot more than me,' I tell him, and yeah, I raise my voice, because I'm now seriously fucked off. 'But they don't need you. They need a support system, and adults who are there for them, but that doesn't fall on you, okay? And don't tell me they need you more than I do because they'll *always* win that argument if you let them.'

'What am I supposed to do?' he asks. 'I can't let this go south for them. If I don't help, Judy might have to cancel the party—there's no way I'm letting that happen.'

'Honey,' I say. 'It's not incumbent on you to make sure

that place looks after itself. I know it means a lot to you, but you've pumped so much time and money into it already. You gave up two weeks of your time for it last month—that's a *lot*. If you're so worried about it not being able to run itself then throw some more money at it and hire a fucking full-time manager who'll be available for all these emergencies. *It's not your problem.*'

'It's just a one-off,' he pleads. 'I'll make it up to you. We can go away next weekend. Or—I know—I'll fly out late Saturday or first thing Sunday and we can still do our quiet time together. But I told Judy I'll be there tomorrow and Saturday, so there's nothing I can do about that.'

'Wrong,' I bark. 'You should've told her you'd be away tomorrow and Saturday and that there was nothing you could do except maybe offer to hire someone. Don't go breaking your word to me like it means nothing and then make me feel like I'm being a selfish bitch for calling you out on it. You and I had a trip planned. You don't get to go all unilateral and cancel it without checking with me first. It's just so fucking *rude*.'

'I get that you're upset,' he says, pacing back and forth in his office. 'But it's an emergency. I'm sure you've had work emergencies you've had to cancel stuff for in the past.'

'Yeah, because it's my business,' I say. 'And if it was a crisis at Totum, I'd get it, because your duty is to your investors. But you're not these kids' parent. You need boundaries, Aide. There's always going to be something with these kids. You can't just toss aside your plans and your personal life and my feelings anytime there's a hiccup. *Jesus.*

'It's like you can't bear to allow yourself a weekend of indulgence when other people are out there suffering. I get it! But at the level of wealth you've got to, there will always be that conflict, and you've got to find a way of squaring it off without thinking you have to sacrifice all your own pleasure in this desperate attempt to keep everyone else afloat.'

I pause, because I'm out of breath, and I'm so angry I'm shaking, and I'm also so angry that I can't actually keep my train of thought straight in my head. I am fucking furious that he's bailed on me without a backwards glance, and I'm equally furious that in his head he's some sort of martyr whose focus on the greater good is so unwavering that it makes people like me, who just want to have a good time, look like they have their priorities wrong.

If it was a real crisis I'd be understanding. Of course I would. I'd be gutted, but I'd give him my blessing. But I know, I just *know*, he's doing this out of some fucked-up lack of boundaries rather than because there is no practical solution.

Aide's a fucking tech genius. If anyone can find a practical solution that doesn't involve him missing the wedding weekend, it's him. I recall a phrase I read once. *If you can afford to solve a problem, you don't have a problem.* Of course he could throw some money at this situation and get it sorted. But he just can't help himself.

'I wish I could get out of this, but I can't,' he says in this martyred, patient tone that makes my palm twitch, because *fuck* is it self-righteous and irritating. 'If I thought there were options, I'd have called you up first. But I'm doing this, and I'm just really fucking sorry I'll be missing out on our trip. I know you'll have a blast. Think of me when you're partying away, yeah? I'll probably be clearing squashed sausage rolls off the floor.'

'Don't you dare play the hard-done-by card with me,' I tell him through gritted teeth. 'It's very clear that you're doing exactly what you want in this scenario, and that's wading in to play St Aidan again instead of treating the commitment you made to me this weekend as anything remotely sacred. And don't even think about trying to fly out on Sunday. I'll speak to you when I'm back.'

And with that, I end the FaceTime and immediately put my phone on Do Not Disturb mode. It's childish, and churlish, but I can't take another second of the smug self-righteousness on that gorgeous face of his.

36

LOTTA

There was an empty spot in my bed last night where St Aidan, Christian martyr, should have been, and now there's a very luxurious and very empty seat next to me on The Montague Group's private jet, which is even more shit. He bombarded me with voice notes and texts and calls yesterday, but I only allowed myself to respond once.

> I'd rather not talk to you till after the weekend. I know you believe you're doing the right thing, but you've completely failed to consider my feelings, and that's really hurtful. I'll speak to you on Tues.

We're in the Montagues' jet thanks to my old friend Theo. I was at uni with him, I've known him forever, and we even fucked back when I was, like, seventeen. His family owns a massive group of high-end hotels, and Theo was the nightmare middle child and exhibitionist playboy until he reconnected with his now-fiancée, Nora, who was also at uni with us. Unlike Theo, she's the most sensible person who has ever lived, and she's been an amazing influence on him.

The man is besotted.

Also on the jet is my friend Honor Chapman, who we know through our gorgeous bride-to-be, Elle, and Honor's husband, Noah, aka Dr Noah Thierry, aka Aide's mate, at whose massive family vineyard the wedding is. While I'm always happy to see these two, I really hope Noah doesn't go too Team Aide on me.

For his own sake.

'Am I being unreasonable?' I ask my friends, having filled them in on the sorry story of my absentee boyfriend as we took off. I cast a desolate look at the unoccupied expanse of soft cream leather beside me before taking a decent slug of my mimosa. Aide's missing everything, including this flight, getting to know Nora and Theo, and the incredibly cute peony-print Zimmerman sundress I chose as my travel ensemble. I feel so hard done-by I'm tempted to throw a full-on tantrum. 'And, obviously, *yes* is not an acceptable answer.'

'Absolutely not,' Nora says, sipping her drink. She's willowy and gorgeous, with glossy light-brown hair and big green eyes. 'I'd like to see Theo pull a stunt like that on me.'

Theo's *I wouldn't fucking dare* grimace makes me giggle, because I'd like to see him try, too.

'It's not cool in the slightest,' Honor agrees. 'But it's incredibly irritating that he's off doing good. It kind of gives him a *get out of jail free* card, you know?' She's the ultimate private jet traveller in a sleek cream jumpsuit, her shoulder-length chestnut hair immaculately tonged and her full lips a perfect matte scarlet.

'Exactly,' I say. 'Look, I know it's a new relationship. We're still trying to work out how we fit, but it's not a great start to pull out of our first trip together so he can go off and sate his saviour complex.'

I may have muttered the words *saviour* and *complex* together far too many times in the past twenty hours.

'It's not a bad turn of phrase for Aide,' Noah says. 'It's a real thing. But I suspect with Aide it's more a case of good, old-fashioned guilt.'

'Yeah,' I say despondently into my champagne flute.

'That guy spends his life acting like he can't believe he got a place on the lifeboat, so he won't rest until he's pulled every last person out of the sea,' Noah observes.

That gets my attention.

I raise my head and gape at him.

'Even if it means he capsizes himself, I reckon,' he adds.

'Jesus Christ, darling,' Honor says with an eye-roll. 'That's a bit fucking depressing.'

'Seriously,' I mutter. That's the kind of analogy that makes me want to burst into tears, because if Noah's right, my gorgeous, huge-hearted Aide can't turn this off. He's so consistently focused on the gap between what he has and what others don't that he can't enjoy his success, or even justify it to himself, unless he feels he's acting to bridge that gap.

That's going to burn a guy out pretty quickly.

'Sorry,' Noah says, putting his arm around his wife and shooting me the kind of radiant, competent, sincere smile that single-handedly explains how he bagged himself one of the most beautiful celebrities on the planet. 'You spend as much time as me with people who are dying, you tend to fancy yourself as an armchair philosopher.'

'You were right,' I tell Honor. 'The worst part of this is that I'm sitting here, on a private jet, slagging my gorgeous, amazing boyfriend off for being a thoroughly decent person.

And I know he is. It's one of the things I lo—adore about him the most. I'd just like to come first when it counts. And Theo'—I hold up a finger sternly—'don't even think about making an innuendo.'

Theo smirks. 'Actually, I was going to say you should remind him that charity begins at home.'

'That would be marginally less obnoxious if you weren't sitting there drinking your parents' Dom Perignon while you said it,' Nora tells him, shooting him a look so contemptuous that I snort.

'Ugh,' I moan when I've recovered. 'I won't talk about him all weekend. I promise. I just miss him.' I pick at a fleck of something on my dress. 'I kind of wish he was just a nice, straightforward, hot builder, after all.'

'How do you mean?' Nora asks, leaning forward to daintily spear a slice of mango from the fruit platter with her fork.

'Oh.' I realise they don't know the full details of our backstory. 'Well, when I showed up to do the community centre refurb thingy, I thought he was just this grumpy dickhead called Aide who was also unbelievably hot.'

'You're kidding me,' Noah says, his jaw falling open.

'Nope. As a matter of fact, when you turned up I don't think I knew who he was—no, I didn't. He was so chippy and judgemental—he obviously didn't approve of me. But then he kept making inappropriate comments about my boobs, and all I could think about was how much I wanted to rip off his stupid vest and lick those insane biceps, and finally we, you know, fucked. But I threw him out right afterwards because I'd found out right before that he'd been lying to me.'

'Bloody hell,' Honor says, her gorgeous tiger eyes wide. 'What happened then?'

I sigh. 'I went to his office to have it out with him and it was all a bit embarrassing, actually, because it turns out we'd met before, years ago, and my dad was actually his seed investor. So the joke was on me. And then he fucked me on his office sofa and we made up.'

Theo winks at me. 'That's my girl.'

'And ironically,' I continue, 'he's the first actual billionaire I've dated.' I blow out a breath. 'I thought it'd be more fun.'

'Something tells me you're not with him for his money,' Noah says softly, 'so I'm sure you can have fun without him this weekend. And you two will hopefully get a chance to talk through all this properly when you've had the weekend to put a bit of space between you.'

'Noah's right,' Nora says. 'You've always been the biggest party girl I know. We're going to have a blast. It'll be amazing! I'm telling you—it's the wedding of the century. There's no way you won't have fun.' She pauses. 'And if what you and Noah say is true, then it sounds like you've found yourself a seriously amazing guy. But maybe he'd benefit from you spelling out that you need him, too. You're so confident and dazzling. He probably thinks you've got this without him.'

I shrug. 'I'm sure you're right. What the hell.' I hold out my glass for a mimosa refill. 'Half of Hollywood should be there, right? There's no way I'm moping my way through a weekend like this. It's his loss.'

I'll have an amazing weekend. I'll dazzle and party and shine like I always do, and I'll try not to think about my beautiful boyfriend and the fact that, right now, he's in that community centre, working his arse off for those poor little kiddies.

37

AIDE

'Baby's here!' Judy shouts, bustling into the kitchen and brandishing her ancient iPhone. It's probably, like, an iPhone Three, if that ever existed.

I stand up and shut the fridge with a grimace. I've been bent over, trying to fit in every last item of food from the massive delivery we've received.

'Thank fuck,' I say. 'What is it?'

'A little girl.' She beams. 'No photos yet. Or a name.'

I close my eyes. *A little girl.* A tiny granddaughter for Sylv. That is just fucking amazing. It makes me want to well up. 'Everyone doing okay?' I ask huskily. 'Mum and baby?'

'Sounds like it.' She looks at her phone again. 'The baby's going into the neo-natal ward, but Sylv says the docs are happy.'

'Well, I think that calls for a coffee break,' I say. 'What do you reckon?'

'Abso-fucking-lutely.' She puts her phone down on the work surface and heads for the Nespresso machine. Sylv wasn't the only one Lotta got hooked on this stuff.

The mere sight of it makes my chest ache.

I've felt torn in two since I spoke to her. I know what I did to her was seriously shitty, and I one hundred percent deserved for her to call me out and, to be honest, for her to put some distance between us. But it didn't make it any easier.

I hated being apart from her last night, I hated hearing that hurt and disappointment in her voice, and I hate even more knowing she's en route to France with her friends and I'm not there by her side.

I can't even imagine how pissed off I'll feel tomorrow night, knowing she's ripping up that dance floor with proper movie stars. Davide de Luca's going to be there, apparently. So's Brad Burton. It'll be like the Cannes fucking Film Festival over there.

And something tells me my girl won't be short of attention.

I grit my teeth and set to work with the Nespresso machine.

'Everything okay?' Judy asks as I wearily usher her out the kitchen door and into the yard area in front of me.

'Fine.' I rub my eyes as I put my cup down on the shitty uneven table. 'I'm just tired.' I'm exhausted, actually, because doing what I thought was the right thing did not sit easily with me last night and upsetting Lotts sat even less easily. Ergo, sleep was not my friend.

'I see.' She sits down heavily and I observe, not for the first time, that she's getting frail. Stiff. 'And how's Lotta?'

'She's fine.'

She purses her lips. 'How excellent that everyone is *fine*. What's going on?'

'Nothing.'

'Nothing. Jesus Christ, you dimwit. You realise you two getting together is one of the most exciting and happy things that has ever happened in my life?' She glares at me. 'You're the son I never had, and she'd damn well better be my daughter-in-law at some point, so don't fuck this up. What. Is. Going. On? Where is she this weekend?'

I sigh but stop short of an eye roll because I value my safety. 'She's in France,' I concede.

'How nice. And what's she doing there?'

'She's at a wedding.'

'Delightful.'

This fucking woman.

'Did you not get invited to the wedding?' she asks with an innocent sip of her espresso. She's even holding her pinky out. Honestly.

'I did,' I tell her, 'but this is more important.'

'I see. Is that the thing you said you had on when I texted you yesterday?'

I hesitate. 'Yeah.'

She sets down her cup.

Uh-oh.

'Let me get this straight,' she says in a faux-pleasant voice that doesn't fool me for a second. 'You are supposed to be at some, presumably glamorous, wedding in France, but you pulled out to help me?'

'To help everyone,' I clarify. 'I didn't want it being a nightmare for you or a washout for the kids.'

'And what does Lotta think about this?'

'She's really fucked off,' I admit.

'Shocker.'

'Judy.'

'Don't you *Judy* me, young man.'

I try again. 'I understand why she's upset with me, and I feel awful. But I know she'll be fine. It's some huge, ridiculous celebrity wedding, and they're her friends, and—'

Her gasp stops me. 'Do *not* tell me it's Josh Lander and Elle Hart's wedding.'

I wince. 'Yeah.'

'Oh my *God*.' She whacks me hard on the bicep, and it fucking hurts.

'Ow!'

'You stupid fucking dipshit,' she howls. 'God, I want to physically hurt you. What is wrong with you?'

'What's wrong with me? I pulled out because I couldn't leave you in the lurch! You told me it'd be a shitshow without me.'

She tuts. 'Fuck's *sake*. You know me. Of course I'm always going to give you a sob story, but Jesus, Aide, I would have worked something out. And *you* should be in France with your beautiful, probably soon-to-be-ex girlfriend.' For good measure, she jabs me with an evil forefinger right in the spot she just walloped.

'It's too late,' I say. 'She's probably almost there already, and you were in a tough spot. It was the right call. Honestly, I don't mind.'

That makes her slump. She buries her head in her hands and groans before looking up at me and laying a gnarled hand gently on my forearm. For some reason, it's more ominous than the physical pain she just inflicted on me with seeming pleasure.

'Aide,' she says. 'You are a good boy. You've always been *such* a good boy. You're also the cleverest kid I've ever seen. But sometimes you are thick as pig shit.' She shakes her head sadly.

'Hey,' I protest.

'No. You need to hear this. Aide, sweetheart, the more you give, the more people will take. Even me. I gave you a sob story and now I feel horrible, but I would have thought you'd have the common *fucking* sense'—she taps her temple pointedly with her other hand—'to know when to say no. You should have said no. You should have told me it wasn't your problem. You had somewhere to be with your lovely girlfriend, and it wasn't fucking here. Got it?'

It's incredibly frustrating when you try to do the right thing and everyone gives you a hard time over it. 'But you needed me,' I say, trying to be patient.

'Nope.' She shakes her head. 'Wrong answer. Because it was not your problem. You've already funded the whole bloody party. You need to learn to say no, boyo. Otherwise everyone in this godforsaken world will keep on asking you to jump, and you'll keep on asking *how high* like a total fucking idiot. *You need to learn. To say no.* Because everyone will always want a piece of you, and that includes us lot and your fancy business friends.' She pauses. 'And most definitely your family.'

I go rigid.

'Yep,' she insists. 'While I'm telling you things you don't want to hear, I'll tell you this. That brother of yours is a useless, freeloading piece of shit, and Veronica, God bless her, has had a shitty time of it and still leans on you far too much.'

I go to protest, but she holds up a hand. 'As do I. We've all got so used to being taken care of by you, Aide dearest, because you're very good at it. But we forget, because you're so loyal and hardworking and never complain, that we're taking the piss, basically.'

'You're not,' I say hoarsely. 'None of you are. I'm glad to do it. It's important to me.'

'I know it is.' She nods. 'But, for once, you should go and look after number one and that lovely girlfriend of yours.'

'Thank you,' I say, and I mean it, because even if it

doesn't change anything, hearing the words, knowing my efforts are seen and appreciated, that I've helped someone, makes a massive difference. 'But I'm here now, so let's forget it, okay? I'll make it up to Lotts. She'll have the time of her life, so don't worry about her.'

'Oh, but I do worry,' Judy says, 'because her boyfriend is too fucking stupid to worry. You know Davide de Luca's going to be there? You think these Hollywood sleazeballs won't be all over her like a rash? And she'll be feeling rejected, and lonely, and maybe in need of some comfort from a nice-looking film star who has enough of a brain to know a good thing when he sees one...'

She tails off and purses her lips at me with her signature unimpressed look.

I have to say, it'd wither a lesser man.

'Come on, mate,' she says, when I remain outwardly impassive. 'Lotta won't cheat on you, more's the pity, because you don't deserve her. But she *will* miss you, and if you want any future with her, that has got to be more important than always being here whenever anyone wants a bit of you.

'So I'm going to make it crystal clear, because you're obviously more of a thicko than I thought. The only person you have an obligation to this weekend is Carlotta. *So go and get her.*'

'But what would you do?' I ask, my mind starting to whirr with possibilities.

'I will get on the volunteers WhatsApp group and give them an even bigger sob story than I gave you,' she says. 'And I'll pin someone down. One of the cooks at the school will probably do it—they're always happy to make a few bob on the side.' She gives me a pointed look. 'You're paying.'

'Obviously,' I say. I spread my palms on the table,

looking at her with dawning hope, and astonishment, and not a little emotion, because I feel like I've been set free.

Absolved.

It's the strangest sensation.

And suddenly I cannot wait to see Lotta.

'How am I supposed to get there?' I ask.

She looks up from her phone. 'Jesus Christ. I'm trying to organise this fucking party. Don't you have a jet on speed dial or something?'

'No,' I say. 'They're awful for the environment.'

She rolls her eyes and returns to her texting. 'You are by far the most disappointing billionaire I've ever met. Make some calls. Go on. Shoo.'

38

LOTTA

Not only am I at one of the most iconic restaurants the past seven decades have produced in France, but I'm being chatted up by an actual sex symbol. Like, a guy who's been voted GQ's Sexiest Man Alive.

Davide de Luca, groom Josh Landers' best buddy, Hollywood superstar and delicious male specimen from the top of his tousled dark head to the tips of his loafer-clad toes, is making it abundantly clear that the only dessert he's interested in later tonight is *me*.

And what do I feel?

Not a *thing*.

Fucking Aide.

Tomorrow evening's ceremony and party will be under the stars at the beautifully-named Chateau des Anges— Castle of the Angels—but tonight, the great and good of the movie world have gathered at Le Club 55 on St Tropez's famous Pampelonne Beach.

The sky is a gorgeous haze of azure melting into golds and pinks and peaches. The Mediterranean sea is still as a mill-pond, a sparkling, blush-coloured mirror broken only the enormous white super-yachts dotted around. Several of our guests have, in fact, arrived by tender this evening and will head back out to their floating gin palaces when the night's festivities are done.

But I doubt that'll be for quite some time. Beachy, abstract remixes of Françoise Hardy are playing overhead, and the rosé and champagne are flowing, except to our pregnant bride, Elle and those who, like Josh, are in recovery.

The throng of beautiful people is thick, and the conversation is loud. Le Club 55 has always had a low-key vibe— think Demi back in the day with a single button of Bruce's linen shirt fastened over her bikini. But tonight, we've kicked it up a notch. The uneven wooden boards covering the sandy floor of the restaurant may call for flat sandals or bare feet, but the resort-wear people are sporting is nothing short of fabulous.

Still, I'm holding my own. My skin is glowing from the past few weekends spent sunbathing by The Saint's pool, and my silk jersey dress is comfortable yet sexy, with a plunging neckline and a daring thigh slit. Its gorgeous, deep coral shade shows off my tan and matches my lip gloss. Mr de Luca is definitely eyeing my exposed skin with approval.

I've long held a view that real, A-list celebrities tend to fall into two camps. The coked-up ones who can barely hold eye contact, or the really good ones who make everyone feel like they're the only person in the room.

Unfortunately for me, Davide is the latter.

Unfortunately for him, my only reaction is to muse that this guy would probably do well if he ran for office.

He's not even up his own arse. His latest movie, the one that premiered at Cannes a couple of months ago, is tipped for an Oscar nod, but is he blathering on about it?

Nope.

Instead, he's peppering me with thoughtful, intelligent questions about the top end of the residential property market in London. He even mentions he's considering buying a pied-à-terre there. If I gave a single shit, I could probably sign him as a new client.

But I don't give a shit, and it's really fucking annoying. Obviously, I'm tickled to have attracted such a massive star's attention. If it wasn't for my fucking, do-gooder boyfriend, I would one hundred percent fuck this guy and enjoy every minute of the experience. Elle would be thrilled—she's had me earmarked for Davide for months, and since the invitations went out, it's been a bit of a running joke between us all that I should hook up with him. With Nora obviously besotted and off the market, I was Elle's Great White Hope for a fellow Cambridge-Hollywood couple (or at least hookup).

It is no exaggeration to say I've been looking forward to this wedding for months.

Fucking Aide.

I'm not one to mope, though. Nor am I one to waste an experience this incredible on feeling a little heartbroken and a lot let down by a guy.

Even if the guy is the single most miraculous person I've ever met.

So I throw myself into it. I mingle. I drink. I enjoy the delicious canapés that are being handed around. I allow myself to soak up the unmistakable scent of the sea, and of the nearby pines, and of the incredible food being cooked up for us.

I revel in the atmosphere of this once-in-a-lifetime event at a place that has so much history. God, some of the guests here tonight probably decorate the walls along with Bardot.

I admire the understated perfection of the view, not only of the sparkling sea in the early evening sun, but of the restaurant itself, with its ancient, white-cushioned benches, its uneven wooden tables, and the faded white sheets that, when strung over the beams overhead, offer much-needed shade during the day. Tonight, those sheets are pulled to one side so we can feast under the stars as night falls.

Davide ushers me over to the edge of the crowd, off the boards and down onto the sand, so we can admire the view. I let my eyes drift closed and absorb the sounds, the smells. I've already referenced Aide several times in our conversation, but either he doesn't think an absentee boyfriend is a problem for him or he's genuinely happy to chat to someone who's not available. Who knows?

'Do you come here when you do Cannes?' I ask him.

'Yeah, if I can,' he answers. 'I usually have someone take me on their boat.'

'Makes sense,' I say. Getting here by boat from Cannes takes under an hour, so it's easily do-able. 'It's probably still a circus, though?'

'The whole of the Cote d'Azur's a circus in May,' he says. 'I've been here in September before, when all the Parisians have gone home but the beach clubs are still open and the heat is a little less intense—it's beautiful then. I think it's one of the most beautiful parts of the world.'

'Not as beautiful as Italy,' I say automatically, and he laughs.

'Totally. My *nonna* would kill me if she heard me say I preferred France.'

'Nothing scarier than a *nonna*. Whereabouts is your family from?'

He's just getting started telling me about his Neapolitan origins when I hear my name called behind me.

Lotta.

The voice is achingly familiar.

Achingly *desperate*.

I turn.

~

OH MY GOD.

I don't know how I thought I could function without him, because now he's here, every part of my starving soul eats the sight of him up.

The man is a sight for sore eyes. He's dressed like he just stepped off a yacht, in off-white trousers and a sky-blue, open-necked linen shirt that not only enhances his tan but makes those blue eyes of his look even more piercing.

Actually, I think they'd be pretty piercing without the shirt, because right now they're boring into my very soul.

It's the expression in them that makes my heart hurt. They are... God, so many things. Beseeching. Hungry. Fearful.

Lost.

And... I think... loving?

'Sweetheart,' he says hoarsely, holding out his arms and taking a stride towards me.

I don't think about the A-list movie star standing next to me, or how pissed off I've been with Aide, or anything else, except how staggeringly relieved I am to see him. How miraculous it feels to have him standing here, right in front of me, like this magical place has conjured him up for me.

His arms are there, waiting for me. I fall straight into them, because there's nowhere else I belong. And oh my God, when he wraps them around me, and tugs me right into the heat of his huge body, the cradle of it, kissing the crown of my head, I know I never, ever want to be anywhere else.

It's such a cliché, but I've been standing here, in an iconic restaurant in a heavenly part of the world, surrounded by the rich and famous and being gently flirted with by a movie star, for fuck's sake, and all of it is totally pointless without him, a fact that's been really irritating me all evening and is now making me so, so happy I could burst.

Because he is here.

He came.

We do this unsteady little dance together as he rocks me in his arms. 'I'm so *sorry*, sweetheart,' he says brokenly into my hair. 'God, baby, I'm so *fucking* sorry.'

'It's okay,' I manage, because the weirdest thing is happening. I've gone all floppy and shaky, and if Aide wasn't holding me tightly I might actually fall down. It's as if I've been holding myself together this entire day, and last night, to be fair, and now he's here and I can just collapse.

I don't need to put on a brave face anymore, or dazzle anybody, or make an effort to be the life and soul when, deep down, I've felt the polar opposite.

It's seriously emotional, being here in his arms when I've accepted not seeing him for days. I'm sure there's lots to say, but I don't give a fuck right now, because his actions are all that matter.

He chose me, which sounds awful, because I don't want to win a battle against some poor little impoverished children. But he chose us for this weekend.

And it really does mean the world.

I pull away just enough to raise my face to his. He's a little blurry, because my eyes are teary, but he's so bloody magnificent, especially because his face breaks into an ear-to-ear grin at what he sees. The soft rays of the sunset are hitting his jaw from the west, and, even better, that wariness is gone from his eyes, and it's a wonderful thing. We stand there, grinning at each other like fools.

'There she is,' he says, reaching one hand up to brush my hair off my face with the gentlest fingertips. 'There's my girl.'

He bends his head towards me and all my inner cheerleaders go *yes! yes! yes!* But before he can kiss me, there's a polite cough.

'I'll just—' Davide says, and I jerk my head in his direction.

'Oh my God,' I'm so sorry!' I pat Aide on the waist to signal he should release me.

'Not a problem,' Davide says with a dashing, and probably trademarked, grin that would have most humans with a pulse swooning. 'You guys catch up.'

'Oh, fuck,' Aide says.

I glance up at him and almost laugh at the star-struck expression on his face.

'Mate,' he says, hugging me against his side and sticking his hand out for Davide to shake. 'Sorry. Aidan. How are you doing?'

Davide takes Aide's hand graciously. 'I'm doin' great. You're a lucky guy.' He nods in my direction.

'Yeah.' Aide hugs me harder and swallows audibly. 'I know.'

Davide raises his glass to us. '*Santé*. Have a great evening and I'll see you guys around.'

As he saunters off, Aide drops his forehead to mine and slides a warm, strong hand around the back of my neck. 'Twenty-four hours and you find yourself a fucking mega celeb,' he groans. 'Jesus Christ. But who can blame him?'

'It's called karma,' I tell him chirpily.

'I deserved that.'

'He's very attractive.' I tilt my head upwards. 'But I only have eyes for one man, no matter how much that pisses me off. I may have dropped your name into the conversation about twenty times.'

'Good,' he growls, and then his lips are on mine, firm and hungry and relentless. I melt against him, opening for him, wanting everything he has to give me. The solidity of his body, the intrusion of his tongue—it's all so incredibly welcome. I don't want anything except this.

I don't want anyone except him.

I suspect we're putting on quite a show. He's insatiable, kissing me thoroughly, licking his tongue deep into my mouth, reminding me who I belong to. As if I needed reminding. One hand's still holding me around my neck while the other slides down my body till it finds my arse and squeezes it hard.

Um, that squeeze isn't the only thing that's hard.

I break the kiss. 'How did you get here?' I ask breathlessly, roaming my hands down the front of his firm chest. He really is so delicious. So hyper-masculine.

'Net Jets,' he says sheepishly. 'Totum has a Marquis card.'

'Wow,' I say innocently. 'Imagine how fewer carbon emissions you could have caused if you'd just come with me in the first place.'

He slaps my bum lightly. 'I'm offsetting it so much I could probably replant the Amazon.'

'Glad to hear it.' I say. I stand on my tiptoes so I can kiss him. 'And I'm *very* glad you're here.'

'You can thank Judy for that,' he says. 'She gave me a proper bollocking.'

'I'm sorry I missed that.' I smile at him. 'But you can tell me about it later. Let's get you a drink and we can explain to our lovely hostess why you've turned up out of the blue.'

'Noah's already let her know,' he says bashfully. 'But yeah, I'm keen to apologise to her.'

I narrow my eyes at him. 'Is *apologise* a code word for *ogle one of the most beautiful actors on the planet?*'

'Nope,' he says. 'I have no fucking interest in anyone but you. But I might extend the apology to cover all the inappropriate things I intend to do to my girlfriend under the dinner table and on the dance floor later.'

'I'd just seek forgiveness later, if I were you.' I let my head drop against his chest. The sound of his heart beating steadily against my ear may just be the best thing I've ever heard, and the smell of *him* through freshly laundered linen puts the work of the chefs here to shame.

Heaven isn't here.

It's him.

39

LOTTA

Aide's already in our suite's huge bed when I emerge from taking my makeup off in the bathroom. I'm tired from too much food, wine, and dancing. When half of Hollywood takes over Le Club 55, you're in for one hell of a party. The vibe got so rowdy, so infectious, after dinner that even Aide fell foul of it and ended up dancing on the tables with me.

It was one of the best evenings of my life, and it had nothing to do with the glamour of the scene and everything to do with letting rip with my gorgeous, sexy boyfriend.

Oh, and it turns out the man can *move*.

Not that that's a huge surprise given his mastery of rhythm when he's horizontal.

Tired I may be, but the vision of Aide, those massive arms crossed behind his head, looking tanned and hairy and fucking gorgeous against the crisp white Provençal linen is a far more compelling siren's call than sleep. I undo my robe, letting it drop to the floor, and crawl naked across the expanse of bed towards him. I'm not sure a man has ever looked more appreciatively at a woman's body than he's looking at mine right now.

I crouch over him, loving how his face tilts up to meet mine, and drop a kiss on his lips.

Mmm.

I go to settle on top of him so I can kiss him more deeply, melt into him, but he halts me with a firm grip on each of my upper arms.

'Not yet.' He glances from my face to my boobs, which are hanging right there in front of him, and back to my face with difficulty.

'Why?'

'Verbal apology first,' he says, gently manoeuvring us both onto our sides, 'and *then* comes the physical apology.'

Oh.

God he's sweet. It's probably pathetic, but all my anger and frustration has melted away because he's here with me, and that's all that matters.

'Just the physical apology is fine,' I say hastily, and he laughs, rolling us further so I'm on my back and he's ranging over me.

'Nope. That's not how it works. Though the physical apology will be very thorough.'

I open my legs so he can settle between them. He braces himself on his forearms and I gaze up at him like a lovesick moron. 'If you're planning on saying anything, don't bother, because I won't be listening to a word you say. Not when your dick's *right* there.'

At least one part of him is anxious to be inside of me.

He grins, but it's pained. 'Fuck.'

'Maybe go into caveman mode?' I suggest. 'You're very good at single syllables and two-word sentences when you're horny.'

His smile softens. 'Okay.' He dips his head and rubs his nose with mine before pulling back so he can look me in the eye. 'How about this? I'm sorry.'

I nod approvingly. 'Perfect.'

'And...' Those incredible pale blue eyes are so intense. 'I love you.'

The swell of emotion hits me like a rubber mallet over the head. For once in my life, I'm utterly speechless.

I stare at him. 'I—'

'Wait,' he says. I've seen this man smile with pleasure and mirth and affection and all the rest, but he's *never* smiled at me like this. Like he's holding nothing back. Allowing every last one of his emotions to flood through him. To show in that smile of his, to shine in those eyes. And it's like nothing else. It's spellbinding.

He's spellbinding.

And *he loves me.*

Before he turned up and surprised me, I'd resigned myself to the fact that Aide didn't choose me this weekend. Not only has he chosen me, but he loves me.

'Don't say anything until I've finished telling you how I feel,' he continues. He's still braced above me, his forearms framing my face. He smooths my hair off my temple with the gentlest of touches. 'Because I'm so in love with you, and I know it's no excuse, but I think maybe my little stunt the other day was about holding myself back. I freaked out.'

'Why?' I ask through my tears. I stroke my hands down the sides of his firm body.

He coughs out an embarrassed little laugh. 'It's going to sound ridiculous.'

I lick my lips. 'Try me.'

'Well, you're magnificent. You're honestly like no one I've

ever dated. I think the women I've gone for in the past have been… needier than you. What?'

I'm trying hard not to laugh. 'Nothing. Sorry. It's just—needier? You shock me.'

'Okay, okay. I have issues.'

'You don't say.' I raise my eyebrows at him.

'Anyway, you're definitely not… needy. You're so amazing, and impressive, and strong. You're the most badass woman I've ever met—apart from Judy, obviously. But you seem so independent.' He shakes his head, and I can tell this is difficult for him. 'I got hold of my therapist for an emergency chat at the airport, and she said I was probably scared because I don't know how to show up for someone who doesn't really need me, and…'

'And?' I prompt softly.

'And she said something about love language.' He shifts on top of me. 'Like, I have this fucked-up view that people love me because they need me, or more like I feel most loved when I'm most needed. Which is really unhealthy, because I should be allowed to feel loved even when someone's not bleeding me dry.

'And I shouldn't be trying to earn people's love by, you know, making them need me. She said I've allowed some people to manipulate me, but by making myself indispensable I've also been manipulating them.'

I stare at him as his face crumples with emotion. Fuck me, that's a lot. And it makes me fucking furious to think a human being as full of integrity and generosity as Aide should have fallen foul of this dynamic. That he should ever have been allowed to get himself to a place where he felt beholden to actively earn love. To keep it.

'Aide,' I whisper. 'I have to tell you something. You're

right. I don't need you—I don't *depend* on you. Not in the way other people in your life do, maybe. But'—I take a deep breath—'I *love* you.'

His face is a beautiful mess of conflicting emotions as he absorbs what I'm telling him on top of wading through all the epiphanies he's been processing these past few hours.

I keep talking. 'And just because I don't need you, it doesn't mean I don't want you. I've looked after myself for a long time. I'm a big girl. But I wanted you with me really badly this weekend. It was important to me.'

'I know,' he manages.

'If I didn't make that really clear, then I should be apologising, too.' I extricate a hand from between our bodies so I can touch his cheek. 'Everything's better when you're here, honey. I'm trying to make you understand that's all I need from you. I don't need you to *do* anything for me. I just want you close.' My bottom lip trembles. 'Otherwise I get really, really sad. Because I miss you so much when you're not around.'

'Fuck,' he grits out low and harsh, his mouth finding mine to kiss me, and *God* it's so good. I could easily let myself succumb to this, to his tongue sliding decisively past my lips, but there's one more point I have to make.

'Do you see the difference? I want you. I love you. I hate it when you're not around. But I don't want to be another person adding to your list of obligations.'

'You will never, ever be that,' he chokes out. 'But you love me?'

I smile against his lips. 'I do.'

He hums approvingly. 'The other thing she mentioned was that I was probably self-sabotaging. You know, because of what she said about me being scared to love someone who doesn't need me. But she also said it was encouraging that I'd fallen for someone strong and independent. She said it sounded like you had excellent boundaries.'

I preen. 'Did she, now?'

'I told her they were good, but not as excellent as your tits.'

'Classy guy.'

'Fuck, that was a lot of words.' He bends to nuzzle at my neck.

'I'm not sure where my caveman's gone, that's for sure.'

'Ug.'

I laugh. 'You can use your body now,' I say helpfully.

He grins. 'I love you.'

And then he's pinning my wrists above my head and sliding down my body so he can suck on my boobs in the hungry, skilful way only he can.

There's a lot more to say.

Aide has a lot of work to do on himself. And I have work to do if I want to be there to support him when he acts in his own best interests while nurturing the generous, open-hearted side of him that made me fall so hard.

But words have their place and time. And right now, he and I need to find solace and pleasure and transcendence in each other's bodies.

He gives my nipple a decadent suck and releases it before collapsing on his back. I gasp at the absence of his mouth.

'Come here,' he says, and I pull myself upright so I can straddle him. 'Sit on my face.'

Oh, God. I look down at him, my pussy clenching at the mere thought of Aide eating me this way.

'Come on.' He slides his hands around my hips and gives my bum a little slap. His eyes are burning, his entire face ravenous as he takes in the sight of me on top of him. 'Get on my fucking face, sweetheart.'

I smile and shimmy forward as he practically drags me up the bed. I hover right above him.

'You might not think you need me, sweetheart,' he tells me in a low, possessive rasp, 'but don't forget your pussy always needs me, just like it needs me right now. Got it?'

'Yes,' I manage. My voice is breathy, and—dammit— needy as fuck.

He's right.

I'll always need him like this.

'Tell me you need me,' he demands. God, his eyes are practically all pupil.

'I need you,' I tell him. 'I need your dick. My pussy needs your mouth on it. Fuck, Aide, I need you to make me feel good so badly.'

'Yes you do,' he mutters. 'So don't be shy. Ride my face.' He grips my waist, slamming me down onto his face. His tongue finds my wet centre instantly, and his big hands come up to palm my boobs. Fuck, his hands are calloused, and the way he drags them over my skin has me arching into them as I push down against his mouth.

The thrusts of his tongue are harsh, fevered, as he laves me. *Fuck*, it's so intense like this. His mouth and my sex are rubbing, pressing, heat coming off us in waves, our wetness combining in a slick slide. It feels like he's touching every single millimetre of my needy flesh. I sit astride him and grind against him, writhing wantonly so my tits and my pussy get every ounce of attention they require.

He wants to be needed?

I'll show him need so white-hot it'll drive him over the edge.

I've been gripping the sides of his head, I realise.

Holding it to my hungry sex. I release it and brace one hand on the headboard for balance while I arch back enough to find his dick with my hand.

Jesus, it's hard. I slide the pad of my thumb lightly over his crown, smearing the pre-cum around as my fingers grip him. His dick jolts, and his anguished growl vibrates right through my centre before he licks me even harder.

This is definitely the kind of reciprocity I can get behind.

I ride him shamelessly just like he told me to, taking and taking, so flooded with desire and so desperate for release that I can't think of anything else except rubbing myself against his face until I get what I need. His ravenous grunts and the slick hardness of his cock in my hand tell me he's taking too, that he's every bit as into this as I am.

And when the heat sweeps through me, engulfing me, taking every sense prisoner, I take that, too. I allow it to splinter my consciousness into a million perfect shards as suns rise and set behind my eyelids. I cry out Aide's name and am dimly aware of his muffled grunts of pleasure as I grip him harder and shudder my orgasm out above him.

As soon as the fog of blinding ecstasy begins to clear, I'm pulling away from the grip of his hands and sliding down his body so I can impale myself on his cock. I'm soaked from my arousal and Aide's mouth, so when I position his crown right at my entrance and lower myself down, I yield to him more easily than usual.

Still, stuffing myself full of Aidan Fucking Duffy is no mean feat. I'm reminded once again that my boyfriend is a real man, a real handful, as I breathe my way down his length. He lies there, his face contorted with hunger, eyes heavy-lidded, hands running up my thighs in encourage-ment as he watches me fill myself up with him. And when I get him all the way and sit down heavily, we both moan.

This is where I belong.
This is where he belongs.

40

AIDE

'So delicious,' Lotta's friend Nora says, holding up a huge strawberry and taking a bite out of it. She moans softly, causing her fiancé Theo to grunt out a strangled *fuck's sake, Belle* and overtly reach under the table to adjust himself. Nora looks outraged, drops what's left of the strawberry like it's a hot coal, and slaps his hand away from his crotch.

I've spent one evening and about half an hour of break-fast with these two, but that's been plenty of time for me to work out their dynamic, and it's fucking hilarious.

As far as I can tell, they're ridiculously hot for each other, but she tries gamely to maintain an air of propriety that he insists on blowing up. He calls her Belle, and she calls him Romeo.

Not confusing at all.

Lotta and I glance at each other. She rolls her eyes and smirks, and I grin and tug her in more tightly against my side.

This is the life.

I don't know why the fuck I don't do this kind of thing

more often, but it's something I suspect the hedonistic love of my life can help me with. Most of us are staying at this hotel in Ramatuelle, Villa Marie. That includes Noah and Honor, as Josh and Elle's families have taken over Noah's parents' chateau for the weekend.

We're sitting on a shady terrace overlooking the pretty pool. Just through the French doors are tables groaning with an excellent breakfast, and I'm slowly and methodically making my way through the spread. Lotta and I worked up an appetite with morning sex that quickly ramped up from sleepy to athletic, and I'm fucking starving.

I didn't eat much last night, even though the food was incredible. I was too amped up from my mad dash to get here on time and too nervous about mustering up the courage to tell Lotts how I felt about her. Now I'm making up for lost time. I've had a massive bowl of fruit and yoghurt, shitloads of charcuterie, and probably an entire wheel of Camembert on what feels like a whole baguette. I'm now putting away an alarmingly large number of tiny pastries, but if I'm going to act like a self-indulgent bastard for a few nights, I may as well do it properly.

Last night was... unbelievable. Literally. I can't believe how big her heart is. Can't believe I bled myself dry and she accepted all of my shit.

Can't believe she loves me.

I glance down at her, and she smiles up at me. Her sunglasses are dark, but I know that smile reaches her eyes. She strokes the hand I've got slung over her shoulder with her slender, ring-dotted fingers, and I silently vow to add two more rings to that collection in the not-too-distant future.

I fucking love seeing her like this. She's drop-dead gorgeous, as usual, but her vibe is relaxed. Undone.

Just-fucked.

She's in some kind of red halter-neck beach cover-up thingy over a tiny string bikini—also red—under which her fantastic tits sit freely. Her hair's up in a messy bun, and she's leaning into me like there's nowhere she'd rather be.

I can deal with that.

'Honor and I had an illicit lunch here,' Noah says casually, draping an arm over the back of her chair. 'Right after we—uh—got together.'

His wife raises a shapely eyebrow. 'Got together? Is that what the kids are calling it these days?'

I chuckle along with everyone else, because I have clear memories of Noah recounting the whole sorry tale over whisky in the square one night. Honor's husband was publicly cheating on her with his then-co-star and now-partner when my mate decided to try out his gallic charm on her and persuade her to 'level the playing field' (his preferred turn of phrase for how things went down).

'Ancient history now, though, right?' I say, stretching. As I do, I take the opportunity to drink more of the view in. I swear, the South of France is good for the soul. And not only is this place idyllic beyond belief, but I'm noticing that simply putting distance between me and London is helping me to put stuff into perspective.

I'll never, ever abandon the community centre, or my friends, or my family. But it doesn't hurt to examine my motives for helping out in the centre more closely and see what a healthy relationship with it looks like going forward. I allow myself a sigh of pleasure as I bury my nose in Lotta's sweet-smelling, still-damp hair.

I'm roused from my happy little zone-out by Noah humming *Here Comes the Bride*, and I look up to see Elle and Josh approaching. They both look freshly showered and really fucking happy. They must have stayed here last night —maybe they're keeping the chateau's bridal suite for tonight.

'You're not supposed to see each other before this evening,' Theo points out through a mouthful of croissant.

'Fuck off, man,' Josh says with a good-natured shove on his shoulder.

'Ooh, I love it when you go all alpha on me,' Theo says. 'Is he like that in the bedroom, Elle?'

'A lady doesn't tell,' Elle says with a smirk on her face so wide it leaves no one in any doubt as to the answer. I saw those two on that period drama, *Grosvenor*, a couple of years ago when Mum made me watch it.

They definitely have chemistry.

'Lady,' Theo scoffs. 'Right. You planning on wearing white today? Because the jig is up.'

He nods at her baby bump, and everyone laughs.

'Tosser,' she says, and she smacks Theo on the arm. Lotta told me they're cousins, and I can definitely see it in their easy banter.

'The mother of my unborn child *is* wearing white,' Josh confirms, 'and she'll be the most radiant bride to ever walk down the aisle. And I'll be the proudest fucking guy on the planet.'

He bends and kisses her forehead as she leans into him, her hand on her bump. They're so high profile it's ridiculous, and I'm not sure how they can juggle a wedding and a pregnancy with this new Pixar movie they've both got coming out. Seeing them like this, though, they're just like any loved-up couple. Delirious. Hopeful. Excited for the future.

I don't count myself as soppy at all, but there's something about the two of them that moves even me. It's probably because I'm so obnoxiously happy. But love is in the air at this table, and it's not just me and Lotta. Nor is it the bride and groom. These people at this posh resort are a world away from Gaz and Sylv and Judy and the gang, but they share one massive feature, and that's heart. There's romantic love here, and platonic love. Chemistry and friendship.

Despite the almost-constant ribbing, they've all got each other's backs.

Maybe, when family falls short, it's okay to let your found family rally around once in a while.

~

LOTTA

Elle does wear white—Valentino couture, to be precise —and she looks like an angel sent from heaven. When Josh sees her, his face is a picture. I swear, I've never seen a man happier to be getting married. There's a full photography, paparazzi and phone ban in force today, but *Hello!* magazine has won the exclusive rights to shoot the event, with all the proceeds going to Crohn's Disease charities. It's a cause close to Elle's heart.

I can't wait to see the money shots they get of Josh's face as he watches her glide towards him in a sea of ivory silk and lace. With her perfect five-month-old baby bump, she's a vision of beauty and fertility and general gorgeousness, and she takes my breath away.

If Aide hadn't turned up, I suspect I'd be spiralling about now.

Pathetic. But true.

I'd be sitting here in my stunning, diaphanous Chanel gown of palest aqua tulle, feeling like the dress of a lifetime was wasted because he didn't come. I'm not proud of myself, but I can't deny it.

The ceremony is underway. It's five o'clock and still very hot, but in this open-sided marquee, banked by white flowers and greenery, we're perfectly shaded. Even Nora, who's a wedding planner for a gorgeous resort in the UK and by far the most anal person I know, is gobsmacked by the beauty around us.

It's a small wedding by Hollywood standards—only two hundred and fifty people. The chateau is built on cliffs over-looking the Med and flanked by pine forests and its own spectacular olive grove. This part of France is verdant and heavily wooded. The scent of pine is everywhere, the elevated position offers a light breeze, and behind Elle and Josh and the officiant is the Mediterranean, sparkling azure like the coast it gives its name to.

We have Noah and Honor on one side and Theo and Nora on the other. Theo's supposed to be sitting up-front with his family—his mum and Elle's mum are sisters—but he said it would be more fun with us. Everyone's so in love, and it's impossible not to get swept up in it.

And while I'm ecstatic for my friends and adore their other halves, this many Happily Ever Afters in such close proximity could be a bitter pill to swallow.

If.

If I didn't have the world's most beautiful man sitting beside me, looking every inch the ultimate female fantasy in his tux.

If he wasn't holding my hand against his rock-hard thigh as if he's scared I'm going to run away.

If he didn't keep glancing at me from under those thick black eyelashes in a way that's loving and conspiratorial and oddly vulnerable.

Then, yeah, I'd probably be feeling totally miserable and lovesick. As it is, I feel like I'm floating in some kind of bubble. I'm swept up in the magic, not only of Elle and Josh's fairytale, but of my own. Caught up in the excitement and the anticipation of what lies ahead for me and Aide.

We've only just scratched the surface. It's been carnal and desperate and lust-fuelled up until now, and I don't expect things to get less explosive between the sheets anytime soon—or ever—but I'm even more excited about what we can achieve together outside of the bedroom.

What does the future hold with Aide by my side? How can I be there by *his* side, to love and support him while he goes through the world, trying to make it a better place? How can I possibly sit here and attempt to imagine what we can achieve together?

All I know is that my world is a brighter place with him in it. I am a better person with him inspiring me every day. And there's nothing I care about more than making Aide Duffy happy as he navigates life hellbent on giving back.

He needs someone who's as focused on his welfare as he is on everyone else's.

Shit. Those are the kinds of sentiments wedding vows are made of.

~

MY MAN SCRUBS UP WELL. For some reason, it keeps hitting me this evening. The irony, that is. The irony of the fact that he had me at hello with his grimy vest and his power tool. He scratched an itch for something I didn't know I needed.

And now he's here with me, in one of the most beautiful spots in the world, surrounded by the rich and famous and beautiful, dazzling everyone he meets with his conversation even more than with his movie-star good looks and Tom Ford tux and bank balance, and I'm swooning.

Maybe it's not ironic.

Maybe it's just a function of the fact that he's so ridiculously hot and impressive and articulate and kind and dripping with integrity that he's irresistible in every persona he embodies. That he has me useless and smitten and aroused and pathetically infatuated simply because, in every guise, he is himself.

He's inimitable.

We've drunk champagne and eaten lobster in the open air, surrounded by potted ancient olive trees and rambling roses. We've wished the happy couple well, and laughed with friends, and watched Aide and Theo have a dance-off to Rihanna's *Work,* which was apparently played in tribute to Josh and Elle's scorching hot dance floor meet-cute at the Cannes Film Festival.

It's impossible to dance like that and not work up a heat, so Aide's lost his jacket and rolled up his sleeves. His shirt's open at the neck, showing off his cross, his tie's hanging loose, his hair's still oiled except for a couple of escapee strands over his forehead, and he looks so fucking hot that I could ride him here and now, in front of everyone.

He caught a little sun today as he passed out by the hotel pool after breakfast, and he's bronzed and gorgeous. I may have dubbed him an all-man man when I met him in full Bruce-Willis-meets-Henry-Cavill glory that first day on site, but weirdly the black tie ensemble doesn't remotely take the edge off his raw masculinity.

If anything, it makes it all the more stark. The perfectly cut shirt showcases those broad shoulders. The massive arms and the tapering waist. He's still got his leather bracelets on. Those chunky rings still decorate his large workman's hands. They're a welcome reminder that the civility of tonight's dress is a thin veneer.

Underneath, just like he promised me that first time in his office, it's all the same. It's all *real.*

His blue eyes are fixed on me, and only me, as I cavort with Nora. The expression in them is nothing short of predatory. He hooks a strong arm around my waist and pulls me in towards him. I go willingly, planting my palms flat on his chest and gazing up at him adoringly. His hand slides down to my arse and he kneads it hard.

I'm expecting some veiled threat about what awaits me later in our suite.

What he plans to do to me when he gets me alone.

I'm *not* expecting the words that come out of his mouth when he puts it close to my ear.

'Just warning you,' he growls. 'I want this for us someday, and I'm not planning to wait too long, okay?' His breath is hot on my skin, but goosebumps erupt all the same. *'Because I'm not letting you go.'*

There he is.

My very own caveman.

41

EPILOGUE - AIDE

A noise from the bathroom has me surfacing from sleep. My knee-jerk reaction is to reach for my phone before I realise it's Saturday.

Heaven.

My gaze snags on the black-and-white photo on my bedside table: Lotts and me on our wedding day. She's a vision, obviously. I look like the happiest fucker who ever lived, and behind us, Lake Como sparkles. It never fails to put a smile on my face.

I collapse back on my pillows, folding my arms behind my head, and observe idly that my morning wood game is as strong as ever this morning. I very much hope my wife comes back to bed soon. The mere thought of her is enough for me to harden even more, but when she emerges from a cloud of steam, naked and wet-haired and holding a bottle of body lotion, my interest is instant.

'Need some help?' I ask, and she smiles seductively.

'Definitely.'

Jesus, I am so royally fucked when it comes to this woman. I'm her slave. I am totally fucking useless around her. All I can do is marvel at her and be endlessly grateful that she comes home to me every night.

It seems I'm also good at putting babies in her.

I clamber over the bed towards her as she throws the bottle down onto the sheets and stretches, combing her fingers through her damp hair so she can pull it up into a big, messy bun on the top of her head. Happily, this affords me a fucking excellent view.

If I thought the version of Lotta I met two years ago was hot, this version of her is mind-blowing. Pregnancy has taken those curves that brought me to my knees at the community centre and put them on steroids. At eighteen weeks along, our baby girl has her stomach swollen into a perfect, smooth, bronzed bump.

Yeah. We're having a girl.

A little baby girl who I just know will look exactly like her mother.

Told you I'm fucked.

And if Lotta's bump has me obsessed, don't get me started on her tits. They are a fucking miracle. They've grown three cup sizes already, and I cannot keep my hands off them. Her nipples are bigger, too, and slightly darker. They are quite simply the most beautiful things I've ever seen.

This time, we went bra shopping together. Lotts thought it would be hilarious to go to Harrods, given my experience there, so I humoured her.

Yeah, we saw Audrey again.

Yeah, she remembered me, even though it'd been *two fucking years* since the incident I'd tried to carve out of my memory. I know this because she pointed a finger at me and said *I remember you* while my wife snorted beside me. Lotta then proceeded to wrap Audrey around her little finger while they went off to the fitting rooms together and left me hanging around the lingerie, trying not to look too much like a pervert.

Afterwards, Lotts informed me that Audrey, disloyal little horror that she was, had recounted the entire story to her and told Lotta she'd never seen a man in such a state. Apparently they had a great laugh at my expense, which I'm sure I deserved.

These days, the only lingerie I buy her is stuff with a lot of holes in it. Stuff that *enhances* our sex life.

I reach her on my knees and tilt my face up for a kiss.

'Morning,' she says right before she kisses me, and that single word is filled with love and affection. She rakes one hand through my hair and scratches my beard lightly with the other.

'How are my girls?' I ask, releasing her mouth and crouching so I can kiss my way down between her tits and wish my baby girl good morning.

'We're good,' she says dreamily. Her hands roam downwards, stroking my shoulders. We stay like that for a moment, me with my head bowed in worship against the shapely swell of her belly, marvelling at the fact that my two favourite humans exist in one sublime body.

'I had an idea,' she says, and I raise my head to look at her. She's fresh-faced and glowing, and she's never looked so beautiful to me as she does in this moment.

'Yeah?' I palm her bump, though I can't feel anything. Lotta's started feeling some tiny internal flutters—she said they feel like goldfish flipping inside her—but it'll be a while before I'll be able to experience our child moving inside her.

'Mmm-hmm. Sit down here.'

She pats the edge of the bed and takes a step away from

me. I plant my arse, swinging my legs over the edge of the bed and watching with great interest as she sinks to her knees in front of my angry erection. Even pregnant, she's graceful.

Blow job, I think as she guides my knees apart so she can close the gap between us. *Little beauty.* But she reaches past me for the bottle of body lotion and holds it up for me. 'Lube up my boobs,' she says, a smile playing at the corners of those luscious lips of hers. 'You know what to do.'

Fuck, yes. Tit wanks are definitely something my beautiful wife has treated me to in the past, but with her tits so engorged at the moment, they've reached another level of pleasure for me. Happily, they're even more erogenous for her during her pregnancy, so she loves it too.

Yeah. I know what to do. I shake the bottle upside down and open it, feverishly squeezing a huge blob of lotion onto my hand with a wet farting noise that makes Lotta laugh.

'You in a hurry?'

'For you?' I reply. 'Yep.'

I toss the bottle and rub my palms together before putting them on her tits.

Fuck, they're glorious.

They're heavy and ripe in my hands. I smear the lotion over them before scooping. Weighing. Smoothing the crease underneath. I work over her nipples with my thumbs as I let my mouth brush over her hair, and she groans below me. I drag a hand between them, making sure that space is nice and slippery for my cock. If I wasn't dangerously close to blowing already, I'd happily do this all day, or for as long as Lotts let me.

'I think they're good to go,' she says with a laugh, and I kiss her head smilingly.

'Oh. Yeah.'

Then she's edging forward on her knees and I open my legs as wide as I can, shuffling my arse to the very edge of the bed. I plant my hands behind me so I can move my weight backwards, gazing down and watching in rapt fascination as my wife takes her gorgeous tits in her hands and squishes them around my rock-hard dick in a slick, pillowy cradle that's total nirvana.

I grit out a strangled *fuck* as she starts to move, because it's like nothing else, this.

Being surrounded by her flesh.

Seeing my dick disappear as it's swaddled in the greatest tits I've ever had the privilege of knowing.

Hearing her moans as she wanks me off. Watching her work her tight nipples with her thumbs as she goes.

Having the unique pleasure of my wife bend her beautiful face and stick out that little pink tongue to lick at my angry, desperate crown when I thrust it up near her mouth.

Yeah, I manage to thrust, but she's doing most of the work here, and it's a sight I'll take to my grave. The pleasure building through my balls, my dick, is so great I'm tempted to let my eyes drift closed, but I don't want to miss a thing.

For some reason, I have a flash of memory. Of Lotta, when I first met her on that volunteer project—high maintenance and inappropriately dressed, but with tits I would have got on my knees for, right from the start. She had me mesmerised from that first day, but I'd never have guessed she'd be kneeling in front of me in our bedroom, my diamonds sparkling on her fingers and my baby growing in her womb, grinding those magnificent, greased-up tits up and down my dick.

The thought has me shuddering extra hard through the next exhale. What she's doing is perfect—*so fucking perfect*—but I need to be inside my wife. I crave that closeness. That certain knowledge that she's mine, and I'm hers, and we're exactly where we're meant to be.

With restraint I barely knew I possessed, I whisper *I want to fuck you, sweetheart*, and I haul her up from her knees.

~

LOTTA

I swear there are tears in Aide's eyes, and awe on his face, as he sweetly helps me up. He stands with me, holding my slippery boobs and my little baby bump tight against the hardness of his body as he kisses me hungrily.

He gets emotional like this sometimes. More often since I got pregnant. I swear he's got more pregnancy hormones than I do swirling around in that huge body of his.

But when Aidan Duffy trusts you enough to get vulnerable with you, that's gold, and there's no side of him I love more than my giant softie. I take his hungry, adoring kisses as his cock jerks angrily between us, and then I turn and clamber onto the bed, crawling a little further away than is strictly necessary, before I stop on my hands and knees and look over my shoulder.

Yep. The awe is still there. He's so sweet it kills me.

'Come get me, honey' I sing-song, and on he jumps. But instead of ramming his dick straight inside me, as I expected, he crouches behind me, nudging my knees apart, spreading my cheeks with his hands and burying his face in my centre.

Oh Jesus. I am such a lucky bitch.

My husband's tongue is as taut as it was when he kissed me just now, his licks just as ravenous as he slices through my flesh. He tongue-fucks me for a few seconds before taking pity on me and finding my clit. The sensation of his mouth on me, his beard abrading me, is so perfect I practically shoot off the bed. But the grip of his strong fingers is tight on my bum, so I get my outlet with a low, agonised moan as I attempt to grind my pussy against his face. He chuckles against my flesh, pleased at having reduced me to this, before ramping up his ministrations.

It's so perfect. *God, he's perfect.* His grip eases so his hands can roam over my bum in a way that's loving and proprietorial in equal measure, and then he truly lets me have it. He slides a couple of fingers inside me, his tongue growing even more taut, and it flicks at my clit with military precision.

I squeeze my eyes closed and collapse down onto my elbows so I can press my fists into my eye sockets as I ride out this orgasm he's building inside my body. He rewards me with harder finger fucks and a more merciless onslaught against my clit, and I writhe with pleasure in his expert hands, because no one can handle me like my husband.

I won't last, but I can tell by the ravenous noises he's making that Aide needs inside me, and quick, so that shouldn't be a problem. I let my body take over as the heat he's stoked courses through my body in waves so powerful they suck me under. I'm lost to sensation, but I need more.

'Fuck me,' I cry, and immediately he's on his knees behind me, pushing all the way in with a single, powerful stroke. The feeling of fullness is so *right*. It's everything. It's life-affirming. I stretch my arms out in front of me and claw at the sheets so I can hold steady for him.

I love my husband in every moment, in every way, but nothing else compares to having him inside my body. Nothing compares to him ramming that thick cock home over and over, his huge form hulking over me. I may not be able to see him like this, but I couldn't feel closer to him. His hairy thighs are between my spread ones, his huge hands are gripping my hips, moving them to meet him every time he bottoms out in me, and, despite my arousal and all the relaxin in my body, his dick is such a tight fit that it feels like the best kind of invasion.

And the friction—the friction, the drag, of his cock in and out of my still-shuddering, still sensitive inner walls is pure perfection. It's always carnal with Aide. With my caveman. When we're connected like this, our appetite for each other never seems to wane.

'Fuck, you're so beautiful,' he moans as he thrusts into me. His drives are measured, but he's not holding back. Every one is perfect. Every one hits the way I need it to. 'I love you.' *Thrust.* 'So fucking much.' *Thrust.* 'My beautiful, amazing wife, who needs it hard.' *Thrust.* 'I can't get enough of you.' *Thrust.* 'Feel that, sweetheart. Feel your husband's dick deep inside you.'

My *hot builder* kink isn't my favourite anymore.

My favourite is my *husband* kink. Therefore, whenever Aide says the words *wife* or *husband* when he's fucking me, it unlocks something primitive. Because being fucked by Aide is amazing. I mean, come on. The guy's a god.

But being fucked by Aide, my *husband*, has me spiralling to another plane. I need him on every primitive, elemental level. I need him to claim me with his body just like he did with his heart and his words and his ring and his vows and this baby he's put in me.

So when he says things like that, it makes everything wind even tighter inside me, and not only because my favourite caveman's graduated to multi-word sentences when he's fucking me.

'Oh my God,' I gasp, which is far less hot than what he's

saying, but it's all I'm capable of right now, because the friction is so fucking amazing, and his drives are so powerful they're obliterating my basic executive function, and all my greedy inner walls can think of is *more, more, more.*

'*Harder!*' I scream, and fuck does he really let me have it. He digs his fingers in so hard I'll have bruises on my hips tomorrow, and he rams into me, over and over, invading my body till I'm a senseless mess, conscious only of the bright white glow that's built and built somewhere deep inside and which my husband's dick is stoking.

When I let go this time, it's more profound, more elemental, and I'm only vaguely conscious beyond the roaring in my ears of Aide shouting my name as the contractions my body's producing trigger his own obliteration. His own epiphany.

After he's eased out of me and cleaned us both up with a wad of tissues, we lie down on the bed together, two happy, spent commas curled up into each other, nose to nose.

'Fuck, Lotts,' he whispers as he brushes a damp tendril of hair off my forehead. His face is soft. Open. Those extraordinary eyes, which I will never get over as long as I live, see only me. And they're wet, his eyelashes starry with unshed tears.

'Hey,' I whisper, winding a leg around him and tugging myself closer. 'It's okay.'

'I know.' He winds his top arm around me like a vice while stroking my bump with the knuckles of his other hand. 'It's just... I love you so much. And I love our daughter. You two are my whole world.'

'You're my world, too,' I tell him. 'Remember that independent woman you fell for, who you thought didn't need you? *Gone.*'

That gets me a laugh.

'I need you every second of the day, in every way,' I tell him, 'and our daughter does, too. We're nothing without you. So buckle up, mister.'

'Our daughter will be like her mother,' he tells me. 'Strong, and beautiful, and amazing. She won't need me, but she'll have me kneeling at her feet, worshipping her, even so.' He shudders. 'Shit, I really need to get more pointers from your dad.'

'He's useless,' I tell him. 'I've got him wrapped around my little finger.'

He sighs. 'Yeah.'

I gaze at him. I may have noticed his incredible beauty first, but the heart inside Aidan Duffy's sculpted torso is by far his most precious feature. He is what I suspected from early on—a good, good man. He'll make such a wonderful dad that just thinking about it makes me well up.

'I'm glad you took a chance on me,' I whisper.

He smiles, and that smile speaks of infinite love. Then it turns to a wolfish grin. 'You basically stuck your tits in my mouth. I didn't really have a choice. No one could say no to those tits, Carlotta Duffy.'

'True,' I muse, trailing a finger over his soft beard. 'But you thought I was a spoilt brat. I had to pull out all the stops.'

'You didn't, actually,' he tells me. 'I would have caved. I wouldn't have let you walk away from me. You had me entranced from the start.' He kisses me gently. 'I never stood a chance against you.'

I let my eyelids flutter closed as his kisses turn less gentlemanly.

I see my husband every day. I wake up with him each morning, mainly in this beautiful home he built—the home that's become our much-needed sanctuary—but sometimes in our flat in London.

I go to sleep each night, wrapped up in his arms.

I share an office with him at least twice a week when I'm doing what he refused to do properly and marketing the hell out of the man behind Fresh Start: Aidan Fucking Duffy. And yeah, I do it really well. It helps me sleep better at night, knowing my entire week hasn't been spent selling eight-figure properties to people who are richer than God.

My point is, I get to see, to enjoy, all the facets of the extraordinary man I fell in love with.

The animal.

The husband.

The entrepreneur.

The philanthropist.

The father-to-be.

And it gets me thinking. It gets me reminiscing about how angry I was that time, what feels like long ago now, when I found out he'd been lying to me about who he was.

Turns out, the only things he'd failed to disclose back then were his surname, his day job, and his bank balance.

He never lied to me about the man he actually *was*.

He was right when he told me, that day in his office, that he'd shown me the real version of himself. Everything Aide has done, and said, and shown me, has been authentic. The man doesn't have a false bone in his body. He's incapable of subterfuge. He's incapable of not wearing that huge, beating, bleeding heart of his on his sleeve.

He is the realest man I've ever known.

THE END

Thank you for reading! If you'd like to see how Aide

proposed (clue: it was very Diet Coke™ ad) check out my bonus scene here.

https://BookHip.com/QRSKRWF

YOU CAN READ Honor's and Noah's, Nora and Theo's and Elle and Josh's stories in my Love in London boxset here:

http://mybook.to/loveinlondon

COME and join the fun and games with my amazing Nerds in my FB group. Search for **Sara Madderson's Book Nerds**

ACKNOWLEDGMENTS

Hi!

Thank you for reading Aide and Lotta's HEA. I've loved every minute of kicking off the Elgin series with many, many bangs. If you've read my Love in London books, I hope you enjoyed catching up with those characters again. I adored revisiting Josh and Elle, Nora and Theo, and Honor and Noah.

Do you remember meeting Lotta briefly in Wilder at Heart? She hosted the fabulous Studio 54-themed birthday party where Nora and Theo got frisky on the dance floor... I've been excited to give her her own HEA for a while now, and I'm both ecstatic and revoltingly jealous that she found Aide.

You'll meet Santi and Sabrina again in my Christmas book, The Christmas Billionaire, when Sabrina takes up the position of Santi's dad's wellness consultant over the festive period. It's an opposites-attract, fish-out-of-water romance and I have the BEST cover photo for it—I can't wait to share it!

I have some very important thank yous to say.

Firstly, thank you to my amazing Facebook reader group, my gorgeous Nerds, for encouraging me and making suitably enthusiastic noises every time I've shared any sneak previews of Aide and Lotta. I love you guys!

In particular, thank you for all the hilarious and amazing (and worryingly, often fact-based) suggestions they came up with for Aide and Gaz's school pranks and for the idea of having a sports teacher called Mr Hell.

Thank you to Jezebel Nightingale for suggesting medical data security as the sector for Aide's software company. I was definitely drawing blanks on ideas on that front—software's not exactly my area of expertise.

Thank you to my wonderful ARC team for reading this first, for always being Team Sara, and for your insightful and generous feedback, typo spotting and reviews. Having you as my initial port of call makes every launch easier and better.

Thank you to Lyndsey and Stephanie, my amazing beta readers who read this book as I wrote it and egged me on when I needed it.

Thank you to Wander Aguiar, Andrey Bahia and team for the beautiful cover photo. Sadly my cover model, Jose K, does not seem stalkable on social despite my very best efforts, but there are lots of delicious pics of him on Wander's Book Club, including several of him shirtless or in a vest that I found, ahem, inspiring. https://www.wander bookclub.com/jose-k.

Finally, thank YOU for reading, reviewing, following me on social and generally supporting this indie author! I have the best readers and I couldn't do it without you.

Sara x

Made in the USA
Las Vegas, NV
18 January 2025

16587905R00204